A KNIGHT'S LIFE IN DAYS OF CHIVALRY

AMS PRESS

NEW YORK

A KNIGHT AT PRAYER.

(Reproduced by permission of the Director of the Victoria and Albert Museum).

A KNIGHT'S LIFE *in* *the* DAYS *of* CHIVALRY

BY

WALTER CLIFFORD MELLER, M.A., S.C.L.

ST. JOHNS COLLEGE, OXFORD

Author of "A Royalist Raid," "Ballads of the '45," "The Boy
Bishop" and other Essays on Old Time Usages and Beliefs

" Vous qui voulez l'ordre de Chevalier
Il vous convient mener nouvelle vie."

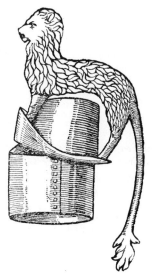

HEAUME AND CREST OF THE BLACK PRINCE

LONDON
T. WERNER LAURIE LIMITED
30 NEW BRIDGE STREET, BLACKFRIARS
1924

Library of Congress Cataloging in Publication Data

Meller, Walter Clifford.
  A knight's life in the days of chivalry.

  Reprint. Originally published: London: T. Werner
Laurie, 1924.
  Includes index.
  1. Chivalry. 2. Knights and knighthood. I. Title.
CR4509.M35   1982   929.7   78-63506
ISBN 0-404-17155-9   AACR2

Reprinted from the edition of 1924, London. Trim size and text
area have been altered. Original trim: 16.1 × 25.1 cm.; original
text: 11.9 × 20.7 cm.

MANUFACTURED
IN THE UNITED STATES OF AMERICA

TO

The Rt. Honble. JOHN FRANCIS, 33rd EARL OF MAR
MY DEAR AND LONG-TIME FRIEND

PREFACE

HISTORIANS no longer sit down, as once they were wont, to write twenty volume works in the style of Hume or Lingard, embracing a dozen centuries of annals, they employ themselves now on certain epochs.

In this work, as the title denotes, I have devoted myself to the age when Chivalry was in flower; more especially that period of it when feudal fetters, becoming loosened, a free and more individual Chivalry became paramount, which not only is a more romantic but more interesting a study.

There are very few books extant that fairly portray this period and its Chivalry.

On the one side we find the learned French writer Gautier and the English Everard Digby, but because the knights belonged to the old Faith they can see nothing evil in their lives and actions, and so, their writings are exceedingly prejudiced; on the other, a host of writers of a lighter literature who have followed far off the steps of Scott, have made of Chivalry and her knights what they degenerated into in the reign of Elizabeth—a mere spectacular and theatrical institution. I hope in these pages I have avoided both these errors.

To the general reader this book may be of some use and interest as a very great portion of the material is drawn from books difficult to obtain in the usual libraries, and also, when found, in old and difficult French. Many of the ballads quoted are from a French author less known than our English Chaucer. I have preferred quoting the former for the very reason that he is less known, though in drawing the characters of those he depicts he is far inferior to the English poet. It may be well to say a few words concerning this writer— Eustache Deschamps, otherwise Morel, who lived during four reigns, namely, Philip IV., John le Bon, Charles le Bel and Charles VI. from 1328 to 1422. He was educated at the University of Orleans and at an early age was appointed by Charles V. one of his " écuyers-hussiersd'armes." In 1381 he was made Castellan of Fismes and soon after Bailli of Senlis. Montaignon, a commentator on his work, says of him he rarely troubles to analyse the ideas and sentiments of those who are the characters in his verse, he is too much occupied in portraying their outward features and the events passing before his eyes. For this reason his poems are very useful as illustrating the customs of his time to any historian of the Middle Ages.

In giving reference to many excerpts from the Romans and Gestes I have for the sake of uniformity and possible utility to the reader grouped most under the English word " Lay " or " Lays." To those who are not familiar with these poetic distinctions it may be briefly said that the word " Romance " in its original meaning was far from corresponding with the definition now assigned. On the contrary it signified merely one, or other, of the popular dialects of Europe, founded upon the Roman, that is the Latin, tongue. At an early period (1150) it plainly appears that the Romance language was distinguished from the Latin and that translations were made from the one into the other. An ancient Romance on the subject of Alexander says it was written by a learned clerk :

" Qui de Latin la trest, et en Roman la mit."

Most of the metrical tales and chronicles of the Middle Ages were composed in the Romance language which, being spoken at the Courts of France and England under our Angevin kings became, in a peculiar degree, the speech of Love and Chivalry.

" Romans " were chiefly occupied with describing adventures of Chivalry where love was the mainspring and reward. So the old poet says

> " Oyez, signor, tout li amant
> Cil qui d'amors se veut penant
> Li Chevalier, et les pucelles,
> Li daimoisel, les damoiselles ;
> Se mont conte volez entendre
> Moult le porrez d'amors apprendre."

" Chansons de Geste," on the other hand, were poems which celebrated the heroes of a country, such as Charlemagne, Roland, Arthur, etc., or a nation's wars, such as those of Charlemagne or the Crusades. They embalmed all the legends of the battle-field and its warriors. They were greatly in vogue with the knight-troubadours and sung on many a winter evening in a castle hall or moated manor-house. It was such that Taillifer sung before the Norman host on the battle-field of Senlac. He sung of Roland and his knights

> " Taillefer, qui moult bien chantout
> Sor un cheval gi tost alout
> Devant le Duc alout chantant
> De Karlemaigne et de Rollant
> Et d'Oliver et des vassals
> Qui morurent en Rencevals."
> —Roman de Rou of Wace.

If the chapters dealing with the amusements, the Chace, the Tournaments, the War Customs and Arms, the Crusades and the Troubadour-knights, may be considered too brief, the subjects of them all are so extensive that, if fully treated, they would demand volumes to themselves. The object of this book has been to describe a knight from his birth to his death, and these subjects have been only treated in such a manner as incidents in that scheme.

CONTENTS

LIST OF ILLUSTRATIONS

The surcoat we see here is very different to earlier
fashion : it now generally reaches to mid-thigh, with
sleeves shortened to the elbow. It ceases to fall in folds,
but is of silk or other material often padded to hang
stiffly. Above it here we see the gorget of laminated
plates, furnished with sliding rivets to allow the maximum
of freedom. The skirt of mail can be traced here at the
bottom of the surcoat. The skirt of mail was a marked
feature of the period. It was of fine mail, and, in all
probability, only a skirt fastened round or below the waist.
This mail skirt had been growing in favour for some
time. We see it upon the brass of Lord Audley, 1491,
in Sheen Church, Surrey, also on that of Edward Stafford,
Earl of Wiltshire, 1499, in Luffwick Church, Northants.
On the genouilléres at this period often much ornament
was displayed—roses, etc.—as seems to be on the knight's
in this illustration. The heaume is probably a tilting one
fitted with a baviere.

Here we find the first example of the nature of a crest
on his cap, also the heraldic lions on his shield, perhaps
the earliest specimens of armorial bearings.

The coif-de-mailles is thrown back in this effigy, and rests
upon the shoulders in folds ; the ailettes are square, and
the sleeves of the hauberk are thrown back off the hands,
and are shown depending from the wrists. Beneath the
hauberk the quilted undergarment called the haqueton
appears. The genouillères are of plate, and a stud is
shown that fastens them to a strap behind the knee.
The singular name of Septvans (seven fans) is from his
cognizance, i.e., fans used for winnowing wheat.

LIST OF ILLUSTRATIONS

Here the coif-de-mailles upon the head—which coif goes under the heaume—descends to the shoulder, while the hauberk is prolonged to cover the hands, the fingers undivided. Over the mail is a loose, soft surcoat, divided at the back to facilitate riding. Later a surcoat was worn much stiffer and without folds, as seen in the brass in the Fitzalan Chapel of John, Earl of Arundel. Stowe, the old chronicler, writes : " These earlier surcoats of silke did by reason of their folds and pleats confound the marks (heraldic) painted on them, so they were afterwards made plaine " (to be seen easily in battle).

Many instances are found of married ladies displaying on their robes their paternal arms and not those of the family they married into. Here Sir Peter's wife displays the arms of Bohun, azure, a bend argent, cotized or between six lyonceux rampant of the last, and not those of Arderne. Later we find the " coats " of husband and wife impaled, as it were, on the latter's dress—her paternal on one side, her husband's on the other. It is so on the brass of Elisabeth, wife of John Shelley, in the church of Clapham, Sussex. She bears on one side a falcon for Falconer, her paternal coat, on the other whelk shells for Shelley.

Ecclesiastics were forbidden to personally take part in a judicial wager of battle. They appointed out of their households either knights or squires or others to take their place. Here on the brass we see the effigy of the Bishop of Salisbury and his champion, who did so well for him that the Bishop ordered he should be commemorated on his brass with himself. On page 118 of this book is the account of another prelate, Bishop Richard de Swynford of Hereford, and his champion.

This form of swaddling children in knightly families seems to have been derived through Gaul from the ancient Romans. See page 14 in this book.

LIST OF ILLUSTRATIONS

There are only a few authentic great heaumes in existence which are of the fourteenth century. One of them is the above, the upper part of which is covered by a cap of maintenance bearing the heraldic lion. No breathing holes are shown, and the " occularium " is extremely narrow. These immense crests followed on the fan-shaped ones of an earlier period. They were almost invariably made of cuir-bouilli, which, besides being light, allowed itself to be moulded into any desired shape. That crests were common in Chaucer's days is obvious from his description of Sir Thopas :

> " Upon his crest he bare a tour
> And therein stiked a lily flour."

A KNIGHT'S LIFE IN DAYS OF CHIVALRY

CHAPTER I

THE ORIGIN OF CHIVALRY

THERE can be little doubt that the original of chivalric forms and institutions may be discovered in the military customs prevalent amongst nations anterior to the Middle Ages. The Roman Equites formed in the earliest ages of the republic the great ornament of its army. They were distinguished by a gold ring, which was presented by the State, and provided with horses at a public charge.

In the rude ceremonial of the Germans, youths were admitted into the assembly of warriors, when we observe a still nearer approach to the observance of a knightly institution. They were endowed with the spear and the shield, and from that time forth attached themselves with devoted constancy to some particular chieftain. " The noblest youths," says Tacitus, " were not ashamed to be numbered among the faithful companies of celebrated leaders, to whom they devoted their arms and service. A noble emulation prevailed among the leaders to acquire the greatest number of bold companions. . . . In the hour of danger it was shameful for the chief to be surpassed in valour by his companions, shameful for the companions not to equal the valour of their chief. To survive him if he fell was irretrievable disgrace. To protect his person, to increase his glory by their own triumphs, were the most holy of their duties."

When these Northern hordes were converted to Christianity it had little effect in softening their war-like spirit. It was the famous Earl Siward who, when he felt death approaching, cried, " Alas, that I have escaped death in so many battles, to yield up my life now at home in this tame disgraceful manner like a cow ! I beseech you, my companions, to dress me in my coat of mail once more, to gird on me my trusty sword, to place my shield in my left hand, my battle axe in my right, and to place my helmet on my head, that I at least may die in the dress of a warrior, though I cannot have the happiness of dying on the battle-field."

A military caste has therefore subsisted among all these races that then populated Europe before the time even of Charlemagne, to whom must be credited the introduction into his vast dominions of the feudal system. Even in our own country, King Alfred is said to have admitted Athelstan to the military dignity, by clothing him in a

1

A

purple vest with a belt set with gems and a sword sheathed in gold. But despite any religious rites, which the Anglo-Saxons grouped round the giving of knighthood, it soon became corrupt. The chronicler, John of Salisbury, after observing that a knight to be a good one, should inure himself to labour, to run, carry weights, bear the sun and the dust, and be content with hard living, and coarse food, says : " Some think that military glory consists in this, that they shine in elegant dress, that they make their clothes tight to their bodies, and so bind on their linen and silken garments as to seem a skin colour, like their flesh. Each is boldest in the banquet-hall, but in the battle everyone desires to do the least ; they would rather shoot arrows at the enemy than come to close fighting—if they return home without a scar, they sing triumphantly of their battles and boast of a thousand deaths." From these few proofs it seems certain that from the age of Charlemagne, and even earlier, the sons of chiefs and kings and the higher nobility assumed manly arms with some sort of investiture, and were a class apart from the ordinary soldier. But these ceremonies which began to surround the entrance into military life of a young soldier would have done little perhaps in themselves towards forming that intrinsic principle which characterized the later and more genuine Chivalry.

In the reign of Charlemagne, however, we find a military distinction that appears in fact, as well as in name, to have given birth to that institution. Under the Carlovingian dynasty property was of two kinds. The holders of Allodial lands enjoyed them absolutely and independently ; on the other hand benefices or fiefs (from the Anglo-Saxon word " feof," cattle or money) were granted by a lord to a person who, in return for that grant, and for the protection the lord afforded him, obliged himself to do some military service. In its early days, therefore, Chivalry was founded on feudal obligations and closely bound up with the military service of fiefs. " Caballarii " in the Capitularies, " Milites " of the eleventh and twelfth centuries, who followed their lord into the field. Land thus held in England was called " a Knight's fee," in Normandy " fiefs de haubert," from the coat of mail which it entitled, and required, every tenant to wear. Military tenure was said to be " by service and chivalry."

To serve as a soldier, mounted and equipped, was a common duty of vassals from the highest to the lowest. It implied no personal merit. It gave of itself no claim to civil privileges. It was before everything obligatory and dependent on the will of another, and as long as he and his descendants held the fief, so long those duties were demanded. Three principal ceremonies characterized these relations between the lord and the vassal. The latter, when doing homage to the former, knelt before him and placing his hand in that of his future lord, declared that he would become his man, and as such acknowledged himself bound to defend his life and his honour. He then took the oath of fidelity, having previously removed his sword and spurs. This was called hommage-lige and bound the vassal to military service for an unlimited time and on whatsoever territory the lord thought fit to lead his dependents.

For circumstances and at epochs when war was permanent, or nearly so, the hommage-lige prevailed. Thus in the code of laws known by the name of " Assises de Jerusalem," drawn up after the taking of the Holy City by the Crusaders in 1099, hommage-lige is regarded as the rule, even though at that time the obligations of feudal service were becoming obsolete and free knighthood was becoming prevalent. The " hommage simple " or " franc " was of a less stringent character: it implied military service only for the space of forty days yearly, within the limits of the fief—and with permission of performing that service by deputy.

The vassal did homage standing, wearing his sword and spurs and placing one hand on a copy of the Evangels. The ceremony once over, the tie between the lord and the vassal was complete, and an interchange of duties, services, and obligations became the necessary result; but the chief of all these obligations in this older form of chivalry (called by French writers on the subject " l'ancienne Chevalerie ") was military service. But other services were also called upon on certain occasions from the holder of a fief, *i.e.*, to help to ransom his overlord if taken prisoner; to help in dowering the over-lord's daughter in marriage; to do the same when that chief's elder son was made a knight, or he himself about to start on the Crusades.

Estates might, and often did, change hands; others were con-fiscated, or left without owners on account of the death of the heir: hence ensued fresh and heavy duties paid over to the lord. If the vassal were a minor the suzerain became his guardian, and as such received the income. The daughters of the vassal were obliged to receive husbands at the hand of the lord, unless they paid forfeit. Even in England, where the feudal system was dying out, the obliga-tions of those holding manors—which represented somewhat the Norman fief and was left by them untouched—were obtained.

The above obligations of the feudal system—besides those, such as the lord's right to make his tenants bake their bread in his feudal oven, to grind their corn in his mill, to make wine in his press—show how hardly all feudal service fell upon the vassal, and if in these common details of ordinary life they were so, much more in the con-stant military services as a soldier that the vassal was called upon to render. This feudal service, as long as the fief remained in a family, was passed on from father to son, and for this reason some of the French writers call it " une chevalerie de naissance," which often, to the casual reader of their works, might lead him into the belief that knighthood was hereditary. As we have said, the fief itself, unless forfeited for not complying with the obligations it carried, or for treason in the holder of it, was hereditary, but the dignity of knight-hood was never so—it was untransferable and simply personal. Thus in a Rescript of the Emperor Frederick II. quoted by Pierre de la Vigne, it was laid down " Licet generis nobilitas in posteros derivetur non tamen eqistris dignitas." So also there are numerous instances extant of youths of noble and of even royal birth who, if they had possessed knighthood by right of birth, would never have afterwards sought it; whereas they constantly did. Thus Henry, King of England, sent his son Edward to the court of Alfonso of Castille, to receive the order of knighthood at his hands, in the city of Bourgos (Walsingham).

From these brief remarks on the ancient feudal obligations attached to knighthood (1) it can easily be understood how cramped and fettered a brave man's soul became by such restrictions, and how, though he longed for military glory, he longed to gain it where, and how, he willed, and not at the beck and call of an overlord. (2) The vast upheaval that the first Crusade in 1095 made in the Christian countries of Western Christendom fostered and helped the growing spirit in Chivalry of freedom from feudal restraint. The cry that went forth to the military caste was not made by the feudal lord, or if it was so made to his vassal, it was left to the latter's individual decision to obey it or not—for it was considered in that age, this cry came from God Himself, it was "Diex el volt." (3) Again the multiplication of fiefs, by their subdivision, helped to swell the ranks of knighthood at this period—this subdivision impoverished greatly the owner's family, and the younger members of it eagerly sought a knighthood, which was not dependent on a fief. A younger brother, leaving the paternal estate in which he took a slender share, might well look to wealth and dignity in the service of a powerful lord. Knighthood which he could not claim, as not holding a fief as his legal right, became the object of his chief ambition. It raised him in the scale of society, equalling him in dress, in arms, and in title, to the rich fief-holders. As it was only bestowed for his merit, it did much more than make him equal to those who had no pretensions, but from their wealth, and these same territorial knights became by degrees ashamed of assuming the title of knights, till they could challenge it by real desert.

This class of noble and gallant cavaliers, serving commonly for pay, but on the most honourable footing, became as we have said above, far more numerous through the Crusades. In these wars, as all feudal service was in abeyance, it was necessary for the richer barons to take into their pay as many knights as they could afford to maintain.

During the Crusades we find chivalry therefore acquired its full vigour as an order of personal nobility, and its original connection with feudal tenure, if not altogether effaced, became in a great measure, forgotten in the splendour of the form which it now wore.

(4) Again it was at this period—the Crusading period—the Church stepped forward and as these warriors were about to engage in what she considered a holy warfare, freed them, while engaged in it, from the feudal obligations of that of their fiefs. In this holy war of hers, they were the free agents of the Cross, and so it was now we find coming into universal practice, at the making of a knight, those more religious and complicated ceremonies, henceforth bound up with Chivalry of Knighthood.

(5) At this period, while the cities in Western Europe were throwing off their feudal chains, they did not gain individual freedom; they only exchanged them for the collective and communal freedom. As societies they were free, but as individuals unemancipated. The peasantry also on the seigneurial estates were still chained to the wheel of labour, even though they were ceasing to be serfs; the craftsman was ruled by his guild, by the parish in which he worshipped, and the quarter of the city in which he dwelt; none of these had individual freedom, the only outcome for this rising spirit of individual freedom was that to be found therefore in the new knighthood.

The ancient knighthood or Chivalry therefore, the embodiment of the feudal system, now had its place taken to a very great extent, by this nobler chivalry founded on individual freedom and religion, and being free, and being religious, cast into shade, as it gained its zenith, the old obligatory knight-service of the earlier ages. However, it was strictly enforced under this newer and freer phase of knighthood, that none should receive the accolade unless tracing their parentage or descent from these feudal families—in other words from the military and ruling class.

Thus Charles II. of France, by an Ordinance of his in 1294, declared " quod nullus possit accipere militare cingulum nisi ex parte patris saltem sit miles "—(here the order of knighthood is allowed to a man, if he can prove on one side that he comes of a feudal family).

Again the Emperor Frederic by an Ordinance made at Naples declared " ad militarem honorem nullus accedat qui non sit de genere militum," and this obligation, for a neophyte in knighthood, of showing he was of the old feudal military caste, remained intact till from the decaying force of chivalry, a sovereign, or prince, permitted often the citizen class to receive the accolade. This may be considered as one out of the many reasons why knighthood fell into ridicule and loss of influence. So Gautier in his work on Chivalry well says, " On avait ouvert les portes de la Chevalerie a trop de candidats indignes. On l'avait embourgeoisée. A force d'être prodigué, le beau titre de chevalier était avili " (p. 94).

Before considering the up-bringing of a future knight, or his after career, it would be well to remember what that warlike age was like when chivalry was in flower. It was essentially a different age to our own. It was one in which Force was paramount, and the sword, and not the law-courts, the chief arbiters of justice. The extinction of the ancient Roman civilization by the inroads of the barbarians had been effected by the sword; that tradition had not died out. The reign of Charles the Great introduced a certain revival of letters, it is true, in those lands nearest to his Court, but by bringing in the feudal system he again, by its obligations of military service, made the sword paramount.

In these Northern lands in which chivalry chiefly flowered most brightly, though Christianity had greatly taken the place of ancient heathendom, many of its rites and beliefs were still kept alive. All those manifestations which we now know are due to nature were then ascribed to the supernatural. The rise of comets, the eclipses of the sun and moon, the Black Death that often ravaged Europe, the storms that swept over the great forests, were all the work of the supernatural, or of an offended God, who was to be propitiated by offerings vowed, and prayers made, to many doubtful saints who filled the places of the ancient gods. It is no wonder, therefore, that the sword was supernaturally supposed to be an effective element in the courts of justice. Trials by battle, between conflicting suitors, were common. Here Force—the strongest sword, the strongest arm, and the strongest horse—decided the issue.

The time chivalry, the new chivalry of a freer sort, arose, was the period of the first Crusade. That Crusade and the subsequent ones, by familiarizing the Northern soldiers with the civilization of the Saracen and the Moor, though it brought with it an amelioration of their rough living and education, brought with it also a great laxity of manners between the two sexes. Woman, as she was in the Moorish

5

Empire, became the object of knightly vows, but she lost much of that older and simpler life of the past generation. At this period women were no longer kept in seclusion within the walls of home-life, but were present at festivals, at tournaments, and sat (so Hallam says) promiscuously in the halls of their husband's castles. The " Lay of Perceforest " tells us of a feast where eight hundred knights had each of them a lady eating off his plate. In the " Lay of Lancelot du Lac," a lady, who was troubled with a jealous husband, complains that it was a long time since a knight ate off her plate (Le Grand, t.i., p. 24). This phase of the chivalric age was every day exhibited by its Churchmen as well as its laymen, and if the former could discover the method of reconciling the apparent discrepancy, an adventurous soldier was not the most unlikely person to take advantage of the invention. Nor does it seem to have entered into the minds of the venerable chroniclers, who have recorded the deeds of their favourite knights, that they might tarnish the brightness of their fame by telling the errors they committed. The same pride and seeming consciousness of noble truths appear to have dictated the anecdotes of licentiousness at which we nowadays blush, as those which incline us to admiration. The famous history of the " Knights of the Round Table," while they are glowing with the praises of their devotion, record with the greatest particularity, and in the same tone, the violation of the principles of morality. While their heroes are sent in the most devout spirit to search for the Holy Grael, we find them recreating themselves from their toils by the most depraved pleasures, and the knights whose characters seemed to have been portrayed in the manner best calculated to fill us with respect, suddenly rise before us as the worst of hypocrites. Notwithstanding all this, we have to acknowledge that the age of chivalry was one essentially of Faith, a Faith that hallowed all the smallest vocations of life, and it is no wonder therefore, that the free and individual chivalry which now arose was impregnated with it, and knighthood was essentially Christian.

In this it differed from men previously banded together for military purposes, and whose life was the sword, both in the ages before its appearance, and after its decadence, e.g., (1) The Roman world had its Equestrian Order, but it was not a religious body. (2) The ancient Teutons had their warrior class, admitted by certain rites to take their places in its ranks, but it was not a religious class. (3) The earlier Chivalry had an admission of members, in order to hold fiefs and take upon them all the obligations of feudality, but such was not for religious purposes. (4) In later times, up to our own, men were raised in armies to higher rank for valour and experience in their profession but never for religion's sake, pure and simple. (5) Even the modern conference of knighthood is given for secular and not for religious reasons; but the knighthood we are considering differed essentially from all these, because it was the Flower of the Ages of Faith, and its very life-blood was drawn from the Cross. It was the temporal and earthly image of the Church Militant, as the latter was of the Eternal Mysteries. Emblematic and numerous as were the observances of the latter, they were equalled by those adopted by these new Christian knights.

Thus the sword was made in the form of a cross, in token of the cause in which it was to be used, and as it was always to be employed

in the θείεnce of justice, it was to be cutting on both sides. The
spear was straight and even, because truth is so, and its iron head was
significant of strength. The pennon, which must be seen afar, was
the sign of courage which wished not to be hidden. The steel helmet
was emblematical of modesty. The hauberk was a castle or a fortification against the powers of evil. The leg-armour was to keep the
feet free from the peril of evil ways. The spurs were tokens of
diligence and swiftness in all honourable designs. The gorget signified
obedience, and, as it encompassed the neck, so should the commands
of his lord encompass the knight. The mace represented strength of
courage, and the knife (or misericordia) with which the combatant
despatched his enemy when other arms failed—the mercy of God and
trust in His aid. The shield was typical of the knights standing
between the prince and the people, or between the prince and his
enemies, as the safeguard of the former. The gauntlets, in using which
he lifted up his hand on high, were to remind him of prayer to God,
and that he was not to be guilty of putting his hand to a false oath.
The saddle of his horse betokened surety of courage, and the great
charger which pertained to chivalry, an emblem of courage and readiness in daring. (Book of Chivalry.)

Despite therefore many shortcomings in its high ideals, as is ever
the case in all the fallible conceptions of men, knighthood, when in its
glory, was essentially religious; not perhaps in the sense in which we
should apply it when speaking of it in modern times, but when it
signified the presence of a strong devotional spirit, the influence of
awe, hope, and the mysterious interpositions of aid from the supernatural. In this light the period of which we are speaking was more
distinguished for its religious character than any other of which the
history of the world makes mention. This feature which belonged to
its society in general was the property of almost all its individual
knights. It infused into the light love-strain of the minstrel a deeper
pathos, giving a soft and solemn beauty to many of the customs of
domestic life, and blending the soldier's splendid dream of glory with
one of immortality and paradise. So, in all the ancient poets of this
age, the aim of every knight seems to have been, to obtain the guerdon
of a rest in heaven. To these hardy men who traversed countless
roads, suffered toils innumerable under different climates—cold and
heat, sunshine and snow—and passed whole days without unlacing
their helmets and easing themselves of their hauberks, the idea of
eternal rest was an unfailing appeal. To rest on a good bed may not
be a very spiritual or a very elevated idea, but it was alluring to the
tired warrior. " For each of you who shall die shall a bed be prepared
with the Holy Innocents," said the Bishop of Puy to the assembled
knights under the walls of Antioch. " In spacious Paradise your
places are all prepared," wrote Turpin, upon the battle-field of
Roncevalles. The future recompense to other brave knights is represented under the form of a beautiful garden where repose the soldiers
who have died in Christ's service. " Those who die here shall have
above a crown of flowers," so runs a verse in the Lay, " Le Charroi
de Nimes "; " Tant fist en terre qu'es ciex est couronez." So
in another " Lay of Renaud de Montauban," he is brought before
our Lord crowned. " Par devant Nostre Sire est couronné portant."

It is little wonder with the celestial rewards ever held before their eyes, that our forefathers, of the twelfth and thirteenth centuries, looked upon the institution of Chivalry as possessing a divine sanction. Its work, it is true, wrought Here, but its reward Beyond. So often stricken on some field of battle this Rest, promised him by his faith, made the knight willingly pour out his life-blood for its truth. " Qui muert pour l'amour Dieu louer en un moult grant "—(who dies for the love of God receives a great reward.—Renaud de Montauban). Is it any wonder the soul of chivalry—medieval Faith—long dead, its shrivelled bones alone remaining, has become a grotesque thing in the eyes of our own generation ?

. . . .

France and England, pre-eminently the homes of chivalry, were not so safe as now, but much more picturesque, adventurous and joyous.

These countries presented the feature of interest which those among us who have the means to travel now find in more distant lands. There were vast tracts of primeval forest, wild and unenclosed moors and commons, and marshes and meres. The towns were surrounded by walls and towers, and the narrow streets, of picturesque gabled timber houses, were divided by spaces of gardens and of grove, above which rose numerous steeples of churches and abbeys, full of artistic wealth. The narrow lanes were full of merchants and buyers, while the many sign-boards, over the booths and merchandise, gave colour to the scene. A contemporary poet describes to us, in the following lively manner, his walk through one of these gatherings of tradespeople and artisans :

> " Au bout par deça regratiers
> Trouve barbiers et cervoisiers
> Taverniers et puis tapissiers
> Assez près d'une sont les merciers,
> A la côté du grand chemin
> Est la foire du parchemin,
> Et apres trouvai les pourpoints
> Puis la grand pelletrarie,
> Puis m'en revine en une plaine
> La où l'on vend ouirs crus et laine,
> M'en vins par la feronerie,
> Cordouaniers et boureliers,
> Selliers et frenieres et cordiers."

(At the end beyond the stalls of retail grocers
I found the barbers and dealers in beer,
The eating-houses and furniture shops,
Near them are the Mercers,
By the high-way side
Is the parchment fair,
Then I found the jackets (tailors)
Then the dealers in furs,
Then I returned by a plain
Where is sold raw leather and wool.
I came next to the quarters of the iron-workers,
Then I found the copper-smiths,
Shoemakers and dealers in horse-hair
Saddle-makers, farmers, and rope-makers.)

8

DAYS OF CHIVALRY

Fairs played, of course, a great part in medieval commerce. The principal French fairs were those held at Falaise in Champagne and at St. Denis, near Paris. The villages consisted of a group of cottages, often mere hovels, scattered round a wide green, with a village cross in the middle. In England, close to the villages was the moated manor-house. This was occupied by the lord of the manor, or by his bailiff, or seneschal, and was often held from overlords. When this overlord was the king, the manor was said to be held " in capite."

Here are a few of these old services taken out of many, which demonstrate the quaintness, and in some, the childishness, of these days.

(1) Rowland le Sarcere held one hundred and ten acres of land in Heiningston, Co. Suffolk, by sergeantry, for which on Christmas Day, every year before our Sovereign Lord the King of England, he should perform altogether, and once, a " Leap," a Puff, and a Fart, or as in the Norman French, " un Saut, un Pet, et un Syflet." (Pla. Coron. Ed. I. Rot. 6.)

(2) Henry de la Wade held ten pounds (a pound is supposed to contain 52 acres of land) in the county of Oxford—by the service of carrying a Gerfalcon every year before our lord the King, when he should please to hawk with such falcons at the cost of the said lord the King. (Pla. Coron. Ed. I. Rot. 26.)

(3) Sir Walter de Hungerford held the castle and barony of Homet in Normany in special Tail—rendering the king and his heirs one Lance with a fox-tail hanging thereat yearly—upon the Feast of the Exaltation of the Holy Cross, and finding ten men at arms, and twenty archers to serve him during his wars with France. (Rot. Norman 6 Hen. V.P. 1. M. 2.)

(4) Peter Spilman paid a Fine to the king for the lands which the said Peter held by the Serjeantry of finding an esquire with a Hamergell (or coat of Mail) for forty days in England, and of finding Litter for the king's bed and Hay for the king's Palfrey when the king should be at Brokenhurst in the Co. of Southampton. (Fines. Hil. I. Ed. II. Wilts.)

(5) Henley, in Co. Warwick, was held by Edmund Lord Stafford by the service of three shillings, or a pair of scarlet hose. (Escaet. 24. Ed. I. N. 59.)

(6) Hamo de Hatton holds the Manor of Gateshull, Co. Surrey, of our lord the king, by Serjeantry, of being Marshal of the Whores when the king should pass into those parts, and he was not to hold it but by the will of the king. (Plac. Coron. 19. Hen. III.)

(7) Salamon de Campis holds certain lands called Coperland and Atterton in the county of Kent of our lord the king, " in capite," by the serjeantry of holding the head of our said lord the king between Dover and Whitfond as often as he should happen to pass over the sea between those Ports towards Whitfond. (Plac. Coron. Ed. I. Rot. 45.)

(8) King John granted to William de Ferrers Earl of Derby, a house in London, which was Issac's the Jew of Norwich, to be held by this service—that he and his heirs should serve before the king, and his heirs, at dinner on all annual feasts with his head uncovered, without a cap, with a garland of the breadth of a little finger upon him. (Ex. libro Magno ducat.)

9

Some of these services are religious. Greens-Norton was held by a family called Green—" in capite " from the king, by the service of lifting up their right hands towards the king yearly on Christmas Day wheresoever the king should be in England. (Fines 18. Rio II.)

Thomas Winchard held land in Connington, Co. Leicester, " in capite " by the service of saying daily five Paternosters and five Ave-Marias, for the souls of the king's progenitors. (Inquis. 27 Ed. III.)

Richard Paternoster for his Relief said three times, before the present Barons of the Exchequer, the Lord's Prayer, with the Salutation of the Blessed Virgin, as John his brother had done. (Rot. Fin. Pasch 31. Ed. III.)

If in England these strange services were required from vassals, in France even stranger ones occurred. We read of such being forced to descend to the humiliation of beating the water of the moat of the lord's castle in order to stop the noise of the frogs during the illness of his lady. We find elsewhere the lord required them to hop on one leg, to kiss the latch of the castle gate, or go through a lewd and doubtful play for his amusement, or sing a broad song before his wife. At Tulle all the rustics who had married during the year were bound to appear on the Puy, or mount St. Clair, at twelve o'clock precisely, when three children came out of the Hospice, one beating a drum violently, the other two carrying a pot full of earth; a herald called the names of the bridegrooms, and those who were unable to assist in breaking the pot, by throwing stones at it, paid a fine. (Lacroix.)

At Perigueeux two young couples had to give the lord's bailiff a pincushion of embossed leather of different colours. A woman marrying a second time had to present him with an earthen pot containing twelve sticks of different woods, but should a woman marry a third time, she had to give him a barrel of cinders, passed thirteen times though a sieve, and thirteen spoons made of the wood of her fruit trees. (Lacroix.)

The castles where the knight, as overlord, exacted these services, varied considerably in England and France, but for the most part partook of the characteristics of a prison; their frowning donjons, their impassable moats, their embattled walls, their jealously guarded portals, were suggestive of war and of rapine. Their interiors, to our modern standard of comfort, were cold and churlish. Through narrow loopholes and unglazed windows—for oiled paper or horn, or wooden shutters alone were then used—the winter blasts blew. The mailed foot of the knight and the silken slipper of the chatelaine reposed upon the undressed flags, whose coldness was somewhat relieved by a covering of straw or green herbs. The intimate association and domestic character arising from a sparse population, ever in danger of raids and battles, removed, in a knight's menie, all suspicion of menial service, or what to-day we intend by that word, to convey. The household fed together with the exception that the knight and his lady sat above the salt, or, if of the noblesse, on a dais above the floor. To counteract the bareness of the walls and to give some protection against incessant draughts, hangings of silken velvet embroidered with gold, were suspended against them. Golden

10

and silver plate ornamented the sideboard, which varied in the number of its shelves according to the rank of the owner. In times of peace the knight and his lady were decked out in rich furs and silks and velvets.

If it may be asked, how in this country and France, so destitute at that time of manufactures, these rich materials were obtained, the answer is they were obtained either by private purchase or at one of the great fairs, from the outcast and down-trodden Jew. To the Jew the knight in need of money turned as we should now turn to our bankers, but the borrower when the bill became due, was enabled by the detestation both lord and cleric felt towards them, often to repudiate the debt if he chose. Such addressed themselves to their lord and often obtained a writing from him that no interest should be paid on their debt. The King of England, as then Duke of Normandy, gave such a letter to the wife of the lord of Conches, Roger de Tosny. " The King of England Duke of Normandy to Henry of Greyss, we command you that you cause Constance Lady of Conches to be quit of a debt of 21 silver marks which she owes Benoit the Jew of Verneuil upon the payment of the principal. This is why we desire she do not pay interest on the debt. I myself witness at Liagle June 20th."

From this outcast race the ladies obtained their jewels and their furs. The Jews' trade was cosmopolitan. It ramified through Europe and the East. He bought amber on the Baltic, he sold slaves in Constantinople, he exchanged the goods of sunny Spain for the furs of Russia, and the pearls and incense of Yemen. In France he found a profitable market for jewels, spices, and cochineal, which was used extensively to dye the scarlet robes of the knights in times of peace. His intimate and extensive relations with the great markets of the East was one of the most important factors of his success. In that quarter of the globe, enjoying the protection and the confidence of the rulers of Persia, Syria and Egypt, were to be found the most wealthy and powerful of his race. He had obtained a network of communication over all the lands East and West. From the East he bought rare products, which commanded fabulous prices in the Middle Ages in Europe; costly gold and silver tissues, gems, aromatics, and he furnished every article needed, from the crown of the king to the sandals of the pilgrim. The law forbade him to sit among Christians without invitation from an ecclesiastic, but the bishop was often compelled to purchase of him the sacerdotal vestments which his race anathematized, and often the sacred furniture of the Church, and even the Crucifix, was supplied through the Jews. The Hebrews of Provence paid their tribute to the Church in wax and provided the tapers used in the great religious festivals, while the shameless trade of Church vessels by Ecclesiastics to the Jewish merchants of France became at one time so notorious as to call forth the indignant denunciations of the Holy See.

In the South the influx of the Moors from Spain also brought many luxuries into France, and so they filtered into England. Narbonne had long been the capital of the Moors in France, and they, and the Jews, abounded there. Montpellier entertained stricter relations with Salerno and Cordova than with Rome. In the time of the Crusades the upper portion of Languedoc had inclined towards the Mediterranean, and her counts of Toulouse were also counts of Tripoli. The beautiful coins, the beautiful stuffs, the rich spices of the East, even the chivalry of the Moors in battle, had done much to reconcile the Crusading knights, who were weary of their toils to regain the Sepulchre, with the world of Islam. Even Richard of England, their determined enemy, wore at Cyprus a silk mantle embroidéred with crescents of silver, the work of the Saracens.

So far had religious antipathies in Languedoc given way, that the bishop of Maghelone and Montpellier coined Moorish money, and had the profit in the minting, and discounted, without scruple, coinage with the impress of the crescent.

Both Pope Clement the IV. and St. Louis exclaimed against this outrage, and, in 1268, St. Louis wrote to his brother Alphonso of his astonishment that it was continued.

From this it will be seen, that cold as was the climate, rough-hewn as were the medieval castles of the North, unskilled as they were in the finer arts of peace and manufacture, their halls never needed—thanks to the Jewish merchants—rich tapestries to hide the walls, rich silks and velvets to prank themselves in, noble armour and embroidered surcoats for their tourneys, and even beautiful vessels for their oratories, all supplied by these despised Hebrews. Yet in these castles, even up to the reign of Edward IV, squalor mingled with splendour. We read of priceless hangings and costumes that cost each a small fortune, yet Erasmus described the floors in knights' and lords' castles and manors as sometimes encumbered with the refuse of twenty years. King Edward IV. was provided with a barber who shaved him once a week, and washed his head, feet, and legs only if he desired. So primitive were the manners even as late as his reign, that a young lord had to be instructed not only to hold his carving-knife with his thumb and his two fingers, but also not to dip his meat into the salt-cellar, or lick the dust out of the dish with his tongue, or wipe his nose on the table cloth. (See the Babees' Book.)

Into such a world of lights and shadows, much good and much evil, in one of these grey weather-beaten old castles in France or England, with its tiny town or village of retainers nestling at its foot, was born the heir of future knighthood. His was to be a warlike yet a religious vocation, sworn to fidelity to Holy Church, and the champion of the widow and the fatherless; fitly he was the outcome of the bridal-night when the nuptial bed had been blessed by some aged lord or grandfather. A certain curé, Lambert of Ardres, in his curious chronicle of the little Seigniory of Guisnes and Ardres, permits us to be present at the benediction of such a marriage bed. He writes : " At nightfall, when groom and bride were placed in the same bed, the count of Guisnes, filled with the zeal of the Holy Spirit, called me and my two sons Baldwin and William, and also Robert, curé of Andruicq, and asked us to sprinkle the pair with holy water. We therefore passed completely round the bed swinging our censors filled with precious spices, and called down upon them the benediction of Heaven. When we had performed our office with the greatest possible care and devotion, the count, still filled with the grace of the Spirit, raised his eyes and hands to Heaven, and after blessing them, he added, ' My dear son Arnoul, who art the eldest of my children and whom I love above all others, if there is any blessing which a father gives a son, and if it is true that a tradition of our ancestors gives us this right, then I bestow on thee, with clasped hands, the same favour of blessing which God the Father formerly gave to Abraham.' Arnoul bowed his head towards his father and devoutly murmured a paternoster, we all responded Amen, after which we left the nuptial chamber and each went to his home." (N.B.—The last item of Lambert's chronicle belongs to the year 1203.)

In those days of constant warfare, whether between conflicting countries, or the petty feuds hardly ever ceasing between neighbouring barons and knights, the birth of a male child was a valuable asset, both in a knight's family and for the lord's banner under whom he might ultimately serve. Battles in those days, it is true, even the more important ones, measured by modern ones caused very little loss of life, and those who were slain were chiefly archers, men at arms, and camp followers, the others of a higher class, such as the knights and squires of high degree, were nearly always held for ransom, still a certain amount of them in these constant little battles fell, and it was therefore requisite to look for children to be born to fill up these gaps.

The vassals also saw in the birth of a male child a future protector and the fief remaining in the possession of those under whom they were accustomed to serve, for if instead of a son, a daughter were born, they must expect—no other issue forthcoming—that the overlord would one day take her into his wardship and bestow her hand and lands on some alien knight.

We suppose therefore a male child just born. News is brought to the impatient father pacing up and down the great rush-strewn hall, littered with hounds and the implements of the chase.

" It is a son ! " one cries. " Par le foi que vos doi, une damoiseaux est né," so exclaims the Duchess Parise in the Lay that bears her name. When the father hears it, rejoicing already, he thinks of the valiant future of his little boy, " Dans quinz ans mon fils sera chevalier," thus the old knight Fromont whispers in the " Lay of Garins li Loherains."

The announcer of the event, too, looks forward. " Il est né, le seigneur dont vous tiendrez vos terres, il est né celui qui vous donnera les riches fourrures, le vair et le gris, les belles armes et les chevaux de prix."

So again in the ancient Breton ballad of " The Clerk of Rohan " (1241) the knight about to go crusading looks forward to his new-born child to do likewise some day.

" With that he took his little child
From off the lap of the ladye mild,
Between his arms the babe he took
And he fixed on its face a loving look.
' How say'st my son ? when tall and stout
With thy father wilt to battle out ? ' "
—Ballads and Songs of Brittany.

In England the person who brought news of the birth of a child was well rewarded. " Rumours " the news was called. The first who arrived with the grand news received a heavy fee according to the pleasure of the giver. King Edward I. gave fifty marks for news of the birth of his granddaughter Margaret de Bohun in 1303, but appears to have reduced the sum to ten for her sister Alianora the next year.

The birth of his grandson Edward Monthermer in 1304 found him more generously disposed to the extent of forty marks (Issue Rolls 31, 32, Ed. I.). Edward II. was more lavish; he settled £80 per annum on John Launge for news of the birth of his eldest son, afterwards Edward III., and gave a pardon for a debt of £80 due from Robert de Stanton for tidings of the birth of Princess Joan (Patent Roll 15, Ed. II.).

Edward II. gave £13 6s. 8d. for tidings of the birth of the Black Prince, and settled forty marks a year on the Queen's varlet, Thomas Priour. For John of Gaunt's birth-announcement, he paid £100 to be divided among three ladies (Issue Roll 27, Ed. III.).

Immediately after birth, this much desired child was bathed— the father often superintending it—and as his son was placed in the water, it reminded him of that bath that he as candidate for knighthood had once long ago entered. Then in many folds the infant was swaddled, his tiny arms bound close to his side, while his feet were held together by ligatures of linen; in the same fashion as before time the ancient Romans bound up the limbs of a new-born child; indeed the medieval miniatures of such a child are exactly similar to the fresco of an infant so swaddled found at Pompeii. " Quand les dames l'auront molt bien emmaillotée " we are told in the " Lay of the Knight of the Swan." So Quicherat in his " History of Costume " confirms this custom being the outcome of the ancient Romans. " Tous les enfants ont les bras enfermés dans leur maillot."

" Chez les Romains, les enfants étaient emmaillotés exactement de la même façon."

In being swathed in these tight ligatures the medieval child differed from his ancestors, of whom Tacitus writes : " In every house you may see little boys, sons of lords or peasants equally ill-clad, lying about or playing among the cattle." Tradition records of such that the first morsel of solid food was put into the baby-boy's mouth on the point of his father's sword, that he might be a valiant warrior and die on the field of battle. (Godfrey's " English Children in the Olden Time.")

Covering over the swathed infant was generally thrown a rich robe, so in the " Lay of Tristan de Nanteuil " we are told " Doon the son of Guy de Nanteuil did not know who was his father. He had as a babe been exposed in the forest, and found and taken care of by a forester, who one day said to him as he was asking who his father might be, ' Child, I will give you the robe in which you were wrapped when I found you.' The child seized on the robe when he saw it, for it was beautiful and embroidered in gold, and cried, ' Beautiful mantle, seeing you I know I was never begat by a family otherwise than noble,' and he covered it with kisses."

But before anything else was further done, this child, so treasured, must immediately be made a Christian. Before even he was allowed to take any nourishment, it was often the custom, that baptism must first take place—so in the " Lay of the Knight of the Swan " we are assured this was the case. " Ains qu'il ait en son cors nulle viande entrée," and stranger still, in the western provinces of old France, the parents refused to even embrace their new-born child till it had been christened (Gautier " La Chevalerie "). This rite of baptism was in the age of chivalry perhaps more highly thought of than ever before or since, for till the infant was immersed in the font, it was an evil thing—when it was lifted from it, it was not only a Christian, but had, in its heart, the making of a Christian knight.

During the thirteenth and fourteenth centuries custom varied as to the number of sponsors at a child's baptism. At one period one alone was thought best, to signify the Unity of God; three at another, to represent the blessed Trinity, so it is laid down in the Council of Salisbury 1217; Treves 1227; Worcester 1240. In the " Lay of the Knight of the Swan," the child has three godparents, the Abbé, who baptised him, the Duke of Montbas and a rich woman (" une rice dame qui a nom Salomas "). The Council of Trent at last decided that two sponsors only should be appointed, thus ending differences, but doing away with the mystical numbers of one or three.

Sometimes after Baptism the child's warlike destiny was prefigured. Thus after the second son of Charles V. of France, in 1371, was baptised, the Constable du Guesclin, his godparent, placed his bare sword in the naked infant's hands (nudo tradidit ensem nudum), so also the Duchess of Burgundy's infant, in 1433, was immediately after baptism admitted a knight of the Golden Fleece.

The day when the knight's lady was able to leave her chamber and repair to the nearest church, to offer her thanks and gifts, was made a great day of rejoicing. She was accompanied by a great throng of relatives and friends, and after hearing mass she made her appointed offerings. St. Elizabeth of Hungary is said to have offered a lamb and a wax taper, but this seems the only instance in medieval chroniclers of departing from the usual gifts of gold or silver or wax for the many altars.

Previous to setting forth to the church she was gorgeously apparelled in her chamber, often in an overdress of ermine, a mantle over it of grey fur ornamented with tufts of sable. (En son dos ot vestu un pelichon hermine. . . . Ses mantiax estoit gris orlés de sebelin.) During this robing a carol suitable to the occasion was frequently sung. We are told that when thus dressed " la contesse est plus bele que fée ! " Returning to the castle, troubadours and jongleurs congregated with the guests, and sang and played till the day declined, " et nobles jogleors, grant joie demenerent tant que li jors decline " (Godefroi de Bouillon.) At the end of the long feasting a herald stood forth and announced a tournament to be held on the morrow (ce hiraut s'escria a moult grant alenée . . .) (Brun de la Montaigne) as a suitable termination for a brave knight's hospitality on behalf of a young life born to one day enter the lists of chivalry himself.

The guests before leaving the castle universally left gifts for the new-born child. The godfather frequently gave his in gold or silver (or et argent lor donna à plenté) (" Amis et Amiles," v. 24). The godmother furred robes and frocks and shoes (un mantel d'escarlate et d'ermine fouré, et un pelicon rice, bien fait et bien ouvré) (" The

15

Knight of the Swan.") These gifts were often afterwards distributed to the poor even to a late period of French history (see Montesquieu, p. 45).

The child all this time was not left alone. Immediately at his birth a foster-mother was waiting to give him nourishment, for the knightly ladies hardly ever suckled their own children. In the history of Godfrey de Bouillon it is mentioned that his mother did so—but as an exception to the rule. The author of the " Lay of the Seven Wise Men " regrets this prevailing custom, but while expressing his regret declares that if the custom is to continue then a nurse should always be chosen according to the rank of the child's father. Thus the son of a king should be suckled by a Duchess; the son of a Duke by a Countess; that of a vavassour by a citizeness, and so on. " Look," he cries, " how the race in our days is going down; we find a woman of the streets giving nourishment to the son of an admiral! "

This practice of surrendering her baby to the care and nourishment of another than herself, can hardly be condemned when we remember how extremely youthful the high-born lady-mother often was—a mere child, we should nowadays consider her, married often, not for love, but to satisfy the policy of her parents. Her surroundings too, in the grey weather-beaten castle, hardly tended to the cultivation of maternal duties—the hall and entrances and tiny sleeping apartment filled with armed men, or giddy pages, often, except a bower-woman or two, she the only woman in a household of rough men, who looked upon her with favour only when she carried on those strange passages of feigned love the knights expected, to give them an object in their tourneys, and a vow for their enterprises.

So few high-born mothers suckling or attending to their children themselves, the nurse was a very important person. Some of their names are still on record as regards the English Princes. The nurse of Henry III. was named Helen of Winchester (Close Roll 15, Henry III.) and was the wife of William Dun. She was in receipt of a pension as late as 1237. The nurse of Edward II. was Alice de Lethegrew and the wardship of Geoffrey de Scotlands was granted to her in 1284 for her services (Patent Roll 18, Edward I.).

Edward III.'s nurse was Margaret de Daventie, and judging from his grants to her and his foster-sister Hawise, he seems to have been much attached to them.

Richard II. was one of our two medieval kings who were nursed by French women. His nurse bore the curious name of Mundina Danes or Danos, once it is spelt Denys (Patent Roll 1, Richard II.). We are distinctly told she came from Aquitaine.

Henry IV. was nursed by an Irish woman, Margaret Taaf of Dublin. Highest in rank of royal nurses was Anne de Caux, the French nurse of Edward IV. His brother Richard III. conferred on her a pension of £20 per annum.

It would perhaps be an incomplete notice of the childhood of a knightly son, if no mention of the belief of the time that children in their early years were peculiarly under the influence of the fairies. These were believed to haunt the fountains and woods outside the castle, often appearing to favoured mortals in lovely guise and to enter the sleeping chambers of the children within the castle. Sometimes they were accused of substituting one of their own elfin race for the lusty little heir, sometimes in a more pleasant humour endowing him with gifts of wisdom and strength. It was customary in some places to leave towels and clean water by the fire, after the child of the house had been bathed, for the fairy mother to use for her own elfin child.

To guard the crib many spells were used, and cradle songs made. But not alone were these fairy guardians round the child, or later the young page or squire, but they were woven in the life of the knights themselves. Thus in the "Lay of Parténopeus de Blois," the fairy "Melior," after sleeping with the nephew of Clovis, to prove to him the sincerity of her love and kisses, professes her faith in Christianity and before leaving him gave him as a knight this excellent advice:

> "Honorez Dieu et sainte yglise
> Et maintainez li sa franchise
> De Dieu aiez crième et peor (crainte et peur)
> Ce vos croistra pris et honor.
> Seur (tout) querrez chevalerie
> Et Dieu arez en vostre aïe (aide)."

Then this strange fairy in order to give her beloved greater confidence repeats the creed:

> "Je croi en Deu le fils Marie
> Qui nos raienst de mort à vie
> Et por lui prie que vos m'ames,
> Tos commandements tenes
> Por tant seres de moi ames
> Se contra hesu faites rien
> Ja puis ne seres de moi rien."

The truth is that at this period the frontier-line between the two beliefs—the magical and the Christian, the spells of fairy enchantment and the intervention of the saints—was hard to delimit. The nurse of the sleeping infant as well as the knight his father, to ward off troubles, as often as not tried to placate the fairy folk as they did the saints in the Calendar, recommending themselves to whichever invisible being they thought at the moment most efficacious for this purpose.

In the "Lay of Daurel and Beton," we have a charming picture of one of these noble little children. We are told at the age of three, Beton had a lovely face, and his locks gold, his eyes as the falcon in her prime, his mouth as sweet as the rose, his skin white as snow. At four years old, he was very precocious—he presented a pair of gloves, embroidered with gold, to the king, who brought him up. At five years old he was able to play at chess, and to throw the dice.

In the twelfth and thirteenth centuries a young boy not seven, learnt to walk on stilts, rackets and kite-flying; also bowls and hoop-driving (les bagues) and often, after the midday meal, to play at games of chance or at marbles (a la billette jeuent, "Charroi de Nimes") and also at shuttlecock. In the castle the child found every day the game of chess, beloved of his knightly father, being played, in which, at a very early age, he was instructed; or else there was

the game of " tables," supposed to be backgammon, " c'est le trictrac
ou le jacquet." He was even taught to throw the dice, " où il aprist
asés eschés et des dés " (Gaufrey).

At the age of seven the child was removed from his nursery and
from the care of females, and generally from his home, and placed in
the household of some powerful lord or knight, where he was to learn
the whole discipline of his future profession, and imbibe its emulous
and enthusiastic spirit. Eustache Deschamps confirms this usage and
depicts a mother sorrowing over the loss of her child:

> " Il y a jusques à VII ans
> Et plus encor trop de péris (perils)
> Mais il n'en chant à nos maris."
> —Poesies (XIV. siècle.)

The law which enforced the leaving children in the hands of
women until the age of seven years was originally decreed by the
Emperor Julian, and was incorporated into the laws of medieval
France.

This custom was an inestimable advantage to the poorest nobility,
who could hardly otherwise have given their sons the accomplishments
of their station, and the latter thus placed in the centre of all that
could awaken their imagination in the creed of Chivalry, gathered
indelible impressions to last through their lives and a thirst to join
in those rude but glorious tournaments and battles, they daily
saw their lord and his squires ride forth from the castle gate to
join in.

The dress of these children was a tunic cut off at the knee and
usually bare legs if not with long hose. In some cases leg-bands wound
round. A short mantle was fastened on the shoulder with a gold
brooch or clasp. The cap setting close to the head was usually of
leather, in winter trimmed round with fur. The hair was cut to the
poll straight across the forehead.

At the early age of seven, under the chief huntsman or falconer,
they were taught the rudiments of the chase. In the gentler art of
falconry they received the four first rules—how to fly a hawk; how to
feed it in its mews; how to call it back when on wing, and how to
retain it when it had returned. So the boy Huon de Bordeaux says,
" I know now how to ' mew ' the sparrow-hawk; how to chase the
wild boar and stag, and how to blow on the horn when I have killed
the beast, and how to give the quarry to the hunting dogs." So
intense was the love of the chase, even in lads, that when an old
chronicler wished to describe the thirst for future glory in youthful
Godfrey de Bouillon, he makes him say, " I long for a battle against
the Infidel more than the possession of gold or silver, or of the love
of a girl, or the flight of my falcon " (" Chanson d'Antioche ").

So, too, in the " Enfance Vivien," the hero is offered a fine
horse, as a youth, and he replies, " Nay, I care not for a horse but for
two dogs and a falcon." We need hardly remind the reader in the
immortal combat of Roland and Oliver under the walls of Vienne, the
whole quarrel was about a hawk. Thomas à Becket afterwards so
famous, son of the Portreeve of London, nearly lost his life as a boy
for the sake of his hawk, when he plunged into a mill-race in the

Thames where it had fallen, to save it (Green's History of English People).

Another pastime in the open air of these noble boys was to venture on the destrier, the knight's great war-horse. They clung on the great croupes and made the unwieldy horse gallop round the castle-yard (" et quant ils en ont sis bien galopent destrier ") (Guy di Nanteuil).

At the age of seven began the knightly boys' so-called education in letters, or what may be called the scant portion of it then in vogue for the children of knights. The colleges under ecclesiastical patronage, and the monastic schools, were only frequented by those of the lower ranks of Society, such as the citizen and, in some few cases, the villein, and most of their scholars were destined for the church or the law.

That villeins attended these schools is apparent from the fact that a petition was addressed to Richard II. demanding that they are restrained from sending their children to school because the ambition to rise in life by becoming a " clerk " was taking many workers from the land. The request was refused.

The education of a knight's or lord's children was conducted by the private chaplain. In some households, particularly if the owner was fond of music, there was attached to the private chapel a number of singers, priests and officials; in the smallest castle there was always the oratory and with a chaplain to serve it. In the poem of Eustache Deschamps the latter knew everything of his lord's intimate affairs. So " honour," says one, " all the clergy, and speak to them with reverence, but no more." Again, " Attend every day at Mass but carry no news to the monastery " (Doon de Mayence).

The scion of knighthood, as a rule, was well instructed in his religion, even though his secular knowledge was small. When Doon in the Lay of his name, was lost in the forest, the little boy hid himself in the bole of an oak and is depicted as making the sign of the cross and after that his prayers, and we are told afterwards he felt no fear though he was a lost child and away from his mother. In the " Lay of the Seven Wise Men " we are told of a chaplain who rebuked in his pupils a love of excessive eating, teaching them courtesy and good manners and never quitted the side of such till they went to bed. In the curious " Babees Book " (temp. Ed. IV.) out of which we give some quotations, is found the sort of education in manners that had long existed for noble boys, and is similar to that described in the household Ordinances of that king for those under the charge of a chaplain or aged knight—their " maystre," who should " teach them to ride cleanly and surely, to draw them also to jousts, to learn to wear their harness, to have courtesy in words, deeds, and degrees, deligently to keep them in rules of goings and sittings, after they be of honour." They were to learn also harping, piping, singing and dancing.

In the before mentioned " Babees Book " (*circa* 1475) the rules are laid down very exactly for conduct. We insert a few. " Take no seat, but be ready to stand until you are bidden to sit down. Keep your hands and feet at rest. Do not claw your flesh or lean against a post in the presence of your lord. Make obeisance to your lord always when you answer, otherwise stand as still as a stone unless he speak to thee. . . . Be ready, without feigning, to do your lord service and so shall you get a good name. Also to fetch him drink, to hold the light when it is time, and if you should ask a boon of God you can desire no better thing than to be well-mannered.

"When ye be set (*i.e.*, at your own dinner) keep your knife clean and sharp that so ye may carve honestly your own meat" (this refers to the meat being as was then the custom not on a plate but on a slice of wholemeal bread four days old, upon which it was served. Later these bread platters were made of wood). "When ye have done, look then ye rise up without laughter, or joking or boisterous word, and go to your lord's table and there stand and pass not from him until grace be said and brought to an end."

Despite all this seeming education, certainly as far as the eleventh and twelfth century is concerned, it is extremely difficult to determine how much or how little that might be called "letters" a child knew, and consequently when he grew up and attained knighthood, what amount he possessed. Antiquaries differ in their verdict, but it is tolerably clear that a certain number grew up unlettered men in the twelfth century. It was a Great Chamberlain, Jean de Nanteuil of France, who was obliged to confess in the reign of St. Louis he was unable to read; on the other hand many of the bravest knights in the Romances and Lays were far from having to make this confession of ignorance.

In the "Geste des Lorrains" the heroes Hervis and Garin knew how to read both in the vulgar tongue (Romance) and in Latin: "Bien savoit lire et Roman et Latin." We have the testimony of O... ic Vitalis that children were taught to read and to write on tablets of wax (parchment being too costly). "Osbertus Rector ecdesice Uticensis juvenes valdé coercebat eosque bene legere et psallere atque seribere verbis, et verberibus cogebat et tabellasque cera illitas prœparabat." ("Oderic Vital." Bk. III., Chap. VII.)

We are again assured in the "Lay of the Duchess Parise," her son could read and write. So, too, the three children of Guy de Mayence—"bien savoit Aiols, lire et embriever et latin et romans savoir parler" ("Aiol," v. 275).

To sum up this question of a knightly boy's education "in letters," it appears, in order to judge rightly, that the mean is the safest to take, *i.e.*, certain number of lads, as to-day, preferred to remain in ignorance, or their fathers or the lord under whom they were placed were themselves ignorant of any of the polite arts and so did not trouble about the boy's education; while on the other hand, and probably the greater portion of them, were sufficiently taught to enable them to read a romance and to write a letter, and, some few, to understand languages foreign to their own. Thus the Duke de Nevers in the "Lay of Gaufrey," was able to boast he could speak in French, German, Italian, Spanish, Poitevin and Norman.

The great end in view, however, in training these noble boys was not a proficiency in letters—that was left to the bourgeoisie and clergy —but for his future career as a knight, to be brave in the field, to endure hardness, to be expert at the mimic war of the chase; this every old knight who trained the boys—and this even the chaplain who loved with his brother ecclesiastics of that age, the chase—had in view. Even as late as 1517 an old writer, Pace, in his work "De

Fructu," tells us how one of those whom we call gentlemen always carries some horn hanging at his back as though he would hunt during dinner and how one such said, " I swear by God's body, I would rather that my son should hang than study letters. For it becomes the sons of gentlemen to bear the horn nicely, and to hunt skilfully and elegantly, to carry and train a hawk. But the study of letters should be left to the sons of rustics."

Sometimes it seems so great was their ardour to arm themselves like their elders, that they were pacified by giving a religious significance to these arms they so wanted, an armour even as boys they could don. Thus so bent on the chase were some of these noble lads in the Middle Ages, that we find to humour their tastes and yet impress them with religion, a Chaplain of King John of France writes, at the king's desire, a book on the subject for his son the Duke of Burgundy (Philip) in 1359. In a passage in it the chaplain compares the weapons used by a boy, to his spiritual armour :

> " Plates aures d'humilité
> Afin que parmi le cousté
> Orgueil ne te puisse bleçer
> Au cueur ne nullement toucher
> De patience soit.
>
> Les plates soient bien clouées
> Et les bouglettes bien fermées
> Et garde bien que en l'escu
> Il n'ait nul defaut de vertu
> De raison feras bacinet
> Tu ne porteras point de lance
> Pour ce qu'es encore en enfance
> Mais auras une belle espée."
>
> (Steel plates shalt thou have of humility
> So that through thy side
> Pride cannot wound thee
> To the heart, that nothing shall touch
> If Patience be the shield.
>
> The plates must be well clamped
> Into the well-closed buckles,
> And take thou heed that in the shield
> There be no flaw (want of virtue),
> Of Reason thou shalt make the bassinet,
> Thou shalt carry no lance
> For fear that thou art yet too young.
> But thou shalt have a fine sword.)
> —St. Palaye, Vol. III., p. 850.

The title bestowed on these boyish sons of the knights was that of " varleton, damoiseau, or page," so the " Order of Chivalry " lays down. " Le chevalier doit avoir Escuyer et Garçon ou Paige qui le servent, et prennent garde de ses Chevaux."

In the well-known medieval romance of " The Little Saintré," at the age of thirteen he was received into the household of the lord of Preuilly where he is described as " paige et enfant d'honneur," he is also called Valet or Valleton, and is sometimes by the speaker addressed as " Maître " or " Sire," or " Beau Sire." When it was announced to the assembled household young Saintré had been advanced to the grade and honour of Esquire, they exclaimed, " He has been, and is, a good Varleton ! " As such a page or varleton, the celebrated knight Bayard when a boy, was placed by his parents in the household of his uncle, the Bishop of Grenoble, and accompanied the latter to the court of Savoy, where " durant icelui (dinner) estoit son nepvue le bon Chevalier qui le servoit de boire très-bien en ordre et très mignonnement (delicately, courteously) se contenoit " (" Vie du Chev. Bayard "). But this office of serving the cup at the high-table seems generally to have fallen to the young squires and not to the pages. Perhaps as nephew of a great Ecclesiastic Bayard was given the honour, though only in rank a varleton.

Somewhat similar to this incident of a young varleton performing a squire's duty is that recited in Joinville's " Life of St. Louis," where he says he carved before that king, the usual office of the squire—though he was not at that time such. At all events it seems so, for he appeared neither in the dress nor " hauberk " of a squire (il n'avoit encore vestu nul haubert).

The duties of these pages were those found generally in domestic service about the person of their lord and lady. They accompanied them to the chase, in their journeyings, in their visits to neighbouring castles, in their walks, and often carried messages.

The chief lessons inculcated were—love due to God, and (strange juxtaposition)—love due to the ladies. So in the before-quoted romance of " The Little Saintré," we find the ladies charging themselves to teach him his catechism and also the art of love. In defence of the latter there is no doubt in the earliest ages of Chivalry this love inculcated was pure and platonic, and possibly prevented youth from falling into regrettable disorders. The wave of ardent and often unplatonic love from Provence had not yet penetrated into the northern castles of France or England. As practice is better than precept, the boy was bidden to choose one of the fairest and most virtuous ladies about the court or castle he served in, and to look on her as his soverayne-lady. To her he was to confide all his thoughts and actions, and she, in return, looked after his welfare and upbringing. The close companionship engendered by the castle walls promoted among the boys thrown together many close and enduring friendships, which were helped by having a similar object in view—to become one day a valiant knight in the service of their present lord or future king. Nor had this gratuitous reception of a brother-knight's lads into his entourage as page or squire no reward to the knight who received such. On the contrary, as it was from such a brave knight the boys imbibed their first lessons in chivalry, and, in his person and bravery, saw the standard of knightly virtue, they rendered him the greatest obedience during their education, and ever afterward, when their days of instruction were over, tendered it to him by following his banner to the wars from their own free-will.

At the age of fourteen the boy was considered of an age to be admitted as an Esquire. Such were allowed a greater intimacy with their lord and his lady than they had enjoyed as pages. Religion stepped in and a certain religious service, not so elaborate or so solemn as that used in conferring the higher grade of knighthood, was held. The future squire was presented to the priest before the altar by his parents, each holding blest tapers in their hands, which afterwards they presented as gifts to the church, and after certain prayers and blessings upon a sword and belt, which was henceforth to be his own, it was girded on the youthful squire's side. It is probable that it was this simple ceremony used when raising a page to an esquire that the early kings of the time of Chivalry bestowed on their children, and lords on their sons, and not as some writers on the subject seem to have thought, the conferration of knighthood. (St. Palaye.)

Before entering into the various offices and degrees of esquire-hood, it may be mentioned that the old French and Norman name " écuyer " is constantly used also in the language of the Chase to denote, just as much as it does in Chivalry, the subordination of youth to age. Thus in a book on the Chase by Gaston Phœbus it is laid down, " Ecuyer, en terme de chasse; jeun cerf qui accompagne et fuit un vieux cerf." But the more obvious meaning of the word evidently is from the squire's duty of carrying the knight's shield. Yet if the resemblance to the martial squire is to be found in the chase, so it was to be found in the Church. The strict upbringing that hedged in the education of the young esquire in the castle was not without its copy in the monastic schools, and strengthened the resemblance that the ancient writers sought to draw between Chivalry and Religion. Each bishop thus congregated round him, in the monastery, or ecclesiastical palace, a bevy of youths emulous for the priesthood; these had daily and particular duties, often menial and personal to the lord-abbot or bishop. A strict code of morals, and of exercises were laid down for them, and they were presided over, as the youthful esquires in the castle, by those older and more learned in their vocation. (Cf. Fleury, Hist. Ecc.)

It may be of interest to the reader before entering more into detail of these young squire's or damoisel's duties to know what their appearance generally was. In the charming account Chaucer gives of such a squire the poet paints his portrait, and it will be found in treating of his duties, a little later in this book.

Except in the case of a few descriptions found in the old chroniclers and poets, the beauty of damoisels or young squires is of a fair or blond type. In the " Chansons " nearly all the heroes are fair. An exception to this rule is mentioned in the " Lay of Ogier " (v. 4612) " noir ot la teste com more de morier."

The ideal lad of both mothers and ladies was one perfectly proportioned and graceful, slender, lively, with regular features and " traitis," having locks as yellow as gold, and these curled, frizzed and plaited, and his eyes beautiful like a falcon's, of a grey, changeful hue (vairs) " des elx ot vairs et la viaire cler " (Ogier). These eyes should be large and dashed somewhat with his proud spirit, and yet in them nothing displeasing. Accompanying these foregoing charms his complexion should be as white as his cheeks rosy (blanche et rose) or as silver or the crystal (" et ot sa char plus blanche que argent ne *cristal* ") (Gui de Bourgogne, v. 2208). His nose should be straight and slender (le nés et lonc et droit) with a laughing mouth; perhaps above it the down of early manhood. As to his body—his chest and shoulders, they should be broad and strong (" gros par les costes, grailes par le baldrer) (Ogier). His arms should be full of muscle and sinew in order to give a ready blow, while his hands should be kept white and his fingers tapering, and his legs should be long and shaped well for the saddle (" les piés voltis et lès ") (" Jerusalem," v. 2325).

But if to the reader such a description may appear effeminate, let such remember it was a picture of only one side of a young esquire's character and life. If the frizzled hair, the clear complexion and golden tresses were the means of furthering " courtesy " as it was then called, which embraced all we know now of graceful dalliance on a lady's whims and smiles, there was always underlying it the sterner and more martial one of military training and of aspirations for what every noble lad so earnestly looked forward to as the consummation of his years of training—a knight's spurs, and career.

Such a youthful " damoisel," reared up in his father's or a neighbouring lord's house, gained a vocation for chivalry without effort. Everything combined to foster it. The conversation of his elders, their tales at the end of the lengthened banquets, the reading of the only books available—the old romances of Charlemagne or Arthur and his Knights—the very painted arras draping the old walls depicting fights of warriors in a bygone age. With every breath he drew, the young esquire drew in the spirit of the chivalrous life. Indeed there was no choice for a noble lad to take but two, the helmet or the tonsure, and he generally preferred the former. For if, as sometimes happened in these lordly halls, a tradesman or a craftsman was mentioned, he was made a gibe by these sons of the sword, and held up to ridicule by the wandering minstrel who was playing before them.

It is no wonder, therefore, that a noble lad of fourteen, just girt with the baldric and the sword of squiredom, grew up longing for the active life of Chivalry. The knight's departure from the castle gate to battle or to tourney every day intensified that longing, sometimes to break into unrestrained activity.

Scott in " Marmion " refers to this youthful ardour:

> " Behind him rode two gallant squires,
> Of noble name and knightly sires,
> They burned the gilded spurs to claim,
> For well could each a war-horse tame,
> And draw the bow, the sword could sway,
> And lightly bear the ring away;
> Nor less the courteous precepts stored,
> Could dance in hall, and carve at board,
> And frame love ditties passing rare,
> And sing them to a lady-fair."

In the " Lay of the Narbonnais " a lad of fifteen is depicted on the beleaguered walls of the city of Orange, whom the Countess Giubourc, his aunt, in vain seeks to restrain from exposing himself to the enemy. He seizes a war-horse (destrier) and gallops off out of the town-gate and engages with the foe. The Countess sends a hundred squires of a maturer age to bring him back, but he refuses to do so till he has proved, by stroke of sword and facing the enemy's ranks, his mettle. On his return, for his reward, he begs knighthood at her hands—which the story tells us she confers. If this narrative is worth nothing else, it seems to show on some unusual event of bravery, knighthood was conferred at an earlier age than the required one of twenty-one, and that a female, if she was of highest rank, was supposed to be able to confer it.

It was probably during their apprenticeship as varlets or esquires that many of those beautiful and life-long friendships were contracted between knightly souls. The yearning after something beyond ordinary intercourse seems to have often been felt in the Middle Ages, and led to various characteristic practices, among which one of the most remarkable was that of sworn Brotherhood. Two men, generally knights, who felt a sufficiently strong sentiment towards each other, engaged, under the most solemn vows, in a bond of fraternity for life, implying a constant and faithful friendship to each other. This practice enters largely into the plot of several of the medieval romances, as in that of " Amis and Amiloun." The desire for this true friendship began when pages or young esquires, living together, was not unnaturally fostered by the general prevalence of hateful feuds. In the Romance of " Garin le Loherain " there is a beautiful passage which illustrates this sentiment—" Begues was in his castle of Belin and beside him sat the beautiful Beatris, his wife. In the middle of the hall she saw her two sons, ten and twelve years old, laughing and playing with six damoisels (older boys). The duke looked at them, and while he looked, sighed. Beatris, observing this, chided him and said, ' Why have you sorrowful thoughts, you possess gold and silver, rich clothing, fine horses and houses and loving sons. What more do you require ? '

" ' Dist le dus, dame, vérités avez dit ; mais d'une chose i avez moult mespris ; N'est pas richoise né de vair né de gris, né de deniers, de murs, né de roncins, mais est richoise de parens et d'amins ; Li cuers d'un homme vaut tout l'or d'un pais."

(Wealth consists not in rich clothes nor in money nor in buildings, nor in houses, but it consists in kinsmen and friends. The heart of a man is worth all the gold of a country.)

These youthful esquires were divided in their lord's household into different classes, or employments. There was :

(1) The Squire of the Body—that is to say he who rendered personal service on the knight's person and his lady's.
(2) There was a Squire of the Chamber or Chamberlain.
(3) The Squire of the Table or Carver.
(4) The Squire of the Wines (?).
(5) The Squire of the Pantry.
(6) The Squire of Honour or " The Honorus."

Of these probably the most honourable were the first and the sixth, *i.e.*, those who were appointed to wait on the persons of their lord and lady, and those who were appointed to the " Honours " as they were called.

The first were admitted to great familiarity by these distinguished persons. They took part in their courts and assemblies; they were enabled to mould their conversation and conduct by those they mixed with; they accompanied them when they made visits to their neighbours; they often took part (instead of those detailed for that duty) in the Honorus. They were enabled by this constant personal service in the more refined presence of their master and mistress, to become skilled in elegant manners and modes of speech, and to cultivate by their bright example, modesty, learning, and a facility in witty conversation.

Secondly, those who were esquires of the Honours were so named as taking part and marshalling the ceremonies of the lord's court. The word " honours " here signifying the ceremonials of such, and the articles pertaining to these stately functions. Thus the esquire of honour carried his lord's sword of honour; he stood by the lord's chair or throne of state; he carried his master's helmet of honour; he led his state horse with all its glittering caparisons; he carried (if not worn) his lord's mantle of state, and had besides all the duties thrown on him of any great Reception at which the lord's neighbours and vassals were entertained. Perhaps the duty they most thought of was their duty of carrying their knight's banner and of raising his battle-cry, as we find such depicted doing in the life of the celebrated Du Gueslin. In addition to these duties, these esquires often were despatched in the place of heralds, and indeed often took the office of such—to throw down their master's " gage " of battle before his adversary (see Hardouin de la Jaille in his " Book of the Battle-Field," fol. 43).

Thirdly, the Esquire of the Table had many onerous duties, such as we now look on as those only fit for persons of a low degree, but were then considered as marks of honour and to be sought after by youths of noble lineage.

To enforce the submission of high-spirited youths to these menial offices the " Order of Chivalry " in its dissertation " How to Acquire Knighthood," lays down: " It is fitting that the son of a knight while he is an esquire should know how to take care of a horse, and it is fitting that he serve (at table) first, and be subject before he himself is a lord (or knight) for otherwise he will never know the nobleness of his knighthood when he comes himself to be a knight. For this reason should every knight put his son into the service of another knight so that he may learn to carve at table and to serve thereat, and to arm, and robe a knight in his youth. Thus like a man who would learn to be a tailor or a carpenter it is fitting that such a one should have a master who is a tailor or a carpenter; so too it is fitting that every nobleman who loves the order of his knighthood should have had first a master who was a knight."

To serve, therefore, whatever his family's rank, at his lord's table, was one of the usual duties of the young esquire told off for that purpose.

Sometimes—if his pupilage was conducted at home—this service was rendered to the knight his father. Chaucer's description of such a young esquire carving before his father is one of the most charming pictures he brings before us of that age:

> " With him there was his son, a young squire,
> A lover and a lusty bachelor,
> With locks crulle (curled) as they were laid in presse
> Of twenty years of age he was I guess.
> Of his stature he was of even length
> And wonderly deliver (nimble) and great of strength,
> And he had been some time in chevachee
> In Flanders, in Artois and in Picardie,
> And bore him wel, as of so litel space
> In hope to standen in his ladies grace.
> Embroidered was he, as it were a mede
> Alle ful of freshe flowres, white and rede.
> Singing he was or floyting alle day
> He was as freshe as in the month of May.
> Short was his gowne, with sleves long and wide
> Wel coude he sitte on hors and fayre ride.
> He coude songes make, and wel endite
> Juste (joust) and eke dance, and wel portraie and write.
> So hot he loved that by the nightertale
> He slep no more than doth a nightingale.
> Curteis he was, lowly and servisable
> And *carf before his fader at the table*."

In the same fashion Froissart tells us the young Count of Foix served at Gaston de Foix, his father's, table. " Le comte de Foix s'assit à table en la salle, Gaston son fils avais d'usage qu'il le servoit de tous ses mets, et faisoit essai de toutes ses viandes."

So, too, Eustache Deschamps tells us of these squires:

> " A table et par-tout servoient."

Another set of them, besides carving, offered water to the assembled guests to wash their hands—a very necessary performance in days when the meats were generally eaten in the fingers. So the old Breton ballad has it:

> " Light down my lord into the hall
> And leave your laden wains in stall.
> Leave your white horse to squire and groom
> And come to sup in the dais-room;
> To sup, but first to wash, for lo
> E'en now the washing horn they blow."

(This practice of sounding the horn for washing called in old French " corner l'eau," is still kept up at the Temple in England.)
So in the " Lay of the King ":

> " Après manger se sont déduit
> De paroles, puis si ont fruit;
> Et après le manger laverent
> Escuier de l'eve (eau) donerent."

(After dinner they amused themselves
With words, then there is playing
And after dinner they washed,
An Esquire presented water.)

Other young esquires offered the wines, and Eustache Deschamps makes one of them say :

" Il n'est esbatement
Où je ne soye la premiere.

Je sers Vin le Roi de France
Les Ducs, les Comtes, les Barons.

Les Dames et les Chevaliers
Les Damoiselles et Escuyers,

Par moy est coulez l'ipocras."

(There is no entertainment where I am not the first.
I serve with wine the King of France,
The Dukes, Counts and Barons,
The Ladies and the Knights,
The Demoiselles and the Esquires.

By me is poured out hypocras.)

Other wine beside hypocras they served. Thus claret which then was a drink composed of wine and honey mingled. Then again " piment," another mixture probably having a greater mixture of wine in it than " claret," for the " Statutes of Cluny Abbey " lay down an injunction against the monks partaking of it.

" Statutum est, ut ab omni mellis ac specierum cum vino confectione, quod vulgari nomine pigmentum vocatur . . . fratres abstineant." (Du Cange.)

These young esquires were also told off to see their lords or guests had refreshments before retiring for the night.

" Les lis firent li Escuyer
Si coucha chacuns son Seignor."

(The esquire is to see to his bed his lord).

Then to offer the " sleeping " cup (so in the " Lay of Gerard de Rousillon ") :

" E las tablas son messas e van maniar
Quant au menjat, s'en prendon à issit,
Et plan devan la sala s'en van burdir
Qui sap chanso ni fabla enquel là dir;
Chevalier a burdir i à vandir.

28

DAYS OF CHIVALRY

E Gerard e lhi feu a esbaudir
Entro que venc la nuh aufre desir.
Lo coms demander vi e vai durmir,
Elevet lo mati à esclarzir:
Siei dozel l'aiuderan gen à vestir."

(And the tables are set and they go to dinner.
When they have eaten they begin to go out.
In the court before the Hall they begin to tilt,
Whosoever knows song or fable that he relates.
And Gerard and his folk take (their) pleasure
Until the night becomes chilly.
The count calls for wine and retires to rest,
And rises in the morning at dawn.
His esquire helps him then to dress.)

The duties of these young esquires were not only confined to these domestic duties. In a warlike household the pre-eminent duty of such was to attend his lord's convenience when preparing for joust or battle, and the arming of the latter before a fight. Doubtless the armourer was needed, when chain armour was discarded for plate, to rivet the many pieces which made a knight a veritable man of steel, but he was always overlooked by the faithful squire. Such, too, when on a journey, carried—till the knight needed such to meet his adversary—the arms of his master. Some young esquires therefore bore after him his steel gauntlets, the armpieces of his coat of mail, others of them bore his lance, and his sword and his pennon, or if entitled to that as a banneret—his square banner. They also, unless slung on the saddle bow of his destrier or war-horse, bore his helmet, ready to give him at the least approach of danger—and with the exception of bearing the pennon or banner, the most coveted distinction of these youthful squires was adjudged to be his who carried the lord's shield.

Not less a service was that assigned to the varleton or esquire who led the great war-horse, ready covered with plates of mail for any knightly adventure which demanded strength rather than speed.

It might not be out of place here to touch on the horses employed by the knights during the Middle Ages, as they enter so frequently into all the noble contests of arms and the Lays of the troubadours. Perhaps no animal is so intimately mixed up with the history of mankind as the horse, certainly this was the case in the age of Chivalry.

The Anglo-Saxon travelled much on foot, and as far as we know, the great importance of the horse, as far as England was concerned, began therefore with feudalism. In the old romances and poetry the knights are generally mounted on Arab steeds, won in conquest of the Saracens. In the thirteenth century they were obtained from Turkey and Greece, and at a later period from Barbary. France also had its native breed, which had a high reputation, especially for its fierceness in battle. Gascony, and on the other side of the Spanish frontier, Castile and Aragon were much celebrated for their horses. The Gascons prided themselves greatly on their horses and they displayed this pride sometimes in a singular manner. In 1172

29

Raymond de St. Gilles, Count of Toulouse, held a grand "cour plénière" and as a display of ostentation caused thirty of his horses to be burnt in presence of his guests.

It may be mentioned that a male horse only was ridden by knights, to ride a mare was looked upon as a degradation. French knights' horses were nearly always docked both in ears and tail. The kind of horses most commonly in evidence in the age of chivalry were the "palefroi," the "destrier," the "roncin" and the "sommier." The "destrier" was the knight's heavy war-horse, the palfrey that on which he often rode when not in immediate warfare or engaged in a tournament, while his esquire or page bestrode the "destrier" carrying his helm and armour. The "roncin" belonged especially to his "menie" or servants, while the "sommier" carried his luggage. Ladies of course rode the palfreys. The Orkney Islands appear to have been celebrated for their "destriers," Brittany for her palfreys. England seems not to have been celebrated for its breed of horses in the Middle Ages, and those her kings and nobles possessed seem to have been imported from the continent.

At this time a horse was considered the handsomest present that could be made by a king or great lord, and horses were often given as bribes. Thus in 1227 the monks of the Abbey of Troarn obtained from Guillaime de Tille the ratification of a grant made to them by his father in consideration of a gift to him of a mark of silver and a palfrey. The monks of St. Evroul in 1165 purchased a like favour from the Earl of Gloucester by presenting to him two palfreys. The widow of Herbert de Mesnil gave King John a palfrey to obtain the wardship of her children; and one Geoffrey Fitz-Richard gave the same king a palfrey to obtain a concession in the forest of Beaulieu. In 1172 Raymond, Count of St. Gilles, gave his overlord, the King of England, as tribute, ten "destriers." Of the colour of horses in the days of chivalry, white seems to have been prized most highly, and after that, dapple-grey or chestnut. The same colours were in favour among the Moors.

To be a skilful rider was before all things necessary to a knight. From the time he had been taken as a page till he rose to be a "valet" or squire, his daily exercises were for this end. One of the feats of horsemanship practised ordinarily was to jump into the saddle in full armour.

> "No foot Fitzjames in stirrup staid,
> No grasp upon the saddle laid;
> But wreathed his left hand in the mane
> And lightly bounded from the plain."

As to horses' adornment, not only were they defended in war or tourney by plate armour, but it was a great point of vanity in the Middle Ages, certainly in England, to hang small bells on the caparisons of the horse, which made a jingling noise as they went along.

In the Romance of "Richard Cœur de Lion" (Weber, II. 60) a messenger coming to King Richard has no less than five hundred such bells suspended to his horse.

> "His trappys wer off tuely sylke
> With five hundred belles ryngande."

And again in the same romance we are told, in speaking of the Sultan of " Damas " that his horse was well furnished in this respect :

> " Hys crouper heeng al fulle off belles
> And hys peytrel, and hys arsoun ;
> Three myle myghte men here the soun."

The bridle, however, was the part of the harness usually loaded with bells.

According to Chaucer a custom particularly affected by monks, that

> " When he rood, men might his bridel heere
> Gyngle in a whistlyng wynde cleere,
> And eeke as lowde as doth the chapel belle."
> —Cant. Tales I. 169.

Fine horses were at this period, as now, much prized.

And in the " Romaunt of the Rose," a youthful knight is portrayed as even preferring theft to having his stables without good steeds :

> " A youth of fairest goodlihead,
> He loved fine mansions, castles fair
> And jewels rich and vestments rare,
> Grand stables, horses past all price,
> And sooner were he charged with vice
> Of theft or murder, than 'twere said
> His stables harboured crock or jade."

In the romance " Perceforest " (fol. 3.) two of the breed of horses in medieval use are described :

> " Si voit venir Monseigneur Gauvain et deux Escuyers dont l'ung menoit son destrier en destre, et portoit son glaive, et l'autre son heaume, l'autre son escu. Quant il entra en la forest il rencontra quatre Escuyers qui menoient quatre blancz destriers en dextre. Lors rencontra ung varlet qui chevauchoit ung roncin fort et bien courant, et menoit à dextre ung destrier noir."

(He saw Monseigneur Gauvain coming and two esquires, one of whom led his steed by the rein.(his destrier) and carried his sword, and the other his helm, the other his shield. When he entered the forest he met four esquires who led four white horses by the rein. There he met a varlet, who was riding a well-made swift pack-horse, and he led a black steed by the rein.)

It was often the custom of a knight victorious in a tournament to offer his adversary's dearest possession next to his sword—his " destrier " or war-horse—to his own lady-love. Thus in the Romance of " Floire and Blanceflor " (MS. di St. Germain, fol. 41) she says :

> " Mais mon ami est bel et gent,
> Quand il vait à tournoiement,
> Et il abat un chevalier,
> Il me présente son destrier."

31

(But my love is fair and fine
When he goes to the Tournament
And lays low a knight
He presents me with his war-horse.)

Often the knights who had conquered their opponents in the tourney (and whose armour and horses were by the laws of the tourney forfeited) presented them to those poor knights, who otherwise could not be mounted. (" Perceforest " Vol. I.).

So a fayre lady seeing this generosity remarks :

" Mon tenant donne à aucun destrier
A l'autre donne palefroy ou courcier."

(My champion gives to one a war-horse,
To another a palfrey, or a courser.)

So again, in the romance entitled " Le Court Mantel " of a Court " plénière " held by King Arthur :

" Qui fist aux Chevaliers donner
Robes moult riches et moult beles,
Et grant plante d'armes nouveles
Et moult riches chevaux d'Espaigne
De Hongrie et d'Alemaigne
Ni ot si poure Chevalier
Qui n'ait armes et bon destrier."

To the custom of hanging small bells on the horses' harness, according to some old writers, is to be traced the origin of the heraldic term " vair " ; and so to the fur " vair and gris " which as only permitted to be worn by knights, is often used in the medieval romances to denote a certain person was knighted. In the " Dictionary de Menage " the word " vair " or " vaire " is derived from the verb " variar " to change or variegate. " Vair " therefore was a fur of variegated colours. But this fur by its very name, demonstrates it was not natural but made by the art of the furriers, and was composed by them chiefly of two skins, one white, the other grey, lapping over each other, figured over by small pieces in the shape of little bells arranged opposite each other, grey and white, in rows, so as to make one entire skin. The origin of this ornamented fur is to be found in the custom of ancient Chivalry. The explanation by another old writer (Beneton de Peyrins) is extremely curious :

" It is necessary," he says, " to remember the way horses about to enter a battle or tournament were dressed. Over their caparisons—or coats of iron which they wore to shield them from blows—they wore a long caparison or cloth of rich material emblazoned with the armorial bearings of their knightly owners. If the knight's coat was of one colour, so the horse cloth, if of many—so the horse's. (The whole horse cloth was also garnished with little bells of two shapes, intermingled together. In imitation of the ancient knight's plumes on his helmet and on his horse's head, we find still in countries abroad where the mule is driven the feather still decking his often weary old head, while round his collar the bells still survive of another age. These rows of little bells which ornamented the horse cloth of the ancient knight were called ' bellfreys,' like the veritable belfreys

GEOFFREY, COUNT OF ANJOU. Father of Henry II.

Died 7th September, 1150.

From an enamelled tablet in the Museum at Mans, formerly in the Church at St. Julian

From Foster's "Some Feudal Coats of Arms."

that gave warning so often of the border or robber bands, about to fall on some hapless village or town. After a time, however, these little rows of real bells became discontinued and it became a custom to embroider them only in rows of two different shapes on the rich horse cloths. This gave the idea to the knights and the furriers to imitate in fur—by, as we have shown, using two colours of skins, alternately facing each other—these discarded and literal bells, and they gave to the fur the celebrated name so associated with the knightly order ' vair,' and which no one except of that degree was allowed to wear. Thus by an ordinance of the King of France in 1294 no burgher or his wife is to wear ' vair,' nor grey (fur) nor ermine, and if they have such they are to render them up at the approaching Eastertide."

Though horses were seldom used except for war and travelling, yet it may be of interest to mention, according to the old Romance of " Bevis of Hampton," the knights rode sometimes for wagers on them, as, in this romance, over a three mile course on steeds and palfreys, for " forty pounds of ready gold." This was in the reign of Richard I. In the reign of John " running horses " frequently are mentioned in the Household Expenditure, and Edward III. had also a number of these " running " horses.

Referring again to the colour of medieval horses, white or grey, which was called " Lyard "—were the favourite colours, but " Favel," a chestnut, was also held in great admiration. A bay horse was called " Bayard "—a dark roan or mulberry colour, " Morel." As to the " Favel " a very old proverb has it :

> " He that will in Court dwell
> Must curry Favelle;
> And he that will in Court abide
> Must curry Favelle back and side."
> —Hart. MS. 425, fol. 93.

To " curry Favel " meant at that time to be subservient to the caprices of a patron in hope of advantage to come; nowadays we have forgotten what Favel meant, and have corrupted the phrase into " curry favour."

Nor must it be imagined in that rough and ready age, horses were neglected or their intelligence not rightly esteemed. Indeed a knight's feats at a tournament or in battle very greatly depended on these qualities of his destrier. In a very interesting extant illumination of this period, a good knight is depicted resting in his tent, pitched in a meadow, after some great tournament. The tent door is open, so we see him in it waiting for his supper, with two candles set on the table. But he is shown as a good chevalier and a humane one to his horse, for the latter is sharing the shelter of the tent and eating in it out of a trough—the tent striped gold and red, green and blue; the good knight's armour laid aside, in his robes of peace and having just been to vesper, he is waiting from the hands of his young squire his well-earned supper.

That too, these chevaliers and those to whom the jongleurs recounted their tales, appreciated the intelligence and faithfulness of their charges we have evidenced in the " Lay of Graelent," where towards the end of the story Graelent is borne away into the land of

Faery but we are told " his destrier grieved greatly for his master's loss." He sought again and again the mighty forest, yet never was at rest by night or day. No peace might he find, but ever he pawed with his hoofs upon the ground and neighed so loudly that the noise went all the country round. Many a man coveted so noble an animal and sought to put bit and bridle in his mouth, yet never might one set hands upon him, for he would not suffer another master. So each year in its season the forest was filled with the cry and the trouble of this noble horse, which might not find its lord.

And the Bretons made a Lay thereof and still sing that the good knight Graelent who went to the land of Faery with his love, shall be seen again bestriding his faithful horse as he did aforetime long ago. (" Medieval Romances," Mason.)

A knight's destrier cost him £20 in 1375, but of course at the present day value of money this was a large sum. The palfrey cost in 1303 about £12 12s. A bay one bought for Queen Marguerite of France—second wife of Edward I.—was bought for this sum, and a Ferrand, or bay one, for £6 (Issue Roll. Micha 31. Ed. I.). The sumpter horse or mule which carried the luggage was from £4 to £8. Henry V. expended " for a dapple-grey horse and a black horse £16 13s. 4d., for a white one and a sorrel one £10, and for two white horses £10 (Issue Roll. Easter 9. Henry V.).

Horses indeed not alone for the knight as " foaming steeds on the golden bridle gnawing " (Chaucer) but for his lady and his " menie " were of the greatest value and use in the Middle Ages, whether for battle, for passengers, or baggage, they shared the work with the sumpter mule.

Carriages were slowly formulated. The sledge-type was the earliest. Then the cart. It took many a century to arrive at the Roman " biga," though that indeed was but a poor improvement on the original Assyrian chariot. Travelling was irksome—dangerous and lengthy. To take one example. It took four days for Sir Thomas Swynford, the good knight, to reach London from Pontefract, riding with his utmost speed, in the reign of Edward II., and of course when a knight was encumbered with his menie and large household gear, which they took—even to their beds, from one castle to another—the time taken—with no roads and constant water-courses flooding the track—was many a long day's journey. No wonder the journey taking so long and inns few and far between, hospitality at some country knight's house or sturdy yeoman's grange, was so often sought by the medieval travellers, when in Chaucer's words they did not ask in vain :

> " His table dormant in the hall alway
> Stands ever covered, all the longe day."

Or that the numerous religious houses, which then were scattered broadcast through England and France, took in, as a matter of course, these weary medieval travellers. Each such had its " hospitium," where those needing rest and refreshment asked and obtained it. The monastery or abbey, originally founded in a wilderness, became a nucleus or news and traffic. The large estates, too, of such, brought artisans together, and so, round its walls, grew up a town, such as St. Albans or St. Edmundsbury.

DAYS OF CHIVALRY

But to return to the duties of youthful esquires, not only did they superintend the arming and carrying of the armour when unrequired of their lord, but they of course accompanied him to the frequent tournaments of the time. Hardouin de la Jaille, in his book " Du Champ de Bataille " (fol. 50 ult.), thus expresses himself on the subject : " One of his esquires should walk his horse in his part of the lists, about half-way, and the other esquire a little more in front, taking care that the horses do not annoy each other, nor fight, which they might do ; nor need they restrain them further than when it comes to mounting (or when they proceed to mount) in order each one to aid his master and to go beyond the pavilions."

A very good description of these young demoisels' or squires' duties before attaining knighthood is given by Eustache Deschamps (Vol. II., p. 216, cccviii., Lay V., line 55, etc.) :

" Les jeuns gais poursuioient
Lances, bacinez portoient
Des anciens Chevaliers,
Et la coustume aprenoient
De chevauchier, et veoient
Des armes les trois Mestiers,
Puis devenoient Archiers,
A table et par-tout servoient,
Et les malectes troussoient
Derrière culx moult voluntiers,
Ainsi adonc le faisoient,
Et en i cuisine s'offroient
A ce temps les Escuyers.

Puis gens d'armes devenoient,
Et leurs vertus esprouvoient,
Huit ou dix ans tous entiers,
Et grands voyages aloient
Puis chevaliers devenoient
Humbles, fors, appers, legiers
En honourant estrangiers.
(Par honour se contenoient
Aux joustes puis tournoient)
Pour ce furent tenus chiers
Et les Dames honouroient
Qui pour leur bien les aimoient.
S'en furent hardis et fiers
Encontre leurs ennemis
Et courtois à leurs amis."

(The young men followed
Lances and bassinets they carried
Of the older knights,
And learnt the way
To ride, and they saw
The three modes of arms.
Then they became archers.
85

At table and everywhere they served
And the baggage (malectes) they packed
Behind them right willingly;
Thus they used to do
And in the kitchen did offer themselves
The esquires at this time.

Then did they become men-at-arms
And proved their worth
Eight or ten years altogether.
And they used to go on long journeys
Then they became knights (*i.e.*, fitted for knighthood)
Humble, strong, prompt, agile,
In honouring strangers.
By Honours they maintained themselves,
At jousts then they tilted,
For this were they held dear,
And they honoured the ladies
Who for their well-doing loved them.
They moreover were bold and proud
Against their enemies,
And courteous to their friends.)

Yet in these outings and more domestic duties in which the young esquires took their share, whether in tourney or enterprise, theirs was always a secondary place. Their education was not over, and till it was, immediately after attending their lord afield, they returned to his castle or manor to engage again in their military training. There they practised putting on the chain-mail and, later in the century, plate armour to accustom their limbs to bear its weight and confinement. There they put on the heavy gauntlets of a knight and practised holding a battle-axe and lance in such. There they learnt to use a shield deftly in mimic warfare with their companions. There they used to ride on the destrier fully armed and at full tilt as against an adversary in a tourney. Often purposely they were without a fire in winter in the hall, to accustom themselves for future forays and encounters in the open country. They practised leaping and scaling walls, to fit them to make good war on beleaguered and fortified towns in the future.) All these martial trials and exercises, despite their youth and sometimes almost a girlish figure and face, were deemed essential to the training of a future good knight, and were eagerly pursued day after day by these lads (St. Palaye, Vol. I.). And despite their youth, many arduous tasks even outside in the world were often confided to them—such tasks continually appear for the young varleton in the old Lays and in the pages of Froissart. And despite their youth too, their lords seem to have had great confidence in them. They used to confide the prisoners they took in a tourney or tournament to their keeping to hold as such for ransom. Thus in the " Lay of Brut " it is said of them

" Les prisòns firent arrester
   Et en lieu seur tourner
   A leurs Escuyers les livrerent
   Et à garder les commanderent."

DAYS OF CHIVALRY

(The prisoners they caused to be arrested
And instead of turning back (*i.e.*, to put them in ward)
To the squires they delivered them
And to guard them they bade them.)

In a march, the esquire was generally mounted on a " roncin " and preceded his lord :

> " Le chevalier erra pensant
> Et Huet Chevaucha avant
> Sor son roncin grant alcure."

> (The knight wandered in meditation
> And Huet preceded him on the foray
> Upon his palfrey at a great pace.)
> —St. Palaye, Vol. I., 50.

Again, the knight on an adventure or journey was in the habit, if he passed a church or oratory, to enter and say his orisons—while he did so, it was to the youthful squire in his train he committed his valued destrier. Thus did Peter de Monrabey (" Lay of Gerard de Roussillon ") arriving at the castle of Roussillon :

> " Intret en Rossilho pèl pon prumier;
> E dissen a l'arc vout sot lo clochier
> A sas armas corregro li chevalier,
> E sa spasa command à son Escudier
> E puis intret orar dins lo Mostier."

(By the entrance of the castle by the first bridge was an arcade standing under the clock where the knights congregated; he confided his horse to the care of his esquire till after he had entered the church to pray.)

Strange as it may seem, considering how stringent were the rules laid down for squires to educate themselves for and proceed—when of the fit age—to knighthood, and considering also how this " free " knighthood introduced was an improvement on the old knighthood with its feudal obligations in opening out a career for the gallant youths of that time—we have to confess that many cases are able to be cited where knighthood was deferred, and sometimes never taken up at all.

The celebrated Chandos was certainly not a youth under the age of twenty-one when he led the English troops of the Black Prince to the assistance of Pedro the Cruel. The four squires of Lord James Audley, whom he so generously rewarded out of the Prince's largesse to himself, were far advanced over twenty-one years of age. (Froissart c.c. 142).

Several things may have delayed or prevented certain of these squires seeking knighthood, *e.g.*, the consciousness that they were unfitted owing to a licentious life or an unreadiness in command, or from their own or their family's poverty, from being able to enter this exalted state. The largesse alone a knight was expected to give was a considerable outlay yearly. The brilliant entourage he was also expected to bring with him on entering, or holding a tournament, was another. The large " menie " he was called upon in his hall or castle every day to provide an open table for—all these demanded wealth. Even in the case of the poorer knights they had a destrier, a palfrey and a squire to keep, and in certain places a tax was levied on their knighthood. Thus in the " Coutume de Hainaut " it was laid down : " Un Chevalier, non pair " is to pay " sept livres dix sols." The knight, however, got some return in another county, for in Brabant according to the " Coutume de Brabant " if a peasant struck a knight he lost his hand, though if his squire was struck, the peasant lost not his hand but his money, being heavily fined.

In a MS. illuminated " Romance of King Meliadus," one of the Arthurian companions of the Round Table, there is to be found a picture of one of these elderly squires very different to the slim, graceful, frizzled-haired lad one is accustomed to associate with that degree. He is a clumsy enough looking man, with a jocular face, on his head a cap containing one long feather. Now the artist portrayed a squire often seen at that period. The illuminators drew men and women as they saw around them. In this these old and delicate illuminations are so valuable, just as are the old stained glass left in Gothic cathedrals in France and England, providing us with what otherwise we should have failed to learn—the dress, armour and figures of the Middle Ages.

Chaucer, who noted too the life going on around him and then wove it into verse, had such a squire—rough and faithful but getting on in years when he wrote :

" A worthy man
That from the time he first began
To ridden out, he loves Chivalry
Truth and honour, freedom and courtesy in his lord's war,
And thereto had he ridden, no man farre
As well in Christendom as in Heathenesse
And ever honoured for his worthiness."

That these older squires who had not ever risen to knighthood served for hire, Leber, in his " Collection Relative to the History of France," gives an instance of in a curious passage asking a knotty question. " A knight has two squires hired for the tourneys and for a year. The said knight comes to a town where he finds it necessary to enter the lists hastily, and he cannot find his squires, so hires two others on the eve of the tourney, but when the morrow comes these two squires hired for a year turn up before the hour of arming, and present themselves to their master, to serve him. But the master says, ' Not so, as far as to-day,' for this day he had hired these two others now. Thereupon these two squires, hired for a year, go out and seek their livelihood with other masters for that year, and they say they are justified in doing so. But their first master says, 'Not so, they are still engaged to him.' How would this be decided by the Law of Arms for Tournaments ? " This passage is valuable as it shows that squires older than twenty-one—or they still would be in tutelage and not, as these were, able to do what they chose—existed ; and also that not only for pure honour but for subsistence, a good sword was then bartered.

DAYS OF CHIVALRY

If it be asked how the younger squires accompanied their lords to battle or tourney, we mean those still in training for the knightly degree, all contemporary writers declare that they did so unarmed—with the exception probably of the sword they received on being admitted to the rank of squire, and also probably with the short knife or poinard they carried at their side, and which is constantly seen in pictures of them at this period.

There is an instance—which seems to be an exception to this rule or he could hardly, so armed, have survived—of a lad still an esquire and aged nineteen, going unscathed through the French war.

In 1357 we find the celebrated poet Chaucer, varleton in the household of Elizabeth de Burgh, wife of Lionel, third son of Edward III., fighting for the king in his French wars. He was taken in the long run prisoner and the following year the king ransomed him.

The young squires, in fact, were quite cumbered sufficiently by carrying the different pieces of armour—the lance and the shield and pennon—belonging to the knight they served. Again it is laid down in all the Laws of the Tourney—when such were rigidly enforced—that no one under the degree of a knight should take part in them. The esquires at that time were therefore merely spectators, and stood ready to assist their lords if dismounted by leading in a fresh horse, or carrying them off the lists, if incapacitated or wounded.

The evening before the Tournament it was a custom to allow the young esquires to compete in the lists among themselves. In the " Lay of Perceforest " these young lads under the name of " la jeune Chevalerie " are stated at the hour of vespers to so muster " pour célébrer les vespers de tournoi de la haulte journée au lendemain." These contests were named " essays," sometimes " escrimie " (fencing matches). The weapons employed by these young esquires were light and easily handled and the lances often blunted in order to avoid wounding.

Again it seems that often in the second day of a tournament, which generally lasted three days, esquires were allowed to appear on foot and engage among themselves in light contests. So, too, in those less formal and less sanguinary games of arms, held by the " Knights of the Round Table," which never partook of a serious character or ending, the young esquires were permitted to engage. After a lapse of years, however, the esquires became more assertive and infringed on the old law that none under the rank of knight should take part in any tourney. They began to push their way into the lists with the knights, they began to wear their own cognizance and armorial bearings, and no longer acted that subordinate part which when knighthood was in flower was alone theirs.

Thus it is that one learned writer on the decay of Chivalry attributes among other reasons its gradual decay, " Les Escuyers usurpèrent successivement et par degrés les honneurs et les distinctions qui n'appartenoient qui aux Chevaliers, et peu-à-peu ils se confondirent avec eux " (M. le Laboureur), and no doubt this bold defiance of the esquires in breaking the ancient laws of Arms and Chivalry contributed to its fall. For whenever the world sees any of a caste that has long kept itself aloof under ancient and definite rules, suffering these rules to be broken, it ceases to have the same high opinion of it, and its ultimate downfall is assured.

These assumptions of the squires to infringe on the privileges and rank of knighthood were greatly helped in England by the king there summoning the knights of the shires to parliament to sit with the burgesses. While it debased the knight's rank, it gave encouragement to the squire's—originally far below him—to assume a position which in the zenith of Chivalry had never been heard of. As a squire thus obtained a position with its privileges his ancestors never obtained, he ceased to be anxious to proceed to knighthood, which entailed often military service and fines. The elevation of the squires contributed therefore greatly to the decay of the ancient Chivalry, so much so that our later kings had to insist on knighthood being taken up.

Again, the practice of the heralds, when they obtained royal sanction for their college, was to establish on quasi-legal footing the squire's right, if of gentle descent, to coat-armour.

In older days it was sufficient honour to the squire that he carried his lord's or knight's own shield when he required it, but in these later days he aspired and asked for his own.

The heralds granting this—while they raised the state of an esquire—debased the state of a knight.

In old days should a squire carry a blazon of his own that blazon was generally some form or portion of his lord's, who had granted it him for some good service. But when every family of gentle blood though only of squire rank obtained from the herald a coat of arms, irrespective of any service in war or otherwise they had done, the service of the sword which was essentially the knight's became dimmed by the service for nothing of the squire.

To return to the elderly esquires. These who had not been able, or were unwilling to gain knighthood, seem to have been permitted to carry certain arms of war of their own, other than the sword which was the only arm the damoisel or young squire looking forward to, and trained for, knighthood, was permitted to wear.

The "Capitularies" call these arms "arma patria." They consisted in a lance and a shield. It is probably from the personal blazon on the latter that by the laws of heraldry, a squire who had the right was dubbed "armigerous." Armed with these they accompanied their lords to field and tournament. The "Capitularies" lay down for such "Nullus ad Mallum vel Placitum, nisi arma patria, id est, Scutum et Lanceam portet." So we find in the Council of Mayence allowed to them such arms when they went into the Church. "Laicis qui apud nos arma patria portare non prolubemus quid autiquus mos est et ad nos usque pervenit."

We have before mentioned the fact that on the decline of the ancient laws relating to Chivalry, the squires usurped many functions peculiar to the higher order—among the rest, assuming his own coat of arms; but St. Palaye says "the squire that took the coat of arms before he was made knight was, in olden times, for ever excluded that honour." Many valorous deeds therefore of squiredom failed to be handed down, because unemblazoned on his coat, to his posterity. Some instances there are of great lords granting their squires liberty of bearing arms, but it was generally their own cognizances with a mark of difference. Thus James Lord Audley, after the battle of Poitiers, granted as a reward for the fidelity of his four squires, Delves, Dutton, Hawkeston and Foulthurst, permission to bear his own armorial bearings. This general inability of a squire to bear a device of his own in ancient days precluded, as we have said, many from transmitting to their children records of their brave deeds, and it is probable that their desire to do so in the only way they could, by acquiring the right as a knight to blazon the tale on their shields, was another reason why the young squire so ardently looked forward to knighthood.

The grade or status of esquire which was held necessary to obtain knighthood was dispensed with frequently when the postulant for the latter was of royal or princely birth. Thus the celebrated Dunois, Bastard of Orleans, was created a knight banneret, though he had never been an esquire; so Geoffrey of Anjou in 1127 obtained knighthood at the hand of his father, King Henry, without passing through the grade of squire. Either for their high birth considered to be unfitting for the menial condition of an esquire, or for their special valour on the field of battle, such as these were excused the long years a squire received of training ere he obtained knighthood. Princes and kings often waived this ordinary rule—of a candidate being an esquire before receiving knighthood—in the case of noble children whom at a very early age they conferred knighthood on. Thus Charles of Valois, brother of Philip le Bel, passing through Bologna in 1301, conferred knighthood on Philip and Albert Degli Asinelli, one boy twelve, the other fourteen, who had never attained the rank of esquires. So, too, he conferred it on Francis Bentivogli who was only thirteen.

In Gherardacci's " History of Bologna " we find Jean de Pepoli, son of the governor of the city, conferring knighthood on the two boys of a certain Macagrano, lately deceased, on account of their dead father's great services to the State, and knighting them on the day of his burial, at his tomb, and neither of these lads, of course, had previously passed through squiredom.

However, with such exceptions which were not rare, and also in the case, as has been noted of older squires who refused to receive knighthood, some in their early youth, and some during their whole lives, the necessity of passing through the rank of esquire, ere knighthood was conferred, was held obligatory on all those who would win their spurs. And it was a wise provision for as we have seen, brought up in a military household from the day they entered it as pages, taught in all martial science by their preceptors, their bodies, by constant exercises hardened for a knight's life in battle and in tourney, they, on attaining knighthood, were perfectly fitted to carry out all the duties that high dignity demanded from them.

From the above description of the early training of a child through the grades of pagedom and squiredom, the reader will easily perceive that that training was carefully undertaken for one purpose—to enable the youth when he had attained the proper age to receive the semi-sacred rite of knighthood. It was a romantic and glorious career opened up to him, the highest ideal that warlike age possessed for a perfect Christian and a perfect gentleman. In the " Fablieaux ou Contes " of the twelfth and thirteenth century (see Vance's " Romantic Episodes of Chivalrie and Medieval France ") that ideal is well brought out. " Who," asks the narrator, " is this gentle knight, engendered amid the strife, brought forth upon the field; suckled in a tent, cradled on a shield, swathed in its hide and built up of the flesh of lions? Who, who is he, in whom are met the lynx's eye, the dragon's front, the lion's heart, the wild boar's bristling ire, the tiger's vengeful spite? Who is he, intoxicate with the fight, yet slumbers in the pealings and the thunderings of the storm? Who is he the whirlwind of the fray will pierce; his foe espy as the falcon her prey through the mists of the morning, as the lightning the oak, rip the man, rip the steed, or tumble them powder as the grist of the mill? Who is he who sooner than rot his days through in peace will traverse not the Rhone but Albion's wintry waves, or needs be scale the rugged heights of Jura? Is he on the field of battle, as the chaff to the wind, sending the foemen before! Doth he tilt? Not foot in stirrup will he deign to put, yet horseman and horse will he pin to the dust; buckler and helmet even cleave to their midst. There is nothing can avail before him; neither shield nor buckler, basenet, lance, nor coat of mail. On the nostril of the fume of the steed as he gasps, on the givain, the gash, the prey, the battered shield, the shivered lance— these things are the sights his soul gloats on. Alone, on foot, 'tis his delight to scale the lofty mountains, to prowl through the forests, the bear to grapple, the lion to rend and to take prisoner the stag. His helmet is never from his head and when he sleeps 'tis his pillow. All he possesses is what is given him—it is ' largesse.' "

Feigning himself as such, it is no wonder that the Damosel earnestly desired the hour when he was dubbed a knight. Such a career gave him power to become honoured by his fellows and his lord; it gave him the means whereby to gain his lady's heart; it gained for him, if he took the cross, a blessed eternity, and lastly if a younger son and without a fief or manor, a means of subsistence. That the latter was often the case, we find in many instances. Thus in the Fabliaux (" Montaiglon et Raynaud," VI., 69) a knight is described, who, having " ne vigne ne terre " lived on what he could make at tourneys, and was reduced to poverty when he no longer could do so. William the Marshal on his deathbed estimated that he had taken prisoner five hundred knights in tourneys, and twelve horses with their saddles, often intact with gold and jewels, also their equipments, as profit (Lines, 3368-3374).

Paul Meyer in his introduction to the Norman French poem of " Guillaume le Marechal " (Vol. IV.) points out that tournaments were sources of income to the needy knights: that certain knights obtained means of subsistence as knights-errant, offering their swords to whom they would. In the above " Lay of Guillaume le Marechal " it is stated peace was made between the two kings, Henry II. of England and Louis VII.; the Chamberlain William de Tancarville and his menie returned to Tancarville and so arranged matters that the knights were allowed to go where they chose to seek their fortune, " and he who would win a prize set forth, if he had the means thereto." Again, which will be referred to later, the lords under whom the young knights often served, were—if they were poor—considered bound in honour to see that what they needed, they had from their " largesse."

For these several reasons knighthood was a state earnestly desired by the youthful esquires. It was at their attaining the age of twenty-one and after serving successively as a page and an esquire, that knighthood was bestowed. At that ripe age the youthful postulant for that coveted honour was considered, by the military education and military exercises he had passed through, to be suitable to enter the ranks of Chivalry. As has been noted above there were exceptions, frequently and principally among royal persons, to this rule.

Thus Fulk of Anjou was knighted by his Uncle Geoffrey when he was seventeen only. In the Lays and Romances frequent instances occur of lads being knighted at the age of fifteen, but for the generality, twenty-one was the obligatory age. It was when attaining this age that the heir—if his father was dead—was allowed to enter on the paternal or ancestral fief, which latter, entailing service in the overlord's wars, demanded from the holder of the fief, strength and aptitude to fulfil those obligations successfully. So at least it was laid down in certain Ordinances promulgated by the reign of St. Louis.

CHAPTER II

THE most usual time for bestowing knighthood was at one of the five great Festivals of the Christian year, *i.e.*, at Christmas, Easter, Ascensiontide, Pentecost or the Feast of St. John the Baptist. Christmas, occurring, however, in the winter, did not commend itself so readily as the others. Chivalry was especially for the young and spirited—emblematic of the spring of the year, and therefore Easter or Pentecost was considered the most suitable. It was at Pentecost that Fulk Rechin was armed as a knight by his uncle, Charles Martel (Hist. Andegar, fragm by Fulk, Count of Anjou). On that feast Henry, the son of William the Conqueror, was knighted. So also on that day his father knighted Geoffrey Plantagenet. On the Festival of the Ascension Renaud de Montauban in his chronicle says: " Many young men were knighted." In the " Lay of the Knight of the Swan," he is represented to have created five or six knights on the Feast of St. John the Baptist.

Besides the Church Festivals there were many other occasions on which the accolade was conferred.

Thus on the marriage or baptism of a prince, or on the latter himself receiving it.

Thus when Geoffrey, son of the Count of Anjou, was knighted by Henry, the English king, twenty-five noble youths also were. (Marmontier.)

The field of battle—the most glorious place to win the golden spurs—often saw, after an engagement, these conferred on some gallant squire. Then places, held in great sanctity, were considered peculiarly adapted for conferring this high honour of knighting. The pilgrimage to the Holy City and the Tomb of the Holy Sepulchre were held in high estimation for this purpose. When the English Earl of Essex was there with Lord Robert de Severino he created several knights. Count Rudolph de Montfort created there Albert IV., " the Patient " Duke of Austria in 1398. Nicolas III. d'Este Lord of Modena would not put his spurs on when at Golgotha, or on those he created knights—he created several therefore on the Holy Sepulchre. Frederic of Brandenburg in 1453 created twenty-four of his followers knights on the Sepulchre. There the Duke Ernest of Austria was created knight in 1414 with twenty-six of his companions.

Sometimes the place chosen was after a battle when a knight was taken prisoner. As it was the rule a knight could only yield to a knight—the captive would knight his captor before he surrendered to him. " Are you a knight and gentleman? " asked the English

A KNIGHT'S LIFE

Earl of Suffolk when four hundred years ago he yielded to his captor, the French Regnault. " I am a gentleman," said Regnault, " but not yet a knight." Whereupon Suffolk bade him kneel, dubbed him knight, received from him the accustomed oaths, and then—and then only—gave up his own sword to the new Chevalier. (Doran.)

We now inquire into the question, who were deemed fitting to confer knighthood? It was, and has always been held, that every knight, whatever his social circumstances, has in himself the inherent power of creating others to his order. Many instances are to be found in the old Chronicles of such knights using this power, yet it can well be understood to the youthful aspirant for knighthood, when all the future of his life seemed unknown and strange, one of the most likely persons he would wish to confer this grace upon him was often his own knightly father. So in the ancient Lays nothing is more common than this conference by the father. In that of Hervis de Metz (Bibl. Nat. fr. 19160) he is thus armed and knighted by his father, Duke Pièrre. In another Lay the young hero is knighted by his father before starting for the court of King Louis. His mother is depicted as standing weeping at his going, and exclaiming, " My son, forget not while away thy father who is ill and left here alone." Thereupon the sick man, raising himself up, gives his son the accolade.

Sometimes instead of the father, the uncle creates the nephew a knight. Thus in the Lay " Li Covenans Vivien " (v. 12-19) William of Orange is portrayed giving knighthood to his nephew " Vivien Guillaumes ot Vivien adoubé."

Another conferrer of knighthood and generally preferred by the parents to their own relative, to give the accolade to their son, was some rich and powerful lord in the vicinity, just as often such are now chosen, with a like view, as sponsors in baptism—with a view of their powerful assistance afterwards, in peace as well as in war, to the youthful Chevaliers they had created. Thus in the " Lay of Girart de Rousillon " it is clearly stated that such was their obligation. " The young warriors said the war is over, there will be no more skirmishes, no more wounded knights, no more broken shields ! " " That none be discouraged at that," said Lord Fulk, " I will willingly give them more." Fulk spoke to Girart to go to King Charles Martel : " Now," said the latter, " see to it that each of you Counts and rich Barons give the poor young knights enough to assure their subsistence. Let some more of them be enrolled for the defence of the land as has become the fashion, and if there be any rich avaricious man, a felon at heart, who thinks their maintenance and gifts cost him too much, he shall be deprived of his Fief and it shall be given to a more valiant, for hoarded treasure is not worth a coal."

Perhaps the most popular person to confer knighthood was a prince or king; receiving the accolade from such in the midst of a brilliant court, the newly-created chevalier became the cynosure of all fair eyes—or mounted on his horse, or engaged at the martial game of quintain, he became the admiration of the populace standing round the castle green. And it was open to him as then knighted to take a vow to perform some chivalrous service for the fayre one he then picked out, or if he was to be a troubadour knight, sing her praises at many a castle and manor through the land.

Other conferrers of knighthood in rare cases seem to have been certain ladies themselves. For instance, Cécile, daughter of Philip I. of France, and widow of Tancred, Prince of Antioch, not only conferred knighthood on Gervais, son of the Count of Dol, but also on many more esquires (Odericas La Rogue " Treatise on the Noblesse," Ch. 97). It is also said that Blanche, mother of St. Louis, a little before her death in 1343, conferred knighthood on the Seigneur de Saint-Yon.

In 1343 Joan, Queen of Naples, on behalf of Andrew, her then husband, conferred knighthood on James Leparito. In the " History of Du Guesclin " (published by Menard) Jeanne de Laval, widow of the celebrated Constable of that name, girded her husband's sword on André de Laval, a mere boy, and so made him a knight (" lors fort jeune et le fit chevalier ").

But is it not possible despite the Chronicle giving the word " Chevalier " that he meant " écuyer " or the rank of " squire," where—as before seen—youths (damoisels) admitted to that rank had the sword girded on? This seems the more probable, as it appears the only instance to be found of a lady, not of sovereign rank, giving the accolade.

We may here mention that towards the later Middle Ages women themselves were admitted as members of certain orders of Chivalry; but if they were so, certainly not admitted to knighthood. Probably they were " honorary members," and as such had certain privileges of rank and service. Thus they were admitted into the Spanish Order of St. James of Compostella; so into the Order of St. John of Jerusalem. An Order entitled " The Servants of Virtue " was instituted for them, in Italy, by Eleanora de Guzman, but only to such of the highest rank. Anne, last Duchess of Brittany, instituted for widows the " Order of Cordeliers," the Cord of St. Francis indicating their profession of continence. In 1158, King Sancho III. of Castile founded the " Order of Calatrava "; women were admitted to such under the name of Chevalières de Calatrava.

It seems extremely doubtful if the rank they thus acquired was any other but honorary. That they did get some " prefix " appears in many cases certain, such as " equitissa " and " Chevalière." In a Charter of the year 1379 Mary de Bethune is called " Chevalière." A Seigneur of Yvaroux named Breton had, we are told, six sons all knights, and two daughters who are described as " Chevalières." A writer—Hemericourt—cited by Honorie de St. Marie says, that women who were not married and yet inherited fiefs were created knights in order to perform the obligations those fiefs carried with them to the overlords. But this seems highly improbable, for whenever a fief thus fell into the hands of a female, the overlord claimed the right of wardship, and her future marriage was always arranged so that her husband should fulfil the military obligations her lands carried, and if she in the very rare event remained unmarried, kept the lands in his own hands.

Again the question of women being able to confer knighthood seems only to have been (1) when knighthood itself was not in its pristine glory, at a time when its sacramental character was gradually being forgotten. In its earlier and first blossom the person who conferred it must himself have been a knight and by the accolade he created a spiritual state, analogous, in some ways, to the Church's.

holy orders. Now in the latter, no woman was ever held to be capable of conveying any sacramental grace. (2) In those rare cases when women do seem to have conferred knighthood, they were in all cases, we believe, rulers, and of sovereign rank. It is for this that the learned French writer, St. Marie, finds their capacity to do so (" Dissertations on Chivalry," Vol. I., p. 269). He argues as sovereign ladies could confer and appoint to Magistracies, General-ships and Governerships of Provinces, so they could confer Knight-hood. For this he cites " Orderic Vitalis," Bk. II., p. 85, which says : " A feminis interdum militaire cingulum indulsum militibus reperitus." Is it not possible that as these females to become sovereigns had been blest, crowned, and anointed, and so received a sacramental grace, this same sacramental unction was held to convey, in these isolated cases, the virtue flowing from it, power to give the accolade ?

(3) Another conferrer of knighthood, as its initiatory ceremonies developed as the years went by, was a representative of the Church. The young squire fell into the habit of placing his arms on the altar of some church to endue them with a sanctity—the priest was asked to bless his sword (though not gird it on him). As we have seen, the great Festivals of the Church were generally chosen as the times to confer knighthood ; almost imperceptibly the mitred bishop often began to take the place of the neophyte's father or overlord, and it was he who bid him " Rise a knight," and it was he who gave him the accolade, not indeed with the vigorous blow of the rough knight but with a touch of his gentle hand.

In a Synod held at Westminster, 1102, Abbots were forbidden in this country to make knights, probably from the dangerous increase it gave to ecclesiastical power.

Again from the habit often in this warlike age of bishops and monks· themselves arming and joining in the feudal battles, either to defend their patrimonies or else siding with the cause of one of the princes whose lands surrounded their own, the hard line was broken down which had existed between an ecclesiastic and a layman—and if the former was a powerful and warlike prelate knighthood at his hand was considered no disgrace but an honour.

This custom was helped on by the Crusades—these were accounted holy wars—what more suitable than that the men wearing the cross should often receive from holy hands their accolade ? Thus Martin V. conferred knighthood on Nicholas, Ambassador of Venice. The Patriarch of Aquilea in 1289 conferred it on Albert of Goritz, Henry Pampers and Nicolas of Cividale.

The historian of Aquilea, when writing of Friuli, gives an account of one of these ecclesiastical knightings. " The patriarch after celebrating mass mounted a step in sight of all the people, and, after a discourse on the duties of a true knight, solemnly blest the young squire who sought it, and called upon God to protect him because he would never engage in any but just wars ; then he threw over his neck a chain or collar of gold (the knight's usual collar) and girded him with the sword. The young knight, leaping thereupon to his feet and drawing his consecrated sword out of its sheath, swore to defend the Church and never do anything unfitting to a Christian knight. He swore also to protect the widow and the fatherless and the servants of

A KNIGHT'S LIFE IN

Jesus Christ against the Infidels." (L'Abbé Paladio " Hist. du Frioul." Part I, 1-6.)

Such ecclesiastical knighting both the Patriarchs of Jerusalem and Constantinople conferred. It was the custom particularly at the time of the first Crusade for those seeking knighthood and who had made the pilgrimage overseas to the Holy Land, to seek the accolade at the hands of the chief ecclesiastical dignitary in the Holy City or some knight of great prowess who happened to be there.

Again from the immense lands which the Church in Western Christendom gradually became possessed of, and the military service those lands were called upon to afford to the prince or overlord, in whose country or kingdom they were situated, it became the custom for the Abbeys to retain in their service men at arms and squires and knights who should lead to the field the men when called upon for military service. Hence often a brave squire was raised, in gratitude, by the lord abbot for his good services to the rank of knighthood.

A famous example of ecclesiastical knighting is that of Amauri, son of Simon de Montfort, who was at Castelnaudary at the time of the Feast of St. John with the two bishops of Orleans and Auxerre. He asked the former to confer knighthood upon his son by putting the baldric on him. The bishop for a long time refused, says Peter de Vaux-de-Cernay; he knew it was contrary to the usual custom, and that ordinarily only a knight could create a knight. However, at the insistence of the count, he ultimately consented. It was in summer-time. Simon de Montfort pitched large tents on the plain outside the city wall which was much too small to contain the spectators. On the day fixed the Bishop of Orleans celebrated Mass in a tent. The young Amauri, his father on one hand, his mother on the other, approached the altar. His parents offered him to the Lord, and asked the bishop to consecrate him knight in the service of Christ. Immediately the two prelates knelt before the altar, belted the sword on him and sang the Veni Creator with profound devotion. The chronicler adds these significant words, " What a new and unusual way of conferring knighthood." However, this mode of conferring it is not so extraordinary as Peter of Vaux-de-Cernay thought, for in the Roman Church—drawn up at the beginning of the eleventh century—there is already the formula of prayer to be used by bishops conferring knighthood. (" Social France," by Luchaire, p. 348.)

Again, so much had the spirit of Chivalry invaded even the peaceful fold of the Church, that what to an earlier age would have seemed alien to its spirit—an ecclesiastic making a knight—became an event which was passed without censure. Chivalric terms were so in vogue, and chivalric customs, that they were after used in describing even sacred things. Our English Piers Plowman describing the Crucifixion and speaking of the soldier who pierced our Lord's side, calls him " a knight," and says " he came forth with his spear in hand and jousted with Jesus." Afterwards, for doing so base an act on a dead body he is pronounced " a disgrace to knighthood," and our " champion chevalier chief knight " is ordered to yield himself " recreant."

So too, in the " Morte d'Arthur " Joseph of Aramathea is called " the gentle knight "; so also St. James of Compostella is named, in

DAYS OF CHIVALRY

one Chronicle, " the Baron St. James." Even God Himself received a knightly title; Joinville the faithful companion of St. Louis translates the words, " ad te levavi animam meam," which words the king had used, into " Beau Sire Dieu j'éleve mon ame vers toi."

In the Harleian MSS. (2169) our Lord's " arms," just as if He were a knight, are given heraldically, *i.e.*, " His figure portrayed as with a helmet crowned or, with roset mantling and wreath a crucifix, or, pierced by three nails, at the top a scroll inscribed I N R I, all between, on the dexter a birch, and on the sinister, a scourge."

Even as late as the eighteenth century heralds still clung to the ancient mixture of Chivalry with the Church. In Bettesworth's " Rudiments of Honour," dated 1720, it is stated, " Abel the second son of Adam bore his father's coat quartered with that of his mother Eve, she being an Heiress, *viz.*, Gules and argent. And Joseph's coat was ' party per pale, argent and gules! ' " We need hardly remark how to a very late period the clergy in this country had the knightly prefix of " Sir " before their names. Perhaps one of these chivalrous prelates of the Middle Ages would point out that even in apostolic times there was a sanction for this blending of chivalry and religion, for did not St. Paul himself write : " Take unto you the whole armour of God, the sword of the spirit, the breastplate of righteousness, the helmet of salvation ? "

We have seen that in the pristine days of Chivalry it was absolutely necessary that those who were to be made knights should be what we should now call " of gentle birth "—sprung from one of the old military feudal families. There were, however, other qualifications— moral ones expected to be found in each young squire when knighted, and before proceeding to an account of that ceremony, it may be as well to state them here :

(1) Truthfulness—a virtue unknown to the ancients. " Fins cuers ne puet mentir," says the writer of the " Lay of Raoul de Cambrai," written, it is true, in the thirteenth century, but imbued with all the fine feelings of the tenth. Raoul in the Lay goes to Persia, and falling into friendship with the son of the king there thus addresses him, " Amis gart toi de mentir, car c'est une tache qui moult fait repentir." Again, when a certain Count William of Orange returning from Palestine, having suffered a defeat, gathered fresh troops and was departing with them—he swore to his wife none should tempt him from his fidelity to her while overseas, and to keep his oath and to diminish his attractiveness to the fair sex, made himself hideous with long hair and beard till his return to her side. The code of the ancient knight was founded on respect for his engagements which led him to loathe a lie. It mattered not whether his oath was given on the book of the Evangels or relics of the saints, or sworn to with his bare uplifted hand—his word was sufficient, " De ta main nue te vi—je fiancier."

A curious confirmation of this is to be found among the epitaphs then common, of God. The most usual one is, " By God, who does not lie." In the " Lay of Jerusalem " it is said " Miex volroie estre mors que ele fust mentie " (death is preferable to telling a lie). The high moral character—which is characterized by an absence of deceit and lying—is well expressed by a ballad of Eustache Deschamps.

49

D

A KNIGHT'S LIFE IN

" Vous qui voulez l'ordre de Chevalier,
Il vous convient mener nouvelle vie ;
Devotement en Oraison veiller,
Pechié fuir, orgueil et villenie ;
L'Église devez deffendre,
La vefre aussi, l'orphenin entrepandre
Estre hardis et le peuple garder ;
Prodoms, loyaulx, sans rien de l'autrui prendre
Ainsi se doit Chevalier gouverner.

Humble cuer ait, toudis doit travailler
Et poursuir faitz de Chevalerie
Guerre loyale, estre grant voyagier
Tournoiz suir (suivre) et jouster pour sa mie ;
Il doit à tout honneur tendre
Si c'om ne puist de lui blasme reprandre
Ne lascheté en ses œuvres trouver ;
Et entre touz se doit tenir le mendre
Ainsi se doit gouverner Chevalier.

Il doit amer son Seigneur droiturier
Et dessus touz garder sa Seignourie ;
Largesse avoir, estre vray Justicier ;
Des prodommes suir la compaignie,
Leurs diz oit et aprandre,
Et des vaillans les prouesses comprandre
Afin qu'il puist les grands faiz achever
Comme jadis fist le roy Alixandre
Ainsi se doit Chevalier gouverner.''

(You who would (take upon you) the order of knighthood,
It is fitting you should lead a new life ;
Devoutly watching in prayer
Fleeing from sin, pride and villainy ;
The Church you must defend
And succour the widow and orphan ;
Be bold and guard the people ;
Loyal and valiant (knights) taking naught from others,
Thus should a knight rule himself.

He should have a humble heart, should work alway
And follow deeds of Chivalry ;
Loyal in war, and a great traveller
He should frequent Tourneys and joust for his lady love,
He must keep honour with all
So that he cannot be held to blame
Nor cowardice be found in his doings ;
And above all he should uphold the weak ;
Thus should a knight rule himself.

He should love his rightful lord
And above all guard his domain,
Have generosity, be a faithful judge,

50

DAYS OF CHIVALRY

Seek the company of valiant knights,
Hearkening to their words and learning (from them)
And understanding the prowess of the brave
Until he can (himself) do knightly deeds,
As aforetime did King Alexander,
Thus should a knight rule himself.)

Now though this probity in word and deed, this horror of untruth seems to have been a nearly habitual trait in the individual knight during the best periods of Chivalry, it has to be confessed that collectively—or rather in the persons of its princes—truth was notoriously wanting. There is no clearer fact for this than the continual treaties made between the English king, Henry II., and his recalcitrant sons, Henry the younger, Richard and Geoffrey. These treaties were frequently made before the altar, they were considered hallowed to the swearer by touching with his fingers the Holy Evangel —yet hardly was the treaty of truce made, than it was broken. So, too, with the treaties or truces made by our other Angevin kings with their suzerains—the kings of France. The often pernicious doctrine ascribed to Machiavelli in his famous treatise on " The Prince," that moral obligations were entirely different for the individual to what they were for the State, must even in this earlier age have sapped the knightly code of hating a lie and enduring all to keep troth—for princes throughout the Middle Ages were continually becoming foresworn. Certainly they forgot the adage : " Miex volroie estre mors que ele fust mentie."

Whatever was the reason that these princes often failed in this virtue, the knight of old held falsehood and perjury abhorrent to his profession. It was one of those things utterly condemned by his order : " Coutumes exigees d'un Chevalier, savoir sept vertus, dont trois théologales, foy, esperance et charité ; et quatre cardinales— justice, prudence, force et attemprerance." So in great detail the " Code of Chivalry " declaims against perjury and condemns it again and again.

(2) Another virtue inculcated in the same Code was active Charity. Sometimes these rough and mail-clad knights in the licence of a camp forgot this virtue, but many were found to be truly animated with its spirit. Godfrey de Bouillon in the first Crusade, by his obedience to this virtue, was called " A brother of the poor." Hugo of Bordeaux, another knight, was so noted for his charitable deeds that he has been compared to St. Laurence come to life.

" La povre gent servoit a lor manger " (he served the poor before he himself took food).

When in danger, by sea or land, it was frequently the custom of the time for a knight to vow for his deliverance a " Hospittel for the Poor," as Godfrey of Bouillon, in danger, called on the King of Heaven and he vowed to found such for the poor. Though some forgot this virtue, many remembered in those rough ages to practise Charity. Apropos of those who neglected it, a story is told by Peter Damien in the Chronicle of Turpin, also in another Lay, the " Assize of Carthage." There was a certain king of the Saracens who had been taken prisoner by Charles the Great, the latter offered him his freedom if he embraced Christianity and was baptized, or on the

51

other hand, death, if he refused. The Saracen chose death and gave this reason for his choice. " Who are those fat and luxurious men sitting at your table, clothed in furs and fine raiment ? " asked he of Charles. " They are," replied the latter, " my bishops and abbots." " Who again," he asked, " are those thin and wasted men in poor garments of black and grey, who also are fed at your table ? " He was answered, they were the mendicant friars. " Who then," said he, " are those I see sitting on the ground and who get but the crumbs from your table ? " " Those," said the Christian king, " are the poor." " Ah," cried the infidel, " is that the way you honour Him who is the author of your religion ? If that is the way you follow your Christ, I refuse to be a Christian—I prefer death." The obligation of Charity and acts of defence on behalf of the widow and orphans and the weak, was one of those laws down in the celebrated Code or Office of Chivalry (folio 6). " Office de Chevalier est de maintenir femmes veuves et orphelins et hommes més-aises et non puissant." To a knight " errant " it was one of his holiest duties to thus help and befriend the hapless.

(3) Another virtue—at least in the Middle Ages it was considered to be such and it is regrettable it is not in the present age so esteemed—was Courtesy. Again and again, in the Lays and writings of the period, the young knight is bidden to be " courteous." We have in the quaint instructions of the Chevalier de la Tour (folio 5 ultmo) his views on this pleasing virtue, which he had in his youth himself been instructed in. He recommends its practice quite as much towards those of low degree as towards those of high estate, for which he gives the following reasons : " These," said he, " will pay you greater praise and greater renown and greater good than the grandees ; for honour and courtesy that are paid to the great are only done as their due, which must be paid them ; but that which is paid to the lesser degree of gentry—such as honour and courtesy—comes from a frank and honest heart, and the individual of low degree to whom it is paid holds it for an honour and therefore he exalts it above everything and gives praise therefore and glory to him who has done him this honour. And thus from those of lower degree to whom such courtesy and honour have been paid, there comes a great praise and fair renown, and this grows from day to day." The Chevalier cites as an example a great lady whom he saw among a great company of knights and ladies of high degree, make a simple man—a tailor—an ornate reverence. When she was reproached, with this, " I would rather have saluted him than not to have greeted him as a gentleman," she replied. This work contains many other similar lessons in which we may often notice simple, rough and even coarse manners but always pure, honest and reasonable. His advice to his daughters is, " To be of comely yet humble manners—not given to giggling and emptiness nor overbold, nor to gaze lightly at people," and he adds this pertinent advice to these demoiselles, " Many have missed marriage by assuming great airs."

In the celebrated " Roman de Rose " :

> " Whoso would practise true nobleness
> Must cast off pride and idleness,
> Himself to arms or study give

And pure of soul and spirit live
In sweet humility attired."

Again,

" A knight should never shame his sword
Nor ever let unseemly word
Escape his lips."

So Eustache Deschamps (p. 77, col. 1 and 2) speaking of the young knights :
" S'en furent hardis et fiers
Encontre leurs ennemis
Et courtois à leurs amis."

We all know Chaucer's " squire," " Courteoys he was, lowly and reverent."
So in an ancient manuscript, addressing a lady :

" Et quand veuta à ami faire
Et amezunbian clerc débonnere
Qui soit vaillaux, preux et cortois
Ou un biau Chevalier aucois
Qu'en Chevalier et en clergie
Et tretorite la courtoisie."

(And when it shall befall to make a friend
And you love a fair clerk debonair
Who shall be valiant, worthy and courteous,
Or rather a fair knight,
For in knights and in the clergy
Is above (all things) found courtesy.)
—MS. du Roi, 7615.

So, too, Chaucer :

" A knight there was, and that a worthy man,
And that from the time he firste began
To riden out, he loved Chivalry,
Trouthe and honour, freedom and curtesie."

Again :

" And tho' that he was worthy he was wise,
And of his post as meke as is a mayde."

(4) Again, another virtue esteemed in a higher way sometimes than it merited, in the knight, was liberality or " largesse."
This feature naturally is dwelt on in the songs and chansons of the troubadours and jongleurs, for though the former disdained to receive money, he seldom was averse to a rich robe, or good horse or harness from the lord he played before—and as to the latter, he lived by what he could get by his art. But even outside these romantic Lays of

theirs, liberality and generosity were highly esteemed and looked for from all who wore the knight's gold spurs; it was a quality that made him of all qualities most popular.

In the ancient days—ere Chivalry came to its full flower—simple alms to the poor, or gifts to Mother Church was the only form of " largesse " practised. The early military knights had one garment to cover them, one horse to carry often them both together, and slept in one bed—as indeed was often the case with knights as brothers in arms on some expedition—the same in the earliest period of their history—ate herbs and bread and drank water for their sustenance, but this was far from the usage when Chivalry was at its zenith. " Largesse "—which covered profuse hospitality—was the rule, not the exception, and long before admittance to knighthood, the varlets and damoiselles had been accustomed to witness and to help in this profusion. Even the garments in peace, worn by the knight and his friends at these carousels, were of the richest. To line, for instance, a cloak in the period between 1350-1364 for King John II. of France, 670 marten skins were used. One of his sons had 10,000 martens brought to line five such cloaks and five Court ladies' doublets. To line a dress for one of his grandsons 2,700 squirrel skins were procured.

Precious gems were also lavishly used. Pearls were quaintly employed to embroider texts and songs and mottoes on clothes. The robe of state, of Jean sans Peur, of Burgundy, was set with pearls and gems, and valued at 200,000 ducats; his consort's ladies-in-waiting received 400,000 Brabant thalers a year from the ducal exchequer for ornaments.

Nor were the religious houses behind in cultivating " largesse " and bountiful hospitality and ostentation. The cloisters were the homes of good cheer. At their feasts pheasants and peacocks were the favourite dishes. Both are mentioned as such in the kitchen accounts, still extant, used in the eleventh century in the abbey on Lake Constance. Foreign foods and ingredients were also imported by the monks. At Hirschau under the Abbot William (1069-91) a number of foreign fruits and fishes, lemons and figs and spices, such as pepper and ginger, were known and used by the monks at their abbey. So too at Cluny in 1130, and the abbot there desiring a stricter enforcement of the rule, complained of all these luxuries then rife in his abbey.

In France the art of cooking was a well-known science in the year 1300, and onward to 1400 the cooks of the famous cookery-school of Charles VII. and his " cordon-bleu," Taillevent, aimed in making the simplest food attractive and disguising its nature. The peacocks at these scenes of " largesse " and profuseness were brought in to the sound of drum beats and clapping of hands. In England it was the same. During the reign of Richard II. it was a time of luxurious feeding. The ordinary dinner of a lord or wealthy knight at the end of the fourteenth century consisted in three courses of seven, five, and six dishes each, and on feast days, eleven or twelve. When George Neville was raised to the See of York 4,000 cold game pies, 104 peacocks and 200 pheasants were provided.

The " largesse " and profusion of Italian luxury at feasts *circa* 1400 and onwards may be illustrated by a description of the one given by Benedetti Salutati on February 16th, 1476, to the sons of King

Ferrante of Naples. The staircase was decked with embroidered carpets and wreaths of yew; the great hall decorated with tapestries. From the canopy, which was in cloth with the colours of Arragon, two candelabras of carved and gilded wood hung down. Opposite the main entrance, on a gilded platform covered with carpets, stood the dining-table, spread with the finest linen over a worked cover. One side of the hall was taken up by a huge sideboard—the shelves in their number proclaiming, as was the custom, the rank of the owner—on which were set eighty ornamental pieces of plate, mostly of silver, some of gold, and bowls, dishes and plates of richest workmanship.

The " *hors d'œuvre* " consisted of a little majolica bowl, passed round, of milk pudding. Eight silver dishes of capons-breast jelly followed, decorated with coats of arms and mottoes. The principal guest—the Duke of Calabria—received a dish with a fountain in the middle, spraying forth a shower of orange-flower water. The finest part of the banquet consisted of twelve courses of various game, veal, ham, pheasants, partridges, capons, fowls and " blancmange." At the end a large silver dish was set before the duke who took off the cover and released a number of birds (this will remind the reader of the old nursery song, " Four-and-twenty blackbirds baked in a pie ").

On two magnificent salvers there were two peacocks apparently alive, with tails spread, bearing essence in their beaks and the duke's arms attached to silk ribbon on their breasts. The second part of the feast consisted of nine courses of various sweets—tarts, march-pane and light and delicate pastry with hippocras as a drink; the wines, indeed, mostly Italian and Sicilian, were chosen by the guest who studies a list of fifteen brands to choose from. At the end of the banquet every guest was handed, by the pages, fragrant water to wash his hands. Then the cloth was removed and a large dish was placed on the table, containing a mountain of green twigs and blossoms, which gave forth a fragrance to the whole hall. During the meal and after, the guests were entertained by the jongleurs with music and a play in dumb-show. About an hour later dessert was served—spices and sugar-designs in silver vessels with covers of wax sugar on which were emblazoned coats of arms. The feast lasted four hours. (" Roman Life and Manners " by Ludwig Friedlander.)

Barons and knights who were owners of lands sought the fame of possessing a spirit of " largesse " and open profuseness often in strange ways. In 1174 Henry II. of England as Duke of Aquitaine summoned to Beaucaire an assembly of his knights and squires and for their honour Bertram Rambaut, the celebrated troubadour-knight, had a piece of land ploughed and sown with 30,000 " sols " in pennies. Guillaume de Martel, who had a following of three hundred knights, had all the provisions in his kitchens cooked, not on wood-faggots, but on lighted wax-torches. Raimond de Venous showed a cruel prodigality in his boastfulness of being a knight full of the spirit of " largesse," for he had thirty of his horses burnt alive (as fuel).

It is needless to say, after these prodigal feasts, the attendants, particularly the wandering jongleurs, after celebrating in their songs the profuse hospitality of the knight who provided it, crying out " Largesse, largesse ! " received rich presents of money and often splendid wearing apparel. The latter particularly a gift to the troubadour-knight, their master, who refusing money, never disdained a rich robe, a good war-horse or a suit of armour for his skill. Thus in the " Lay of Richard Cœur de Lion," we read that after the capture of Acre, he distributed among the heralds, disours, tabourers and tromposers, who accompanied him, a great part of his march-largesse in money, jewels, and horses and fine robes, which had fallen to his share. It was not only out of a natural liberality princes and knights gave largesse, it was that as these men skilled in song and versification were—with exception of the monkish chroniclers—the only medium to keep alive and hand on their deeds of prowess to another age, they might be encouraged by rich gifts to do so.

It will be seen by the above that the heralds and minstrels are often coupled in the same category, thus Froissart tells us that at a Christmas entertainment given by the Earl (Count) of Foix there were many minstrels as well as his own, as strangers, and he gave to the heralds and minstrels the " sum of five hundred franks " and gave to the Duke of Tourayne's minstrels " gowns of green cloth of gold, furred with ermine, valued at two hundred franks." A sword as " largesse," though often given with harness to a troubadour, was never given to these jongleurs or minstrels, and these latter—unlike the former—were forbidden to carry arms; so in the Statute of Arms for Tournaments, passed in the reign of Edward I., 1295, it is laid down " E qu nul Roy de Harrarunz ne minestrals portent privez armez." Largesse therefore, it can be seen from the foregoing, was a virtue extremely popular. The debts it brought with it were not considered a disgrace but a sign of nobility. In the " Lay of Ogier le Danois " it is said " an avaricious king is not worth a farthing." In that of " Garin " " no avaricious prince can keep his land, there is injury and grief while he lives."

The author of the " Chanson de la Croisade "—William of Tudela —a troubadour—says of himself, " Master William composed this song at Montauban, where he was. Truly if he had good luck, if he were rewarded as so many are of the common players (jongleurs) so many of the cheap fellows, surely no man of courtesy would fail to give him a horse or a Breton palfrey to carry him easily over the sand, or raiment of silk or velvet, but we see the world going so decidedly to the bad that rich men—a worthless lot—who should be gracious (i.e., having a spirit of ' largesse ') will not give the value of a button." War was an immense expense in the age we are treating of, and war never ceased, but peace was no less costly to knighthood, it involved feasts, marriages, knighting and tournaments, and lavish gifts cast broadcast—in a word, largesse.

A fifth virtue, or rather qualification, necessary in a tyro of knighthood was gallantry. We shall later, in dealing with the knightly-troubadours, enter more largely into this very confusing subject to modern thought and modern customs to properly understand. Held originally in a poetic but perfectly chaste manner, its cult became rapidly corrupted from intercourse with Provence and other southern portions of France, which largely felt the licentious influence of their Moorish neighbours. In its incipience it was a good and restraining influence for the young squire and afterwards for the young knight—a lady whom he had taken, as the object of his platonic affection, to serve, honour and obey. To be without such, not to have

DAYS OF CHIVALRY

" gallantry," as it was called, a young damoisel would have been considered wanting, and not really fit for the accolade. Thus in the Romance of " Little Saintry," his protectress realized this, and taught him how needful, even while still a page, it was to have some fair one as the object of his service, and she herself the protectress of his interests. So Brantôme enjoins " Si une honneste dame, veut se maintenir en sa fermeté et constance, il faut que son serviteur n'espargne nullement sa vie pour la maintenir et deffendre, si elle court la moindre fortune du monde, soit ou de sa vie ou de son honneur, ou de quelque meschante parole, ainsi que jeu aye vu en nostre Court plusieurs qui ont fait taire les medisants tout court, quand ils sont venus à detracter de leurs maistresses et dames aux-quelles par devoir de chevalerie et par les loix, nous sommes terms de revoir de champions à leur afflictions."

The symbolic ritual of conferring knighthood when in its zenith, so nearly figured the more sacred ritual of the Church when administering her Sacraments of Baptism, Marriage and Holy Orders, that it is not surprising, considering that about this period the greater Cult of the Virgin was spreading through Christendom, that, woman's place in Chivalry became much more considered, and that a platonic devotion grew up which caused the knight to dedicate knightly swords and knightly adventures to her service.

The Virgin herself, from being the dogmatic Mother of God, was at this period brought forth from her celestial niche in dogma, and made more human, and so more popular by being appealed to with greater freedom of language, while she also became a centre, like her earthly sisters, of poetic fancies and knightly vows. So in a sermon delivered by Stephen Langton, Archbishop of Canterbury, he thus addresses her :

" Bele Aliz matin leva
Sun cors vesti et para
Ens un vergier s'en entra
Cinq fleurettes y truva ;
Un chapelet fit en a
De bele rose flurie.
Pur Deu trahez vus en là
Vus ki ne amez mie ! "

(Fair Alice rose in the morning, clothed and adorned her body, entered an orchard and found there five little flowers. She made herself a wreath of fair flourishing roses. God has drawn you there, you who love not.)

He applies each verse in a mystical sense, to the Virgin, and then exclaims with fervour : " Ceste est la belle Aliz. Ceste est la flur. Ceste est le lis ! " (Roquefort " Posie du XII et du XIII siècle.)

Knights' ladies could not—except as spectators—take their places in tournaments, but so had the platonic gallantry of the age grouped itself round their sex, that the Virgin herself was interwoven in the fierce encounters of Chivalry. It is on record that in a tourney held close to the walls of an abbey (dedicated probably to her) the Virgin took the place of the chief knight—Walter de Birklede—and fought in the bloody mêlée. Gallantry therefore, devotion to the fair sex—

yet in the finest times of Chivalry never more than platonic—was a necessity in him who would be a knight. It embraced the highest ideal of womanhood (the Virgin Mother) as well as the Chatelaines and their daughters.

We may therefore assume that at this period the grand distinction of the Chivalrous character, in regard to the other sex, was gallantry, not love; the one being of a nature to refine manners, throw over the face of society a rich and golden veil, and help the fancy to many sparkling and seductive images, but producing few of those mighty and permanent impressions, either on individuals or communities which love in its strength has accomplished.

Endowed with courtesy, gallantry and largesse, the young aspirant for knighthood stood ready for that high profession. As we have seen in the foregoing, he has passed through the ranks of page, varlet or squire, he has been thoroughly trained to arms, he has received what was considered, at that time, sufficient profane education to write a letter, sign his name, and tolerably read a book in the Roman or Norman language; he also, under the chaplain who resided with him in the castle or manor of the lord who supervised his training, had been instructed in religious knowledge—he therefore was fully ready for the accolade of Chivalry, and to pass through the prescribed formulæ attached to his admittance thereto. These were as follows:

Confession. Previous to their long night vigil with their armour, this was demanded of all those who were about to become knights, as it was during their lives ever afterwards. Before the first charge was made in battle they had to confess all the acts of their past lives—or if time was not given for that, then a short general summary of them. So in the Lay " Le Destruction de Rome " (Romania) " Chescon or se confesse vie doit peschiés celes," " that each of you should confess and that each of you should not hide a single sin, afterwards charge in the battle and kill each one an infidel."

Peter the Hermit thought it useful to tell those who had taken the Cross that " St. Andrew had appeared to him in a wonderful light and recommended him to urge each warrior to confession " (" Lay of Antioch "). Indeed it was always customary in those ages of faith for a knight to confess before he took part in a judicial combat, or before he took ship overseas, or on any occasion where he adventured his life.

This confession took place on the field of battle just before engaging, or in some adjacent chapel or church, or even in one of those cells of hermits found scattered over France and England. Thus in the " Lay of Garin " it is said " that a certain Begue traversing all France to see his brother whom he greatly loved, stopped on his way to make his confession at a hermit's cell at Grantmont." If mortally wounded on the field of battle and a priest could not be found, it was not unusual for a man to make his confession to a brother-knight.

The Church, though she regretted the necessity, did not censure it. " Si "—so wrote Peter Lombard, the master of the sentences— " defuerit sacerdos, proximo vel socio suo est facienda confessio, sed curet quisque sacerdotem quævere qui sciat ligare et solvere."

There is the well-known case of Bayard dying on the battle-field, no priest procurable, he made his confession to his highest servant present. So in the "Lay of the Aliscans," the young lord Vivien, aged only fifteen, on the evening of the great fight, lay a-dying, and no priest present, he raised himself from his dying torpor, and made his confession in the ear of his weeping uncle, the aged Count William. There was also a strange symbolic rite often performed by knights at this period, the origin of which is veiled in obscurity. It was done with three blades of grass, or of a herb, or else three leaves plucked from a tree. Gautier, in his work on "Chivalry," says he could cite twenty or more cases, gathered from the oldest Chivalric poems, of this curious usage. The explanation most feasible seems to be that the three blades or leaves represented the Blessed Trinity. In the "Chanson d'Antioche" it is recorded, "De l'herbe lui a-t-il trois peus rompus—en l'honneur Dieu les use." Again in that of "Raoul de Cambrai," "Savari, après avoir confessé Bernier, lui administre ce sacrament d'herbe." So in the much quoted Lay, "Li Loherans," "Sur le point de mourir, Begue de Belin trois foilles d'herbe a poins entre ses pies." In another Lay, "Daurel et Beton" it is stated a traitor of the name of Guy, wounded in pursuit of Duke Beuves d'Antoine, asked in vain for this strange Communion, so in another "Les Chetifs," "When Hernoul of Beauvais perceived death near, he took a tiny piece of grass, 'si le prist a segnier'" (so he took it to make the sign of the Cross).

Lastly, a more splendid virtue than all others demanded of the young aspirant for knighthood both before, and after, initiation, was the pursuit of good, the detestation of evil, not alone when found in his own soul, but in that of the world. "Le mal abatez et le Bien hauciez" (Beat down the Evil, raise up the Good). The Liturgy of the Church reiterated the same exhortation when youths were admitted to knighthood, thus in the thirteenth century when the Service was re-composed by Durandas—"Grant that this new knight may never draw his sword in an unjust cause, but ever in defence of what is just and right," "omnia cum gradio quo justa et erecta defendat" ("Martine de ant: Eclesiæ Ritibus II"). At Rome, on the creation of a knight, it was even more solemnly said: "Call to mind, O knight, that thou art to be the defender of the Order and the punisher of Injustice. On this condition—the living copy of Christ—thou may reign eternally above with your Divine Model" ("Pontificale Romanum"). But it was necessary not alone to warn the young neophyte "le Bien hauciez" but also, "le mal abatez," for through the Middle Ages had crept in the Manichæan heresy, so prevalent in Provence—as an undercurrent of the Exaltation of Evil. This, as can be expected from its prevalence in the South—the homeland of trou-badour and jongleur—is found most frequently in the Chansons and Gestes. It mocks at the Liturgy of Good, and turns it into a Liturgy of Evil. Thus in the "Lay of Gaydon," a man is bidden not to keep faith with his lord, not to be loyal to anyone, to betray the good and true, to rail at the poor, to disinherit the orphans, to dishonour the Church, to lie with impunity, and to violate all oaths. Well was it with a consecrated sword—a soul absolved—the young knight should be clothed in his spiritual as well as his natural armour.

Perhaps we cannot do better than in finishing these moral requisites in a young man seeking knighthood, to sum them up in the description taken from the Morte d'Arthur, where the excellence of the true knight is well portrayed. Sir Ector in his eulogy over the body of Sir Launcelot du Lac thus bewails him : " Ah, Sir Launcelot, thou wert head of all Christian knights, now there thou liest; thou wert never matched of more earthly knights hands, and thou wert the curtiest knight that ever bare shield. And thou wert the truest friend to thy lover that ever bestrode horse. And thou wert the truest lover of a sinful man that ever loved woman. And thou wert the kindest man that ever struck sword. And thou wert the goodliest person that ever came among a press of knights. And thou wert the meekest man and the gentlest man that ever eat in hall among ladies. And thou wert the sternest foe to thy mortal enemy that ever set spear in rest."

Loyalty, courtesy, liberality and justice were the virtues essential in the estimation of mankind to the character of a knight in the days of Chivalry.

So an eloquent writer (" Pearson's History of England," Vol. I., Chap. XXXIV.) says in speaking of this new and freer Chivalry, unfettered by feudal claims : " The secret of its strength lay in its human elements, its regard for life, and its infinite tenderness. With sympathies so wide it could not restrict itself to the narrow circle of caste. Throughout English history, the man who had won his spurs, by fair conduct on the field, might wear them. The gentleman without fortune might command barons in war, and be called brother by his king. To be brave, loyal and generous established a claim to the title-deeds which were good throughout Europe. This Chivalry invaded the very strongholds of rank and clung like ivy round the grey battlements of feudalism, at once beautifying and destroying it."

It is no wonder that this higher and individual Chivalry displaced its predecessor, fettered as it was by feudalism, or that throughout Western Europe it was loved and sung of by every wandering minstrel. Feudalism had been a confederacy of little sovereigns, of small despots, unequal among themselves and possessing and owing, each towards the other, rights and duties, yet invested in their own domains, over their own immediate subjects, with absolute arbitrary power. This is what feudalism really was, and this is what distinguishes it from every other aristocratic form, from every other kind of government. From the tenth to the thirteenth century, liberty, equality and peace were all wanting. To the inhabitants on a feudal estate their sovereigns—however petty they were—were at their very doors. Not one of them was too obscure for his notice, nor too far removed from his power—and that power on their retainers was often of the most savage kind.

We will take two instances of this brutal excess of power by lords exercising feudality, from the historian Peter of Val-de-Cernay.

" Bernard of Cahuzac, a petty lord of Perigord, spends his life in looting and destroying churches, in attacking pilgrims, in oppressing the widow and the poor. It pleases him especially to mutilate the innocent. In a single monastery, that of the Black Monks of Sarlat, one hundred and fifty men and women were found, whose hands and feet had been cut off, or whose eyes had been put out by him. His wife, as cruel as he, aided in his deeds. She took pleasure in torturing these poor women herself. She had their breasts slit, or their nails torn out so that they would not be able to work."

DAYS OF CHIVALRY

Again, " Foucaud, a knight and a comrade of Simon de Montfort, angered even the warriors by his cruelties. Every prisoner who did not have the means of paying one hundred sous as ransom was condemned to death. He enclosed his prisoners in subterranean dungeons and let them die of starvation. Sometimes he had them brought forth half-dead and thrown into cesspools before his own eyes. It was said that on one of his last expeditions, he returned with two captives, a father and son, and that he forced the father to hang his own son."

Giraud, a troubadour, who wrote at the beginning of the thirteenth century, deplored these habits of pillage, unworthy of men of the sword. " I used to see the barons in beautiful armour, following tournaments, and I heard those who had given the best blow spoken of for many a day. Now honour lies in stealing cattle, sheep and oxen, or pillaging Churches and travellers. Oh, fie upon the knight who drives off sheep and pillages Churches and travellers, and then appears before a lady." Giraud himself, when travelling in Navarre, had been plundered by the men of Sancho the Strong, its king.

But to return to the young squire, the postulant for a knighthood, far removed from that of these feudal and despot obligations. The preparations for conferring Chivalry upon him were of the most strict and solemn nature, indeed they followed their counterpart in the rites of baptism, and marriage.

We have seen above how strict the rule was that confession of sins should be made always and frequently by knights; it is no wonder therefore that before admittance to that order, the young neophyte had to fast the day before his initiation, and make a general confession embracing the whole of his past life.

After this the Vigil began, of prayer, in some Church and watching his armour, during the night preceding his knighting. Thus Helinand in his Chronicle (A.D. 1257) states, " In certain countries the future knight passed the preceding night in watching." In the Chronicle " Geoffrey de Bouillon," he is represented to have kept his vigil " la nuit veilla li enfer el'non Sainte Marie." Again in the Lay " Anseis de Carthage," " a Saint Vinchent va veillier et prier— Trosc' à l'demain qu'il virent le jor cler " (he went to the Church of St. Vincent to vigil and pray until the dawn broke clear next day). This " veille des armes " was very ancient, for in 1039 in the Latin Chronicle of Andemar of Chabannois, he writes of a certain judicial combat where the victor though wounded returns his thanks at the tomb of St. Cibar, where says the Chronicler, " Il avoit veillé la nuit précédente." Indeed the custom first came into vogue when causes were tried by these judicial contests, and, originally, no doubt, to enforce upon the minds of those who were about to place their cause on the judgment of God and the dexterity of their right arms—the gravity of the occasion. Often their vigil was shared in by the young aspirant's godfather in Chivalry (patron) or some friendly priest who through the long night—in the shadows of some great cathedral or ancient church—helped to join in his orisons and serve to keep his drowsy eyes awake.

It would be perfectly easy to multiply instances found in the old Chronicles and Lays to show the nearly universal obligation of this night vigil for those seeking the accolade next day. It corresponded

61

to the neophyte's vigil before the Feast of Pentecost, when he was to receive the sacrament of Baptism. A vivid description is given of the time of the early twelfth century, when young Geoffrey Plantagenet, son of the Count of Anjou, received the accolade at the hands of the English King Henry (1129). Geoffrey was fifteen years old, he was always an expert horseman and remarkably good looking and according to the old Chronicles full of chivalric virtues. They make Henry say to the Count, " Send me your son and I will marry him to my daughter (Maud) and as he is not yet a knight, I will knight him with my own hands." Accordingly Anjou consented and sent his son with five picked companions to Rouen, namely Hardouin of St. Mars, Jacquelin of Maillé, Robert de Lemblançai, John of Charvans and Robert of Blois. Twenty-five noble youths (damoisels) of the same age as Geoffrey went also with him. The King of England who was not used to rise from his seat at any one's approach, rose at the entry of young Geoffrey and throwing his arms around him, showed the greatest affection. But he did not let his feelings overcome his prudence, for he immediately put searching questions to the young Count as to his aptitude in learning and in arms. These being satisfactory the interview was terminated. Night then came ón, it was the Vigil of Pentecost, and the lad was conducted to his bedroom, where he and his five-and-twenty young companions were provided with the symbolic bath. In the morning he was clothed in an inner shift of white linen and over it a dress of cloth of gold, a purple cloak thrown on his shoulders, while his legs and feet were clad in hose and shoes embroidered with golden lions. The same in less rich dresses were his five-and-twenty companions given. Then conducted before the king, he knighted them severally.

Antoine de la Sale, an ancient writer, thus describes the ways an esquire becomes a knight. " L'Écuyer quand il a bien voyagé, et a esté en plusieurs faicts d'armes dont il en est failly a honneur et qu'il a bien de quoi maintenir l'estat de Chevalerie; car autrement ne lui est honneur et vault mieuix estre bon Escuyer que ung poure Chevalier, dont pour plus honnourablement li estre que avant la bataille, l'assaut ou la recontre, où bennieres de Princes soient; alors doit requerir aulcun Seigneur on proud-homme Chevalier que le face Chevalier de Dieu, de Notre Dame et de Monseigneur Saint George, le bon Chevalier a lui baillant son espée nue en baisant la Croix; en autres bons Chevaliers se sont au Sainct Sépulchre de Notre Seigneur, pour amour et honneur de lui. Aultres se sont a Sainte Katherine, là vu ils ont leurs dévotions. Aultres se sont qui soñt baignez en cuves, et puis revétus tout de neuf et celle nuyt vant veiller en l'église on ils doyvent estre en dévotion jusques après la grant Messe chantée Lors le Prince, où aulcan jusques Seigneur Chevalier, lui ceint l'espée dorée, et plusieurs aultres plus legieres façons."

(The squire when he had travelled much and has been on several deeds of arms by which he had attained to honour, and if he has sufficient of what is necessary to maintain the estate of knighthood (for otherwise there is no honour for him and it is better worth while to be a good squire than an impoverished knight). Since that it is most honourable to be made so before a battle, an assault or encounter, where the banners of Princes are, then he might request some lord or noble knight in the name of God, of our Lady and Monseigneur St.

George; the good knight delivering to him his naked sword, kissing the cross. Other good knights are dubbed at the Holy Sepulchre of our Lord for his love and honour, others at St. Katherine, or where they perform their devotions. Others are *made* (knights) who are bathed *in tubs*, and then re-clothed in new (garments) and that night they go to watch in the Church where they must be at their devotions until after High Mass is sung. Then the Prince or some other knighted lord girds him with the golden sword and also in several other easier ways.)

The latter part of this passage is important as mentioning both the Bath and the Vigil and which evidently refers to the more elaborate ritual observed, when being knighted in peace time and not on the field of battle—which the commencement does, where all ceremonious giving of the accolade was necessarily omitted.

In the curious poem " L'Ordene de Chevalrie," purported to be written by Hugues de Tabarie, a prince of Galilee, in the time of Saladin, which will be again alluded to, is the injunction

> " Ch'est droit à chevalier nouvel
> Puir le fist en un baing entrer."

Again :

> " Sire tout ensement devez
> Issir, sanz nule viloinie
> De ce baing."

> (Sire, it is thus that you must
> Emerge, without any stain
> From this bath.)

" By the great God," said Saladin (who in this Lay is supposed to have sought instruction previous to Christian knighthood), " this is a wonderful beginning." " Now," Hughes, his teacher replies, " leave this bath and recline on this great bed. It is an emblem of the one you will obtain in paradise, the bed of rest that God grants to His followers, the brave knights."

The bath here mentioned was no doubt a wooden one. The old Roman baths of marble had long since been forgotten and perished. Metal was never employed, so if ever a bath was used, it was a round wooden tub. So in the " Lay of Bégun and Fromont," when the latter consents to knight his son Fromondin, the lad returns the night before to his lodging and finds fifty tubs waiting his immersion and that of his forty-nine friends, young postulants, too, for knighthood next day.

A fuller description is given of the ceremonial of the Bath which existed in England (see Mills " Chivalry," Bk. I.). When an esquire came to Court to seek the accolade in time of peace, two esquires, sage and well-nourished in courtesy and expert in deeds of knighthood, were assigned to him as teachers. If he arrived in the morning he was to serve the king with water at dinner or else place a dish on the table—this was his farewell to his past services as a squire. His governor then led him to his chamber where he remained till the evening, when they sent a barber to him while his beard was shaven and his head rounded (this shaving seems a mistake, as all illuminations of this period show the young squires beardless, and it was probably, as Lacroix points out, the small tonsure they received before knighthood to show their semi-ecclesiastical position as a future Soldier of the Cross).

A curious analogy to the ceremonies of the Church is to be found in the latter's custom in the medieval Church of treating the Faithful on the Vigil of Easter. In order to prepare worthily for the Feast, the body was purified by baths and the hair and the beard were cut as token of the care with which the Christian ought to preserve the purity of his soul and to remove all vices. (Lacroix " History of Religious Life in the Middle Ages.")

The bath was then brought forward but water not yet put into it, but the squire himself was, and sat, wrapped in white cloths and mantle. This being arranged, the news was conveyed to the king in the words, " It waxeth nigh unto the Even, and our master is ready in the bath."

The king then commanded his chamberlain to take into the squire's chamber the bravest and wisest of his knights, who should instruct and counsel the youth, concerning knighthood.

The chamberlain, preceded by minstrels singing and dancing, went to the door of the squire's room. When the governors heard the sound of minstrelsy they stripped their master and left him naked in the bath. After paying much worship and courtesy to each other, he to whom precedence was given advanced to the bath and kneeling down whispered these words in the ear of the young squire: " Right dear brother, may this order bring great honour and worship to you; and I pray that Almighty God may give you the praise of all knighthood. Lo ! this is the order : Be ye strong in the Faith of Holy Church, relieve the widows and oppressed maidens, give every one his own, and above all things, love and dread God. Superior to all other earthly objects, love the king, thy sovereign lord; him and his right defend unto thy power and put him in worship."

The squire being thus advised, the chief knight his preceptor, took in his hand water from the bath, and threw it gently on the shoulders of his young friend. The other knights counselled and bathed him in a similar manner, and then, with the first knight, left the chamber.

The governors then took the squire out of the bath and laid him on a bed " to dry." When the process of drying was finished he was taken out of bed and clothed warmly (which certainly he must have needed) and there was thrown over him a cape of black russet with long sleeves and with a hood like a hermit. It appears indeed to have been a sort of dressing-gown put on till the shivering squire attained his ordinary temperature, for we are expressly told that white was the colour of the chief tunic the neophyte put on, an emblem—as the Christian catechumen of baptism—for purity. This we gather from the " Lay of Perceforest " (Vol. I., fol. 20, v. 1) was the established custom just as it was so in the case of Kings and Queens of England the night before their coronation to be clothed in white, " que les Rois et les Reines de la Grande-Bretagne avoient coutume de prendre la veille au soir de leur couronnement des habits blancs en signe de pureté." So in the old work to which reference has before been made, " L'ordène de Chevalrie," its author, Hugues de Tabarie, says to the

Sir ROBERT DE SEPTVANS

In Chartham Church, Kent, 1306.
From Foster's "Some Feudal Coats of Arms."

proposed neophyte of Chivalry, " The snow white linen with which
I am clothing you, and which touches your skin, is to teach you that
you must keep your flesh from every stain if you wish to reach
heaven."

> " Car Chevalrie
> Si doit baingnièr en honesté
> En courtoisie et en bonté
> Et fere amer à toutes gens."

> (For knighthood must be clothed with honesty,
> With courtesy and with goodness
> And make itself beloved of all.)

A close fitting vest, " saga," was placed under the white tunic—
as the white represented Christian purity—the inner black one
emblemed death common to the knight as well as the serf; over all
was often cast, after knighthood, a red mantle, symbolical of the blood
the young cavalier should be ready to give for God and His Church.
Speaking of this inner black tunic " L'ordene de Chevalrie " says :

> " La mort et la terre où gisrez
> Dont venîtes et où irez.
> A chou doivent garder votre œil."

> (Death and earth where you will rest
> Whence you came and whither you will return,
> This is what you must keep before your eyes.)

As to the scarlet cloak Sainte Palaye writes : " Le manteau long
et trainant qui enveloppoit tout la personne étoit reservé particulierment
au Chevalier, comme la plus auguste et la plus noble decoration qu'il
pût avoir, lorsqu' il n'étoit point paré de ses armes. La couleur
militaire de l'écarlate."

However, it must be acknowledged that it is extremely doubtful
if this mantle of scarlet was assumed before the squire had received
knighthood; he probably put it on when he sat down at the banquet
following that ceremony, and agreeable to the Church's precedent of
white being the colour of a neophyte for baptism, appeared in that
colour, and that only, when he presented himself before the lord who
was to confer on him that high and semi-sacramental dignity.

When we turn to the following ceremonies that followed the Vigil
and the Bath, there is considerable difference between the more
primitive conference of knighthood and that which was usual when
Chivalry had attained its zenith. In the earlier it was greatly
shortened and almost exclusively un-sacramental; in the latter it was
the reverse. In the former it was lay, in the latter ecclesiastical.
But in each case—with the exceptions we have given of ecclesiastical
knighthood, and the very rare cases of sovereign ladies conferring it—
it was imperative, in the simplest rite, that only a knight should make
a knight. There seems indeed also to have been something mysterious
implied in the manner by which the honour of Chivalry was transmitted from one knight to another. It is no wonder that the

resemblance has been often traced between the admission of knights and Churchmen to their respective functions, and a close resemblance really did exist in the different ceremonies we are considering on the two occasions.

But perhaps the most singular circumstance of the whole is this solemn necessity which in both cases was insisted on as to the validity of the original fountain, and the genuine transmission of the honour, or the sanctity, to be conferred. The ordination of priests by bishops regularly succeeding each other was not esteemed more necessary to the purity of the Church than was the investiture of knights by knights to the propriety of Chivalry.

The instances otherwise were, as it has been pointed out, the exception to the rule, and rare. So the history of Chivalry presents us with a vast body of men of different races and of different countries, who through successive generations, derived their dignity from the supposed inviolable power of their immediate predecessor to confer it.

To return to these initial ceremonies of knighthood. The earlier and simpler form of conferration is to be found in many of the old Chronicles and Lays. Thus the curé Lambert, Chronicler of the County of Guisnes and Seigneune of Ardes, describes the knighting of young Arnoul, son of Count Baldwin II., in 1181. The Count called together his sons, his legitimate and natural ones, besides his friends, to attend his Court. Then in their presence he dubbed his son Arnoul knight, by giving him a light blow with his fist in the nape of his neck, the principal sign of knighthood. This was all. It was purely a brief and a lay conference.

In the same simple fashion another Chronicle (*Magnum Belgii Chronicon* 1247) recounts how the King of Bohemia knighted William of Holland—he conferred it by simply giving the blow with his fist on the young Count's neck, "Rex Bohemiæ ictum impegit in collem tironis."

When young Geoffrey Plantagenet, son of the Count of Anjou, was knighted at the hands of King Henry in 1129, being then fifteen years of age, though he certainly was bathed with his companions the night before receiving the accolade, the ceremony of conferring it was the simplest. Clothed in a rich garment he marched next morning into the king's presence, who thereupon knighted him. William of Malmesbury describing the knighting of William of Normandy by the King of the Franks describes it in the fewest words, "Williemus, ubi primum potuit per ætatem militiæ insigne a rege Francorum accæipiens."

So again in the Chanson of Fromond and Bégon the hero was asked to confer knighthood on a certain man. Here the knighting is extremely simple. "You shall be a knight," Bégon tells the postulant, "only go and bathe and then someone will give you the vair and the gris" (the fur only permitted to knights and often used as an alternative to the word "knighting.") Then Bégon raised the palm of his hand and let it descend sharply on the young man's neck. "What are you doing?" the youth cried out. "It is the custom, it is the act that makes you a knight," said Bégon.

A curious example of the freedom with which the ceremonies of creation were sometimes dispensed with, even in Courts and in seasons of peace, when circumstances rendered it inconvenient to observe them, is related by Favine (" Theatre d'Honeur "). Sigismunde being on a visit to Charles VI. was made acquainted with a quarrel between two of the courtiers, respecting an office which each of them thought himself entitled to enjoy. One day when sitting in court, the claims of the two rivals were argued before the two monarchs, when he who had the greatest interest on his side thought at once to destroy the pretensions of his opponent by representing that he had not the order of knighthood. Sigismunde, to whom the latter had been recommended, immediately directed that he should be brought before him, and then declaring he had the right to knight whom he liked, ordered a sword to be brought, with which he gave the man three blows on the neck. Then taking off one of his own gilt spurs, he ordered it to be put on the heel of the new knight, and lastly, girdled him with the ceinture and a long knife instead of a sword. Here again it was a simple and purely lay conference of knighthood.

Hence are seen instances of the simplest kind and of purely lay character in the bestowal of Chivalry. Far different was the ritual when knighthood had been taken under the wing of the Church, and knighthood had expanded into that glorious body of men untrammelled longer by feudal claims.

It has been seen how the day before they were examined as to being possessed of courtesy, largesse, chastity and fidelity to the cause of the widow and orphan, and dedicated to the cause of Holy Church. It has been seen with what severity a Confession of sin was demanded of each postulant and how afterwards with elaborate ceremonial they received the mystical Bath of Chivalry; the next morning such proceeded to Church and heard the Mass of the Holy Christ and took the sacrament clothed in white, to signify he was the bride of Chivalry. Hence the word " adoubor " (to dub), a kindred word to " espouser " (to espouse).

It was usually customary to hear this Mass and receive the Blessed Sacrament in the Church or Chapel where the young squire had passed his vigil the night before. In the Lay " Hervis de Metz " it is said of Hervis, " Au mostier va le service escouter," so in that of " Godefrey de Bouillon," " Et il ot messe oie a l'autel Saint Martin." A sermon followed, an exhortation to be " preuse, hardi et loyal "—a defender of the weak and of Holy Church.

Generally several squires were knighted on the same day, and the exhortation was shared in by all. So St. Palaye says, " Plusieurs Chevaliers ayant été souvent crées dans une même promotion," and he hints that one reason for this might be that after the ceremony they might, on their fiery steeds, caricole along the course together before the assembled multitude, " en cadence " and show off their horsemanship among the crowd of burghers and others attracted to the Court. (St. Palaye, Part II., page 73.)

After receiving Communion, the young esquire presented his sword to the officiating priest who laid it on the altar, blessed it and returned it. According to one, authority, however, Mabillon, writing on the Order of St. Benedict (Article XCV., page 44), " Le Novice reçevoit la Communion après que le Prêtre lui avoit passé l'epée autour du cou," in other words, the priest hung round his neck this blest sword. Whether this was so or not the novice proceeded to kneel at the feet of the lady who was to arm him and then gave his sword to his patron knight (adoubeur) to whom he now made his knightly vows. He was then invested by the young squires and by the lady whose favour to do so he had previously knelt before and obtained this concession from, with hauberk, brassards, gauntlets, spurs and the rest of his armour, and lastly with the knightly belt and sword.

The spur seems to have been generally first fixed on the right foot. According to a passage in " Lancelot du Lac " (Tome I.) " Éperon dextre chaussé au nouveau Chevalier, comme c'étoit alors la coutume."

The custom of being armed by a fair lady (assisted of course by the squires or armourers riveting the various pieces of the armour together) was a very usual proceeding. In the Lay or Romance of " Don Flores of Greece " a knight about to go into the battle is depicted being so armed by a young " Demoiselle," " qui de ses blanches et delicates mains commença à nouer et lacer es guilettes et courroyes."

The girding on the belt (ceinture) with the sword attached was the most important ceremony of Chivalry. Sometimes a king or queen provided the sword to be belted on. Thus in the " Lay of Lancelot," Arthur's Queen gives him a sword and he becomes in future the knight of fair Guinevere. During his armouring the young squire is supposed to be receiving the sword and the belting with the utmost humility and piety, to lift, during the belting, his eyes to God and his hands to heaven, and to realize the belted sword now round him as the silent memorial ever after of chastity, of justice, and of charity. So it runs in the book, " The Order of Chivalry," " L'Écuyer se doit agenouiller devant l'Autel, et lever à Dieu ses yeux corporels et spirituele, et ses mains au Ciel, et le Chevalier lui doit ceindre l'epée en significance de chasteté, et de justice et en significance de charité." Here we see it is the knight and not the lady, who girds his sword on him. The explanation probably is that the custom was a variable one, and often left to the choice of the young squire about to be knighted.

All this being done the postulant knelt before his patron from whom he received the accolade—that is, three strokes with the flat of the sword on the neck or the shoulder, and the " soufflet " or " colée " (alapa), a light blow on the cheek (as the Bishop gives in the rite of confirmation).

" Cette ceremonie de donner un soufflet s'était prise de l'usage du sacrament de la confirmation qui est une espèce de la Chevalerie Chretienne, ou vertu de ce sacrament, ou reçoit armes spirituelle pour resister aux tentation, pour combattre contre nos ennemis invisibles, et pour souffrir patiemment les injures." (Leber, " Dissertations.")

Another learned writer (Stebbing, " Chivalry and the Crusades ") thinks it is probable that this " soufflet " or blow was a copy of some part of the practices that followed the conferring of fiefs, by which it might be signified that as the tenant thenceforth owed his homage to the lord of the estate, so the new-made knight became the servant of God and the Church. And this seems likely, as the other custom of the patron-knight kissing the cheek of the new-made Cavalier, obtained also in the feudal ceremony, and in " The Order of Chivalry " it is so stated that the patron-knight was in the habit, at this juncture, of kissing the new-made knight (as a mark of brotherly love and fraternity, " le Chevalier doit baiser l'Écuyer qu'il reçoit Chevalier.") The light blow on the cheek was accompanied by the words, " In the name of God, of St. Michael and of St. George, I dub thee knight; be gallant, be courageous and loyal " (au nom de Dieu, de St. Michel et de St. George, je te fais Chevalier; sois preux, hardi et loyal). (The colée or buffet on the cheek are in the Lays and Chronicles frequently used as synonymous with the accolade.) Then followed " largesse " both to the new-made knight from his patron and from himself to his companions and inferiors in token of that noble liberality which has previously been dealt with as one of the virtues necessary in a good knight. Indeed " largesse " and courtesy it was said were the two wings of Chivalry.

The Christian symbolism which accompanied the first steps of the novice, we see from the foregoing, followed and accompanied him in some way or other during the whole of his knightly career. The vigil of arms, the strict fasts, the nights spent in prayer in some lonely chapel, the white garments of the postulant for knighthood, the consecration of his sword, were graven on his memory ever after—a constraining force, against a constraining world. In the words of Hugues de Tabarie, the Prince of then Christian Galilee, " the white girdle which I place around your loins is to teach you to keep your body pure and to avoid luxury. The two golden spurs are to urge on your horse to deeds of daring. Imitate its ardour and docility, as it obeys you, so be you obedient to the Lord. Now fasten your sword to your side; strike your enemies with its double edge, prevent the poor from being crushed by the rich, the weak from being oppressed by the strong. I put upon your head a pure white ' coif ' to indicate that your soul similarly should be stainless." (L'Ordène de Chevalerie.")

Indeed the very word " ordène " otherwise " ordination " implies that the arming of a knight was a sacred ceremony. And the very sacredness of the order of knighthood made its betrayal looked on with horror—an act unforgivable and irremediable, for the culprit was regarded not only as a culprit to his honour, but to the Holy Cross. Exposed on a scaffold in nothing but his shirt, he was stripped of his armour, which was broken before his eyes, and thrown at his feet, while his spurs were thrown upon a dunghill. His shield was fastened to the croup of a cart-horse and dragged through the dust, and his charger's tail was cut off. A herald-at-arms asked thrice, " Who is there? " Three times an answer was given, naming the knight about to be degraded, and three times the herald rejoined, " No, it is not so, I see no knight here, I see only a coward who has been false to his plighted troth." Carried thence to church on a litter like a dead body, the culprit was forced to listen while the burial service was read over him, for he had lost his honour without which a knight could not live, and was looked upon as a corpse. (Lacroix.)

And if this degradation a man suffered who shamed his knighthood seems, in this age, to have been excessive, it must be remembered how high that dignity was held to be. Camden, in his book, notes it is a name of such a dignity that a lord never attained to knighthood. A Baron, he says, till he had expressly been admitted to the Order of Chivalry, in subscribing any deed wrote his name with the simple addition of " Dominus "; that in many ancient documents the signatures of knights are placed before those of barons. The honour, indeed, which it conferred was of such a nature that it seems to have been considered capable of forming a new character altogether in those who obtained it. Even in the very rare case of a villain if he had won this almost unheard of honour by his bravery, he became immediately enfranchised and his base blood henceforth accounted gentle for ever. (Camden.)

After receiving the accolade it was the privilege of the young knight to claim of the patron who had conferred it any boon that was not discreditable to his honour or his order (thus again resembling baptism, where after it, the godfather used to give presents to those assembled and a rich gift to his godson). Indeed, the custom of having these parvains or godfathers is stated to have given another explanation (one has already been given) of the word " adouber," *i.e.*, the young squires to be knighted were adopted children of the knight who gave them this honour—and so the word " adouber " equals the word " adoptare," and the older knight who thus adopted them was bound to look after them in their first and early " passages of arms " and tourneys. (Leber, " Collection de pieces pour L'Histoire de France.")

Du Cange refers to the custom of the godfather knight, and the young Chevalier just knighted giving and receiving gifts thus : " This day of the creation of knights, it is fitting to hold a great feast, to give fine gifts and donations, and to have great dinners, to joust and to tilt and such other things as appertain to the Festival of Knighthood. And the lord who makes a new knight must give unto the new knight and the other knights. And also the new-made knight should give unto the others that day. For whosoever receives such a great gift as is the Order of Knighthood this order is lowered if he does not give as he ought to give."

Again this usage is confirmed in a definite way by a passage in the " Lay of Lancelot du Lac." " As was," it runs, " the custom then, the new-made knight prayed Galahad, who has conferred on him knighthood, to grant him the first gift that he should ask him, and in such case one's new-made knight should never be refused if the demand was not unreasonable or prejudicial to whom it was made. So Galahad promised him and the new-made knight prayed him that he might follow him in the Quest he was about to undertake."

We have before mentioned the vows or promises which the young knight, previous to his admission, made. These vows were varied and to be kept as occasion arose. The first one, according to some ancient writers, bound him, whenever he went on a quest or strange adventure, never to lighten himself of his arms, except for the sake of repose at night.

By the next, he promised that whenever in pursuit of adventure, not to avoid perilous " passes," nor to turn out of his way for fear of meeting powerful Chevaliers, or from any dread of monsters, savage beasts or spirits, or anything which could only harm, or might be resisted by, the body of a man.

Among other rules, similar to those already quoted for the conduct of his life, we also find that having undertaken to defend a lady, he was rather to die than desert her, or suffer her to be offended. That he should be punctual to the day and hour in which he had been engaged to contend in arms with a brother knight; that on returning to court after having been about in quest of adventure, he should give an exact account of all he had done, even if his actions should have been to his disgrace, his knighthood being the forfeit if he should disobey this ordinance. That on being taken prisoner at a tourney he should, besides rendering up his arms and horses to the victor, not again contend without the special leave of the latter, and lastly that he should not, in company, fight against a solitary enemy, nor carry two swords, if he was unwilling to contend with two opponents.

That arms, especially the destrier or war-horse, were rendered up to the victor as his right, we find in the charming little " Lay of Flore and Blanchflor," when the lady says :

> " Mais mon ami est bel et gent
> Quand il vais a tournoiement,
> Et il abat un chevalier
> Il me présente son destrier."

> (Fair and gentle is my knight
> When he rides to tournament,
> When his foe he overthrows
> Me he gives his prisoner's steed.)

Immediately after receiving the accolade the young knight was armed. In the " Lay of Garin le Lorrain " there is a charming picture of the young lad on the morning of his knighting being armed. Although the poet does not say so, Fromondin, the young hero, doubtless passed the night in church, in the Vigil of Arms, for he is described as returning to his quarters after having heard the morning Mass, and then going to bed to sleep. " The day dawned beautifully and the sun beamed. Count Fromont (the father) was the first to leave his bed. He opened the window and the fresh brilliance struck him full in the face. In a moment he was dressed and shod. He went completely armed from his room, ordered his horse and rode through all the quarters of the town waking the knights. He came to his son's lodging and found the lad asleep on his bed. Fromont called Bernard, " Come, see my son. He should have been given a chance to get bigger and stronger, but now he must be clothed in the white Hauberk," and then with a loud voice, " Come, Fromondin, get up, you must not sleep too long, young sire. The great Tournament ought already to be forming." The young man leaped from his bed on hearing the voice, and the squires entered to serve him. They quickly booted and clothed him. In the presence of all Count William of Montelin girded the sword on him with a golden belt. " Dear Nephew," he said, " I enjoin thee not to trust false and dissolute men. Given a long life thou shalt be a mighty prince. Always be strong (hardi), victorious and undoubtable to all thy enemies. Give the vair and gray (i.e., knighthood) to many deserving men. It is the way to attain honour." " Everything is in God's hands," answered Fromondin. Then they led to him a costly horse. He mounted him with an easy bound, and they gave him a shield emblazoned with a lion.

It was often considered, however, a great privilege of the ladies

A KNIGHT'S LIFE

to do this arming. The young daughter of a knight was trained to do this and many other things to help the young cavaliers. If he came to her father's castle, it was she who was told off to greet him and disarm him, with making ready his chamber and his bed, with preparing his bath, and even (we have on this point many unquestionable texts, especially in the " Lay of Girart de Roussillon ") with massaging him in order to help him to go to sleep. And one gathers from the " Chansons de Gestes " that it was these young women who made all the advances in love to knights when thus entertaining them. Maidens thought these youths handsome, and they told them so without the least embarrassment. So to arm a newly-made knight came easily to a young maiden. In the " Lay of Don Flores de Grèce " a knight preparing to go to battle is armed by a young demoiselle, who " de ses blanches et delicates mains, commença à nouer et laces es guilettes et courroyes."

And so Lacroix ("Military and Religious Life in the Middle Ages ") says of such demoiselles, " they unbuckled the knight's armour with their own hands, they prepared perfumes and spotless linen for his wear (on return from warfare or a tournament), they clothed him in gala dress, in mantle and scarf that they themselves had embroidered, they prepared his bath and waited on him at table."

And no doubt arming a knight to go into danger gave to the ladies a deep interest. In the battle of Agincourt four such knights, having been armed by their demoiselles, went into the fight—one, we are told, was killed, one was made prisoner, another was missing after the battle, the fourth saved his life by dishonourable flight.

The lady whom this last one had wakened an interest in felt so much his disgrace and for having placed her regard on a knight who had dishonoured his order, that she declared that she preferred death to longer living. (St. Palaye, Part II., p. 108.)

CHAPTER III

WHAT the armour was that the new-made knight assumed depends on the century in which he lived.

As this work is not a treatise on medieval armour—which is so extensive a subject that it would more than suffice for a book in itself—we shall briefly place here some of the salient points in the chain armour which subsisted from temp. 1066 till end of reign of Edward I., before the introduction of plate armour—which latter, under continual alterations and improvements, lasted till armour ceased to be used. As for chain-mail which is now dealt with, its origin is of remote antiquity. It came from the East and penetrated to the north and west of Europe. As far as this country is concerned, the epoch of chain-mail, pure and simple, may be said to close with the reign of Edward I. From the Norman Conquest down to the introduction of plate armour there was little alteration in a knight's panoply. With the advent of the Normans in 1066 the subject of armour and arms as far as England became more definite to trace and to describe. This chiefly is owing to the famous Bayeux Tapestry, also to the multiplication of manuscripts, carvings, ivories, and brasses preserved in France and England, for both countries, who though often at war, were one in the manner of their armour. Though the date of the Bayeux Tapestry is still disputed as to whether it was the work or not of Queen Matilda and her bower-women, it certainly was begun and completed within fifty years of the Conquest, and its subject—armed men—most useful therefore for students of armour.

To begin with the lance. Here we find the lance's head of the leaf-form, and sometimes of the lozenge shape, and very seldom barbed.

Nearly all the Norman spears were adorned with pennons from two to five points.

The Saxon axe is not seen—but the mace takes its place, even though at a later date the axe again came into favour with the knights.

The sword to the Vikings had been their most precious weapon. Fighting as they did along the coasts of the countries they made descents upon, their weapons alone saved their lives, and such were cared for with the utmost diligence. To them the sword had surrounding it a mystic glamour which was handed on to the medieval knights, their successors, and which lingers yet in regal functions.

At the time of Bayard, the epitome of French Chivalry, this mystic glamour still hovered round the sword. What he considered the greatest reward of all his labours was when his King, Francis I., came and sought knighthood at his hand and full of enthusiasm of the glamour round his sword, that had given that monarch the accolade, he cried to it, " Tu es bien heureuse d'avoir aujourd'huy à

73

lui si beau et si puissant Roy donné l'ordre de Chevalerie; certes, ma bonne espée, vous serez comme reliques gardée et sur toute autre honorée, et puis fit deux saults, et après remit au fourreau son espée." (La Columbière.)

Tradition elevated the forger of Odin's sword into a demi-god. Athelstan, Ethelwulf and Alfred, in Saxon England, bequeathed—as their dearest treasure—their swords to their next of kin. Thence it passed in the Arthurian circle to Arthur's mystic sword Excalibur, which is said in after time to have been presented by Richard I. to Tancred of Sicily. All the better armour in the twelfth and thirteenth centuries was brought from Germany. There, the constant feuds of the Hanseatic and other towns with the neighbouring nobles made the manufacture of arms a personal necessity, and the best armed gained the day. This armour the Jews, the universal providers in the Middle Ages, continually brought into France and England, and among the chivalrous of both kingdoms was eagerly purchased. Later Italian—particularly Milanese armour—was the fashion, but this only when plate had taken the place of the older chain armour. Cologne was a great centre for this warlike commodity, and is spoken of in many an early ballad.

Thus the battle of Otterbourne was fought with swords of " fyne collayne." King Arthur's mystic sword was said to have been made there. " For alle of Coleyne was the blade, and all the hilte of precious stone."

As to France—the sword St. Louis, in the thirteenth century, bore in the Crusade which he undertook, was of German workmanship. The swords themselves were generally cross-hilted, hence often in battle a knight sorely wounded would (as it is said the celebrated Bayard did) place before his dying eyes his sword upright—bearing his last thoughts heavenwards. The two-handled sword seems seldom to have been used; it rarely occurs on the monumental brasses of the period. It required great strength of arm to handle it enough. That redoubtable knight, Richard I., is said to have been a proficient in its use.

The swords in use at this period can be divided into three classes: (1) Those having the character of a broad sword with parallel sharp edges and an acute point and the tang (the prolongation of the blade which fits into the handle is the tang) only for a grip; (2) A similar variety having a cross-guard arm; (3) A sword with the blade slightly curved. The sheaths were usually of leather stiffened with a wooden framing. The sword of the knight varied little in form from the twelfth to the end of the fifteenth century.

The helmet, another necessity in the knight's equipment, was at this period conical with a " nasal " (nose protection). This is seen clearly in the Bayeax Tapestry. The nasal continued in use till about 1140. This conical shape of helmet gradually was superseded by one of a cylinder shape, made of iron with a vertical slit for the eyes, one on each side of the helm, called " occularii." Holes for breathing were rare in specimens left us, the knight had therefore to breathe through the orifices for his nose and eyes.

A fine example of this sort of helmet is to be found upon the monumental effigy of Hugh FitzEudo in Kirkstead Chapel, Lincolnshire. The helmet itself was generally flat-topped and had very much the appearance of a modern chimney-pot. A little more graceful one was brought in at the end of the fourteenth century called the " armet " (from " elmette " or " armette "). This differed from those previously used in that, while the older forms had been put on by lowering them over the head, and the weight had in all cases been borne by the head, the armets opened out their lowest part on hinges, and could be closed round the head and neck, while the weight was transferred to the gorget (collar) and thence to the shoulders. It is very likely the present heraldic way of portraying helmets is derived from this " armet," as singularly alike in both cases. There is a fine specimen of an armet in the Wallace Collection.

The conical helmet, which the armet afterwards often took the place of, was of great weight and so either hung at the saddle-bow or was carried by the squire when not in use. Inside—as all the other forms were—it was thickly padded and went over the mailed " chapelle de fer." On these helmets at first no crest appeared. The earliest form of the latter was a painted emblem on the side of the helmet, such as is found on that of Philip d'Alsace, Count of Flanders, 1181. So, too, on the cap of Geoffrey, Count of Anjou, 1150. The earliest authentic example—predecessor of all others—is that of Richard Cœur de Lion, who shows on his great seal a fan-shaped ornament surmounting the helmet.

The introduction of a crest on the helmet seems to have been originally for defence—from their indented and serrated edges they first possessed—which served to deaden the blow of a sword or mace. The immense crests also used were for an entirely different purpose—that of ostentation and ornament in tourneys and tournaments, and were generally made of painted " cuir bouilli."

" Ailettes " also must be mentioned. These came into vogue towards the end of the thirteenth century. They have often puzzled the uninitiated; they were small shields or defences fastened at right angles across the shoulders, designed to lessen the effect of a sweeping cut from a sword or axe. An early notice of ailettes occurs in the " Roll of Purchases " for the great tournament held at Windsor in 1278, where they were stated to have been made of leather covered with a sort of cloth. Silk laces were employed sometimes to fasten them. It is remarkable that the brass of Sir Roger de Trumpington, who was one of the thirty-five knights taking part in this tournament, should show one of the earliest examples extant of these ailettes. The use of ailettes is rather perplexing; that they were merely ornamental is improbable. The only supposition is that they were little shields for the neck and shoulders, but more especially for the latter. Occasionally for tournaments and pageants ailettes appear to have been made very elaborately. Thus in the Inventory of Piers Gaveston in 1313 mention is made of a pair garnished and fretted with pearls.

The gambeson was another article in the knight's equipment. It generally was worn under the mail, but it also, on one or two brasses, has been found over the chain-mail. It was made chiefly of leather, prepared by previous boiling and so extremely tough, and had various snips and discs of iron sewn on its surface. It, like the coat of mail or hauberk, had a thick stuffing underneath, to prevent it, or the mail, from chafing the knight's skin.

A KNIGHT'S LIFE IN

The tunic was worn under both the gambeson or hauberk. Sometimes the tunic was worn much longer than at other times, so in some sepulchral brasses it is quite clearly seen beneath the ringed hauberk. The hauberk itself was the chief method of bodily defence. Its coif, which went generally over the head and under the chapelle de fer (the other head defence) was generally a part of it, though instances occur when it was placed detachable round the neck, where afterwards the " gorget " was placed. This coif had only a small opening for the face. This almost complete covering of the latter sometimes led to knights in battle mistaking their enemies for friends. Thus Ralph de Courci, in the French wars, mistook the French for his own side, the English, and was taken prisoner. At the battle of Noyon, Peter de Maule and others escaped recognition of the pursuing enemy, and mingled in their ranks. William the Conqueror is said himself to have been reported dead by his soldiers, though he was riding in their midst, until he threw back his coif and showed his face.

The hauberk was generally made to open in front in order to afford convenience in riding. Upon the outside of it was, on the chest part, a square or oblong piece to doubly protect the former. The hauberk was at this period made of chain-mail, and chain-mail was a manufacture, as has before been said, of very great antiquity. Antiquarians have traced it on relics of the Assyrian and ancient Persian dynasties—it was certainly in a lesser degree known to the Romans, who used rings and discs sewn on a strong stratum of tough textile, for arming their soldiery. There is little doubt, however, that chain armour originated in the East, where its comparative coolness and lightness would, as an armour, be peculiarly fitted for a hot country. It came by their depredations, far afield, round Europe, into the hands and use of the North-men, and thence spread rapidly among the Western countries of France and England.

Its manufacture took a great amount of labour and trouble to forge. Different ways appear to have been in vogue to apply the " mailles." Sometimes from how they appear in the brasses of the time, they have rings overlapping each other in the same row; sometimes they look as if each row of rings had been sewn on, and doubtless they often were, upon stout linen or cuir-boilée. Sometimes the rings are interlinked, as in a modern steel purse, so that the coat is entirely of steel rings. The bottom of the hauberk was often scolloped, or gilded.

Another item, chausses of chain-mail, were requisite to preserve the nether limbs of the mailed knight. These came into general use about the commencement of the twelfth century. In some they were short, only protecting the knees and shins of the wearers; in others, they were a continuation of the hauberk and so the latter covered both the legs and feet. To avoid the difficulty of bending the knee " genouillières " were invented, which generally were of cuir bouilli—often highly ornamented. The reason for this defence was not alone the protection afforded. The intolerable drag of chain-mail upon the knee or elbow when flexed prevented freedom of action in each joint, but by the termination of the ringed mail at the upper part of the genouillère, to which it was affixed, and the continuation of it below, an advantage was obtained which was fully appreciated. For the same reason—to free a man's arms from the strain of the mail—a similar device later on was invented to wear at their elbow joints, called "coudieres." These coudieres were frequently elaborately ornamented.

The hands, as before mentioned, at this earlier period, were covered with a continuation down the arms of the linked hauberk and not divided yet into fingers. They were, in fact, ringed mittens. The sword was long and straight with short "quillons" drooping towards the blade. The grip is slightly swelling, and the circular pommel, if not a cross-hilted sword, is enriched with a design. The method of suspending the sword is peculiar to the period; it grips the scabbard in two places, between which a small strap runs as a "guide"; the weapon thus hangs diagonally across the left front of the knight.

The most interesting perhaps—certainly the most showy—of the knight's panoply was the surcoat. It was a sleeveless garment and reached nearly to the heels. It was split up in front and probably behind for convenience in riding. It was originally introduced to preserve the mail from the rain, which from its material was much apt to rust, and indirectly as protection in the Early Crusades, of protection against the heat of Eastern suns. But the chief reason for its adoption was that it afforded a means for recognizing the wearer, whose features now were completely hidden by the helmet, thus rendering it impossible, without a distinguishing mark, to recognize friend from foe. The surcoat indeed took the place of the long flowing tunic, which, as has been mentioned above, has been worn under the hauberk, as shown on the two great seals of Richard I., and it was a natural outcome to transfer the latter to the outermost position, leaving the padded and often mail-set gambeson alone the duty of supporting the weight underneath of the hauberk.

The first English monarch who appears in the surcoat is King John, and he is thus habited upon his great seal, while his rival, the Dauphin Louis, is similarly represented upon the French seal (see Harl. MS. 43). So, too, the surcoat appears on the seal of Alexander II. of Scotland. One writer (Ashdown) says it was of white material, sometimes diapered and nearly always with heraldic charges. Joinville, in his Chronicle, says he spoke to the son of St. Louis then dead, " of the embroidered coats of arms (surtouts) then in vogue, reminding him he had never seen such rich ones in his saintly father's time, and the young prince, then king acknowledged he had such surcoats with arms embroidered which had cost him eight hundred pounds." Joinville told him he could have employed the money better if he had given it to God and had had his surcoat made of good taffeta (satin) ornamented with his arms, as his father had done. Another writer (Gardner) says from the time of King John it was nearly always green, and cites the old adage :

> " With scharfe weppun and schene
> Gay gownes of grene
> To hold theyre armour clene
> And werre it from the wette."

The illuminations extant, however, certainly point to the correctness of the first writer—except that the surcoat in them is not always white; sometimes a brilliant blue, sometimes scarlet, in a prince's, cloth of gold, but in all charged with heraldic emblems.

The shield of the period was kite shape, either flat or a round hollow, so as to encircle the knight's body to some extent. It was invariably made at this time of wood and covered on both sides with leather. The shield's length was generally about four feet long and two feet across. It was often worn not on the arm as in action, but slung round the neck, or carried by the youthful squire for its owner.

Spurs, of course—for they were essentially the emblem of knighthood—completed the Chevalier in armour.

Gilt spurs were fastened on his heels when knighted; they were hacked off by the cook's axe when degraded. At the famous battle of Coutrai in 1302 an immense spoil of these fell to the victors and were hung up by them as trophies in the neighbouring church.

The gilded spurs were not unknown to the Romans. They were one of the marks of their Equestrian order. The earlier form of the medieval spur was of a " goad " type and fastened on by a single strap; they were probably first used singly and were called " pryck spurs." The more modern " rowel " spur appears later in the thirteenth century and is seen in the great seal of Henry III. The number of pricks on the ordinary spur of the rowel type was usually eight; those used at tournaments contained generally sixteen pricks and had very long shanks to reach the horse's flank below the outstanding bards.

As to horse-armour, nothing is more constantly met with in the old Chronicles than accounts of the destructive effects of missiles, whether from bow or cross-bow, upon knights' horses in battle, yet excepting the poetic fancy of Wace in his " Roman de Rou " who mounts Fitzosbert on an iron-clad horse at Senlac

" A co Ke Willame disseit
Et encore plus dire voleit
Vint Willame li fitz Osber
Son cheval tot couvert de fer."

(As the Duke said then
And would have said more,
William Fitzosbert rode up
His horse being all coated with iron.)
—Roman de Rou.

the first mention of horse-armour as far as England is concerned, is at the battle of Gisors in 1198, when Richard I. speaks of the capture of one hundred and forty sets in terms which plainly show that he then met with it for the first time. Indeed no reference is made in English Statutes of horse-armour until 1298, so that it seems certain it was till then unknown. In France its introduction seems earlier, for at this time a man-at-arms received half as much pay again if his horse was barded, and in 1303 every man with an estate of five hundred livres was bound to provide horse-armour. A mailed horse appears in the effigy of Sir Robert de Shirland in Sheppey, and there is a fine figure of a destrier completely clad in mail among the figures of the " Painted Chamber " (published by Society of Antiquarians). One reason why it was so late in its appearance was that the Norman knights copying their predecessors, the Danes, during the civil wars of Henry I., Stephen and Henry II., fought their battles dismounted, rendering horse-armour of relatively small importance.

But later it rose in importance as knights ceased for a time to engage on foot. When Monstrelet wrote it was the pride of the knight to make his destrier's head-front even blaze in jewels. This head-front was called the " chaufron," originally the " chevron." The chaufron bore a spike, a custom dating to the time of Edward III. In the Lay " Anturs of Arthur," it is said :

> " Opon his cheveronne be-forr
> Strode as a unicorn
> Al scharpe as a thorn
> An nanlas of stele."

The charger ridden by Lord Scales in his tourney with the Bastard of Burgundy had a

> " Schaffrô with a large sharpe pyke of steele,"

which penetrated the Bastard's horse and caused him to rear and dismount that good knight. The oldest chaufron handed down is now in Warwick Castle. However, all this is getting beyond the age of chain-mail when barbed horses were never found—or if any were—it was a new, and till then, an untried expedient.

To conclude this short dissertation on the weapons and armour the young knight, now admitted to Chivalry, would be accoutred in, perhaps to the reader such would be better brought home, by taking the description given of the dress and armour of such a knight as described by Chaucer in his " Rime of Sire Thopas," only it must be understood it portrays the fashions of the fourteenth and not the thirteenth century, and therefore of the age of plate and not ringed mail.

> " He didde next his white lere
> Of cloth of lake fine and clere
> A breche and eke a sherte.
> And next his shert an haketon
> And over that an haubergeon
> For piercing of his herte.
>
> And over that a fine hauberk
> Was all ye wrought of Jewes work
> Full strong it was of plate ;
> And over that his cote-armour
> As white as is the lily flore
> In which he wol debate (contend).
>
> His shield was all of gold so red
> And therein was a bore's head
> A charboncle beside ;
> And then he swore on ale and bred
> How that the geaunt should be ded
> Betide what betide.

A KNIGHT'S LIFE IN

His jambeux were of cuir bouilly
His sworde's sheth of ivory
His helm of latoun (brass) bright,
His sadel was of rewel bone,
His bridle as the sonne shone
Or as the moon light.

His spere was of fine cypres
That bodeth warre and nothing pees,
The hed ful sharpe y-ground-e
His stede was all of dapper gray
It goth an amble in the way
Ful softely in londe."

If this is a poetical description of a good knight of the time
we give a description in prose of another knight as shown in his
monumental effigy, that of Sir John d'Aubernoun, existing in Stoke
D'Aubernoun Church near Guildford. It dates from about the year
1277, the fifth year of Edward I. and is one of the most remarkable
brasses in existence either here or on the continent.

It is unique among the brasses of this reign by reason of the
knight being represented with straight lower limbs, the remainder all
having the cross-legged position.

Although the figure is somewhat disproportionate, and the partial
covering up of the lower parts of the legs by the surcoat is unfortunate,
yet as a work of art, and especially as an example of technique and
patience on the part of the engraver, it is unrivalled. Every
separate link of the mail is faithfully represented. The reinforce-
ment of the chain-mail by secondary defences is here exemplified in
its primitive stage, a pair of grenouillères only appearing, which from
their ornamental appearance are presumably of cuir bouilli. The
Coif de Mailles upon the head descends to the shoulders on either side
and covers part of the surcoat, while the hauberk has sleeves which
are prolonged to cover the hands with mail gauntlets, not divided for
the fingers. The mail chausses are continued like the sleeves of the
hauberk, in order to protect the feet as well as the legs. Over the
mail appears a loose surcoat reaching to below the knees and confined
at the waist by a cord from below, which it opens in front and falls on
either side in many folds, being divided also at the back to facilitate
riding. It does not wear any ornament or design, but apparently is of
rich material and has a fringed border.

The sword is long and straight. The " guige " (by which the
shield was often suspended round the neck) bearing here the shield is
engraved with roses, alternating with the mystical Cross (signifying
good fortune and long life) termed the Fyl-fot, in which each arm of
a Greek Cross is continued at right angles; it passes over the right
shoulder, and supports a small flat heater-shaped shield, upon which
the arms appear (azure, a chevron or). The spurs are the usual short
ones of the pryck variety affixed by ornamental straps. The lance
passes under the right arm and displays a small fringed pennon
charged with the same arms as the shield. Here we have the full
equipment of a knight in armour between the years 1250-1328. It
may be remarked D'Aubernoun's legs are uncrossed and from that

might according to the popular belief denote he never had been on a Crusade, but this belief is negatived by the existence of monuments to bonâ-fide Crusaders and to persons known to have visited in pilgrimage the Holy Land who are represented with the lower limbs not crossed. Two examples can be given again of knights cross-legged and cross-armed who neither of them were Crusaders, that of Sir Roger Kerdiston, 1337 at Reepham, and that of Sir Oliver d'Ingham, 1343 at Ingham, Norfolk—both these were benefactors to their respective churches, like others found cross-legged who also were such. It therefore seems probable their effigies appear thus delineated not from having taken the Cross, or on pilgrimage to Palestine, but from being benefactors to a Church.

A more sure sign of a knight having been a Crusader than his crossed-legs is to find on his shield, with his own armorial bearings, some form of the Cross. This was a very frequent practice for such. To take one instance, the Count of Vela, of the Royal House of Arragon, after making the Crusade added to his arms " on a border azure the eight Crosses of the kingdom of Jerusalem." (Argote de Molina I. c. 100.)

To return to the young squire now having received the accolade, and fully armed as described in the preceding paragraphs. The first thing he is represented to have done in the many " Lays " and " Chaussons " was to mount his destrier and by himself, or else with other youths who may that day have been knighted, shown himself in all his new-acquired harness, and bravery, to the fair ones looking on from the castle door, and to the villagers and burghers congregated on the castle green. There two martial games awaited his dexterity, one was the quintain, the other the behourd.

The quintain was a manikin covered with a hauberk and a shield and fastened to the top of a post. The play consisted in the young knight dashing on the post, his horse at a gallop, and his lance couched, and piercing the hauberk and buckler with a single lance-thrust.

Sometimes to increase the difficulty of the play, several armed manikins were arranged in a row, and the point was to run through and overthrow them all. This was the test that was ordinarily imposed upon newly created knights and which took place before the witnesses of dubbing—the ladies and his friends.

As to the behourd, it was simply a form of training for tournaments and was a sort of fencing or tilting on horseback. The knights arranged themselves two by two, and one of them turned upon his partner trying to pierce his shield with a lance. This sometimes became dangerous play for one grew excited in it, and in the heat of the strife forgot that it was an amusement.

In the " Lay of Girart de Roussillon " occurs a description of the game of quintain in the recital of the marriage of Fulc.

" On that day he dubbed a hundred knights, giving horses and arms to each. Then in a meadow which bordered on Arsen he arranged for them a quintain equipped with a new shield and a strong and glittering hauberk. The young men ran their courses, and other people came to watch them . . . Girart saw that they were beginning to quarrel with each other, and in his heart he was much troubled. The crowd pushed towards the quintain. The hundred young men had made their trial; some had succeeded, others had failed, but no one had more than indented the mail of the hauberk. The Count called for his boar-spear. Droon brought it to him. It was the spear which Arthur of Cornwall had carried when formerly fighting in a battle in Burgundy. The Count spurred his horse into the lists; he struck the target and made a hole of such a size that a quail could have flown through it. Then he broke and cut the shield under the ventail. There was no knight who equalled him or could ever have sustained a struggle against him. The Count struck out with such force that with a blow he split one of the straps and tore off the other, all the while holding his weapon so firmly in hand that he again drew it out. And his men said, ' What strength.' When he makes war it is not to take sheep or cattle, that he is intent against his enemies, he had drawn much blood from their bodies.''

These games ended, the whole knightly company sat down to one of those rich banquets already described. It was here that all the superb dresses of both knights and ladies best displayed themselves. The chevaliers in their long mantles of scarlet, which at the end of the fourteenth century on their admittance to chivalry they were accustomed to receive, reviving in these mantles the colour of the ancient military cloaks of the Romans. These, the French kings were accustomed, at the two seasons of winter and summer, to renew for their knights. It was also usual for the king at the time he gave the young newly-created knight a scarlet mantle, to also give him a horse, or if not that, then a bit for the same, ornamented with gold, which represented the pledge used in Investitures, as a sign of an alienated fief. The cost of these mantles, horses, and bits, frequently occur in the Exchequer Rolls of the period—particularly those of Philip le Bel in 1307-8.

At this banquet of his initiation in Chivalry, the knight would, for the first time, put on the gold collar pertaining to that order, here again, in these collars of gold, reviving the practice of the Equestrian order of ancient Roman days. These knight's collars were probably, in the early ages of Chivalry, plain gold circles, and they obtained them, not from the favour of a sovereign lord, but as a personal right appertaining to their status as Chevaliers. This was a right descended from a long ancestry of warriors, for twisted collars of metal and torques are found in the burying-places of all the older dwellers in Northern Europe. The British Chiefs wore them, and golden torques were around the necks of the leaders of the first Saxon, and afterwards Danish, invaders of Britain, and they continued to be worn by the Saxon warriors down to the time of the last King—Edward the Confessor, who was buried with a chain-collar of gold two feet long, carrying a jewelled cross. The quaint chroniclers of the age even gave these gold collars a more remote ancestry. They asserted that Joseph, after explaining Pharaoh's dream, was rewarded with such by the king, on his creation as first minister of the realm. They asserted that the youthful Daniel received the same as a mark of favour of Belshazzar; and Darius the king so rewarded, with a collar of gold, Zorobabel the son of Salathiel. (Leber.)

Afterwards these collars developed often into a more elaborate form, and were greatly superseded by the glittering collars and chains bestowed by the sovereigns who founded and instituted a sort of

DAYS OF CHIVALRY

" imperium in imperio " in knighthood, for their own special benefit. It was perhaps natural, it certainly was a wise action, in nearly every king when knighthood no longer was hampered and held in leash by feudal chains, to try, by setting up these secular orders of theirs, to forge new chains to knit together, to their own interests, groups of free knights. Thus in both France, Germany, Italy, Spain and England these many royal and individual orders arose. The inspiration for such was found in the religious military orders which the first Crusade called into being. The oldest order of Chivalry—whether religious or secular—was that of the Holy Sepulchre, the parent, or the incentive of all the rest, and that owed its rise to certain knights grouping themselves together, out of the rest of Chivalry, in defence of the Sepulchre and the pilgrims who visited it. These secular orders therefore to enlist in their service, and band together, the free knights of different countries in the interest, and for the benefit of, the secular prince who had lost the benefit that feudal service had given him of a constraining power over the swords of the knights, grew up very rapidly in the states of Christendon, and the more brilliant the ornaments of each order, in their chains and collars, the greater attraction the prince found in them to lure the knight to strive under his peculiar banner. The recipient exchanged the feudal chain for the chain of honour or ornament, but it became no less a chain on his actions, " la plupart de ces chevaleries avaient des marques d'honneur, des horées, des devises, et particulièrement des dorures et des fourrures de vair ce qui les fit nommer ' chevaliers dorés.' Ces dorures étaient des ceintures, des chaines d'or, des colliers, des éperons dorés des franges d'or, et autres semblables ornemens." (Leber.)

In both France, Germany and Italy many more collars were invented. The King of Cyprus gave to those he wished to honour or bind to his service, a collar with a sword silver gilt on it; the King of Scotland a collar silver gilt composed of little curbs (gourmettes); the King of the Romans one of a serpent coiled round—out of whose mouth appeared a cross florée, all worn by those who displayed fealty to the giver, and all militating against the newer and freer knighthood which had recently emancipated itself from feudal chains.

However, sometimes it is generous to say that these collars were given as a mark of fraternity, that beautiful virtue ancient Chivalry nursed and cultivated. Those sworn to fraternity usually wore the same clothes and arms, mingled their blood in one vessel, received the Holy Sacrament and kissed the Pyx together. They engaged to support each other in all quarrels. Such brotherhood of fraternity in arms over-rode all duties, even to ladies, except those owed to the sovereign. Thus De Guesclin was brother-in-arms of Oliver de Clisson. The Seigneur de Courcy to De Clisson; Gilles de Brun, Constable of France, was brother-in-arms to Joinville, and in the Romance of " Guy of Warwick " Sir Guy and Sir Urry say :

" Will we now trowthe plyght
And be fellows day and night."

For fraternity Charles V. of France granted in 1378 to his Chamberlain Geoffrey de Belville the right of bearing the collar of the " Cosse de Geneste " or Broomwood, a collar accepted, as from one brother knight to another, by the Angevin kings of England. This French collar—a chain of broom-pods—linked by jewels, is seen in the contemporary picture of Richard II. at Wilton.

Livery collars of the King of France, of Queen Anne, and of the Dukes of York and Lancaster, are numbered in the inventory, made of the royal jewels at the beginning of the reign of the youthful Henry VI. Even non-reigning princes and others invented these collars to give to those they wished to honour, or induce to keep in their service. The House of York had on theirs falcons and fetter-locks; that of Lancaster, the collar of Esses (ss) used by the king's son, Henry of Bolingbroke, as earl, duke, and king. The oldest effigy bearing this collar of dependence and of fealty to Lancaster, is that of Sir John Swinford in Sprotton Church, who died in 1376. As remarked above, others than royalties seem to have had made these collars of cognizance for their friends and household. So Menéstrier writes: " Ailleur que les princes avaient accoutumé de donner des coliers aux seigneurs de leur court, soit pour récompenser leur belles actions, soit pour indiquer qu'ils les faisaient ' hommes liges,' etc."

Thus a brass at Milden Hall shows a knight whose badge is a dog or a wolf circled by a crown, which hangs from a collar, whose edges seem to represent a pruned bough of a tree. Another brass dated 1415 of Thomas Markenfield at Ripon has a strange collar of park palings, with a badge hanging to it, of a hart in a park; and Lord Berkeley in 1392 wears a collar set with diamonds and apparently one peculiar to his own family.

Leber, the editor of Menéstrier, in his " Collection of Pieces Illustrative of the History of France," bears out the assumption that many of these collars and decorations were given as marks of knightly fraternity. " La Chevalrie la plus commune, et qui dure encore aujourd'hui, est celle de la fraternité d'armes, qui était comme une espèce d'adoption, de société et de liason d'amitié, lorsque les princes se liant ces uns aux autres en des occasions d'entrevues, de mariages, de traités, d'alliances et de ligues, se donnaient des marques mutuelles d'amitié, et s'engageait à en porter quelques signes exterieurs, comme frères de Chevalerie. Ils étendaient assez, souvent ces témoignages d'amitié aux principaux seigneurs de leur cours, à leurs favoris et à leurs principaux officiers. Et les symboles de ces chevaliers étaient des ceintures, des bands, des nœuds d'amour, des liens, des anneaux, et autres marques de liason et d'amitié." Thus, in fraternity, Louis Duke of Bourbon, one of the hostages for King John of France's ransom, on being set free in England, and returning to his native country, instituted a Belt upon which was embroidered " Esperance," and bestowing it on many of his knights, said, " I wish to live and die with you." " Je veux vivre et mourir avec vous . . . and I wish that you will wear this device of mine—this belt on which you see writ this happy word ' Hope '; " and so when the redoubtable knight du Guesclin passed through his land, to him he gave also, as a mark of fraternity in arms, this same belt inscribed as he called it " avec un joyeux mot—' Esperance.' "

Here, too, as somewhat a kindred subject may be mentioned " Honours," as they were called. Nicolas Upton in his work " De Militari officio " tells us that the new-created knights of the Bath carried affixed on their left shoulders, a white knot of ribbon which they had to wear till they had performed some knightly deed of prowess and honour, unless some noble and fayre lady requested it to be removed. " Milites qui creantur per balneum portant de consuetudine in humero sinistro suum stigma militare album, quod quidem stigma dictus tyro portabit, quousque fecerit aliquod notabile factum nisi nobilis domnia illud tollat, et docet consuetudo Angliæ."

This knot was in the form of a label hanging down, and from it came, in heraldry, its adoption on a coat of arms to show, placed over the paternal shield, it was that of the elder son and not the old knight, his father. When the latter died, and the heir succeeded, the label was removed. It was considered by that time in his life the heir had proved his prowess and his knighthood, and the label denoting " adventures " was no longer needed.

Kindred to these were the favours or " honours " which devotion to a lady prompted the knights about to tourney to place on their helms or harness. Many of the " legends " inscribed on these scarves or elsewhere were only decipherable to the loved and the loving—all were to show the " devoir " the bearer was to render to the object of his affection. So Menéstrier (p. 244), writing on the origin of amorial bearings : " Il'y a quantite de demi-mots que j'appellé énigmatiques et de sens couvert, parce qu'ils ne sont entendas qui de celui qui les porte ; c'est ce qu'on a affecté en la pluspart des Tourmois où les Chevaliers prenant des devises d'amour se contenoient d'être entendus des personnes qu'ils amoient, sans que les autres pénétrassent dans le sens de leur passion."

Often the amorous knight did more, for he assumed the livery— we should call it " the colours "—of his ladye-love—" l'usage de ces devises a donné lieu à cette fiction des arrêts d'amour. Un amant ayant entrepris de joûter, fit faire harnois et habillement." Instead of their own blazon on their shield they would substitute some device, the meaning of which, though puzzling to those who saw a knight wearing it, was known to the fair one whose device the knight then bore. Hence arose so often in the " Lays " and " Chansons " the fanciful names such as " knight of the Swan, of the Dragon, of the Eagle, of the Lion." For the same amorous reason they assumed, as before said, the lady's livery or colours ; hence we read of the White Knight, the Chevalier noir, the Green Count, or the Red Count, and no woman in that gallant age felt so honoured, as when her device and colours were triumphantly borne by her knight, in tourney and on field of battle, not alone in his own country, but far afield in Europe.

That sometimes, however, a fayre one did not reward the knight is found in an instance given by the author of " Aresta Amorum," where he tells of a certain lady after her chevalier had mounted her colours and liveries and came before her armed and mounted for her benediction, ere he entered the lists, made an excuse for not doing so, on the ground she was too unwell to appear. The " Parliament of Love " before which the case was brought condemned her conduct, and ordered her, the next time this knight rode to the tourney, to robe and arm him herself, and, taking his horse by the bridle, after he had mounted, lead him down the lists, and giving him his lance, say to him, " God be with you, my friend, fear nothing, because I pray for you."

In the earliest and purest age of Chivalry this claim or right (droit) that woman exercised over Chivalry was ever held conditional on their claiming no service unworthy of the high order of knighthood, " il supposoit que leur conduire et leur réputation ne les rendoient point indignes de l'espèce d'association qui les emissoit a cet ordre uniquement ton sur honneur." Happily this wearing of a lady's favours was far from infringing on the honour due to knighthood—reversely it was one of its glories, even if shown in an extravagant degree.   Thus at a certain tournament a knight appeared with strange " honours "—with chains attached to his hands and feet to show that he was chained by his word of honour to his lady (enchaîné à sa parole).   Another came into the lists, chained, one end of the chain held by his lady-love.

At a tournament held in 1388 by the King of Sicily, the knights marched to the barrier, and with them the ladies who then decorated them with coloured ribbons and scarves of their own devices and liveries of silk.   " Elles tirérent de leur sein diverses livrées de rubans et de galends de soye pour recompenser la valeur des ces nobles Champions."

Another instance given by Oliver de la Marche where in a more serious affray yet not " à l'outrance " at the court of Burgundy in 1445 " que le Chevalier qui l'avoit entrepris, chargea pour emprise une manchette de Dame et fit attacher icelle emprise a son bras senestre, à une aiguillette noire et bleue, richemens garnie de diamants, de perles, et d'autres pierreries." (Book I.—de ses Mémoires.)

Sometimes to reward her Chevalier, the lady gave him a costly jewel; these, like the collars given for knightly brotherhood, were very much used in different articles of jewellery between lovers and friends, lords and ladies, princes and those they wished, for the same purpose as they gave collars to, to bind them to their interests and service. " Fermails "—the large " ouche " or " nouche " in the oldest shape like a Scottish brooch, and which the knight used to fasten his scarlet mantle with in times of peace—was a favourite gift between such, in this age.

In the English registers several such appear.   One of the most favourite was composed of " an image of St. George," a gift in this case from the Black Prince (Register of John of Gaunt, Vol. I., 168).   Then too an eagle, a ruby between joined hands of gold, price £8 14s. 2d.; a diamond heart, price £7 7s. 4d.; a white hart in a park (Patent Roll 50, Ed. III.).   A gold " nouche " with three sapphires and three balases, price £15 13s. 4d., was the New Year's gift of the child-queen Isabelle of France to Katherine Duchess of Lancaster in 1398.   The " Fermail " of St. Louis is still in the Museum at the Louvre.   It is of gold enamelled and is enormous, both in size and weight.   One of the most costly of these Fermails belonged to Sir Lewis Clifford and after his death came into the hands of the Countess of Hereford, from whom it was bought by her grandson, Henry V., who commanded £400 to be given her as part payment. (Issue Roll Easter 1, Hen. V.).   The modern value of this sum would be £6,000.   The Duchess of Bretagne possessed thirteen superb fermails; a description of one is " a large fermail with a white griffin, a balas (uncut ruby) on the shoulder, six sapphires around it, six balases around them and twelve groups of pearls with a diamond." (Patent Roll 50, Ed. III., Part I.)

Again referring to collars or necklaces.

DAYS OF CHIVALRY

Henry III. ordered a necklace—a chain, of course—to be made, value thirty marks, with a great " makarus " or other precious stone which was to be sold to the Archbishop of Canterbury for forty marks. (Close Roll 27, Hen. III.)

Richard II. and his mother gave gold chains to the Shrine of St. Alban. A gold chain or collar is round the neck of Anne, Countess of Warwick—wife of the king-maker—in her portrait in the Beauchamp Pedigree. (Sloane MS. 882.)

A superb gold collar was bought by Henry IV. in 1406, worked with this word " Soueignez," and letters of S and X enamelled and garnished with nine large pearls, twelve large diamonds, eight balases and eight sapphires. It cost £383 6s. 8d. (Issue Roll Michs 8, Hen. IV.)

King Henry III. ordered 600 marks to be made into rings and fermails with stones and fine work, to give away for the purposes we have before mentioned—i.e., to bind his friends and knights to his service—when he came to London. (Close Roll 26, Hen. III., Part I.)

The " Circle " too, was a medieval ornament used as the collars to be given as a mark of fraternity or a bribe to those the giver wished to bind to his service, particularly the free knight to the giver's banner. Such a plain circle knights-bannerets were allowed to wear. It might, perhaps, so narrow was it, in the case of those not of royalty, be termed a narrow ring, and was used by nobles of all ranks up to royalty. Thus we find Sir John de Yerburgh, Clerk of the Wardrobe to John of Gaunt, is ordered in 1372 to deliver to Aline Gerberge, maid of the Duchess Constance, one little arch of gold and perry, emeralds and balases, and one of gold and perry. The same Aline was to receive from Juana Martinez—one of her fellow damsels—forty large pearls for a circle for the Lady de Mohun, state governess of the Princess Katherine, and four circles containing 665 pearls were to be delivered to the nurse. (Register I., fol. 166.)

Nor in this description of the collar the knight would wear is to be forgotten the belt of gold—" le Baudrier ou la ceinture d'or," which was always the mark of a Chevalier, distinguishing him from even the nobles who had not attained to that coveted order. Thus St. Gregory of Tours speaks of the knight Macon who wore a great belt covered with precious stones, " Balneum magnum oro, lapidibus que pretiosis ornatum "; often these were shoulder-belts, the custom taken from the ancient Romans of whom Virgil says :

" Humero cum apparuit alto ;
Baltheus et notis sulserant cingula bullis."

The young knight having on some belt and collar of gold as described above, his own, in right of his knighthood and not at this time given as a mark of brotherhood (except that all knights were brothers-in-arms) nor one of these more private collars devised and given by princes to rivet the free knight to his banner and his service, but worn around his neck as an honour he had gained by passing into the ranks of Chivalry, would, in his robe of peace—of scarlet—sit at the high banquet which always followed a knighting. Before has been described when treating of " largesse " the profusion of the medieval feasts which, if quality was sometimes wanting according to modern standard of delicacies, was made up for in quantity.

" The steward bit the spyces for to hye
And eek the wyn, in al this melodye
The usshers and the squyers ben y-goon;
The ete and drinke; and whan this hadde an ende
Un to the temple, as reason was, they wende."

Then the tables laid on tresseles are cleared and they dance,

" Who coude telle you the forme of daunces
So uncouthe and so freshe contenauces ? "

and

" Up-on this daunce, amongst other men
Daunced a squyer biforen Dorigen
That fressher was and jolyer of array
As to my doom than is the monthe of May,
He singeth, daunceth, passinge any man
That is or was, sith, since the world began."

Strange as it may seem, it was a not unusual thing for the young
knights to perform their dances in their armour, removing only their
helmets and throwing back their coifs. For so long a time as young
varlets or squires, had they practised wearing their armour, lifting in
it heavy weights, in it climbing heights and jumping fosses, to accustom
themselves to afterwards, as knights, become familiar and easy in
their mail, that even " treading a measure," in the slow dances of the
period, they were able successfully to accomplish.

Dancing was at this time a very favourite pastime. In the sequel
to Chaucer's " Squire's Tale " we read how the king and his nobles,
when dinner was ended, rose from table and preceded by the minstrels,
went to the great chamber for the dance—the king

" Rose from his bord ther as he sat ful hie
Beforne him goth the loudé minstraleie
Til he come to his chambre of paraments (great chamber)
Theres they soundes divers instruments,
There is it like an Heaven for to here
Now daunces lusty Venus children dere."

But the dances were not always in the great chamber. Very
commonly it took place in the hall, certainly in the earlier ages of
Chivalry because the " great chamber " or " paraments " was not
then built. The tables in these halls—as seen still in the Oxford
colleges—were only movable boards laid upon trestles and at a signal
from the knight, whose hall it was, were quickly put aside, while the
minstrels tuned their instruments anew and the dancing began. In
folio 174 of Royal MS. 2, B. VII., the minstrels themselves appear to
be joining in the dances which they inspired. Certainly before minstrel
galleries were introduced into the halls of the castles and manor-houses,
the musicians played on the ground of the halls, and stood round (as
we can judge from the illuminations left us of such festive scenes)
those engaged in the dance. These minstrels' or jongleurs' proficiency
was not so much their vocal attainments, though now the word
" minstrel " chiefly has that sense, as those gained on instruments.

DAYS OF CHIVALRY

Their skill on them merits a very high position in the history of music. Among themselves and in their own estimate of one another, they looked upon him as the best minstrel who could play the largest number of instruments, who could exhibit the greatest versatility of style in his musical performances and who could render himself, upon occasions, the most amusing and entertaining, when the company were induced to laugh rather than to sigh, or when the wine cup had driven love and its thoughts out of the clouded brains of the hearers; or, as now, their entertainers after some grand pageantry as the conference of knighthood, desired to end the day in dancing. In the Bodleian MS. at Oxford (Digby MS.) the jongleur says, " I can play the lute, the violin, the pipe, the bagpipe, the syrinx, the harp, the gigue, the gittern, the symphony, the psaltery, the organistoum, the regals, the tabor and the vole. I can sing a song well, and make tales and fables. I can tell a story against any mån. I can make love verses to please the damoiselles, and can play the gallant for them if necessary. Then I can throw knives into the air, and catch them without cutting my fingers. I can do dodges with string, most extraordinary and amusing. I can balance chairs and make tables dance. I can throw a somer-sault and walk on my head." In order to please their masters—the troubadours—the jongleurs decorated with as great skill as they could, the composition of such—their employers. They ransacked Europe for instruments and spent endless time in practising them, therefore very expert were these minstrels when called in to some weather-beaten old castle, or ivy-covered manor-house, when, after the accolade had been given to some son of the house, and after the great banquet, they were called to play to the dancers. Yet at all times by the medieval Catholic Church (as to a great extent it has' been since) dancing was forbidden on account of its tendency to corrupt morals; on the other hand it could not complain of want of encouragement from the civil power. When King Childerbert in 554 forbade all dances in his dominions he was only induced to do so by the influence of the bishop. What these dances were, we have little information concerning, they certainly were no longer, in France, the dances of the antient Franks. In any case war-dances appeared at the commencement of Chivalry, for when a new knight was made, all the other knights in full armour, performed evolutions either on foot or horseback to the sound of military music, and the populace danced round them. It has been said that this was the origin of " Court ballets." La Columbière, in his " Theatre d'Honneur et de Chivalerie," relates that this ancient dance of the knights was kept up in his time by the Spanish knights. But Chivalry not only encouraged these war-dances but those others between the knights and the ladies.

The troubadours mention a great number of dances without, unfortunately, describing them. They speak of the " Danse au Virelet," a kind of round dance, during the performance of which each person in turn sings a verse, the chorus being repeated by all. In the Code of the Courts of Love entitled " Arresta amorum " (that is the decrees of Love) the " Pas de Brabant " is mentioned, in which each knight went on his knee before his ladye; and also the " Danse au Chapelet " at the end of which the knight kissed his partner. In the " Romances " or " Lays " frequent mention is made—as has been before referred to—that the knights used to dance with the dames and damoiselles without taking off their coats of mail. In the " Lay of Perceforest " we find that after a banquet while the tables were being removed for the dance, though the ladies went and made fresh toilettes, the knights made no change in their accoutrements. Sometimes a torch-dance was performed. In this each chevalier and lady bore in their hands a lighted taper, and endeavoured to prevent their neighbours from blowing it out, which they each endeavoured to do. (Lacroix).

All the time the Church set herself against these practices of the faithful. Indeed it is somewhat difficult for us in these latter times to realize how religion entered into—side by side with the secular amusements, either by prohibition or approbation—all the recreations of our forefathers. Thus at the marriage of Robert, the brother of St. Louis with Matilda of Brabant in 1237, the minstrels or jongleurs, instead of singing a secular song, gave one of a religious kind—the " Roman or Lay of Antechrist," composed by Huon de Mery (Meran, "La vie au Temps des Trouveres," p. 159) and as each course at table was served so they sang this somewhat strange romance :

> " Quant les tables ostées furent
> Cil jongleur en pies esturent (stood)
> Se ont vielles et harpes prises
> Et de geste chanté nos ont
> Chansons, sons, lais, vers et reprises."

It must always be understood that these jongleurs—or as they were called in England, in the Anglo-Norman speech, " minstrels "— were entirely different and of a lower rank than the troubadours or trouveres. In the Angevin possessions of the Kings of England they went by the name of " menetriers," and so generally in France. In the Netherlands they were known as " ministrele." In Germany they were called " the wandering folk " (varende lute). In Provence under their best known name of jongleurs, they wandered through the breadth and length of the land. Their living was precarious, some clothed in rags, but even then with a peacock's feather high in their caps ; others, by their power of playing or singing or tricks, making a good living. Such an one's very life was in danger owing to him being a wanderer and a jongleur. No protection or support could he claim ; no nation would own him as a countryman. He might be killed, and his murderers would not be brought to justice. (Grimm's " Rechtsalter-thümer," 1-678.) The murder was not of a man, but of a jongleur, a being beyond the pale of the law, less protected by enactment than the swine in the forest. If he was robbed, he had no defence, beaten and maltreated, he had to bear it. If he did wrong he was treated with extreme severity ; as exile was no punishment to such a wanderer, he was branded and maimed. To protect his forlorn state, he gradually joined with his comrades in Guilds, and towards the end of " jongleurie " ceased so much to wander about, and betook himself to the cities and towns where he lived in common with his brothers and sisters (the glee-women) distinct, as the Jews, from the other inhabitants.

As all the medieval Guilds were placed under the tutelage of some saint, the wandering minstrels or jongleurs sought to choose one to put their Guild under. Their practices and songs, however, were far removed from saintliness. At last one merry jongleur hit on St. Julian, as one that might well serve their turn for the following reason :

St. Julian having passed a life of pride and haughtiness, repented at last of his arrogance and wished to atone for his misdeeds in the past by going in the opposite extreme. He made a vow accordingly to take into his house anybody and everybody, and presuming that, among the rest, poor strollers would not have been denied, the jongleurs dubbed him their patron-saint accordingly.

The part therefore of a town was called often St. Julian's, and travellers themselves who were not jongleurs, hearing of this saint of the wayfaring man, frequently on setting out on a journey in the Middle Ages, commended themselves to the prayers of St. Julian. As has been said how very precarious their life was, it was as long as silver pennies were in their pouches, a merry one, but when the pouch —as often—was empty, despite all their songs and tricks that life had dreary intervals. It was for this reason so constantly in their songs they boldly asked the rich and the poor for alms, and if they were refused, held the refuser henceforth up to scorn in their next songs, and so Colin Muset, a jongleur of Lorraine and Champagne in the thirteenth century, is no less backward in complaining—if a lord had no spirit of largesse :

" Sire cuens, j'ai vielé
Devant vous, en vostre ostél,
Si ne m'avez, riens doné
Ne mes gages, aquité :
 C'est vilanie !

Foi que doi Sainte Marie !
Ainc ne vos sieurré mie
M'aumosnière est mal garnie
Et ma malle mal farsie.

Sire cuens, quar commandez
De moi vostre volonté,
Sire, s'it vous vient à gré
Un beau don car me donez.
 Par courtoisie.

Talent ai, n'en dotez mie
De raler à ma mesnie.
Quant g'i vois borse esgarnie
Me femme ne me rit mie.

Ains me dit : Sire Engelé
En quel terre avez esté
Qui n'avez rien conquesté

 Aval la ville ?
Vez com vostre male plie
Elle est bien de vent farsie,
Honi soit qui a envie
D'estre en vostre compaignie.

Quant je vieng à mon hostel
Et ma femme a regardé,
Derier moi le sac enflé
Et je qui sui bien paré
    De robe grise,

Sacluez qu'elle a tôt jus mise
La quenoille, sans faintise
Elle me rit par franchise
Les deux bras au col me plie.

Ma femme va destrouser
Ma male sanz demorer;
Mon garçon va abruver
Mon cheval et conreer,
Ma pucele va tuer
Deux chapons por deporter
    A la sause aillie."

(Lord Count, I have the viol played
Before yourself, within your hall
And you my service never paid
Nor gave me any wage at all,
    'Twas villainy.

By faith I to so many owe
Upon such terms I serve you not,
My alms-bag sinks exceeding low,
My trunk ill-furnished 'tis I wot.

Lord Count, now let me understand
What 'tis you mean to do for me,
If with free heart and open hand
Some ample guerdon you decree
    Through courtesy.

For much I wish, you need not doubt
In my own household to return
And if full purse I am without
Small greeting from my wife I earn.

" Sir Engele," I hear her say,
" In what poor country have you been,
That through the city all the day
You nothing have contrived to glean?

See how your wallet folds and bends
Well stuffed with wind and naught beside,
Accursed is he who e'er intends
As your companion to abide."

When reached the house wherein I dwell
And that my wife can clearly spy
My bag behind me bulge and swell,
And I myself clad handsomely
    In a grey gown,

Know that she quickly throws away
Her distaff, nor of work doth reck,
She greets me laughing, kind and gay,
And twines both arms around my neck.

My wife soon seizes on my bag
And empties it without delay,
My boy begins to groom my horse,
And hastes to give him drink and hay,
My maid meanwhile runs off to kill
Two capons, dressing them with skill
    In garlic sauce.)

However, not to speak of the south of France, which was their true home—if they had any—but in England, despite their lawlessness and avaricious habits, these minstrels or jongleurs were immensely popular. The minstrel Galfrid even received an annuity from the Abbey of Hide, Winchester, in the time of Henry II. to play and sing to the monks. William, Bishop of Ely, Chancellor of Richard I., engaged a number of minstrels to go about singing of him and his renown. We hear that at the Priory of St. Swithin, Winchester, the defeat of the Danish giant and the triumph of Queen Emma was sung by a party of minstrels for the delectation of the monks (Wharton's " History of British Music "). When a bishop went on his pastoral rounds he was very often greeted place after place by bands of minstrels hired for the purpose. When Bishop Swinfield, for instance, was making his episcopal progress through his diocese, we read that on one occasion he gave twelve-pence apiece to the minstrels who played before him. (Roll of Household Expense of Bishop Swinfield. Camden Society II. 155.)

In the accounts of Winchester College we read that minstrels belonging to the king, the Earl of Arundel, Lord de la Warre, the Duke of Gloucester and the Earl of Northumberland, received largesse and recompense from the college for their music. The Countess of Westmorland brought minstrels of her own with her to the college— these, too, received ample largesse.

Royalty itself appropriated some of these minstrels or jongleurs especially for their service. In the Roll of Thomas Brantingham, treasurer to Edward III., we find frequent mention of disbursements to such. Richard II. constantly had jongleurs in his company (Jusserands " Wayfaring Life," 199). When he went the last time to Ireland, he was delayed at Milford Haven for two days, and passed the time mainly with the music and song of these jongleurs.

" Là femmes nous en joie et en depport
Dix jours entiers, attendant le vent nort
Pour nous partir.
Mainte trompette y povoit en oir
Du jour, du nuit, menestrelz retentir."
—MS. British Museum, Harl. No. 1319.

Edward II. received four minstrels in his chamber at Westminster
and heard their songs. When they departed he gave them twenty
ells of cloth. At the marriage of Princess Margaret, daughter of
Edward I., we read that four hundred and twenty six minstrels and
singers were engaged (Wright, " Domestic Manners," p. 181).
Henry V. was so fond of their music that he gave to his English
subjects the lands of the Norman seigneurs who had refused to
recognize him as their lord, on condition that their fees (redevances)
should be paid in instruments of music. Thus Thomas Appleton is
assessed to pay for the land at Asnieres (near Bayeux) " one pair of
flutes yearly, called recorders." (Rot. an 5, Henry VI.)

Richard Geoffrey was king's jongleur under Henry V. and
Henry VI. and we read that he was presented by one or other of these
kings with the estate of Vaux-sur-mer.

Berdic was king's jongleur under William the Conqueror. Rahier,
king's jongleur under Henry I. He was the founder of the Hospital
of St. Bartholemew. But all these royal jongleurs were the
aristocracy, and few and far between the great mass of minstrels or
jongleurs who went from village to village, town to town, and country
to country, " wayfaring men " in the Middle Ages.

Towards the lordly troubadours they held a position such as the
Saxon " glee-men " held to the Saxon minstrels. Often mixed up
with the vast throng which accompanied the Crusaders to the East,
they returned learned from contact with their Eastern brethren with
new ways to extort money. They learnt to practise magic and
conjuring. They copied the Arabic story-tellers in becoming adept
narrators. They learnt to become spies for such as needed information
of a secret character, and, travelling from land to land, the chief
narrators of distant news ; indeed it is greatly owing to them, when
asking and receiving hospitality at the many religious houses sprinkled
over France and England, that the monkish chroniclers—some of
whom had never left the shade of their monasteries—were able to
furnish their accounts with events at a distance, and, in their
Chronicles record them.

Inns and other places of hospitality knew them well. To gain a
dinner they sang, they danced and played tricks. In a curious
manual, " La manière de language," written in French by an
Englishman in the fourteenth century, the traveller of distinction
listens at an inn where the jongleurs are earning their supper by their
varied skill and records, " then came forward into our lord's presence
the trumpeters and hornblowers (i.e., the jongleurs) with their frestels
(flutes) and clarions and begin to play and blow very hard ; and the
lord with his squires begin to move, to sway, to dance, to utter fine
carols till midnight without ceasing." (Meyer in the " Revue
Critique," X. 373.)

If we have chiefly written of the male jongleurs it must not be forgotten female ones—in this country called " Glee-maidens "—also perambulated the country and delighted the people by their music and recitations.   One of the most celebrated of these was Adeline, who received an estate from William the Conqueror for her attainments. Then in the " Lay of Sir Bevis of Southampton " there was the fair Josiane ; while Melior, another glee-maiden of romance, figures in a Lay, as telling her lover " les fais del ancien tems " (Parthenopeus de Blois).   But of all the most distinguished of these female minstrels was Marie de France, who was jongleuse to William Longsword, son of Henry II. and Fair Rosamond.   Whether she were English by birth is unknown, but what is known is she passed the greater part of her life in England.   She was most likely born in Brittany, hence so many of her Lays have a Breton origin.   The " Lai de Lanval " is a beautiful one she composed, dealing with Arthur and his knights of the Round Table.   She dedicated her " Lays," of which there are twelve found, probably to Henry III.   Her second work was a Collection of Æsop's Fables set to verse.   She did this, she says, at the suggestion, and for the love of, William Longsword.

> " Ki fleurs est de Chevalerie
> D'anseignment et curteisie
> Pur amur de Cumte Willaume
> Le plus vaillant de cest royaume
> M'entremis de cest livre feire
> Et de l'angleiz en Roman treire."

The chief musical instruments played on by the jongleurs were : (1) The violin.   The violin had been bred and born among the Saxon glee-men.   Many writers have tried to disprove that England was the original birthplace of this popular instrument.   They have agreed that it was introduced into Europe about the ninth or tenth century.

But if so, how is it that a violin—immature it is true—is drawn in Saxon MS. of the seventh century, and on other Saxon MSS. representing violins in the hands of Saxon kings ?   The violin was probably therefore evolved in Saxon England from the ancient British instrument—the " crwth."   The crwth was played resting on the left shoulder with both hands employed on the strings—the next step was, after the violin had been improved on the crwth, the introduction of the bow.

(2) The bagpipe was also popular with the jongleurs, being known and freely used by the Normans—an instrument of extreme antiquity, familiar to the ancient Assyrians.   It was used in different forms, sometimes the bag in shape of a tortoise, sometimes in shape of a serpent—with a bag that writhed round the body of the jongleur.

(3) The harp has never gone out of fashion ; its special home seems to have been amongst the Anglo-Saxons.

(4) The gigue, a small variety of the violin, was used by the minstrels.   It was a shrill little instrument which they much played out of doors.

(5) The other instrument much in vogue with them was the " gittern "—a guitar strung with catgut ; it was introduced to the West with the guitar from the Arabians, this latter having travelled all the way from Persia to be the joy of Europe and delight of the courtly world of Chivalry.

These were the chief instruments the jongleurs used, though, as the boasting minstrel we have quoted a page or two back told us, there were many more he was an adept on. (See Rowbotham's " Troubadours.")

At the banquet consequent on a young squire—or squires—being admitted to knighthood, jongleurs such as have been described would be present, to play at the feast and afterwards at the dances following, but during the banquet there would be a ceremony or episode almost sure to occur, for it was during these feasts it most frequently took place—the singular action among the knights assembled of making vows and oaths.

The Vow of Chivalry was a mode of calling on God and the saints to witness a resolve, and in so conspicuous a manner as to draw the attention of the world around. Knights vowed that they would not cut their hair, or change their clothes, or sleep in a bed, or eat meat, or drink wine, till they had achieved some particular " emprise."

Edward I. of England, sitting in state in Westminster Hall, caused two live swans with gold chains about their necks, to be brought into the Hall, and laying his hands upon them swore with all his attendant nobles " before God, our Lady and the Swans," that he would be avenged on the Scots.

Sir Walter Manny (1339) vowed before God and the Heron that he would be the first to set foot on the soil of France, and Sir James Audley (1346) that he would be first in the field and the best knight. Joinville in his Chronicle (1250) tells of a knight who, for some private quarrel, had sworn that he would not wear his hair cut after the knightly fashion, but long and parted down the middle as women do till he was avenged. When his enemy was disgraced, he came and sat down on a bench in the hall before the king and his lords, and had his hair cut.

Joceline de Courtenay, Prince of Edessa (1123), took a vow not to change his clothes, eat flesh, or drink wine except at Mass (the Chalice was not then denied to the laity till late in the twelfth century) till he should be relieved of a charge laid upon him by Baldwin II., King of Jerusalem. Jehan de Saintie rode for three years with four knights and squires with helmets chained to their left shoulders till they should have accomplished their vow to defy with sword and lance a like number of knights and squires for the beauty of their mistresses.

And here it may not be out of place to quote the calm and judicial words of a present day writer on these strange oaths of our forefathers—F. Warre Cornish. " Such vows are in part produced by the same spirit of sacrifice and self-mortification which is seen in the self-imposed rigours of the saints ; a sense that no sacrifice can be equal to the debt owed by the soul that is saved ; they bear witness to an intensity of feeling, the expression of which cannot but be extravagant ; they speak also of a pride of personal worth which, if half-savage, is also dignified. They may be compared with the violent gestures—for gesture, too, is symbolical—which often accompanies strong emotion in those days and was not thought unseemly. The tremendous defiance of Henry II., ' God, I will take from Thee that part of me Thou lovest best—my soul ' ; the furious gestures of Becket's murderers ; the transports of rage which Henry II. and his son John gave way to, and which they themselves attributed to the devil's blood in their race ; the savage outrages committed upon the body of Simon de Montfort, and the no

Sir **WILLAM DE RYTHER.**

In Ryther Church, Yorks. 1308.
From Foster's "Some Feudal Coats of Arms."

less savage mode in retaliation by his sons upon Henry of Almaine in the church of Viterbo; the outbursts of fury which stain the lives of the Cid, the Douglas, Edward I., Robert the Bruce, and on the other hand the exaggerated parables by which St. Francis put his precepts into action; all these and many more instances of violent and (as we should call it) theatrical exaggeration are marks of a state of civilization in which passións were more keenly and more dramatically expressed than in our cooler age. Our emotions, like our customs, tend to a level of similarity. Symbolical action was natural then (as in the times of the Hebrew prophets) because life was more pictorial, more vivid and brightly coloured." Then again we must figure to ourselves a state of society which was not ashamed of the joy of living—those who did so became classes apart—anchorites, hermits, the good among the monks and nuns, the greater part accepted human life and loved all its outward signs of joy; so that life without such signs would be to them as silence instead of speech. Ceremony was a language, however it may have been travestied afterwards by heralds, masters of ceremonies and sacristans.

In the account of the vows taken at the Court of the Duke of Burgundy (Philip le Bon) in 1453 the bird chosen to make them on was the pheasant. " Afin," says the writers of the event, " de conformer aux anciennes coutumes, suivant les quelles dans les grandes fêtes et nobles assemblées on presente aux Princes, seigneurs et nobles nommes quelqu'autre noble oiseau, pour faire les vœux utiles aux Dames et Demoiselles qui implorent leur assistance."

The Duke thereupon having heard their requests through his heralds, takes the vow himself. " Je voue à Dieu, mon Creature tout premierment, et la très glorieuse vierge, sa mère, et après aux Dames et au Faisan."

Sometimes these vows, particularly at the Court of our Angevin kings, was made on the swan. These birds were considered preeminently noble by our forefathers, while the peacock and the pheasant, by the brilliance of their plumage, represented to their vivid imagination the royal robes of their princes. The flesh of these birds was therefore considered the most appropriate for those nobly born, and most amenable for a gallant or a lover. In Provence, the ladies there thought the rich feathers of the peacock a most suitable gift to decorate their favourite jongleur or even a troubadour knight. Hence Ménestrier writes in his " Traite des Tournois " (p. 40), " Les Troubadours venoient au septième rang tous couronnés de plumes de paon, qui leur furent autre fois consacrées dans les fameaux cercles des principales Dames de cette Province."

But of all vows in Chivalry the most renowned, because it was the starting point of the Hundred Years War between England and France, was that of the Heron. Its origin probably, though it deals with the Court of Edward III. and the birth of his son Lionel, is of an Anglo-French source. The heron unlike his brother the swan or the pheasant, or the gorgeous peacock, was looked on with disdain—he was the symbol of cowardice. The Lay or Romance opens with reference to the time of year:

> " Ens el mois Septembre qu'estés va à declin
> Que cil oisillon gay ont perdu lou latin (note)
> Et si sekent les vignes."

King Edward sat at his high table; he had at the time no ill will to his brother of France. The inducer to have it was at hand, Robert of Artois, a banished noble from France, who that day went out hawking along Thames bank. His falcon brought down a heron. He hurried back with it to the palace and ordered it to be served at the royal table, when he purposed to get King and Queen, and all the nobles there, to take an oath to invade France. " Now I purpose," said the count when it was served up, " to present the heron to the greatest coward living, namely Edward, who is the rightful heir of France, and yet because his heart fails him will out of cowardice die disseised of his inheritance."

When the King heard this he was greatly troubled. " You call me a coward," said he, " yet hear the vow I make. ' I vow and promise to God in Paradise and to His Sweet Mother by whom He was nursed, " Et à sa douche mère de qui il fu nouris " that before the year is out I will cross the sea, and my people with me, and defy the king in St. Denys, and fires shall be lighted throughout all the land; and I will fight Philip of Valois who bears the fleur-de-lys.' "

After securing the King by his oath, Robert went first to the Earl of Salisbury and to him he spoke very graciously. " Fair sir, who art so full of bravery, in the name of Jesus Christ—to whom the world belongs—I humbly beseech you without delay to make upon this our Heron a vow of right devotion."

The Earl answered, " And why should I not be ready to put in risk my whole body so highly that I might be sure to achieve my vow."

(The Earl was sitting by the fair daughter of the Earl of Derby.) " See you, I serve a maiden of such perfect beauty that if the Virgin Mary were here present and only her deity were taken away from her, I should not be able to make any disseverment of the two. I have asked her for her love but she stands on guard, yet gives me gracious hopes. Therefore I pray this maiden from my heart devoutly that she would lend me one finger of her hand and put it entirely over my right eye."

" By my faith," says the lady, " one who expected of her lover to have the whole force of his body, would act basely if she denied him the touch of one of her fingers, indeed I will lend him two."

Immediately she placed her two fingers upon his right eye and firmly closed it, and then the Earl took oath. " I vow and promise to God Omnipotent and to His Sweet Mother that my eye shall never be opened again, neither on account of wind or weather till I shall have been in France, etc."

Then Robert of Artois made his appeal to the maiden herself, the daughter of the Earl of Derby.

" Damozel," said he, " in the name of Jesus Christ will you now vow upon the Heron the right of this country ? "

" Sir," she replied, " it shall be all at your will : for I vow and promise to the God of Paradise that I will not have for a husband any man who is now alive—duke, earl, sovereign, prince or marquis—before this vassal shall have accomplished the vow which, for my love, he has so loftily adventured. And when he shall return to this country if he escape alive, I give him my body heartily for ever."

After soliciting many of the other powerful knights, Robert

approached the Queen herself, and kneeling down before her said that when she had made her vow upon it, he intended to have the luckless heron cut up and eaten.

The Queen demurred at first, because being married she could not safely vow, as her husband might recall her vows, but the King said, " Swear, my body shall acquit it. Vow boldly, so help you God."

To this the Queen replied :

> " Je sais bien que piecha
> Que sui grosse d'enfant, que mon corps senti la
> Encore n'a il gaires qu'en mon corps se tourna ;
> Et je vous et promette à Dieu qui me crea
> Que nasqui de la vierge, que ses corps n'enpira
> Et que mourut en crois, on le crucifia
> Que jà li fruis de moi de mon corps n'istera
> Si me n'ares menée ou pais par delà
> Pour avaucher le veu que vo corps voué a
> Et s'il en voellh isir, quant besoins n'en sera
> D'un grand coutel d'achier li mien corps s'ochira
> Serai m'asme perdue et li fruis perira."

This briefly translated is to the effect that the Queen soon expected her accouchement, but, unless the King shall have led her over to France when he performs his vow, she vows to God who created her and who was born of a virgin, she will never be the mother of a living child. The sovereigns pass over shortly after to the Netherlands and when they arrive at Antwerp

> " la dame delivra ;
> D'un biau fils gracient la dame s'acouka,"

and thus the fairy lady acquitted her vow. " Le sien vou aquitta."

This covering of the eye by the Earl of Salisbury's desire until he had performed his vow seems to have been no unusual occurrence among the younger knights of the period.

Froissart recounts of several knights-bachelors from England as having each one eye covered with red cloth, " and it was said that these had vowed to certain ladies of their country that they never again would see with both eyes until they had done some prowess with their bodies in the kingdom of France, the which they would in no wise tell to such as inquired of them, so that there was great wonder made at it by everybody."

The belief of our forefathers in these strange oaths, and the sustaining power they seemed to have afforded in many of their enterprises and feuds, was truly astonishing. It is no doubt some solace to one aggrieved to thus bind the mind in a set course to bear the evil; it is also bracing, when the heart falters at the future, to have an oath behind to strengthen its shrinking. Far down the after ages we find relics of these oaths still taken. Thus the aged Lord Scarsdale after the death of his sainted king—Charles I.—swore his hair and beard should never be cut again, as a mark of his continual mourning. The noble House of Traquair, after the rising of the '45, declared after Prince Charles Edward had been under their roof-tree, never should the main gates through which he had once entered, be opened again till the day—if ever—a royal Stewart should again pass through them. Those gates are still closed.

If it be asked if these vows were kept—to quote a very unsympathetic writer on Chivalry (Stebbing " Chivalry and the Crusades ") and so, from such, a more valuable testimony, " The knight never broke his vow." If the vow was an extraordinary one, and required particular labour and hazard to fulfil it he had measured the difficulty beforehand; he had calculated how much admiration and praise he should secure when he had gone through this voluntary trial, and he bore with him, in the peril of the encounter, that pleasant feeling which always attaches to the consciousness of being watched and admired, while combating any danger. Nor must it be forgotten that a large number of vows which the knights made, and obtained the greatest praise for observing, had their origin, not in personal vanity, but in these vows aiding them in the most difficult of their love and adventure.

To vow that he would perform some notable exploit in honour of his lady was the noblest piece of gallantry which a knight could exhibit. It elevated him in the eyes of his brother-chevaliers, contributed to establish the reputation of the charms of her he honoured, and thereby insured him of her smiles even when every other expedient of the lover he had previously found fruitless. To carry out a vow of this sort a young knight should have certain qualifications as a lover. One of the fullest descriptions of what these should be is found in the instructions given to a young chevalier by the Seigneur Arnaut de Marvelk:

" One morning in the month of October when preparing with other noble cavaliers for a day of excellent sport, and just as the pages had brought out the dogs and horses and all was ready for setting forth, a young knight of great beauty and bearing appeared at his castle, and taking hold of his horse's bridle, begged him with great misery on his face, to have pity on his distress. The generous knight hesitated not but ordering back his followers, inquired of the younger knight the cause of his grief, and having found it to be the cruelty of his ladye, promised on the next morning to give him instructions in the gentle science of love. The day was spent in mirth and feasting; and the following morning, seating themselves under the shade of a laurel, the teacher and his pupil began their discourse on the subject of their meeting. The former commenced by saying that he should speak neither of riches nor learning, but that he should reduce the essential qualities of a lover under a vow to gaiety, courtesy and bravery. He then began to give him instructions on his personal appearance. His tunic was to be of linen, fine and white, and his surcoat of the same colour as his mantle and of a proper length, and not to open as to show his neck uncovered. He was frequently to wash his hair and to keep it short. Again, the eyes being the interpreters of amorous sentiments and the hands the ministers of these constant services which faithful love is ever ready to render, he was directed to pay particular attention to their being always of proper keeping with the rest of his dress.

" With regard to his attendants, he was to have at least two squires, who were to be courteous and above all good speakers that they might be able to give a good opinion of their master by the manner they delivered his messages. Whenever he should go to any court he is recommended to spare nothing in ensuring the magnificence of his appearance. He is to have a dwelling always open to all comers. Squires, pages, mendicants and jongleurs are never to be driven away although they come in crowds. In the directions given him as to the games he should play, he is forbidden to use the dice, as only fit for the vulgar or the covetous. If he play at a game he is particularly directed not to be sorry if he loses or to change colour or to twist his hands about as one in a passion, for the instant he does that, he would that moment be degraded from all pretensions to gallantry.

" Again, if he would be happy in love, and carry out his vow it is essential he should have a good horse, swift in the chase yet adroit and tractable in combat, and this horse should be always ready, together with his lance, shield, and hauberk. His horse should be well harnessed and adorned with a splendid ' portrail.' The housings, saddle, and shield, and lance with its banderolle are to be uniform in their colour and device. He must also have another horse to carry his second hauberk, lance and shield, which arms are to be carried as high as possible to make a more graceful and noble appearance.

" His squires should always be on the alert to aid him on the instant and that his arms may not have to be sought for when attacked, for it must needs be known, says his instructor, a lady will never take for her lover a coward or a niggard. She desires that her lover rather should be continually gaining some new accession in glory and to love Chivalry, which ought to be his sovereign good.

" The old knight added, ' Be always ready for the combat, let nothing make you fear. Be the first to strike and the last to give over; you will thus fulfil the duties of true love.' Then directing him to be careful to have good mail, to have his horse adorned with little bells, the sound of which, he says, inspires the rider with courage, he once more repeats that it is the duty of whoever follows the banner of love to be the first in the charge and the last in the retreat, to fight till his arms one after the other fail him, and when he comes to his sword ' to strike his blows so hard and fierce that the noise may rise to God, and that it may echo both through heaven and hell.' " (MS. D' Urfé, quoted by St. Palaye.)

Yet though in this case just quoted and in the innumerable ones in the " Romans " and " Lays " the knightly oath was taken for love's sake, many were also taken, as a knight's own vow on admittance to Chivalry, on a higher and nobler plane—to defend the widow and sustain the rights of the fatherless. Crusade after Crusade, too, heard from the youngest and from the oldest knight's lips, those vows which though many failed by the weakness of human nature to keep, yet many to the death preserved—to cross the seas, and on many a battle-field to rescue " those holy fields over whose acres walked those Blessed Feet which fourteen hundred years ago were nailed for our advantage on the bitter Cross."

CHAPTER IV

KNIGHT-ERRANTRY

THE writer Hallam has cast doubts on knight-errantry existing. Yet whatever a name—if the state existed—the title of it is of little moment except for classification. The question therefore is, did a state exist in Chivalry which that name covers? There seems little doubt that such did. A knight " errant " was a knight who left his castle or manor and estate to seek adventures far afield. Now in the old Chronicles, not to mention the Lays and Romances, hardly a knight there is mentioned who did not at some time of his life set forth on a quest of this sort. He was really bound to do so by the oath he had taken before entering knighthood—to defend the widow and the fatherless, to use his sword in protecting the rights of holy Church, to succour distressed ladies and to carry their favour at the point of his lance to distant places. We can well understand none of these in his immediate neighbourhood might need his assistance. How then? Was his sword to remain in the scabbard, was his knightly oath to be as if never taken? It was not at the bidding of romance but at the bidding of duty such a one had to go out " errant " to fulfil his oath and give play to his sword far afield.

The Romances and Lays, as has been before mentioned, are most useful to us for this reason—the makers of them were always committing anachronisms—they portrayed their knights and other personages in the exact way they saw them around at the time of weaving these stories. St. George, for instance, was clothed in chain-mail; the patriarchs in the dress of the burghers and knights then living, and so on. Now these Lays and Romances are full of the stories of knight adventurers—or knights-errant—can it be conceived, as all these other characters were then portrayed faithfully as they saw them around, this portraiture was imaginative and false? Knights-errant—" wandering " knights or whatever historians like to call them—existed and played their part in the kaleidoscope life of the Middle Ages. So an old English poem lately unearthed and translated runs :

> " O'er wild ways of the world rideth Gawayne
> Grace gotten of his life, with horse and mail,
> Sheltered of times, oft camped in open plain
> Beneath the stars, adventuring by vale,
> To court he comes at last a knight all hale
> And Queen and King greet him with a kiss."
> —Sir Gawayne and the Green Knight.

The knight-errant was usually some young knight who had lately

102

A KNIGHT'S LIFE

been, as has before been described, dubbed, and who, full of courage and tired of the monotony of his father's castle or manor, set out in search of adventure. One could envy him as, on some bright spring morning, he rode across the sounding drawbridge, followed by a squire in the person of some young noble lad as full of animal spirits and reckless courage as himself, or perhaps some steady old soldier practised in the last French war whom his father has chosen to take care of him. We sigh for our own lost youth as we think of him, with all the world before him—the medieval world, with all its possibilities of wild adventure and romantic fortune—with caitiff knights to overthrow at spear-point and distressed damsels to succour and princess's smile to win at some great tournament; and rank and fame to gain by prowess and hardihood, under the eye of kings, in some great stricken field. Such a knight was known to be a knight-errant by his riding through the peaceful country in full armour, with a single squire at his back. " ' Fair knight,' says Sir Tristram (" Morte d'Arthur ") ' ye seem to be a knight-errant by your arms and your harness, therefore dress ye to joust with one of us,' for this of course was inevitable when knights-errant met. Again, Sir Tristram and Sir Ray rode within the forest a mile or more, and at the last Sir Tristram saw before him a likely knight and a well-made man, all armed, sitting by a clear fountain and a mighty horse near unto him tied to a great oak, and a man, his squire, riding by him leading a horse that was laden with spears. Then Sir Tristram rode near him and said, ' Fair knight, why sit ye so drooping, for ye seem to be an errant knight by your arms and harness, and therefore dress ye to joust with one of us or with both.' Therewith that knight made no words but took his shield, and buckled it about his neck, and lightly took his horse and leaped upon him, and then he took a great spear of his squire and departed his way a furlong."

And so we read in another passage, " Sir Dinadan and Sir Tristram rode forth their way till they came to some shepherds and herdmen and they asked if they knew any lodging or harbour thereabout. ' Forsooth,' they answered, ' there is a fair castle near but to be received and entertained ye must first run a tilt with the knights therein for such is the custom there, and if ye be vanquished ye shall have no harbourage.' "

Often in the old illuminated manuscripts these knights-errant are portrayed, overtaken by night, and sleeping in the open and what is curious, their heads, as so often in their monumental effigies are supported, in lieu of softer pillows, by their helmets, as if to signify they soon should go on that last Great Adventure every man must take.

According to La Columbière (" Theatre d'Honneur," VIII. and IX.) the word " errer " which these knights bore is a counterpart of " chercher," because the reason of their wandering was in search for an adventure—so in the " History of Marshal Boucicaut " the word " errer " is used in speaking of his voyaging and marching, and " chercher " in reference to the battles he had come to seek in Holy Land.

These knights-errant in the earliest times adopted green as the colour of their dress (surtouts) and as it was the rule for a knight's horse, if caparisoned, to have the same colours as the rider, the horse, too, would be trapped in green—that is when he appeared in a tournament abroad. Thus in a tournament which Charles VI. of France, in 1380, gave at St. Denys, it is said, " Ils avoient l'escu verd pendu au col, avec la devise en or du Roi des Cates . . . ils attendèrent les Dames que le Roy avoit destinées pour les conduire aux lices, et qui s'y étoient preparées avec des habits de la même livrée, qui étoit d'un verd brun." Probably the young knights' adoption of green when " errant " was to show they were young and in the spring of their life, or would be as some of the clans of Scotland have a hunting tartan of green to wear when following the deer and passing over the hills where their enemies lurked, to whom their usual bright-coloured tartan might afford a mark, the knight-errant adopted green to pass more securely through the vast forests on his way, and the possibly lurking foemen in a foreign land. Or thirdly, it may be some colour—and green was adopted—was used to cover the knight-errant's own bearings on his shield, so that as an unknown knight he might bear off in tourney and some high enterprise the prize for the sake and love of his far-off ladye. At all events no one seems to know exactly why in the earlier ages of knight-errantry this colour was adopted. A good horse under him, good mail on his body, a ready lance and sword, with one faithful squire, these young knights wandered over Europe; they were in the modern phrase—cosmopolitan.

A thousand years of Christianity passed without any softening of the severity of war till Chivalry brought in the idea of a universal bond of knightly brotherhood. A knight was a member of an order analogous to the order of priesthood; the priest was vowed to preach, and the knight to defend the helpless and the church in every part of the world.

Whatever may have been the practices in an age in which travelling was difficult and dangerous, when every sea was beset by rovers, and every forest by outlaws, and when robber knights and barons rode down from their castles to spoil shipmen faring on the river, or travellers on the roads, or shut them up in their castles to be held for ransom—to ride in search of adventure was part of a true knight's " devoir." So among the duties of a knight is reckoned :

" Estre grant voyagier
Tournaiz suir, et jouster pour s'amie."

His absence from home is explained :

" En autre terre est allé tournoyant."

Froissart describes as the right estate of a knight, to be able " bien chevir et gouvener du sien, et servir son seigneur selon son état, et chevaucher par les pays, pour avancer son corps et son honneur."

Henry, the eldest son of Henry II., is described by the troubadour Bertrand de Born as " the best jouster and man-at-arms since Roland," because he had ridden for three years as a knight-errant over many lands and borne away the prize of all tournaments (Dirz, p. 204). As has before been said, the Lays and Romances are almost totally taken up with these knightly adventures. In these Babylon (Cairo), Damascus, Byzantium are in themselves as familiar

DAYS OF CHIVALRY

names as Rome and Spain. To take a few instances, William of Palerme visits Rome, Spain, Greece and Italy; Guy of Warwick fights and jousts in Normandy and as far east as the land of the Emperor. Arthur fights with Romans, Allemans and Gauls. As Chivalry was common to all Christendom, so its laws and customs belonged to Christendom, not to this or that nation. In the same way when the knights in their wanderings visited these out-land countries they found in each a home in Chivalry there as in Holy Church there. This unity and fraternity was not a mere convention, it was a reality and was understood in war and peace.

It is easy to say the aim of a knight-errant was an " ignis fatuus," leading them to a land of chimeras; that it had no relation to the love of God and man, to the misery of the world, that it was founded on pride and at best but a soldier's virtue. At any rate, it aimed higher than the common scope of the world. The pride of the true knight-errant was pride in his order, not his own deeds. If his obligation of courtesy, for instance, was too much confined to his own rank, it taught him self-control, self-respect and consideration for the weak; it was better than the gross licence out of which it sprang.

The fraternity of Chivalry bound, as nothing else did in the disorganized states that then formed Europe, individuals and nations together. Granted it often was fantastic and extravagant it was more noble than modern money-making. Granted, particularly in the south of Europe, the young knight-errant carried his love of ladies too far and fostered a way of living which often destroyed domestic life, yet it was better than the animal passion of barbarous Huns, Goths, and Northmen.

But to return to the quests of the knights-errant. It was not always necessary that they should leave their own country to meet with enterprises. Every castle offered hope, not only of hospitality but also of a trial of arms; for in every castle there would be likely to be knights and squires glad of the opportunity of running a course with bated spears with a new and skilful antagonist. In many castles there was a spear tilting-ground. So we read in the " Morte d'Arthur " : " Sir Percival passed the water and when he came into the castle gate, he said to the porter, ' Go thou unto the good knight within the castle and tell him that there is come an errant-knight to joust with him.' ' Sir,' said the porter, ' ride ye within the castle and there shall ye find a common place for jousting, that lords and ladies may behold you.' " At Carisbrook Castle in the Isle of Wight, the tilting-ground still remains. At Gawsworth also the ancient tilting-ground remains to this day. But in most castles of any size, the outer court afforded room enough for a course, and at the worst there was the green meadow outside the castle walls. In some castles they had special customs, just as in old country houses people used to be told " it was the custom of the house," so it was " the custom of the castle " for every knight to break their lances or exchange three strokes of the sword with the lord. Thus in the " Romance of Sir Tristram " he and " Sir Dinadan rode forth their way till they came to some shepherds and herdsmen and there they asked if they knew any lodging-house thereabouts. ' Forsooth, fair lords,' said the herdsman, ' nigh hereby is a good lodging in a castle, but such a custom there is that there shall be no knight lodged there but if he first joust with two knights and if ye be beaten and have the worse, ye shall not be lodged there and if ye beat them, ye shall be well lodged.' "

But if adventures happened in castles, so often in lowlier manor-houses they were found. From the same source as the last extract we read: "Then Sir Lancelot mounted upon his horse and rode into many and strange and wild countries, and through many waters and valleys and evil war he lodged. And at last, by fortune, it happened him against a night to come to a poor courtilage and therein he found an old cavalier which lodged him with a goodwill, and there he and his horse were well cheered. And when time came, his host brought him to a fair solar chamber to his bed. And there Sir Lancelot unarmed him and set his harness by him and went to bed, and anon he fell in sleep. So soon after there came one on horseback and knocked at the gate in great haste. And when Sir Lancelot heard this, he arose up and looked out of window and saw by the moonlight three knights that came riding after one man and all three lashed upon him with their swords and that one knight turned on them knightly again and defended himself." And Sir Lancelot like a knight-errant " took his harness and went out at that window by a sheet," and made them yield and commanded them at Whit Sunday to go to King Arthur's court and there yield them unto Queen Guinever's grace and mercy; for so knights-errant gave to their lady-loves the evidences of their prowess and did them honour, by sending them a constant succession of vanquished knights and putting them " unto their grace and mercy."

Often though the young wandering knight would be overtaken at nightfall in the great forests that then covered Britain and France, and found no shelter but under one of the trees with his helmet for a pillow. Sometimes instead of this rough couch, he would take refuge for the night in one of the many little hermitages that then abounded. So in Malory's " Morte d'Arthur " it is written: " The good knight, Sir Galahad, rode so long, till that he came that night to the castle of Carbnecke, and it befel him that he was benighted in an hermitage. And when they were at rest there came a gentlewoman knocking at the door and called Sir Galahad, and so the hermit came to the door to ask what she would. Then she called the hermit. ' Sir Ulfin, I am a gentlewoman that would speak with the knight that is with you.' Then the good man awaked Sir Galahad and bade him rise ' and speak with a ladye that seemeth hath need of thee.' Then Sir Galahad went to her and asked what she would. ' Sir Galahad,' said she, ' I will that you arm you and mount upon your horse and follow me, for I will show you within these next three days the highest adventure that ever knight saw.' "

In the language of Chivalry these adventures of knights-errant were called " emprises," and the young knight engaged in such, sometimes for six months or a year, would wear on his leg or arm or on his helmet the sign of his " emprise," such as a scarf, a sleeve, a bracelet, a chain, a star, whatever in a word gave him to the beholder a marked individuality, hence the word " emprise " from the other word imprese which was given to these " devises." There was also the " emprise " of a suspended shield. " C'était, dit

DAYS OF CHIVALRY

Moisaut de Brieux, un exercise de l'ancienne noblesse, qui gardait des pas on passages (hence ' pas d'armes ') sur des ponts et grands chemins, où les chevaliers pendaient leurs écus, et se tenaient préts à joûter contre tous ceux pareille qualité qui viendraient toucher ces écus du bout de leur lance." Sometimes they placed their helmets above these suspended shields, and this writer then says : " De la est venue peut-être, la coutume de timbrer les armes de heaumes, et voilà pourquoi l'on voit si souvent des écus pendans." (From thence came perhaps the custom of displaying helmets on coats of arms (in heraldry) and that is why suspended shields are so often to be seen with them.)

(Hulme in his " History of Heraldry " says the different forms of helmets placed over shields heraldically were not used for the purpose of distinguishing rank in England till the reign of Elizabeth.)

Sometimes to procure an " emprise " a young knight-errant would take up his abode at a wayside cross where four ways met in order to meet adventures from east, west, north and south. Notice of adventures was sometimes affixed upon such a cross as we read in " Morte d'Arthur." " And so Galahad and he rode forth all that week ere they found any adventure ; and then upon Sunday, in the morning, as they were departed from an abbey they came unto a cross which departed two ways. And on that cross were letters written which said thus : ' Now ye knights-errant that goeth forth for to seek adventures, see here two ways,' etc."

Whether housed in castle or manor, sleeping with his helmet for a pillow in the forest, or taken in by some wayside hermit, this careless gipsy life had immense attractions to the youthful knights of the period. So much had it become the vogue that Henry III. in 1241 proposed to levy a tax on knight-errantry as was levied on tourneys.

In a passage given from the Raymbaud de Vaqueiras—a southern knight-troubadour—the wanderers accept cheerfully many of the discomforts arising from a quest. " Galloping," says he, " trotting, leaping, riding, vigils, privations and fatigue will henceforth in errantry be my pastime. Armed with wood, iron, and steel, I shall endure heat, cold, frost ; scattered meadows will be my dwelling-place. Discords and severities must serve the place of love-songs and I shall maintain the weak against the strong."

Often these wandering knights, as the above, had on journeyings to subsist on the wild fruits of the forest or animals they trapped, such as the smaller deer which they pressed between two stones and thus extracted the blood, and this meat was called in the Romances and Lays of the time " chevreaux de presse," and " nourriture des Heraux." As has before been mentioned, the knight-errant usually travelled alone with the exception of one trusty squire, though in the " Morte d'Arthur " frequently two—sometimes three—such knights are spoken of as together. The custom of travelling singly was to avoid observation or interruption in a quest. For this reason they often disguised their arms or their shield and their horse's trappings.

Among the Normans both in France and England this longing to roam and love of adventure had been inherited from their northern forefathers. Among the latter, the young men set out annually on adventurous quests—either from being outlawed for their unruly ways or wishing to make their fortunes (as young men emigrate to-day). They went from Scandinavian lands usually in bands but occasionally would set forth alone. Byzantium was a favourite resort of wandering Northmen and the Varangian Guards received many recruits from these northern lands.

Sweyn, son of Earl Godwin, was outlawed and became a wanderer and afterwards a pilgrim. Hereward the Wake is said to have been outlawed, and his adventures certainly come under the classification of a soldier " errant." In " De Gestis Herwardi Saxonis " it states that when Gisebritus de Gant heard of his banishment he sent for him, for Hereward was his godson, and he set out beyond Northumberland and came to him abandoning his own province and inheritance, travelling with a single servant Martin, whose surname was Lightfoot. They were knights-errant who founded the Norman kingdom in Sicily. The incentive for this expedition shows us how often it was the same in many cases that made the sons of a knight at home, knights-errant. Tancred of Hauteville had twelve sons—three left their home in the Cotentin in 1038, weary of their swords rusting and an impoverished estate, to carve out their fortunes in foreign lands. Already some of their race had penetrated to the rich fields of Southern Italy. Thither the brothers went, and in 1042 " William of the Iron Arm," the eldest, had won the lordship over the Normans already settled in Apulia. Robert Guiscard, the younger, went down to Italy to join his brother in 1046. But the brothers required no more knights-errant and he had to take service with the Prince of Capua against the latter's rival at Salerno. He ended by becoming Duke of Apulia and lord of all Southern Italy save Capua. His younger brother hearing of his brother's success, took his lance and wended his way as a knight-errant to Italy. This was the celebrated Roger, who in 1060-1101 made himself master of Sicily. It appears that all these sons of Tancred, who were such successful warriors in Italy, originally left home as knights-errant—and perhaps of all successful and rich quests that any young and unattached and wandering knights in Chivalry ever attained, these sons of Norman Tancred won the greatest and the fairest. No lady's evanescent smiles, no carrying off a useless jewel in a tourney, ever produced the solid prizes their lance and their sword procured—rich and noble lands, and a kingdom the most fertile and beautiful in Southern Europe.

Another historical event a knight-errant is recorded to have performed, not to gain, as above, a kingdom, but to honour a sovereign. Brantome in his " Discours sur les Duels " relates that Galeazzo of Mantua was received by Queen Joanna of Naples at her castle of Gaeta, and after feasting him presented her hand to the young knight Galeazzo to lead out in the dance. This being finished he knelt down before his royal partner, and in order to show his gratitude for the honour she had done him, took a solemn vow of knight-errantry to go through the world wherever deeds of arms were done until he had defeated two valiant knights and brought them as prisoners before her, to be disposed of at her pleasure. After a year spent in errantry in Brittany, France, England and Burgundy he returned with his prey, and presented two knights his lance had overcome, before Joanna. The Queen graciously received the gift but declined to impose rigorous terms on the captives. She gave

them their liberty without ransom and bestowed on them rich
" largesse."

As we have seen in the case of Tancred's sons, these quests
undertaken by the younger sons, generally without the prospect
as the elder one had of succeeding to the paternal lands, were
not always for love of a fair one, or simply for a love of adventure,
but to pick up by the wielding of their good swords and lance a
subsistence. To such the constant feuds and petty wars of the
Middle Ages was always a welcome discovery. To find no war, no
joust, no tournament was to many of these young and poverty-
stricken wandering knights, a great loss. So in one of the French
Fabliaux the distress of such a one is well described.

> " Listen, gentles, while I tell
> How this knight in fortune fell;
> Lands nor vineyards had he none
> Jousts and war his living won;
> Well on horseback could he prance,
> Boldly could he break a lance,
> Well he knew each warlike use;
> But there came a time of truce,
> Peaceful was the land around,
> Nowhere heard a trumpet sound;
> Rust the shield and falchion hid,
> Joust and tourney were forbid;
> All his means of living gone,
> Ermine mantle had he none,
> And in pawn had long been laid
> Cap and mantle of brocade,
> Harness rich and charger stout
> All were ate and drunken out.
> —Barbazan's Fabliaux, Vol. III.

Nor were these young impoverished knights wandering from place
to place ashamed that their good swords often procured them
subsistence. They often called the sword which they used in some
tourney they happened on, their " gagne-pain " or bread-winner. So
in de Deguileville's " Pèlerinage du Monde " :

> " Dont i est gaigne-pain nommée
> Car par li est gagnies li pains."

Bridges, as before mentioned, were favourite places for knights
out on adventures to hang up their shields on, for with the constant
use the roads had, being few and far between in the Middle Ages, and
from the bridges by law kept in repair by the neighbouring lord or
abbey—or sometimes a hermit who was permitted to have a chapel
on the bridge in return for keeping it in good order—it was an excellent
place for this purpose. The knight-errant would compel every one
of his degree to there defend his honour or declare himself a craven.

There is a curious verification of this in the annals of the Eastern
Empire. When Alexius Comnenus received the homage of the
Western Crusaders, seated upon his throne, previous to their crossing

the Hellespont, during the first Crusade, a Frank baron seated himself by the side of the Emperor Alexius. Upon being reproved by Baldwin, he answered in his native language, " What ill-taught clown is this (meaning Alexius) who dares to keep his seat when the flower of the Christian nobility are standing round him." The Emperor, dissembling his indignation, desired to know the birth and condition of the bold Frank. " I am," he replied, " of the noblest race in France. For the rest I only know there is near my Castle a spot where four roads meet, and near it a Church where men desirous of single combat spend their time in prayer till someone shall accept their challenge. Often have I frequented that chapel but I never met one who dared accept my defiance."

So the Bridge of Rodomonte in the " Orlando Furioso " is made the scene of the armed defiance of the hero to those who would contest his challenge. Scott in his " Essay on Chivalry " mentions the curious fact that even as late as Elizabeth's reign, Bernard Gilpin recounts finding in his Church of Houghton-le-Spring, near the Border, a glove hanging over the altar, which indicated a challenge of the sword to all who should take it down.

Before ending these particulars concerning knights-errant and their quests, it would seem more than fitting to touch on a quest which has become world-renowned and yet whose origin is born of Romance, and can hardly even come under the heading of legendary truth—yet from its beauty and pathos and its high teaching has been the theme of many a noble achievement. We mean the quest of the Holy Grail, with the young knight Galahad as its hero. Originally probably of Celtic origin the dry bones of the legend were brought from Ireland to Wales, and from Wales to their kindred Brittany. Two different knights were in different versions named as seekers of the Holy Grail before Galahad was introduced—Percival in one version, Gawain in another—and there is little doubt that when the legend was re-dressed and given a Christian purpose, both these knights were discarded on account of their characters, in Arthurian Romance, being of doubtful morality, which this new conception of the knight who was to seek and find this Holy Grail must possess. The time Galahad was substituted as a young knight-errant " sans peur et sans reproche " was when the platonic love which at first a knight had conceived for a ladye, and for whose fair sake he had taken up some difficult quest, had degenerated into a love sensual and earthly.

To set up therefore a lofty ideal for the troubadours and trouveres to descant on in their Lays, who better than a young knight as Galahad in the very flower of his age, and to interest, in castle and hall, these lascivious knights and dames? It set up against an immoral love, a heavenly—against a quest for short-lived triumphs in a tourney, the attainment of a glorious Relic of the Passion of the Lord. The legend, as the poets and thinkers of the twelfth century fashioned it, allured the hearers while it brought in on lives fast deteriorating under sensual love and living a loftier aim. When it came it seemed a breath from that spirit of Celtic romance which, born in the green isle of Erin, still seemed to dwell in her mist-girt mountains—filled with mysterious yearning for the truth and beauty of the Infinite. Born the last, perhaps, of her legends, her youngest, yet the most beautiful, that still appears in its undying beauty to each generation to work out their quest and to realize, if not in life, but as death opens the gates of the Life Beyond—that there is the end of the quest and there the Holy Grail is found.

Three different accounts of the Grail which came into the possession originally of Joseph of Arimathea exist :

(1) The Grail is the vessel in which Christ's Blood was received as He hung upon the Cross. This vessel Joseph had had made.

(2) The Grail is the vessel which had been used by Christ at the Last Supper. It was used afterwards as a receptacle for the Blood of Christ after His Body had been taken down from the Cross.

(3) The third version is the same as the last with the exception Joseph found the Holy Vessel himself.

We learn from one of these versions that Joseph having obtained this sacred relic was wont to pray before it. In consequence he was imprisoned in a high tower by the Jews. In another version he is said to have been visited by Christ in his dungeon—" Qui estoit horrible et obscure "—who hands him the Grail. Whereat Joseph is much surprised as he had hidden this Holy Grail so none might find it. Christ promises

> " Tout cil qui ten vessel verrunt
> En ma compeignie serunt
> De cuer avunt emplissement
> Et joie par durablement."

> (All those who see this vessel
> Will be of my company
> They will be satisfied in their hearts
> With joy everlasting.)

With the passing of Joseph this mysterious vessel disappeared— now and again as a flash of supreme beauty it was seen to pass through forest and hall but none could attain to it, till one, as Galahad, innocent and young, yet full of a knight's noblest aims in errantry, should set forth on this holy quest to find It.

In the version called " Le Grand Queste " we are told of the physical gifts of this Holy Vessel, how as soon as it entered the door of a castle hall, the whole court was filled with fragrance, while over every place It hovered, perfume broke forth—sometimes in the deep forest among the rustling leaves at night—sometimes high up over the shadowy hills It was seen to hover, ever it set up a quest and ever escaped till Galahad, the perfect conception of a Christian knight-errant, died as he found it.

It may not be thought perhaps by the reader out of place in leaving this story of spiritual errantry to quote the enthusiastic words of Dr. Furnivall—a learned writer on the Holy Grail. " What is the lesson of it all ? " he asks. " Is the example of Galahad and his unwavering pursuit of the highest spiritual object set before him, nothing to us ? Is that of Percival, pure and tempted, on the point of yielding, yet saved by the symbol of his Faith, to be of no avail to us ? Is the tale of Bors who once sinned but by a faithful life after partaking of spiritual sustenance consecrated his after days to God—nothing now ? This bodily chastity of the young knight Galahad not wanted still, raised as it was in the quest above every other earthly virtue ? Is it not founded too on another virtue—a deep reverence for woman which is one of the noblest and most refining sentiments of man's nature which no man can break without harm to his spiritual life ? " (Furnivall " The Holy Grail.")

As to the legend itself, those who altered the fragments in the original Celtic romance to a deeper Christian colouring, no doubt intended to give an Allegory of the Blessed Sacrament. Thus the good offices Joseph rendered to the Body of Christ were symbols of this : the hewn Sepulchre—the altar; the Sheet in which the Body lay—the corporal; the Vessel (the Grail) in which the Blood was received—the chalice; the Stone upon which the Body rested—the paten; and Galahad—the pure Soul of a man seeking the invisible glory Beyond. The monks of Fecamp who long boasted to possess the relic of the Holy Grail were probably those who gave this Christian character to the old Celtic legend it was founded on.

CHAPTER V

THIS may be a suitable place to mention certain privileges which a squire attaining knighthood obtained, for, as Leber says in his "Collections of Papers Relative to the History of France": "A knight's title was not one simply of honour but carried with it many prerogatives, privileges, and franchises, which often later in the Middle Ages were particularly named in the letters of the sovereign who made the squire a knight."

(1) That of jurisdiction. The knight was empowered—as such—to assemble his retainers for services in any war he might be about to engage in; and also, on such vassals of his, to dispense justice both of the high and the low kind (moyenne et basse) or as the old Saxons expressed it, "outfang and infang."

(2) Another privilege, in France, was when the different estates of the province or realm assembled, knights took precedence of all those not such—so in the Parliament of the year 1322 in the forest of Vincennes, those who were knights were first announced. So in the Parliament of Paris all those councillors who were knights had precedence of those who were not.

Constantly from their privilege of precedence in courts of justice, they were called to the assistance of the sovereign, so in an old piece of verse entitled "Manteau d'ounour" it is said in speaking of such:

> "Qui que Preudomme ait conseiller
> Soit Rois au Quens, je lì conseille
> Pour s'onnour, croire son conseil," etc.

(3) In France a knight had bestowed upon him the prefix of "Monsieur" or "Monseigneur." In Gascony "Mossen," in Spain "Dom" or "Don," in Italy "Messer," in England "Sir."

The wives of such, in France, obtained the prefix "Madame," but anciently that of "dam," which had been the older prefix of knights themselves, so we find in the old French chronicles "dam chevalier." In England the wife of a knight evidently obtained her prefix from this, as she was called "Dame." In the "Life of St. Louis," by Joinville, we have examples of both ways of addressing a knight. Thus he speaks of "Monsieur de Valery, y doit aller luy trentième de chevaliers," and "Li connetable ira entresi luy quinzième de chevaliers, es mêmes conditions que messire de Valery ira."

(4) Another privilege attaching to knighthood was to go into battle fully armed, not alone themselves, but when "barding" (or

113   H

armour) came into vogue, for their horses also to be thus equipped. Indeed it was one of the privileges of a new-made knight to be granted money, for a knightly mantle and a horse, " pro pallio et palafredo novæ militiæ " as the entries read in the Treasury Rolls of the years 1247-1288. A sum of eight livres six sous were paid out of such for the sons of Philip, Duke of Burgundy, when knighted, for their mantles and horses, " pro liberis Philippi Bourbourg qui fierant milites."

To revert to one of these knightly privileges—that of a knight being able to be fully armed. The account of Geoffrey of Anjou's arming will be found a sufficient example : " On a mena des chevaux," writes the monk of Marmoustier in his Chronicle, " on apporte des armes, on le revétir d'un bon et excellent haubert a doubles mailles, et a l'épreuve des lances et des traits les plus forts ; on lui mit des grèves de fer de bonnes doubles mailles et des éperons d'or on lui mit au cou un brouchlier sur lequel étaient peints on graves des lionceaux. Le casque qu'on lui mit sur la tête était orné de pierres precieuses, et d'une si bonne trempe que nulle épée n'eut pu le fausser. On lui mit en main une lance de frene (ash) avec un fer de Poitiers, et on lui apporta une riche épée tirée du trésor royal."

It has before been mentioned that the furs, the " vair " and the " gris " were the peculiar privilege of knighthood.

(5) From earliest times even among the Lombards in A.D. 571 the sons of princes and the highest nobles were not permitted to sit at the table of their parents, unless of Chivalric rank, but from that time onwards and during the noblest time of knighthood, a belted knight was permitted not alone to sit at his lord's, but even at a king's table, when invited to do so—without having received the accolade, however high his birth, he could not do so. Thus when the marriage had been arranged between Maud, daughter of Henry I. of England, with Geoffrey of Anjou, Count Fulk, his father, besought the king thereupon to knight Geoffrey, in order that he might be qualified to sit at the high table, and enter into the festivals proper to his rank— " ut ibidem cum coævis suis arma suscepturus, regalibus gaudiis interesset " (in " Vita Godfredi Ducis Norman.").

(6) Knights, particularly in Germany, were allowed, at Mass, to unsheath their swords, and hold them aloft during the Gospel to demonstrate they were ready above all men, by their knightly oath, to defend the Christian faith with their lives.

But if these were some of a knight's privileges there were the reverse, and knights might be degraded, without combat, when convicted of a heinous crime, which was patent to all men. In Stowe's " Chronicle " we find the following minute account of the degradation of Sir Andrew Harclay, created Earl of Carlisle by Edward II. for his valiant defence of that town against the Scots, but afterwards accused of traitorous correspondence with Robert the Brus and tried before Sir Anthony Lucy. " He was ledde to the barre as an Earle worthily apparelled with his sword girt about him, horsed, booted and spurred and with whom Sir Antony spake in this manner : ' Sir Andrew,' quoth he, ' the king for thy valiant service hathe done thee great honour and made thee Earle of Carlisle since which tyme, thou as a traytor to thy Lord the King, leddest not people that should have holpe him at the battell of Heighland, awaie by the county of Copland, and through the Earldom of Lancaster by which means our lorde the king was discomfitted there of the Scottes, through thy treason and falseness; where as if thou haddest come betimes, he hadde had the victorie—and this treason thou committedest for ye great summe of golde and silver that thou receivedst of James Dowglasse, a Scot, the king's enemy. Our lorde the king will, therefore that the order of knighthood, by which thou receivedst all thine honour and worship uppon thy bodie, be brought to nought, and thy state undone, that other knights, of lower degree, may after thee beware and take example truly to serve.' Then commanded he to have his spurres from his heeles, then to break his sword over his head, which the king had given him to keepe and defend his land therewith when he made him Earle. After this he let unclothe him of his furred tabard, and of his hoode, of his coate of armes and also of his girdle; and when this was done, Sir Antony sayde unto him, ' Andrew ' (quoth he) ' now art thou no knight, but a knave—and for thy treason, the king will that thou shalt be hanged and drawne and thyne head smitten off from thy bodie, and burned before thee, and thy bodie quartered; and thy head being smitten off, afterwarde to be set up on London bridge, and thy four quarters shall be sent into foure good townes of England, that all others may beware by thee.' And as Sir Antony hadde sayde so was it done in all things, on the last daie of October.''

CHAPTER VI

As knights-errant, as the champions of those oppressed, frequently were called upon to fulfil this office in judicial ordeals of battle, it may be here the place to notice these contests.

In Saxon times, as we find in the preamble to King Ethelred's Laws, A.D. 980, two ordeals of fire and water were a recognized institution. " Ordeal " is a Saxon word signifying " a great judgment," that is by the judgment of God. The ordeal by fire was reserved for freemen and those of a better condition, that by water was kept for bondmen and rustics. Both were done away with in the reign of Henry III. Another ordeal—wager by battle—was introduced some time previously by William the Conqueror, and seems to have been the only real change he made in the legal system of England. Like the other two ordeals it was called the judgment of God and was represented as an appeal to, and an acknowledgment of, the unerring wisdom of Providence. It was not so absurd a method of settling disputes as a more advanced civilization rendered it. It substituted one conclusive trial of strength between two representative champions for a succession of murderous acts of vengeance committed by private families or men. It compelled the rival parties to bring their quarrel to a public legal issue; for the result of a combat, like the result of a trial at law, was, that the side that suffered defeat was forced to submit to a verdict at law. If the accuser failed in the encounter he had to suffer the penalty, that, if he had succeeded, his adversary would have suffered. This was a great check on unwarranted accusations. The demandant for such a wager of battle, if it was a civil suit, could never engage personally in the combat, he had to fight in the person of another. In criminal suits both accuser and accused could meet, and when first introduced by the Conqueror, this ordeal was intended only to be applicable to criminal accusations. If the principle of this rough combatant justice be once admitted, it must be acknowledged that a spirit of wisdom dictated every possible precaution to render the inconveniences as few as possible. The ordeal only took place, at least in France, when a crime punishable by death had been committed, and then only when there were no witnesses to the crime, but merely grave suspicions against the supposed criminal.

All persons less than twenty-one or more than sixty years of age were dispensed from taking part in these combats, so too, were priests and women, who were allowed to be represented by champions. If

A KNIGHT'S LIFE

the two parties to a dispute were of different ranks in life, certain regulations were drawn up in favour of the plaintiff. A knight who challenged a serf was forced to fight with a serf's weapon, that is to say, with a shield and a staff, and to wear a leathern jerkin; if, on the contrary the challenge came from a serf, the knight was allowed to fight as a knight, that is to say, on horseback and in armour.

It was customary for two parties to a judicial combat to appear before their count or lord, when, after reciting his wrongs, the plaintiff threw down his gage—generally a glove or gauntlet—which his adversary then exchanged for his own, as a sign that he accepted the challenge.

Both were then led to the seigniorial prison, where they were detained till the day fixed for the combat, unless they could obtain substantial sureties. On the day fixed for the combat the two adversaries, accompanied by their seconds and a priest, appeared in the lists mounted and armed at all points, their weapons in their hands, their swords and daggers girded on. They knelt down opposite to one another with their hands clasped, each in his turn solemnly swearing upon the Cross and upon the Evangels that he alone was right, and that his antagonist was false and disloyal, and he added, moreover, that he carried no charm or talisman about his person. A herald-at-arms then gave public notice, at each of the four corners of the lists, to the spectators to remain perfectly passive, to make no movement, and to utter no cry that could encourage or annoy the combatants, under pain of losing a limb or even life itself. The seconds then withdrew, and the camp-marshal, after seeing that both antagonists were properly placed and had their proper share of wind and sun, called out three times, " Laissez les aller," and the fight began.

This judicial combat never commenced before noon and was only allowed to last till the stars appeared in the sky. If the defendant held out till then he was considered to have saved his cause. The knight who was beaten, whether killed or merely wounded, was dragged off the ground by his feet, the fastenings of his hauberk were cut, his harness thrown, piece by piece, into the lists, and his horse and his weapons divided between the marshals and the judges of the combat. In Normandy, according to Lacroix, sometimes according to ancient usage—as was the case in Scandinavia—the vanquished champion was hung or burnt alive; while if, as so often, he had fought as the champion of another person, that person was usually put to death with him.

The Church, although she allowed a priest to be present in the lists, never even granted a tacit approval to these ordeals by gage of battle. She excommunicated the successful duellist (Lacroix) and refused the rites of burial to his victim. On the other hand a legal writer (" Lectures on Feudalism," by Abdy, p. 120) states, when dealing with the Ordeals by Fire and Water—" for three days before the trial whether by water or fire, the culprit was to attend the priest, to be constant at Mass, to make his offering and to sustain himself on nothing but bread, onions, salt and water; on the day of the trial to take the Sacrament." Now if this was the attitude of the Church towards those going to suffer the lower ordeals of fire and water, and she allowed them even the Sacrament on the day of their Ordeal, it seems reasonable to suppose she took the same view towards the higher Ordeal of arms and those taking part in it, and they did not die excommunicated.

These judicial combats, as has been said, could not be undertaken by those under age, nor over sixty, nor by Churchmen or women. Champions had to be found for such, and this is why when dealing with knights-errant, these judicial combats here are placed, as the champions for these young, old, and defenceless women and priests were found most frequently in the persons of these wandering knights; and it was an office—if called upon—their vows prevented them refusing even though they knew, if defeated, they would incur infamy and perhaps death. At all events the penalties of failing being so severe, made the knight before he offered himself as champion examine well the cause he was to uphold being a good and just one.

Notwithstanding (though it seems from several authors, those entering as champions in these judicial combats had previously to their meeting the offices of a priest allowed them) these Trials by the Sword were continually condemned by the Church. Her Councils, her Bishops and Popes anathematized those who took part in them in vain. The Fourth Council of the Lateran held under Innocent III. utterly forbade clerics from resolving their disputes by Wager of Battle in the person of a champion.

It may also be remarked though a knight might meet a serf and a serf a knight in these lists, by, if the knight was challenger, adopting a serf's weapons, it was often the case if the challenger was a squire to raise him to equality with his knightly adversary, and make him then and there a knight. Thus in a judicial trial of arms between Philip Boyle, a knight of Aragon, and John Astley, temp. Henry VI., that king gave the accolade to the latter in 1470 to place him on an equality. For the same reason if a champion appeared for an Ecclesiastic not then being a knight, an Abbot or Bishop whose champion he was, often previously knighted him. (Sainte Marie, " La Chevalerie.")

The last judicial combat in England was claimed in the case of Ashford v. Thornton as late as the year 1818. The Court was obliged to allow the claim, but the contest did not take place as one of the men withdrew his case rather than fight. This caused the right to make a claim of judicial combat, which was then a common law right and depended on no Statute, to be abolished by Statute in 1819.

One of the most curious retainers of Richard de Swinford, a Bishop of Hereford, was Thomas de Bruges, the Bishop's champion, who was paid an annual sum that he might fight in that Bishop's name on occasion of any law-suit which might be terminated by a judicial duel—a duel not for cases of felony or crime which resulted in the death of the vanquished, but carried through with staff and shield (cum fuste et scuto). Again in the twenty-ninth year of Edward III. such a duel took place between the champions of the Bishop of Salisbury and the Earl of Salisbury; alas! for the Bishop's champion, when the judges conformably to the law came to examine the dress of the combatants they found that he had several strips of parchment with spells and prayers on them, some even sewn on his clothes, and was disqualified accordingly (Year Book of Edward III., Rolls Series, 32-33 year). To conceal such charms or incantations when entering a perilous undertaking seems from the Ordinance of Philip le Bel common in France, for in 1306 he enacted that one entering a combat should make oath : " Je n'ay ni entens porter sur moy ne sur mon cheval, paroles, pierres, herbes, charmes conjurements ni invocations d'ennemis ne nulles autres choses où j'aye espérance d'avoir ayde ne a luy nuire, ne ay recours fors que en Dieu, et mon bon droit, par mon corps, et mon cheval, et par mes armes." (See also Du Cange.)

CHAPTER VII

VERY akin to those judicial combats, where frequently the knights-errant, in their wanderings, found a widow or an orphan or a serf, whose cause seemed to them an innocent one, and which needed a champion to uphold it in the lists, were those other judicial combats among knights who fell out, or accused each other of some malfeasance and appealed to the sword to proclaim their respective innocence. In these, however, the knights-errant never figured, because both the challenger and challenged were denoted beforehand by their own appeals, and they wanted no wandering brother-knight to uphold their cause, but relied on their own good swords. Inasmuch, as in the jousts for pleasure, two knights were set against each other, it seems not an unfitting place ere we leave the subject of jousting to devote a space to these knightly judicial jousts. As it was not an unfrequent occurrence, a whole chapter might, if space allowed, be devoted to the subject.

In the Lansdowne MS., 285, will be found directions for the complete arming of a man who is to engage on foot in a judicial combat, with a list of the things, such as tent, table, chair, etc., which he should take into the field with him. The MS. (Tiberius, B. VIII.) contains the form of benediction of a man about to fight and of his shield, club, sword. In the *Archæologia*, Vol. XXIX., are a number of illustrations of the year 1400 representing the various phases of the combat. In one it is the knight being armed; in another receiving the Blessed Sacrament in church, before combat; in another the oath in the lists, the combatant seated armed in an armchair with his attendants about him, his weapons around and—ominously enough —a bier standing by, covered with a pall, ready to carry him off the ground. In another place the vanquished is depicted actually laid in his coffin, and the victor returning thanks in church for his victory.

As an example of the Joust of Battle—or Wager of Battle—we take an account of one related by Froissart, between a squire called Jaques de Grys and the knight John of Carougne.

The knight and the squire were friends, and both of the " menie " of the Earl of Alençon.

Sir John went overseas for the advancement of his honour, leaving his lady in his castle.

On his return his lady informed him that one day soon after his departure, his friend, Jaques de Grys, paid a visit to her and made excuses to be alone with her, and then by force dishonoured her. The knight called his and her friends together and asked counsel what he should do.

A KNIGHT'S LIFE

They advised he should make his complaint to the Earl. The Earl called the parties before him, when the lady repeated her accusation, but the squire denied it and called witnesses to prove that at four o'clock on the morning of the day on which the offence was stated to have been committed, he was at his lord's, the Earl's, house, while the Earl testified that at nine o'clock he was with himself at his levée.

It was impossible for him between those two hours—that is four hours and a half—to have ridden twenty-three leagues. Whereupon the Erl sayd to the lady, that she dyd but dreame it, wherefore he wolde maynteyne his squire, and commanded the lady to speke not more of the matter. But the knight who was of great courage and well-trusted and byleved his wife, would not agree to that opinion but he wente to Parys, and showed the matter there to the parliament, and there appelled Jacques de Grys who appeared and answered to his appelé.

The plea before them endured for more than a year and a half. At length the parliament determined that there should be " betayle at utterance between them." This the king confirmed.

" And the kynge sent to Parys, commandynge that the journey and batayle betwene the squyer and the knight sholde be relonged tyl his comyng to Parys, and so his commandment was obeyed. . . . Then the lystes were made in a place called Saynt Katheryne behynde the Temple. There was so moche people that it was a mervayle to behold; and on one side of the lystes there was made grete scaffoldes, that the lordes myght the better see the battyle of the two champions; and so they bothe came to the felde, armed in all places and there eche of them was set in theyr chayre." (In the combat between John Astle and Piers de Massie, the combatants are represented each sitting in his chair—a great carved chair something like the Coronation chair in Westminster Abbey.) " The Erle of Saynt Poule governed John of Carougne, and the Erle of Alençon's company with Jacques de Grys. And when the knight entered into the felde, he came to his wyfe who was there syttinge in a chayre covered in blacke and he seyd to her thus—' Dame, by your enformacyon and in your quarelle I do put my lyfe in adventure as to fyght with Jacques de Grys; ye knowe if the cause be just and true.' ' Syr,' sayd the lady, ' it is as I have sayd; wherefor ye may fight surely, the cause is good and true.' With those words the knyghte kyssed the lady and toke her by the hande and then blessyd her and so entered into the felde. The lady sate styll in the black chayre in her prayers to God and to the Virgyne Mary, humbly prayenge them, by theyr specyall grace, to sende her husbande the vyctory accordynge to the ryght he was in. The lady was in grete hevynes, for she was not sure of her lyfe; for yf her husbande sholde have been discomfyted she was judged without remedy to be brente (burnt) and her husband hanged. I cannot say whether she repented her or not yt the matter was so forwarde, that bothe she and her husbande were in grete peryle; howbeit fynally she must as then abyde the adventure.

" Then these two champyons were set one agaynst the other, and so mounted on their horses and behaved them nobly, for they knew what pertayned to deedes of arms.

121

" There were many lordes and knyghtes of France that were come thyder to see that batayle; ye two champions parted at theyr first metyng but none of them dyd hurte other; and upon the justes they lighted on foote to persue theyr batayle, and soe fought valyaintly, and fyrst Sir John of Carougne was hurt in the thyghe whereby al his friends were in grete fear; but after that he fought so valyaintly that he bette down his adversary to the erthe and thruste his sword in his body and so slew hym on the felde; and then he demaunded yf he had done his devoyre or not; and they answered he had valyauntly achieved his batayle.

" Then Jacques de Grys was delyvered to the hangman of Parys, and he drew him to the gybet of Mount Fauçon and there hanged hym up.

" Then John of Carougne came before the kynge and kneeled downe, and ye kynge made hym stand up before hym, and the same day the kynge caused to be delyvered to him a thousand frankes, and retyned him to be of his chambre with a pencyon of two hundred poundes by the yere durynge the tern of his lyfe. Then he thanked the kynge and the lordes and wente to his wyfe and kysses her and then they wente togyder to the Churche of Our Lady in Parys and made theyr offerynge and then returned to theye lodgynges. Then Syr John of Carougne taryed not long in France, but wente to vyste the Holy Sepulture."

If we wonder at the supreme punishment awarded to the combatant who failed in the arena to uphold his cause, it must be remembered our ancestors, by the very fact of sanctioning these judicial combats, looked upon the outcome as the verdict of God. Again, a combat such as this upon the occasion of the lie given by one or other of the combatants resting on a supposition of dishonour, was justified by the laws of Chivalry, since, as Selden says (the " Duello," page 19), " truth, honour, freedom, and courtesy, were incidents to perfect Chivalry, and, upon the lie given, custom hath arisen to seek revenge of their wrongs upon the body of their accuser . . . ' seul à seul.' "

So long as it was lawful, or at least customary, to fight in the lists " a l'outrance," it was impossible to ensure that private quarrels should not be settled there; thought they were never considered so honourable as contests in the tournaments which were held for simply honour and hardiness. Both Popes and kings made many attempts to abolish them. Louis IX., whose superiority in loftiness of character and clearness of intellect, lifts him far above his contemporaries, attempted to do away with judicial combats, but only succeeded " in suis terris." Edward I. forbade Sir James Cromwell to take up a challenge from Sir Nicholas de Seagrave, whereupon the challenger " dared him in France." Upon a clear quarrel the laws of Chivalry ordained, and the king could not well forbid, that the forms of a judicial combat should be observed, the court being that of Chivalry, while in the Wager of Battle, it was (in England) the Court of King's Bench, but in France, as seen above in the sanction it gave to the judicial combat between de Grys and Carougne, it remained for the Parliament to order it.

It may be mentioned that the Court of Chivalry held under the

High Constables and the Earl Marshal, with an appeal to the king, had cognizance of all military matters, and included in its purview, controversies of coat-armour and precedence, as in the cases of Grey de Ruthven and Hastings (t.r. Henry III.), Scrope and Grosvenor (t.r. Richard II.). It also judged cases where personal honour was impeached.

This Court relied on "honour among gentlemen" to obey its edicts; it had no jurisdiction wherever the common law could give redress; it could not impose or grant pecuniary satisfaction or damages, nor commit to prison. Its sanction therefore was founded on Chivalric honour and sentiment.

At all events questions which otherwise would have been difficult to solve were, in these judicial combats, abruptly settled, and, from these bloody decisions, there was no appeal. In some countries indeed the judge who had sanctioned them had to submit himself to the judgment of God as represented by the judicial duel (Lacroix), and was forced to come down from his seat and contend in arms against the criminal he had just condemned, if the same had not expired in the contest. On the other hand the judge, in his turn, possessed the privilege of challenging the combatant who refused to bow to his decision.

CHAPTER VIII

PAS D'ARMES AND JOUSTS

SOMEWHAT similar to knights-errant were those knights who, not so much sharing in the wandering propensities of the former, still sought adventures. Unlike the knight-errant who, as a rule, rode forth attended only by a single squire, and engaged singly in the contests he provoked or found, these others sought such with brother-knights. The old writers give to the name of their combats the title of " pas d'armes." Some of these adventures were almost similar—except in the number of those engaged—to the knight-errant's. They fixed their shields on bridges, on trees, on palings, with the notice they would contest the passage with all who passed (hence " pas d'armes ") who should touch their shield with sword or lance, and if victorious, they claimed a guerdon from the conquered.

Differing, however, from the knight-errant who generally—except he entered a joust or a tourney—had no one witnessing his combat, except his henchman, these knights often met in public, and, before a full court, ran a course. Princes, too, provided these opportunities and, as was the case in tournaments, proclaimed beforehand that a passage of arms would take place. It was in such a " passage " Henry II. of France received his mortal wound from the lance of Montgomery during the fêtes held to celebrate the marriage of Elizabeth of France with Philip II. of Spain, for in this " pas d'armes " the king and his nobles all displayed their skill.

Very quaint and stirring to a chivalrous mind is the proclamation issued before this passage of arms.

" De par le Roy . . . lequel fait à savoir à tous Princes, Seigneurs, Gentilhommes, Chevaliers et Écuyers qu'en la ville capitale de Paris, (1) le Pas est ouvert pas Sa Majesté très Chretienne, et par les Princes de Ferrare, Alphonse d'Este, François de Lorraine, Duc de Guise, Pair et Grand Chambellan de France, et Jaques de Savoye, Duc de Nêmours, tous Chevaliers de l'ordre, pour être tenus coutre tous venans dúement qualifiey," etc.

These public passages of arms were arranged in two bodies—one the attacking, the other the defending party. Sometimes a mimic castle was erected in the lists to give greater verisimilitude to a real battle—which one party defended, the other assaulted.

These passages of arms comprised challenges—very akin to what is also named by ancient writers on Chivalry as an " apertise d'armes."

An example of the terms in which some of these were announced is given here, being those of the celebrated " Apertise d'armes " in Guienne mentioned by Froissart (3rd Vol.) : " En ce tems y eut a Bordeaux sur Gironde une Apertise d'armes devant les Seigneurs

124

A KNIGHT'S LIFE

Messire Jean de Harpendane et les autres, de deux Chevaliers; c'est a scavoir du Sire de Rochefoucaut François, et de Messire Guillaume de Montferant Anglois, à courir à tout trois lances, a Cheval, et en ferir trois coups, trois d'Épée, trois coups de Dague et trois coups de Hâche. Si furent les armes faites devant les Seigneurs et Dames du Pais, que lors étaient à Bordeaux . . . si s'armèrent les deux Chevaliers bien accompagnez chacun de grande Chevalerie de son côté et avoit Sire de Rochefoucaut bien deux cent Chevaliers; et Messire Guillaume de Montferrant bien autre tant ou plus."

This passage is interesting as showing the weapons and the amount of blows permitted in these combats. These apertises seem to have been held most frequently when no tournaments had been proclaimed and the warlike spirit of the knights, not resting in idleness at home, prompted them to these contests in which they challenged all competitors. From an abridged account of the " pas d'armes " called the " Juste of Saint Inglebert " is gathered the following: The emprise or apertise was sustained by three gallant knights of France—Boucicaut, Reynold de Ruy and de Saimpi. Their articles bound them to abide thirty days at Saint Inglebert, in the marches of Calais, there to undertake the encounter of all knights and squires, Frenchmen or strangers who should come hither for the breaking of five spears, sharp or with rochets (blunted with caps on) at their pleasure.

In their tents they hung two shields, called Peace and War, with their armorial blazons on each. The stranger desiring to joust was invited to come or send and touch which shield he would. The weapons of courtesy were to be employed if he chose the shield of peace, if that of war, the defenders were to give him the desired encounter with sharp weapons. The stranger knights were invited to bring some nobles with them to assist in judging the field, and the proclamation concludes with an entreaty to knights, squires, strangers, that they will not hold this offer as made for any pride, hatred or ill-will; but only that the challengers do it to have their honourable company and acquaintance, which, with their whole heart, they desire. They were assured of a fair field, without fraud or advantage; and it was provided that the shields used should not be covered with iron or steel. The French king was highly joyful of this gallant challenge and exhorted the challengers to regard the honour of their prince and realm and spare no cost for which he was willing to contribute ten thousand francs. A number of knights and squires came from England to Calais to accept this gallant invitation, and at the entrance of the " fresh and jolly month of May " the challengers pitched their green pavilions on a fair plain between Calais and the Abbey of Saint Inglebert. Two shields hung before each tent with the arms of the owners. On the 21st of May as it had been proclaimed the three knights were properly armed and their horses properly saddled according to the laws of a tournament. On the same day those knights who were at Calais sallied forth, either as spectators or tilters, and being arrived at the spot drew up on one side. The place of the jousting was smooth and green with grass. Sir John Holland was the first who sent his squire to touch the shield of Sir Boucicaut, who instantly issued forth from his tent completely armed. Having mounted his horse and grasped his spear, which was stiff and well steeled, they took their distance. When the two knights had for a short time eyed each other, they spurred their horses and met full gallop with such a force that Sir Boucicaut pierced the shield of the Earl of Huntingdon and the point of his lance slipped along his arm, but without wounding him. The two knights, having passed, continued their gallop to the end of the list. This course was much praised. At the second course, they hit each other slightly, but no harm was done; and their horses refused to complete the third.

The Earl of Huntingdon, who wished to continue the tilt and was heated, returned to his place, expecting that Sir Boucicaut would call for his lance; but he did not, and showed plainly he would not that day tilt more with the Earl. Sir John Holland seeing this, sent his squire to touch the shield of the Lord de Saimpi. They couched their lances and pointed them at each other. At the onset, their horses crossed; notwithstanding which, they met; but by this crossing, which was blamed, the Earl was unhelmed. He returned to his squires, who soon rehelmed him, and having resumed their lances, they met full gallop and hit each other with such a force in the middle of their shields, they would have been unhorsed had they not kept tight seats by the pressure of their legs against their horses' sides. They went back to their proper places where they refreshed themselves and took breath.

Sir John Holland, who had a great desire to shine at this combat, had his helmet braced and re-grasped his spear, when the Lord de Sampi seeing him advanced at the gallop, did not decline meeting, but spurring his horse on instantly, they gave blows to their helmets that luckily were of well-tempered steel, which made sparks of fire fly from them. At this course, the Lord de Saimpi lost his helmet, but the two knights continued their career and returned to their places. This tilt was much praised, and the English and French said that the Earl of Huntingdon and the Lord de Saimpi had excellently well jousted without sparing or doing themselves any injury. The Earl wished to break another lance in honour of his lady, but it was refused him. He then quitted the lists to make room for others, for he had run his six lances with such ability and courage as gained him praise from all sides. (Froissart, Vol. IV., p. 143.)

The other jousts were accomplished with similar spirit, and the whole was regarded as one of the most gallant enterprises which had been fulfilled for some time.

This account given of the passage of arms at Saint Inglebert was —in contradiction to a tournament—a joust. In the former a great many more knights were engaged in the general mêlée—in a joust two knights at a time. While it took place the squires saw to their master's arms and horses and stood in readiness to help him in every way short of joining in the contest, which was only allowed in the mêlée. The knights, after mounting, set their lances in " the rest " (a half ring attached to the saddle-bow). The object in a tourney was to strike an opponent, either on the head—the more effectual but more difficult aim—or on the body. The shock of heavy armed men often dismounted both opponents. If both sat firm, the lances were generally shivered, but often it happened both man and horse fell together.

DAYS OF CHIVALRY

If the horses did not swerve and the lances did not break and either knight aimed true and held his lance firm, mortal wounds were often given. If both knights, as in the above " passage " at Saint Inglebert, were unhurt and kept their seats, they wheeled their horses round and charged again with fresh lances till one or both were unhorsed. Often then the victor dismounted and the combat was continued on foot with swords. Two men completely armed in mail might slash at each other with swords for a long time without much injury done.

The combats of such portrayed in the " Morte d'Arthur " and other romances, last for hours, and the knights pause at intervals, drink and get cool, and then begin again, and they always seem ready, so slight are their wounds, to attend the feast in the evening of a tourney.

These " pas d'armes " embraced, as has been said, challenges in lieu of battles. As early as Saxon times Edmund Ironside proposed to Canute to claim the kingdom by eight champions. William of Normandy challenged Harold and accepted a challenge from Geoffrey of Anjou. John sent a cartel to Louis VII.; Edward III. to Philip of Valois; Richard II. to Charles VI.; Francis I. to Charles V.

These challenges, as Cornish well says in his work on " Chivalry," were partly the natural outcome of the military spirit delighting in personal distinction, partly of the nature of an ordeal (like the judicial ordeal before treated of), on the principle, that, God would defend the right. Who does not remember Taillifer the jongleur, or troubadour, riding on Senlac's bloody field before the Norman host, throwing his lance into the air and catching it while he sang the Song of Roland and challenged the opposing Saxons. At the Siege of Jerusalem (1097) one of Robert of Normandy's men attacked the city wall alone and was killed, no man following him.

Peter the Hermit summoned the Saracen lord of Antioch to send him forth three of his knights to fight against three Christian knights. Another knight at Cherbourg (1379) invited three champions, the most amorous knights of the enemy, to fight with three amorous knights, on his side for the love of their ladies. At the battle of Cockerel (1384) an English knight left the ranks " pour demander a faire un coup de lance contre celui des François qui seroit assez brave pour entrer en lice avec luy." Rowland du Boy presented himself " pour luy prêter le colet " and won. At Bannockburn De Bohun burned before his monarch's eye to do some deed of Chivalry, and pricked forth alone against Robert le Brus as he rode along the Scot lines.

The Lord of the Castle of Josselin in Brittany in 1351 (Froissart) " Messire Robert de Beaumanoir vaillant Chevalier durement et du plus grand lignage de Bretagne " called upon the Captain of the town and Castle of Ploermel to send him forth one champion, two, or three, to joust with swords against other three for love of their ladies. Their Captain Brandebourg replied, " Our ladies will not that we adventure ourselves for the passing chance of a single joust, but, if you will, choose you out twenty or thirty of your companions and let them fight in a fair field." So the sixty champions heard them, put on their harness and went forth to the place of arms, twenty-five on foot, five on horseback. Then they fought and many were killed on their side and the other and at last the English had the worst of it, and all who were not slain, were made prisoners and courteously ransomed when healed of their wounds. Froissart recounts he saw sitting at King Charles' table after, one of these Breton knights called Yvain Charnelz, and his face was so cut and slashed that he showed how hard the fight had been.

In " The War of the Disinherited " in 1266, the Barons at Kenilworth disdained to wait behind their defences and kept the Castle gates open in defiance of Prince Edward for ten months, thinking Chivalry more glorious than warfare, that is to say from the morrow of St. John the Baptist to the morrow of St. Thomas (Chron. Petriburg).

These jousts or " pas d'armes " served in times of peace to keep alive a knight's spirits when tranquillity might have gradually subdued them. They furnished him with opportunities of comparing himself with the most celebrated of his companions; and if he had unwillingly contracted a habit of pride, they often afforded him a lesson and a remedy. Above all jousts the fair ones seem to have favoured even more than the tournaments—they enabled them to judge with their own eyes the merits of their cavaliers, to comprehend what their lovers or husbands meant when they told them tales of Chivalry, and to appreciate the value of knightly fame, as they often saw, in such a combat that ended fatally both its glory and its mortality.

It was no wonder therefore, when a " pas d'armes " was announced that valorous knights jousted in them, till one was declared the victor, that the countryside, and often a city, the court and its fairest dames, gathered to the lists. Eustache Deschamps well describes this excitement in these verses of his:

DU TOURNOI LIEU A SAINT DENIS, 1389

Armes, amours, déduit, joye et plaisance
Espoir, desir, souvenir, hardement,
Jeunesce aussi, manière et contenance,
Humble regart trait amoureusement,
Genz corps joliz, parez très richement,
Avisez bien ceste saison nouvelle.
Ce jour de may, ceste grant feste est belle
Qui par le Roy se fait à Saint Denys;
A bien joustes gardez vostre querelle
Et vous serez honnorez et chéris.

Car la sera la grant biauté de France
Vint Chevaliers, vint Dames ensement,
Qui les mettront armez par ordenance
Sur la place toutes d'un parement,
Le premier jour; et puis secondement
Vint escuiers, chascun sa damoiselle,
D'uns paremens, joye se renouvelle;
Et la feront les heraulx pluseurs cris
Aux bien joustans; tenez fort vostre selle,
Et vous serez honnorez et chéris.

... BOHUN, WIFE OF Sir PETER ARDERNE.

Chief Justice Temp. H. VI. and E. IV. and Justice of the King's Bench.
In Latton Church, Essex, 1465-5 Ed. IV.
From Foster's '' Some Feudal Coats of Arms ''

DAYS OF CHIVALRY

Or y perra qui bien ferra de lance,
Et qui sera de beau gouvernement
Pour acquerir d'armour la bienvueillance,
Et qui durra ou harnois longuement;
Cilz ara los, doulz regart proprement
Le monstrera; Amour, qui ne chancelle,
L'enflambera d'amoureuse estincelle.
Honneur donrra aux mieulx faisans les pris;
Avisez tous ceste doulce nouvelle,
Et vous serez honnorez et chéris.

ENVOY

Servans d'amours, regardez doulcement
Aux eschaffaux anges de paradis,
Lors jousterés fort et joyeusement,
Et vous serez honnorez et chéris.

(Arms, Amours, joy and pleasure,
Hope, desire, remembrance, hardiness,
Youth also, manners and bearing
Humble glances cast lovingly
Fine persons and fair, adorned richly
Bethink ye of this new-come season
This May-day, this great and beautiful feast,
Which by the king is held at St. Denys,
Joust well and maintain your cause,
Thus will ye be honoured and held dear.

For there will be the great beauty of France,
Knights are coming and ladies also
Who will present themselves armed as is ordained
At the proper place all in gala array
The first day; and on the second
Come the squires with each his demoiselle
In tournament array and the joy is renewed,
And there will the heralds utter many shouts
To those who joust well, " keep firm in your saddles
And ye will be honoured and held dear."

Now there may be those who wield well the lance
And who manœuvre skilfully
To gain Love's favour
And who will bear harness a long time
These shall have praise and fair looks;
Rightly shall such be shown them;
Love who wavers not shall enflame them with amorous aspirations,
Honour shall be given them (and), to those who do best, the prizes,
Take heed, all, of this sweet new thing
And ye shall be honoured and held dear.

L'ENVOY

Servants of love! look longingly
On the angelic Beauties of Paradise,
Then joust manfully and joyously
And ye shall be honoured and held dear.)

But not always were these " pas d'armes " made before a royal court and before the applauds of the fair sex—they were made in sight of an armed force of warrior knights, intent on battle. This was the case—as has been mentioned of De Bohun who rode out of the English ranks in the Scottish war to tempt the Bruce to single combat—this was the case of a knight in the English army commanded by Sir Robert Knowles when passing near Paris in the French wars of Edward III. Froissart says: " Now it happened one Tuesday morning when the English began to break camp and had set fire to all the village wherein they were lodged, so that the fires were distinctly seen from Paris, a knight of their army who had made a vow the preceding day that he would advance as far as the barriers and strike them with his lance, did not break his oath, but set off with his lance in his hand, his shield round his neck, and completely armed except his helmet, and spurring his horse, was followed by his squire on another, carrying his helmet. When he approached Paris he put on his helmet which his squire laced behind. He then galloped away, sticking spurs into his horse, and advanced prancing to strike the barriers. They were then open and the lords and barons within imagined he intended to enter the town, but he did not so mean, for having struck the gates according to his vow, he checked his horse and turned about. The French knights who saw him then retreat, cried out to him, ' Get away, get away, thou hast well acquitted thyself.' " Froissart adds, " As for the name of the knight, I am ignorant of it, nor do I know from what country he came, but he bore for his arms ' gules à deux fousses noir,' with ' une bordure noir non endentée.' "

As to the weapons used in jousting. If only a friendly trial of skill was contemplated, the lances were headed with a small coronal instead of a sharp point; if the sword was used at all, it was with the edge only, which would inflict no wound at all on a well-armed man, or at most a flesh wound, but never with the point which might penetrate the opening of the helmet or the joints of the armour, and inflict a fatal hurt. This was the " joute à plaisance." If the combatants were allowed to use sharp weapons and to put forth all their force and skill against one another, this was the " joute à l'outrance " and was of common occurrence.

In a MS. in the Egerton Collection in the British Museum, there is a quaint account how the knights are rewarded after a successful joust. " When the heraldes cry à l'óstel! à l'óstel then shall the gentlemen within unhelme them before the seide ladies and make their obeisaunce and goo home into their lodgings and change them, the gentlemen without comyn into the precence of the ladies. Then comys foorth a lady by the advise of all the ladyes and gentilwomen and gives the diamounde unto the best jouster withoute, saying in this wise—' Sir, theis ladyes and gentilwomen thank you for your disporte and grete labour that ye have this day in their presence—and the saide ladyes and gentilwomen sayn that ye have best joust this day; therefore the saide ladyes and gentilwomen geven you this diamounde, and send you much joy and worship of your lady.' Thus shall be doone with the rubie and with the sauire unto the other two next the best jousters. This doone, then shall the heralde of armys stande up all on hygh, and shall say withall in high voice—' John hath well jousted, Ric hath jousted better, and Thomas hath jousted best of all.'

Then shall he that the diamound is geve unto take a lady by the hand and bygene the daunce, and when the ladyes have danced as long as them liketh, then spyce wyne and drynk and then avoide."

We have above mentioned that though blunted weapons were generally used at tourneys and so few deaths happening, when these weapons were unblunted accidents often took place. Thus in the MS. " Life and Acts of Richard Beauchamp, Earl of Warwick," it states " how a mighty Duke chalenged Erle Richard for his lady's sake and in jousting slewe the Duke and thereupon the Empresse toke the Erle's staff and wear from a knight shouldre, and for great love and favour she sette it on her shouldre. Then Erle Richard made one of perle and precious stones and offered her that and she gladly and lovynglee reseaved it." The Duke perished by his adversary driving his lance half a yard through his breast.

But seldom was the termination of a joust fatal, particularly if it was a " joute à plaisance," such as that which took place in Windsor Park in the sixth year of Edward I., for which, according to a document in the Record Office of the Tower (printed in the *Archæologia*, Vol. XVII., p. 297) it appears that the knights were armed in a tunic and surcoat, a helmet of leather gilt or silvered, with crests of parchment, a wooden shield, and a sword of parchment, silvered and strengthened with whalebone, with gilded hilt. Even if real weapons —as was generally the case—were used in tourneys or single combats little damage was usually done. Froissart describes how the English king, Edward III., " lyghted on the Lord Eustace de Rybemount, who was a strong and a hardy knight, there was a long fyht between hym and the kyng that it was a joy to beholde them. The knight strake the kyng the same day two tymes on his knees, but finally the kyng himself toke hym prisoner." The upshot of this encounter was a merry one. King and prisoner sat at the same banquet given by the prince that night and there rising up before the assembled guests, Edward declared Sir Eustace de Rybemount the most valiant he had ever encountered, and, taking off from his own head a chaplet of pearls which he was wearing, gave it to the knight, saying, " Sir Eustace, I gyve you this chapelet for the best doar in armes in this journey (war) past of either party, and I desire you to bere it this yere for the love of me; say wheresoever ye come that I dyd give it you and I quyte you your prison and ransom, and ye shall depart to-morrow if it please you."

CHAPTER IX

THOUGH the time of Chivalry was one which bristled with feuds and wars, at certain times peace reigned in the disturbed countries of Europe, and it was then, having no foes to fight, the ever restless lance of the knight urged him to those mimic representations of war, the Tournaments.

Many doubts are entertained as to the precise origin of these grand and chivalric exhibitions. Classical tradition abounds in notices of military games and contests instituted for the purpose of displaying in noble rivalship the valour and address of distinguished soldiers. But wide distinctions are found to exist between these and the tournaments of Chivalry, and a totally new origin is, without much necessity, sought for the latter. To bring their commencement nearer modern times, some writers have supposed that they had their beginning in the spectacles and games which were instituted by Charles of Germany and Louis his brother after the battle of Fontenay, on which occasion they became reconciled to each other, and spent some time together in making the most brilliant displays of their mutual regard and riches.

This event occurred about the year 842; but the same objections are made to the exhibitions of the royal brothers, as to the ancient games; and we are referred to a still later period for the institution of the genuine chivalrous tournament. Still the earliest historical instance recorded, and that by Nithard, a co-temporary and grandson of Charlemagne, is that of the above Charles the Bad and Louis the Pious meeting at Strasbourg when the vassals of both princes engaged in contests on horseback. Whether Germany, therefore, or France, was the birthplace of these Chivalrous amusements seems a doubtful point. Geoffrey de Preuilli, a Breton lord, is, however, generally credited with the invention of them in France in 1036, and probably was the first who drew up rules how they were to be conducted.

In France, therefore, tournaments seem first in regular use, and Matthew Paris calls them " conflictus gallici." To England they probably travelled from France, and as early as the reign of Stephen, who is accused of " softness " (mollities) because he could not, or would not, hinder them. Matthew Paris, however, says that Richard I. introduced tournaments into England in order " that the French knights might not scoff at the English knights as being unskilled and awkward " (Tamquam rudibus et minime suavis). This king also got money for the Crusade by granting licences to hold tournaments in

A KNIGHT'S LIFE

certain lawful places and fined Roger Mortimer " quod tornaverat sine licentia."

These prohibitions of tournaments constantly occur in English history and are to some extent an indication of the condition of the country. Edward II. (see Rymer's " Fœdera ") issued a great number of letters forbidding all persons " torneare—burdeire, justus facere, aventuras querere sine licentia nostra speciali." The reason given is for fear of breach of the peace and terrifying quiet people. No tournament, e.g., is to be held within six miles of Cambridge to protect " tranquillitatem ibidem studentium." So, too, in France Philip IV. (1312) forbade all " astiludere vel justare subpœna amissionis armorum " (to engage with the spear or joust under forfeiture of their arms).

That the tournament became a great institution in England it will be sufficient to cite the passage from the English Chronicler, Roger de Hoveden : " A knight cannot shine in war if he has not prepared for it in tournaments. He must have seen his own blood flow, have had his teeth crackle under the blow of his adversary, have been dashed to the earth with such force as to feel the weight of his foe, and disarmed twenty times; he must twenty times have retrieved his failures, more set than ever upon the combat. Then will he be able to confront actual war with the hope of being victorious." The tournament, indeed, was looked upon as a veritable military school, for by these voluntary and regulated combats a tyro exercised himself and trained himself for that offensive and defensive strife which entirely filled the life of the knight. Here, too, he learnt that subtility and " finesse " in fighting which made the knights so victorious in other lands, for it was not so much brute force, but a dexterity in wielding his arms that made those arms bring him victory.

So an ancient writer lays down the law that " Chevaliers doivent avoir sens force, ardement loyaulté et exercise de leur art. Sens de Chevaliers vault plus aucune fois en vicctoire, que ne fait multitude de gens, ne que la force de ceul qui se combatent."

We may cite the Normans in their conquests of England and Sicily to prove this. Far from being the colossal height of the heroes of romance, they were small men. The Germans, who opposed them in Italy, derided their shortness of stature, " Corpora derident, Normannica qua breviora esse videbantur " (Guill. Apul. ap Muratori). Even as sailors these descendants of Rollo and of Senlac show themselves but poor ones, and are greatly alarmed by the tempests of the Adriatic (" Gibbon," X., 289), but they possessed a compound of audacity and stratagem, the constant trials in jousts and tournaments strengthened and made perfect. Scribes, in their better learning to the hordes of Europe; shaven, like priests, they carried their lances victorious through Europe, and by such skill and training raised their hero, Robert Guiscard, to the ducal throne of Apulia and Calabria, and were apt exemplars, in later days of Chivalry, how each knight should cultivate like qualities even in the mimic wars of the tournament.

In tournaments too, the training of younger knights was accomplished. They were well called, therefore, " Schools of Prowess." The elder knights, who often in them took the rôle of instructors to the younger ones, got to know the fighting capacity of these youths of the

younger generation.   They trained them to the word of command;
they taught them there to reflect well before making a charge, to
group and move themselves together to the best advantage before
engaging—lessons they themselves had learnt the expediency of, on
many a real battle-field, and encouraged them also to invent new ways,
in the lists, to circumvent their opposers.

Thus it was that contemporaries justified the tournament when it
was attacked, and why both in England and France it was so
flourishing.   In the latter country in the historical ballad " Guillaume
le Maréchal," the recital of tournaments occupies three thousand of the
twenty thousand verses; the author describes fifteen tournaments
which followed one another within a few years in the lands of
Normandy, Chartres and Perche.   He says : " I cannot keep up with
all the tournaments that take place; it would take great trouble to do
so, for almost every fortnight there is a tournament in some place or
other."   Gilbert of Mons informs us that every creation of new
knights, every great marriage, had almost necessarily to be accompanied by a tournament in which the young barons could exhibit their
strength and bear their first arms; and so in the Lay " Garin le
Lorrain "—" Sire," said the Messenger of Count Fromont to King
Pepin, " the Count has sent me to request a tournament for to-morrow.
His son Fromondin is a new knight, the father wishes to see how he
will bear arms."   And indeed if one bore oneself well in a tournament,
one could well hope to bear oneself well in the real battle, for the
tournament differed little, when it was fought " à l'outrance " from
the former.   True there was not in it, as in a war, systematic pillage
of fields and massacres of peasants, otherwise the noble knights armed
themselves, if it was thus fought " à l'outrance," for the tournament,
exactly as in a real battle; if they usually strove to capture others for
the sake of taking profit from their ransoms, it still happened that they
wounded and often killed each other.

The word " outrance " used in these more bloody contests comes
from the word " utterance," and signifies the extremity or completion
of the contest by the death, flight, or confession of defeat by one of
the parties.   The opposite to " à outrance " was " à plaisance."

In 1208 when Philip Augustus decided to knight his son Louis—
that is to emancipate him—for the sake of precaution he caused him
to subscribe to certain promises, among others, never to take part in
a tournament, so dangerous they often were.   One of the reasons for
the Church's prohibition of these warlike games was simply that they
were dangerous and even fatal to the nobility, and often incapacitated
them from their wounds taking part in a Crusade when it was
published.

In these encounters it was not, like those in jousts or " pas
d'armes," a question of individual tilts between picked knights, but
often entire small armies entered the lists to charge eagerly on one
another.   In the tournament at Lagny-sur-Marne more than three
thousand knights were engaged, composed of French, Flemings,
Norman Angeours and Burgundians.   Considering the number of
combatants, a tournament like that of Lagny, which was fought in the
open field, exactly represented a decisive action of real war.

According to the biographer of William Marshall, who recounts
this engagement, the knights who were taken prisoners mattered more

than those, many though they were, who were killed in it or grievously wounded. "Banners," he writes, "were unfurled; the field was so full of them that the sun was concealed. There was great noise and din. All strove to strike well. Then you would have heard such a crash of lances that the earth was strewn with fragments, and that the horses could not advance further. Great was the tumult upon the field. Each corps of the army cheered its ensign. The knights seized each other's bridles and went to each other's aid."

Soon, the account goes on, the young King of England, the eldest son of Henry II., gave the signal for the grand mêlée. Then began a desperate strife in the vineyards, the ditches, across the thick forests of vine-stocks. One could see the horses falling and men sinking, trampled under foot, wounded and beaten to death. Always William the Marshal distinguished himself; everything he struck with his sword was cloven and cut to pieces; he pierced bucklers and dented shields. He was associated with a daring companion called Roger of Gaugi, and the two made their clerks prove in writing "that between Pentecost and Lent they took three hundred knights prisoners without counting horses and harness."

Curious incidents in this account of the Marshal are related—the exchange of visits by knights on the eve of the tournament, at the inns where they chatted gaily over two jugs of wine; the Marshal running through the crowded streets of a little village at night in pursuit of a thief who had taken his horse. This same knight had had his helmet so dented in the tournament that he could not take it off after the battle, and was obliged to seek a blacksmith and put his head on the anvil, so as to free himself from this unlucky headpiece by hammer blows.

If we compare this historical tournament with the poetical one found in "Garin le Lorrain," the same fierce fighting took place. The plain seemed to be nothing less than a forest of glittering helmets, above which floated brilliant pennons. The two armies having come face to face slowly approached each other until they were not separated further than the range of a bow. Who would make the first attack? Who would be the first to make a sortie from the lines? It was the young Fromondin. His shield hard against his breast, he encountered a knight and unhorsing him, hurled himself on another, whom he likewise overthrew. His lance was shattered, but with a fragment he still thrust and threatened. Already order in two armies was gone, the mêlée became general. Each lance crossed another, and the earth was covered with their débris; the vassals were thrown and their terrified horses fled; the wounded uttered horrible cries, and it was not in one place but in twenty or forty that they thrust each other to give or take death. Five times Fromondin fell and remounted another horse. With one blow he cut down the Flemish knight Baldwin, with a second Bernard of Naisil; finally covered with sweat he went to a place where no one could follow him. There he was able to unfasten his helmet and refresh himself for an instant.

In these combats "armes courtoises" were never used in the mêlée, and, as we have just seen, they were often the occasion of much bloodshed. When Edward I. was on his way from the Holy Land (1274) he spent some time in France and was present at a great tournament at Châlons. He was assailed by a knight who tried to drag him from his horse. The king was the stronger of the two, he lifted the man off his saddle and rode away with him. His party tried to rescue him, and the fight became so fierce on both sides that the mêlée was called " the little battle (parvum bellum) of Châlons," so much did it resemble one. Indeed the mêlée often was a combat for life and death, closed only by the defeat of one party, or by the heralds, or the prince, giving the word to cease. " The king hath thrown his warder (truncheon) down," was the signal to stop the battle in the lists at Coventry, when Mowbray and Bolingbroke met.

As a rule tournaments before taking place were proclaimed, that is to say, published à cor et à cri, either when a promotion of knights, or a royal marriage, or a solemn entry of a prince into a town took place, and the character of these chivalrous festivals changed according to the time and place at and in which they occurred. The arms used on these occasions varied in a similar manner. In France the tournament lance was made of the lightest and straightest wood, either fir, aspen, or sycamore, pointed with steel and with a pennon floating from the end; whilst in Germany and in Scotland they were made of the heaviest and toughest wood, with a long iron pear-shaped point. England followed the French fashion.

Eustache Deschamps gives in one of his poems a good description of the proclamation of a tournament; he writes of one held at Saint Denys.

" Tuit Chevalier et escuier estrange
　Et tous autres qui tendez à renon
　Oez, oez l'oneur et la louenge
　Et des armes grantdisime pardon;
　C'est de par le chevalier
　A l'Aigle d'or, lui trentième à destrier
　D'uns paremens, joustans en sa compaigne
　Et delivrans tous ceuls de leur mestier
　A lendemain du jour de Magdelaine.

A la noble cité, ainsi l'entenge,
　Qui de Paris porte le propre nom,
　Royne y aura parée comme un ange
　Trente Dames d'uns habiz et façon.
　D'Isle Celée nuncier
　Vous fait son nom; le dimanche dancier,
　Et le lundi jouster à bonne estraine
　Tant de lances c'om vouldra emploier
　Au lendemain du jour de Magdelaine.

Le mieulx joustant dehors, sanz faire change
　Aura pour pris chapel d'or bel et bon,
　Et de dedenz dyamant en losange
　Dont la Roine fera présent et don
　Et si auront estrangier
　Quinzaine avant et quinz à repairier
　Bon sauf-conduit hors traison villaine;
　Ainsi le fait l'Aigle d'or publier
　Au lendemain du jour de Magdelaine.

DAYS OF CHIVALRY

Après ce jour tuit escuier se range;
Car le mardi autres joustes raron
D'un escuier, lui trentième en sa range;
D'uns paremens seront li compaignon,
Pour les rans faire et drecier,
Et damoiselle au gent corps et legier,
Soy trentième d'uns habiz et demaine,
Pour les joustes veoir et adviser
Au lendemain du jour de Magdelaine.

Le mieulx joustant dehors n'aura pas lange,
Mais d'argent fin chapel à son bandon,
Et de dedenz fezmail d'or sanz meschange
La Damoiselle leur donrra, ce dit-on.
L'Aigle d'or donrra à mangier
Lundi au soir et vouldra festoier;
Le noble Roy de France aura court plaine
Mardi au soir; la feste a fait crier
Au lendemain de jour de Magdelaine.

ENVOY

Princes, qui veult les grans fais esploitier
A telz festes se doit lors conseillier
Aux Chevaliers; lors est temps qu'on empraingne
Grosses choses qui a à guerrier;
Pour ce vueillez sur ces poins adviser
Au lendemain du jour de Magdelaine."

(All stranger knights and squires
And all others who seek renown
Hark, hark to the honour and the praise
And of arms the very great festival;
It is by order of the knight
Of the Golden Eagle, with him thirty on horseback
All garbed alike, tilting in his company.
And ready to (run a course) with any of their profession
On the morrow of the Day of Magdalene.

In the noble city, so it is understood
Which bears the name of Paris as its right;
There will be the Queen adorned like an angel,
Thirty ladies (dressed) after the same habit and fashion
As for the secret isle, the herald
Will give you its name; on Sunday dancing,
And on Monday tilting for splendid prizes,
As many lances as one likes to use,
On the morrow of the Day of Magdalene.

He who jousts best of all without any substitution (*i.e.*, another
    taking his place)
Shall have for prize a chaplet of gold, fine and good
With a diamond set lozenge-shaped therein,

Which the Queen will present and give,
And stranger shall have
Fifteen (days) to come and fifteen to return
Fair—safe—conduct without villainous treason,
Thus doth the Golden Eagle make proclamation
For the morrow of Magdalene's Day.

After the day all squires may present themselves,
For on Tuesday other tilts will be arranged
By a squire and with him thirty in his array,
Equipped alike will be the comrades
So that the ranks may be formed and dressed,
And (a) demoiselle with fair lightsome body
Shall there be (with her) thirty of the same habit and bearing,
To watch and counsel the jousters
On the morrow of Magdalene's Day.

The best jouster of all shall not have a woollen scarf
But of fine silver a chaplet for his diadem,
And within it a clasp of gold without alloy,
The demoiselle will give it them, so 'tis said.
The Golden Eagle will give a dinner
On Monday evening, and will keep festival;
The noble King of France will hold full court
On Tuesday evening; the Festival has been proclaimed
For the morrow of Magdalene's Day.

ENVOY

Prince, who wishes to exploit great deeds
To such festivities thou shouldest counsel
The knights; for it is time that then should be understood
Great deeds by those who have gone to war
For this cause be pleased to advise concerning these matters
On the morrow of Magdalene's Day.)

Previous—as we have seen from the above poem—to a tournament taking place, it was proclaimed far and wide by the heralds-at-arms for a king or lord or noble or knight or lady who designed to give one. These went forth on horseback to castle and town, and sometimes from court to court of foreign countries, clad in their gay insignia of office, attended by a trumpeter, and in every castle-yard they came to, and at every market cross, first the trumpeter blew his blast, and then the herald-at-arms made his proclamation of the coming warlike festival.

The preparations for a tournament afforded an animated and interesting picture. The lists which were at first of a round shape like the theatres of antiquity, were later constructed in a square, and later still in an oblong form. They were gilded, painted with emblems and heraldic devices and ornamented with rich hangings and historical tapestries.

While the lists were being prepared, the knights who were to take part in the tournament, as well as those who were to be only its spectators, had their armorial banners hung out from the windows of the houses they were lodging in, and affixed their coats of arms to the outer walls of the monasteries, castles, and cloisters in the neighbourhood. When this was done, the nobles and the ladies went round and inspected them, and a herald or pursuivant-at-arms named their owners, and if a lady recognized any knight against whom she had any ground of complaint, she touched his banner or his shield, in order to bring him under the notice of the judges of the camp, and if, after inquiry, he was found guilty, he was forbidden to appear in the tournament.

For some time before the tournament, which occurred three weeks after it had been proclaimed, the prince who may have summoned it, opened his hall to the throng of knights and squires who were intending taking part in it. But, as the appointed time approached, strict regulations forbade the presence of the party who accepted the challenge. If they wished to visit any friend or lady within the walls of the city, they were only permitted to do so in disguise, and even that was prohibited on the eve of the festival.

On the eve of the tournament the youthful esquires—as has before been remarked—practised among themselves in the lists with less weighty and less dangerous weapons than those wielded by the knights. These preludes, which were often graced by the presence of the ladies, were termed " éprouves " (trials), " vêpres du tournoi " (tournament vespers), or " escrimies " (fencing bouts), the esquires who distinguished themselves the most in these trials were frequently immediately admitted to knighthood and allowed to take part in the ensuing feats. (Lacroix.)

Tournaments which were real popular solemnities excited the ambitions and quickened the pulses of old and young.

Stands, usually roofed and closed in, were erected at the ends of the lists to afford shelter to persons of distinction in the event of bad weather. These stands, sometimes built tower-shape, were divided into boxes, and more or less magnificently decorated with tapestry, hangings, pennons, shields of arms and banners. Kings, queens, princes, dames, demoiselles and the older knights, the judges of the combats in which age prevented longer taking a personal share—stationed themselves there. The king-at-arms, the heralds, and pursuivants-at-arms who had proclaimed the tournament up and down the country, now stood within the arena or just without it, and were expected to narrowly observe the combatants and to draw up a faithful report of the different incidents of the combat without forgetting a single blow. These officers had to particularly see the blows given did not transgress the laws of Chivalry, e.g. :

(1) A knight should take care not to bear arms in this sport which can strike with the point (in fencing " à l'estoc "), but everyone may carry his sword, his shield and his lance for jousting, and he must beware not to strike a knight from behind, nor should either combatant maliciously injure the other when they happen to be unhelmed.

(2) According to ancient custom the knight who rides outside his course shall be held recreant or overthrown (récréant ou assolé).

(3) It is against the usages of Chivalry to strike an adversary's horse when jousting.

(4) No blow should be delivered too high, or too low; if the blows are aimed too low it is against the laws laid down for tourneys.

(5) In the " Lay of Perceforest," a knight is depicted who was so infuriated with his adversary, and aimed a blow at him when he had lost his helmet. This was, and is, considered infamous and treasonable.

In the ardour of the mêlée many faults unwittingly were made, and many curious incidents arose. So ardent was one unknown knight in a tournament, he was named the " Knight of the Smoke." Another, having lost his helmet, forgetting in the onset what he did, snatched off a demoiselle's hat, and in this strange covering met his adversaries, much to the amusement of those who looked on. (St. Palaye, Part II., note 80.)

The heralds also were to afford encouragement to the knights when engaged, particularly to animate by their cries the younger ones in the mêlée. Monstrelet has a curious passage concerning this. He says : " Il n'est nul si bon Chevalier au monde qu'il ne puisse bien faire une faute, voire si grande qui tous les biens qu'il aura faits devant seront adnillez ; et pour ce ou ne crie aux jousts ne aux batailles, aux Preux, mais on crie bien aux fils des Preux après la mort de leurs pères ; car nul Chevalier ne peut estre jugé Preux, se ce n'est après le trépassement," (Vol. I., Chap. xxix.) That is to say owing to the fallibility of human nature no one in their lifetime can be said to be perfectly " preux " or without fault, and only when they are dead, their errors forgiven, may they claim that word to be said of them. Therefore the heralds shall cry out to the youthful knights, not " on ye Brave," but " ye sons of the Brave."

In the Chronicle of the monk of Vigeoise, he says : " It was also the custom to salute at the tournaments the elder knights with the cry of ' Heroes,' while the younger were ' Sons of Heroes.' These cries filled the heralds' pockets with money. ' Largesse ' was lavishly scattered not only by the knights about to enter the fray but by their ladies in the galleries around." Monstrelet in his account of the festivities and tournament held at the marriage of Mademoiselle de Cleves, niece of the Duke of Burgundy in 1440 with the Duke of Orleans, remarks : " Esquels jours furent moult grands dous a tous les Officiers—d'armes par les Princes dessudits peur lequels ils crièrent à haulte voix par plusieurs fois largesse " (Vol. II., p. 178).

The sergeants (or keepers of the lists) and the squires of the knights were especially entrusted with the duty of keeping order, the former among the rude populace which crowded on the barriers, the latter in replacing broken lances, leading off weary or wounded " destriers," and replacing them with fresh ones, often replacing and relacing portions of armour and specially doing so with the knight's helmet, which often, stricken by an adversary's lance, rolled off.

As our ancestors were great lovers of music it is needless to say that jongleurs and wandering musicians were posted everywhere outside the lists, holding themselves ready to celebrate with noisy flourishes every great feat of arms and every fortunate and brilliant stroke. The sound of their clarions announced the entry of the knights into the lists, stepping with slow and solemn cadence, majestically armed, and equipped, and followed by their squires on horseback.

DAYS OF CHIVALRY

Sometimes the ladies were the first to enter the lists, leading in by golden or silver chains the knights, their slaves, whom they only set at liberty when the signal was given for the combat to commence. Now was the time for the ladies to give those " favours " to their favourite knights, which have before been referred to; these consisted generally of a scarf, a mantle or a bracelet, or even a piece of ribbon which had formed part of their own dress. This was termed an " enseigne " or " nobley " (distinguishing mark) and was placed on a knight's helmet, or lance, or shield, that his lady might know him in the mêlée.

Sometimes the fettering of the knights was the act, not of these ladies, but of a powerful lord. Thus the announcement of " Joustes mortelles et à champs," issued by John, Duke of Bourbon, in 1414, may be given here . . . " desirans d'eschiver oisiveté et explecter (exploiter) nostre personne . . . pensant y acquérir bonne recommée et la grace de la très-belle de qui nous sommes serviteurs "—the Duke proclaims, by heralds, a tournament to be held every Sunday during the space of two years; sixteen lords, knights and squires will meet all comers in equal numbers on foot in joustes à l'outrance, each champion wearing a fetter on his right leg, hung by a chain of gold for the knights, of silver for the squires.

One of the most curious of these incentives of valour given by a lady to a knight was that of her " shift," recounted by Jaques de Basiu, the trouvere. The lady proposes to her three lovers, successively, the task of entering unarmed into the mêlée of a tournament, arrayed only in one of her shifts. The perilous proposal is declined by two of them, the third accepts it, so de Basiu says he put on the shift " qu'il ne changeroit pas la canise contre le plus fort haubert d'Augier le Danois," then " il lace ses chausses, ceint son épée, embrassé son écu monté à cheval met le casque en tête et pour éprouver ses étriers (stirrups) il s'y appuie encore en partant,"—the very thought of his ladye braced up his spirit for the combat, " il a repris tant de vigeur pour l'honneur de sa Dame, qu'il ne craint ni mort, ni blessure; il part au galop, s'enfonce dans son bouclier et charge le premier qu'il s'encontre." Victoriously did the fair one's shift carry him into the thickest of the fight; protected by no armour, covered only by this thin garment he runs many a course in that hard fought tournament, and at last, covered with wounds, the shift soaked in his gallant blood, he emerges victorious from the combat and is awarded the prize of the day. On the morrow the husband of the ladye, for she was married, was to give a mighty banquet to the knights who had taken part in the tournament. Whereupon the wounded victor sends the shift back to the owner with his request that she should wear it over her rich dress on this festal occasion, soiled and torn as it was, and stained all over with his blood. The ladye did not hesitate to comply, declaring that she regarded this shift, stained with the blood of her friend, as more precious than if it were made of the most costly materials. " La Dame tendant la main pour prendre la Canise toute ensanglantée qu'elle est, ' c'est,' dit-elle, ' pour cela même qu'elle est trempée (drenched) du sang de mon loyal ami, que je la considére comme une loyal parure; il n'est or fin, ni pierreries, qui puissent m'être aussi chers que le sang dont elle est teinte.' " Jaques le trouvère, who relates this curious tale, is at a loss to say whether the palm of true love should be given to the knight or to the ladye on this remarkable occasion. The husband, he assures us, had the good taste to seem to perceive nothing uncommon in the singular vestment which his wife wore, and the rest of the guests highly admired her courageous requital of the knight's gallantry. (MSS. at Turin, No. G. 1, 19.)

Notwithstanding the reverence the Church was held in, during the Middle Ages, her prohibitions against tournaments were disregarded, so fully did they meet with the Chivalric spirit of those times and the break they made in, otherwise, the monotonous life the knight in times of peace passed in his feudal castle or moated manor-house. Cornish, in his work on " Chivalry," gives a very apposite example of how eager the nobles were to engage in tournaments from the fact that after the signing of the Magna Charta, when King John had disappeared from sight and was known to be collecting an army and preparing to take the field against them, these barons could find no better way of passing the time than in holding a tournament at Staines, the prize of which was a bear given by a lady to be jousted for.

That the Church prohibited them was constantly the case. Eugenius III., Innocent III., Innocent IV. published bulls against them, Alexander III. at the Lateran Council of 1179 forbade the holding of " detestabiles . . . illas nundinas vel ferias quas vulgo tournamenta vocant " and refused Christian burial to such as fell in them; visions of knightly souls excluded from Paradise confirmed these prohibitions; and as late as the fourteenth century Clement V. renewed at Aragon the prohibition. A contemporary of Philip Augustus, the historian Cæsar of Heisterbach, says in his Dialogues, " Will those who perish in tournaments by that same blow go to hell? That is a question which need not be asked unless indeed they be saved by contrition." A legend of a later time shows us demons in the form of crows and vultures fluttering over the lists where about sixty jousters lay dead, most of them smothered by dust. Ever since the time of St. Bernard Churchmen had only words of reprobation with which to designate tournaments, " those execrable and accursed festivals." Jaques di Vitry, one of the preachers of the regular clergy, is even more emphatic. " First," he says, " the Jousters were brigands since they seized the person of an adversary or at least took his horse away, and further, tournaments always give rise to detestable pillage; nobles despoil their vassals without mercy; wherever they ride they injure the crops. Then comes another charge, they have the mortal sin—these knights—of gluttony, since at tournaments, and after, banquets were held, where they spent their time and substance in profuse prodigality. Lastly comes the sin of lust. Do not Jousters first of all seek to please their mistresses. They even go so far as to wear their colours? "

Neither sermons of this sort, nor terrifying legends, nor thundering anathemas by clerics, influenced the nobility or succeeded in abolishing tournaments. The Church was herself obliged to often relax her rigours and to temporize. An instance of this is found in the letters of Innocent III. The Bishop of Soissons, one of the heroes of the fourth Crusade, an able energetic prelate, excommunicated all Jousters in his diocese and those who had taken part in a tournament at Laon. The knights thereupon refused to take the Cross or to give a penny towards the Crusade fitting out. Innocent III. therefore had to explain his prohibitions against tournaments in the province of Tours. He wrote: " It is not our intention to authorize tournaments, which are forbidden by our holy Canons. But since the measures we have taken have seemed to us for the moment to offer grave inconvenience we have permitted the Bishop to relax the sentence of excommunication both of those whom he himself has sentenced or of any others."

After all these ecclesiastical censures, it is strange to find in 1350 King John of France held a tournament at Ville-Neuve, near Avignon, at which all the Papal court was present (" tota curia papali adstante "). If at the present day we calmly consider this moral question of tournaments, much may be said on that ground in their defence. (1) The Church has always laid down in considering the morality of human action, the intention in which it is done. Except in some rare case when a knight entered a tournament with the intention of meeting with his personal or hereditary foe and slaying him under a disguise of a festal meeting (and even this was safeguarded against by every strange knight who came into the lists giving satisfaction to the heralds he was a " gentleman of name and arms " and taking oath he had no secret weapons, or would use no unfair advantage), none of the knights, even in a mêlée, wished to kill those opposed to them, but to take them prisoners by the valour of their arms and to hold them, after, as ransom. To overcome them in the lists for their vows' sake, or their ladies' honour, was the intention with which they entered into a tournament; a very different intention to what possessed them, on a real battle-field, where, to slay, to dismember, and to exterminate the foe, was their bloodthirsty object. Even here in real battles, to take prisoners for ransom was a greater object than slaying them, and in a medieval battle the numbers of those slain were generally remarkably small.

(2) In that warlike age when from page, varleton, to knight, a noble youth had been educated with the sole object of using his sword well, the tournament often prevented him, by giving him a legitimate exercise of his valour, making raids and joining in that constant petty warfare which desolated some of the fairest lands of Western Europe—they formed, these tournaments, an avenue where youth's hot and fiery blood might, with least harm to the peasantry, escape. They gave such an opportunity of practising on a fallen foe, that virtue a knight from his earliest days had had instilled into him—courtesy and forbearance—and the lists a place where, as we have said above, not for slaying, but for honour, his sword could be unsheathed.

(3) As the different ceremonies of conferring knighthood had a dissimilarity yet a similarity to the ceremonies of conferring the tonsure, and a certain sacredness was held to be in a knight as in a priest, these pageantries called tournaments demonstrated the visible expression of Chivalry's character as the ecclesiastical pageantries of the Middle Ages demonstrated the ecclesiastical. As the Church felt it requisite to teach the ignorant by visible ceremonies of the most gorgeous character, processions through the medieval towns,

miracle plays outside the Cathedrals, grand ritual in her Gothic and lofty fanes—the greatness of religion, so Chivalry—her co-sister in those ages—found the need of outward expression of her life and ethics, in the brilliant festivals called tournaments. Despite therefore the disfavour of the Church when a tournament was proclaimed in the words of Chaucer:

> " For every wight that loved Chevalrie
> And wolde, his thankes have a lasting name,
> Hath praied that he might ben of that game
> And well was he that (thereto) chosen was."

And indeed in the poetry of old romance, if there be anything in which we may indulge as a true picture of chivalrous delight it is in its representations of the pleasure of a young and noble knight setting out to a tournament. In the full glow of youth, occupied incessantly in pursuits that added graces to his figure or joyousness to his feelings, enjoying the advantages of proud associations and encouraged to expect the most brilliant rewards of knightly exertion —he had the brightest materials that hope could possibly possess on which to frame her enchantments. War is to be his glory, but its ancient splendour was to be blended with a milder and more captivating charm. The ponderous sword had a golden scabbard, and the iron lance-head was adorned with a silken pennon. There were other smiles to be won than those of senators and they were those which he was justified by the elder knights in valuing more highly than all other rewards of valour. Yet if this was the bright side of tournaments and the youthful ardour they were entered into, they had also their darker aspects, and these no doubt were the chief reasons the Church set her face against them. It would be easy to mention the names of a great number of knights who met in these combats à l'outrance great misadventures. It may suffice to mention Robert, Count of Clermont, son of St. Louis, who from the injuries he received while jousting was all his life after weak in his head; Raoul, Count of Eu, Constable of France, who lost his life in a tournament in 1344 which was held to celebrate the marriage of Philip, son of Philip of Valois; and the tournament held at Nuys where forty-two knights and squires were slain. Still considering the frequency of these combats and the great number engaged in them, the number of those permanently incapacitated or slain was extremely small.

The last day of a tournament was devoted to the ladies. As the knights-bannerets in actual warfare shouted their individual " crie de guerre," so on this occasion, the gallantry of the knights entering the lists, raised their ladies' names as an incentive in the onset. " Lances des Dames " was on this day the name given to the final tourney.

As a combat on horseback, armed with the lance, was considered the most noble in jousting, it was rightly used in the ladies' tourney. It was an old axiom in considering the relative honourable position that lance had to sword, " la lance affranchit l'épée, l'épée, n'affranchit pas lance " (Menestrier), i.e., a lance being the longer weapon could disengage (affranchir) a sword—whereas a sword could with difficulty parry or disengage the lance, the lance therefore was the superior weapon.

It was in this final tourney more even than the preceding days, the ladies' " devices " adorned each faithful cavalier's helm or armour, and at the end of the " Lances des Dames," rightly it was the ladies' hands handed to the victors the prize. It was then, we are told, a kiss was given them by the honoured knight, " lequel les buisa comme il avoit accoustumé," and we are told this was the usual thing to do—" qu'il est de coustume."

Thereupon in the Court of France he cried, " Montjoie," with a loud voice.

Possibly it was then at the feet of his ladye a young knight would uncover his shield for her to see his nobility and paternity; otherwise it was the practice for all tyro knights, entering a tournament for the first time, to carry their shields whitened over. This custom may have been to show that up to that time their careers had been a blank, and that the shield was waiting till their emprises should blazon it in the glowing colours of a chivalrous life.

It is said by one writer on heraldry (Cornish) that the squires who, the night before a tournament, stood at their knights' tents, holding their shields, if those knights had been admitted to former tournaments, held these shields couché (i.e., not upright but slantwise), at all events from these same squires being often, for that purpose, fantastically arrayed, sometimes masquerading in the furs of animals, the origin of " supporters " to arms in heraldry may be found.

As to esquires, very fully were their duties and obligations to the knights gone into in the chapter dealing with them. Here, therefore, it may be briefly said that to have a good squire was almost as important to a knight in " Chevaucie " and tournament as to have a good horse—on him depended often the knight's life, seeing how important it was that his armour was adjusted properly and securely; on his celerity depended bringing a fresh lance into the lists when his master's was shattered; on him depended recovering the knight's helmet if thrown off by his adversary's skill, or if it was loosened, replacing it before engaging. That squires were good, quick and smart was imperative, and no doubt when the knight was about to attend a tournament he chose out of the many noble lads in his castle who had attained squire's rank, the best. An amusing description, however, is appended by Eustace Deschamps where either the young squire had not been chosen judiciously or the lad's own amusements had lured him away from his duties to his lord.

SUR SON VARLET

Bon fait avoir varlet de congnoissance
Qui soit prodoms et saiges par le pais,
Qui de logier ait bonne diligence
Et qui ne soit fètart ne esbahis,
A court de Roy soit appert et sutils,
Au deslogier treuve son maistre en place
Mieulx que n'a fait Jehannin varlet Eustace.

145   K

A KNIGHT'S LIFE

Car a Nemours sanz cheval et sanz lance,
Laissa illec son maistre, li chetis,
Sanz le querre, dont il fut en doubtance
Qui son varlet ne fust rendu fuitis,
Un cheval noir emmenoit et un gris;
Sa male aussi; son senice li face
Mieulx que ne fist Jehannin varlet Eustace.

A donc faisoit trèsorde contenance,
Et bien sembloit qu'il fust desconfis,
Quant Braguemont de ses gens avance
Après le Roy, lors lui fut bons amis.
Il rapporta qu'il fuioit le logis;
S'a bien mestier d'un autre qui lui face
Mieulx que n'a fait Jehan varlet Eustace.

(Good it is to have a young squire of parts
Who will be brave and prudent on the road,
And be very diligent in camp,
And will not be idle or abashed,
At the king's court he must be alert and cunning,
On striking camp he must be at his master's elbow
Better than Jack the squire of Eustace.

For at Nemours without horse or lance
He left his master, the rascal,
Without asking leave, so that he feared
That his squire (varlet) had given him the slip,
A black horse and a grey he led away;
His trunk also could be packed
Better than did Jack the lad of Eustace.

For indeed he (Eustace) made a very wry face,
And truly it seemed as if he were undone—
When Brequemont and his men came on[1]
After the king, for he was his good friend.
He reported that young Jack had fled the camp,
So there is need indeed of another who will serve him
Better than has done John the young squire of Eustace.)

[1] This might mean that Brequemont to help Eustace as his friend goes in his
stead after the king.

CHAPTER X

BESIDES the tourneys and tournaments proper, there was another description of such that certain of the knights amused themselves with, in times of peace, so called " of the Round Table."

Thomas of Walsingham, also Ménestrier in his " Treatise on Chivalry " (Chap. VI., p. 231) assert that Edward III. first instituted these chivalrous games. Du Cange says that this same king built the Round Tower (la Rose) at Windsor Castle to provide a meeting-place for these knights, that the Table therein ran along the walls of the tower, the guests sitting in one side facing inwards, while in the centre the servers, carvers, and minstrels stood. The editor of Ménestrier's " Treatise " asserts that for a long while travellers were shown the veritable Table Arthur and his knights, the romantic originator of the first Round Table used, and that this was at Winchester. Camden, the antiquary, writes as if he had seen it but says the Table was of a far later date than the supposed times of King Arthur.

One thing seems certain, that before the fourteenth century knights of the Round Table were in existence. Matthew Paris mentions such when he says in the year 1252 on the Octave of the Nativity of the Blessed Virgin, very nigh the Abbey of Wallenden, certain knights of the Round Table held a tourney, *i.e.*, " Anno sub Eodem, Milltes ut exercutis militari, suam peritiam et strenuitatem, constituerunt unamiter ut non in hastiludio illo quod communiter Torneamentum ducitur, sed potius in illo militari, qui Mensa Rotunda dicitur, vires suas, attendarent." This passage is valuable as showing the Round Table tournaments, or jousts, were distinct from the ordinary ones. Yet the differences could not have been great. Both required those engaged should be of knightly degree. Both in their combats contended for honour and the praise of arms. Both gave to the victor a prize, and both, the evening of the Festival, sat down to a feast. Sometimes, too, both were held on the same day. So an old writer : " frequenter tamen, non negaverim junge bantur joci robustiores duo." Who then were these knights ? It seems probable that basing their origin on the Arthurian romances, wherein the king sits assembled with his knights, they were a military confraternity who met together at certain times of the year to joust together and then, after these jousts " à plaisance," sat down in amity at a feast. So Ménestrier says, " The Round Table was a sort of festival

147

of arms, in jousts and tournaments. The lists were arranged for such in a round space, so as to be capable of holding a great number of persons in the form of an amphitheatre. It was in England that these fêtes had their origin, and to render them the more celebrated, were called ' the Court of Arthur and his knights.' "

It has been noted above that certain writers give Edward III. the credit of founding this Chivalrous Company, but according to an old writer, Nicholas Trivat (see " History of Priory of Wigmore "), Roger Mortimer was the first founder, who when he had received knighthood invited all the knights of England and those from over sea, to come to a Tournament and Festival of the Round Table at his Castle of Wigmore. Here the feast was served at a Round Table for more than a hundred knights and their ladies, and lasted three days. The prize was a golden lion. After the festivities at Wigmore, he again entertained the same company at his Castle of Kenilworth. Hardynge, in his Chronicle, thus pictures these Round Table festivities :

" And in the yere a thousand and full then
Two hundred also sixty and nynetene
When Sir Roger Mortimer so began
At Kelyngworth the Round Table was sene
Of a thousand knyghts for discipline
Of young menne, after he could devise
Of Turnementes, and jousts to exercise,
A Thousand Ladies, excellyng in beautee
He had also there, in tentes high above
The jousts, that thee might well and clerely see
Who jousted beste, there for their Lady Love,
For whose beautee, it should the knightes move
In armes so eche other to revie
To get a fame in play of Chevalrie."

Whether Mortimer or King Edward was the founder of this Confraternity of Arms and Social Festivities is of little consequence, but what is, is that the king found in the precedents of the Arthurian Round Table and the Paladins of Charlemagne much instruction before he founded the Garter-Order. For this reason, whether a revival of Mortimer's or from his own initiative, he proclaimed in 1344 as well in Scotland, France, Germany, Hainault, Spain and other foreign lands, as in England, his design to revive Arthur's Round Table, offering free conduct and courteous reception to all who might be disposed to attend the splendid jousts to be held on that occasion at the Castle of Windsor.

This solemn. festival, which Edward proposed to render annual, excited the jealousy of Philip Valois, who not only prohibited his subjects to attend the Round Table at Windsor, but proclaimed an opposite Round Table to be held by himself at Paris. In consequence of this interference, the English meeting lost some part of its celebrity and was diminished in splendour and frequency of attendance. Though the Garter-Order the king afterwards founded on this sub-stratum of the Round Table and its jovial knights resembled the

DAYS OF CHIVALRY

latter in some points, he excluded from the Garter much of the licentiousness and carousing of the earlier confraternity.

In the Preface to the Black Book of the Order of the Garter, it is said it was established by Edward that true nobility after long and hazardous adventures should not enviously be deprived of that honour which it hath really deserved, and that active and hardy youth might not want a spur in the profession of virtue which is to be esteemed glorious and eternal.

That the whole fabric of the Knights of the Round Table of Edward's day was founded on the story of Arthur and his knights, none can doubt, chiefly on that written by Robert Wace in his " Romance de Brut," a translation into verse of Geoffrey of Monmouth's Chronicle. So Wace writes :

> " Fist Artus le ronde table
> Dont Bretons dient mainte fable."

According to the Arthurian legend there were thirteen places at Arthur's Round Table in memory of Christ's Apostles, one always unfilled to mark the treachery of Judas, but the other twelve places were filled in rotation by fifty chosen knights.

In these Arthurian legends there seems some affinity between the Round Table therein set forth and that of the Holy Grail.

As it was necessary that the knight who sought the latter should be of spotless character, so only those the most worthy could sit at the king's Round Table.

In two of these romances—the prose " Tristan " and the " Parzival "—the place of the Round Table proper is taken on a journey by a silk cloth laid on the ground, round which the knights are seated. In that of the Holy Grail a journey arduous and long has to be taken by him who would find it. In the versions most closely connected with the Grail story the name of the chosen knight appears on his seat at the Round Table and there is one vacant place, " the Siege Perilous," continually filled by the Grail winners. A student of this subject (Mott) has pointed out that Round Tables exist in many parts of England, the name being associated with circular trenches or rings of stones, which were employed in connection with the agricultural festivals held at Pentecost, Midsummer and Michaelmas. If so, possibly a remnant of Sun worship—where a round or wheel typified that luminary, and the origin of a Round Table may go therefore back through long ages to the Cult of Baal. In Layaman's Romance a magical Table often appears, and could be carried by King Arthur when he rode abroad.

Although not dealing properly with Chivalry, may be here mentioned the armed contests that in France went under the curious name of Toupineures, which bore a certain resemblance to knightly tourneys and the jousts of the Round Table, although the source of them was entirely different. While those of Chivalry were practised and fostered by princes and nobles, these " les toupineures " or " toupinez " were essentially indulged in and fostered by the burgher classes and those below knightly degree. Under different cognomens such as " The Lion," etc., the townsfolk held martial games where they practised with the weapons allowed to their rank, and endeavoured to copy the jousts and the military engagements of the Round Table. Ménestrier mentions thirty-one of the citizens of Tournay, who held such a toupineure which they called a tournament in that city in 1331. So closely were these inferior and civic games considered to be allied to those of Chivalry, that in an Ordinance of King Louis le Hutin they are prohibited in the same Proclamation as the knightly tournaments were. " Que nuls n'allast à Toumoiemens en notre Royaume, ne hors ou feist ne allast a Tupinez " (A.D. 1312).

In England these games were of frequent occurrence, though of course not called toupineures. They took place at the seasons of the great fairs; on some of the chief Saints' days of the Calendar, on times of public rejoicing. Here, of course, also the knightly sword and presence was wanting, and were supplied by the countryman's staff play and the archers' shafts. For the latter reason, contests between these men were much encouraged by the crown, as schools for these famous " bowmen of England " that so often had turned the tide of victory in her favour.

In France after the toupineures had been held, the combatants (here again copying the knights of the Round Table) feasted together. In some places they each brought contributions of game or other dainties to the common board. In ruder England, the conviviality, after the wrestlings, archery and single-sticks were over, took place at the nearest ale-house or wayside inn.

So fascinating even to the lower orders was Chivalry, that its same imitation by the common people existed in Flanders as in France with its toupineures, and in England with its archer contests. Each town, according to Ménestrier, instituted their fêtes, combats and imitations of Chivalric tourneys, and under fanciful names. In Bruges, they had the festival of the Forester; in Valenciennes those of the Prince of Pleasure, in Cambrai that of the King of Ribalds, and Douai the festival of Asses, and so on. The most celebrated of these bourgeoisie fêtes was that of the Little Thorn (Spinette). John Duke of Burgundy condescended in 1460 to honour them with his presence; and in 1464 Philip the Good with Louis XI. was present at it, when a young boy aged fifteen, son of Jean, seigneur of Crouy and Reuty, overthrew in the lists set up and unhorsed one of the strongest men among the French king's followers—Jacques Moyer. All these citizen festivals were originally copied from the knightly ones of the knights of the Round Table, which, from their conviviality and feastings, appealed to the grosser minds of the lower classes more strongly than the classic jousts and tournaments of the nobler Chivalry.

It may be of interest to mention that in the Public Record Office there is a manuscript covering the expenses of the great Wardrobe of Edward III. from December, 1345, to January, 1349, and that some of the articles scheduled cover robes for the person, which were delivered to certain knights taking part in a Round Table held by the king at Lichfield in 1348 and 1349, viz., for the king's persons and seven knights of his chamber. To each of these two yards of blue cloth for coats and three quarters and half a yard of white cloth for hoods. Similar cloth was also issued to some of the other knights.

The challengers or " tenans " of the Round Table consisted of the king and seventeen of his knights; their opponents, the " venans," comprised fourteen knights under the Earl of Lancaster. An entry in the accounts shows that King Edward wore a harness bearing the arms of Sir Thomas Bradeston on this occasion.

These tournaments were celebrated with great pomp and magnificence.

CHAPTER XI

IF jousts, tournaments and martial games were the occupations of knights when not at war, they also, when these were not held, had milder pursuits in their castles and manors. In the enclosures and pits about the latter they had animals, especially boars and bears, with which they amused themselves by making them fight.

If it was warm they sought the orchard to play at dice, chess or even a sort of backgammon, called often " tables." Chess, one of the most ancient of games, was in high favour with knights and their ladies—with the former, because its tactics somewhat resembled their own in many a real battle-field. Indeed, in the medieval castle, it was all that bridge is to the modern country house, and even more, and, at first sight, its popularity among men more distinguished for physical than intellectual powers, seems little short of incredible. A writer on the game (Murray) says this arose partly in the conditions of life of the feudal nobility, and partly in the general demand for new forms of occupation, which was the result of the definite organization of feudalism and the establishment of a stronger central Government in most of the countries of Western Europe.

However that may be, the chief characteristics of the life of the knight, when not at the tourney or the chace, in peace time, were, from the tenth to the twelfth century, his isolation and his lack of regular occupation, and the bleak monotony of everyday existence. The traditions of his order cut him off from the companionship of all save the members of his own family. When he was not fighting or hunting, time hung heavily on his hands; he had no daily duties, no daily responsibilities. The long winter evenings must have been tedious in the extreme; dense forests often intervened between him and his nearest friend; no wonder the jongleur with his budget of song, romance, and tricks, was everywhere warmly welcomed, and that the war game of chess with its hierarchy of pieces which he brought with him (as the disguised Tristam did) was eagerly studied. Chess had no great rivals to contend with at the time of its rapid diffusion through the West. It became the favourite indoor game of the knights, tables or backgammon and " merels " and various forms of dicing being secondary in their estimation.

From A.D. 1100 onwards, literary references to its popularity became more and more numerous, and by the middle of the thirteenth century when the early prejudices of the Church against an invention of heathenesse (for it was introduced from the East) had weakened, ignorance of chess was regarded as a social disability. Among the knights and ladies chess was a necessary part of " Chevalerie," skill in its mimic warfare being looked upon as a sufficient proof of noble descent. (In a former part of this work we have referred to the fact how early the young noble pages were taught it.) In monasteries and nunneries it was accepted as a welcome alleviation of the monotony of convent life and an antidote to that " sorrow of the world " Dante called " accidie." From the communities of religious centres of all medieval culture as they were, chess reached the wealthy merchants of the towns; it was also a favourite diversion in the ghettoes, though the Jews already knew it well from their Eastern brethren. It was also an essential part of the equipment of the troubadour that he should be a chess player, and he generally carried a board and men with him wherever he went; even as it was said and sung by Sir Tristram, travelling disguised as a minstrel:

> " His harpe, his croude (organ) was like
> His tables, his Ches he bare."

The romances of the age are full of allusions to what was " the game of kings." Even the common folk had in their ballad of " Tamerlane " a reference to it.

> " Four and twenty ladies fair
> Were playing at the Chess,
> And out there came the fair Janet
> As green as any grass."

Even in knightly gallantry chess had its place. In the " Clef d'Amors " and other handbooks on the gay science it was declared no other diversion afforded such opportunities of dalliance and platonic love as chess. So the medieval romances give many examples of the value of chess as a means to bring lovers together, for it was permissible to visit a lady in her chamber or " bower " to play chess with her. Thus in " Raoul de Cambrai," Beatrix falls in love with the young Bernier, but he is too shy to accept her advances, so she invites him to play at chess or tables with her in her chamber in order to give him a chance of declaring himself, which he did, and was rewarded with many proofs of her love. So in the Arthurian Romance, Lancelot visited Guinevere in her bower and Tristram visited Yseult under the pretence of playing chess. Some ladies excelled the men in this favourite game. In " Les Echez Amoureux," there is a lady such, whose skill is thus described in our early poet Lydgates' translation:

> " And this mayde of which I telle
> Had a name and dyde excelle
> To pleyen at this noble play
> She passed alle, yt ys no nay,
> And was expert and knyw full well
> At the maner every dell.
> There was not fonde to reckne all,
> That was in craft to her egall,
> For she surmountede every choon."

Generally speaking, chess was confined to the castles; in the Romances it is mentioned as a matter which no merchant or mechanic could properly understand or appreciate. The fact that a menial knew anything of chess at once aroused suspicion. Thus Huon of Bordeaux, disguised as the servitor of a travelling minstrel, found his word was doubted when he boasted of his skill at chess, and in Gautier de Coincy's " Nouvelles de la Sainte Vierge," written about the year 1230, there is a story how the devil who had disguised himself as a servant, was discovered because he could play chess, and therefore could be no servant. Still chess appears to have been played at taverns, for Wycliff attacks the clergy of his time for going to inns to play " tables, chess and hasard," until " thei han lost there witt."

Another game, that of dice, was in a secondary degree to chess a favourite with the knights, and both dicing schools (scolædeciorum) and gilds existed of dicers. Many of the dice of the Middle Ages were curiously carved in the images of men and beasts. In France both knights and their ladies were very prone to dicing and though St. Louis in 1254 interdicted it, he did so vainly. Some have traced the origin of dice to knucklebones or else to small pebbles played in the old game of " odd and even." That the game had a long ancestry is certain. Virgil, in a poem attributed to him, says :

> " What ho ! Bring dice and good wine,
> Who cares for to-morrow ? "

Dice were forbidden by Councils to the clergy—yet still they played. The tale " Du prêtre at des deux ribauds " tells of a curé who lost his money and even his horse at playing at dice with two fiddlers whom he chanced to meet on his way. The highwaymen had cheated; their dice was loaded and it was with no little trouble the curé obtained his horse, but not his money. Adam of Perseigne, a preacher of the period, among other charges against his brother clergy says, " They play at dice, instead of administering Sacraments, the Churches instead of being holy places, have become market places and haunts of brigands."

If with these games the knights in time of peace amused themselves when either summer heat or winter storm kept them indoors, their days were fully occupied at other times by that, of all amusements most favoured, the Chace. It had the nearest similarity to actual warfare, and shared with the tourney therefore an inexpressible fascination for their warlike hearts. From earliest childhood (as has been noted in a previous part of this work) its orders, its duties, and its delights they had been encouraged to pursue. The wide spreading forests that then covered Europe, including the isle of Britain, the lair of the wolf, the wild boar and the deer, had an inexpressible fascination for all of noble and knightly birth in the days of Chivalry, which we at this distance of time can hardly realize.

This ardour in the chace, not only in England where William the Conqueror devastated whole villages to form a new forest and whence he was said to love the deer as if he had been their father, and where

DAYS OF CHIVALRY

the penal laws against depredations in the forests were punishable with loss of limbs and severe fines, but in France, too, was remarkable. Louis XI. when laid up in his last illness and unable to hunt, made a mimic chace in his chamber and ordered an enormous number of rats to be let loose in it, with an equal number of cats, so the pursuit of his favourite pastime might still go on. Even in books of devotion or religion, terms used in the chace were employed. An Abbé Michel, living in the reign of Francis I. thus begins his book: " I commence with the Forest of Conscience, which contains the chace of spiritual princes and pastors," and so, under the form of hunting he portrays the soul contending against the wild beasts which represent the sins and evils of life. The fear of God, Holy Love, Confession, Penitence, Satisfaction, Retreats, etc., are the Hounds the Christian is to employ in this Spiritual Chace—even to-day, a modern poet's most thought-of work is on similar lines, and is called " The Hound of Heaven," but whether like the medieval abbé inspired by the love of modern hunting, is problematical.

Falconry, one branch of the chace, was indulged in by both the knights and the wealthy clergy, and an extraordinary importance was attributed to the possession, and the use, of these little birds of prey. Property in them was inviolate. They were inseparably connected with the aristocratic and personal privileges of their owner and could not be alienated even with his consent, to make up the ransom of their master if he had haply been taken prisoner. Persons of plebeian station were not permitted to purchase or to keep them. They were usually recognized symbols of suzerainty. For this reason kings, bishops, and noble ladies never went abroad without their birds on their fists. Knights even carried them into battle. Prelates deposited them in the chancel while they recited the service of the altar. A Bishop of Ely in the fourteenth century excommunicated for sacrilege the thieves who stole a falcon from her perch in the cloister of the Abbey of Bermondsey, " the falcon being the bishop's own," and the theft being committed while a service in the Church was going on.

Though it has been stated above no one under knightly rank was allowed to possess or fly a falcon, this statement must be so modified that it applies only to the beautiful ger-falcon, for it is certain others than knights went a-hawking. Their birds were of a different species. For the priest there was the sparrow-hawk, for a knave (squire) the kestrel, for a yeoman the gos-hawk. However, even these sometimes were used by those of knightly rank for the chace. Sir Thopas carried a gos-hawk, and the sparrow-hawk that angered Geraint was not a priest's. Such an etiquette was preserved towards the noblest and lower-estimated birds of all sorts, that there is a story of Louis IX. when he was out hawking that one of his birds, a beautiful and strong bird, dared to attack an eagle. The courtiers praised its valliance but the king seeing it had attacked the noblest of birds—the eagle— ordered it to be killed, " parce qu'il avoit eu la téméraire audace a'attaquer le Roi des oiseaux."

The regulations of falconry constituted a science only to be mastered after months of assiduous study. The education of these birds required the exertion of great skill. Each falcon was carried on a glove which could not be used for any other purpose. It bore the arms of the knight or lord and was often embroidered with gold and precious stones. In many kingdoms the office of Grand Falconer was one of the highest of distinctions. In France the emoluments of this dignity were eighty thousand francs a year. Even on entering on the long and arduous war between his own country and France, Edward III. could not do without his falcons. Froissart says of him : " Et avec ce avoit bien pour lui trente Fauconniers à cheval charges d'oiseaux," also sixty couples of fierce hunting dogs and greyhounds which along the river bank he used for the chace as he penetrated into France at the head of his army. This, of course, was when he had days of peace in his expedition, for the idea of peace in the minds of men of the Middle Ages associated itself naturally with that of the chace. So in the " Lay of Girart de Rousillon," " Now the knights enter upon a long rest ; this will be a propitious time for dogs, vultures, falcons, falconers and huntsmen." On another page of the same poem we have King Charles Martel when he had ceased making war on his vassals or on the Saracens, saying to his barons, " Let us hunt by the river and in the woods ; that is much better than staying at home." The chace was not merely a way for knights to escape inactivity, it was a passion, often even such a mania that the Church was obliged to condemn it, and this for many reasons. First, because the noble knight, preoccupied with roving the forest, forgot even religious services, and then because the harshness of the laws which regulated the exercise of the chace and the forests and game, things sacred and inviolable, became in many respects an intolerable scourge to the peasantry and his crops. For one noble who relaxed the forest laws, far more maintained them with untold cruelty and greed.

Henry II. of England restored all these forest laws of his predecessors, which provided that any man found guilty of hunting in the royal forests, without a licence, should have his eyes put out and his limbs mutilated. This made William of Newburgh, a chronicler of the time, say that Henry II. punished the killing of a deer as severely as the murder of a man. The French were nearly as ruthless. Several years after the death of King Philip Augustus, Enguerrand de Courcy hanged three unfortunate young nobles of Flanders, who had hunted upon his lands. Possibly from these being of noble birth the king committed Enguerrand to prison and did not release him until he had promised to pay a fine of ten thousand francs and make a pilgrimage to the Holy Land.

The fanciful imagination of these ages found a type in different sections of the community in different animals of the chace. The " Third-Estate " or Commons was represented by female dogs and greyhounds, because of their stupidity and want of wit. The Ecclesiastics by stags, because their probity and high character allowed them to march through life like the stag, with his head held high, and because their six fingers held up at the Elevation of the Mass represented the six " points " of a stag's antlers, and the six commandments. On the other hand the wild boar typified the corruptness of the age and had ten bad propensities, which represented the ten commandments of anti-Christ.

Though the infractions of the " forest-laws," both in England and France, were extremely severe, and these vast and leafy hills and dales kept for the use of the king or certain nobles who owned them, licences were frequently given to certain favoured individuals to follow the chace in them under the sovereign's or lord's permission. Thus Geoffrey de Meller, an ancestor of the present writer, in 1257 had from the king, a free grant of hunting in the counties of Nottingham, Northampton and Derby. Richard de Radcliffe received a grant of free warren and of hunting in Bury and lands adjoining from King Edward I. for his services in the Scottish wars. Even as early as the time of the Saxons such grants were issued. Here is a curious one of a grant of forestry and its denizens in the reign of Edward the Confessor :

> " Iche Edward Konyng
> Have given of my forest the keping
> Of the hundred of Chelmer and Dancing
> To Randulph Peperking and to his kindling,
> With Harte and Hinde, Doe and Bokke
> Hare and Foxe, Catt and Brocke
> Wild Foule with his Flocke
> Patrick, Fesaunte-Hen and Fesaunte-Cocke ;
> With Green and Wilde, Stob and Stokk
> To kepen and to yemen by all her might,
> Both by Day and eke by Night
> And Hounds for to holde
> Good swift and bolde ;
> Four Grey houndes and six Raches
> For Hare and Fox and Wild Cattes,
> And therefore Ich made him by Booke.
>
> Witenes the Bishop Wolstan
> And Book ylered many on,
> And Swayne of Essex our Brother
> And teken him many other
> And our Steward Howelin
> That besought me for him."

(Inter Record. de Term, Sci. Hilarii 17. Ed. II. penes Thes. et Camerar. Scaccarii, Camd : Brit. Essex.)

Another grant runs concerning the lands of Hopton, Co. Salop :

> " To me and to myne, to thee and to thine
> While the water runs and the sun doth shine
> For lack of Heyrs to the king againe
> I William king, the third year of my reign
> Give to the Norman Hunter
> To me that art both dine and Deare
> The Hoppe and Hoptoune
> And all the Bounds uppe and doune
> Under the earth to Hell
> Above the earth to Heaven,
> From me and from mine
> To thee and to thine
> As good and as faire
> As ever they myne were

A KNIGHT'S LIFE IN

To Witness that this Sooth
I bite the White Wax with my tooth
Before Jugg, Marode and Margery
And my third son Henry
For one Bow and one Broad Arrow
When I come to hunt upon Yarrow."

("This Grant made by William the Conqueror to the antient family of Hopton I copied out of an old MSS. and John Stowe has it in his Chronicle," so writes Robert Glover the Herald in an MS. of Co. Salop. Cited in "Antient Tenures," by Thomas Blount, 1784.)

Our ancestors carried the art of hunting very thoroughly out and one of the most explicit and curious treatises on it, as far as this country is concerned, is the "Book of St. Albans," written by Dame Juliana Berners. There is also a rare book written by William Twici, Huntsman to King Edward II.; it has been edited by H. Dryden (1908). From these and other sources we find the following were the chief dogs employed by the knights and nobles in the chace :

(1) The Lymer (from the old French word "liamen," "a strap") these hounds being held on leash. They were a heavy smooth-haired black and tan hound, standing about twenty-seven inches high, resembling a bloodhound. Some lymers were white, however, and the Count de Foix in his book on the Chace gives it as his opinion that the White Hounds were imported from Barbary, and in many points showed traces of Spanish pointer blood. The man who held the lymer was called "harbourer," and it was his business to go out early in the morning on his ring-walks and to find by this hound where a hart or other beast had gone into the wood. He then informed the huntsman.

(2) Another breed of dog were the "braches," mostly in colour black and tan, standing about seventeen or eighteen inches in height. They were hunted in packs. Sometimes they were called "ratches." They were dogs that had a sharp scent of the quarry and were much used in hunting the hare.

(3) Then there was the greyhound, also called the "gaze-hound," because it is said "the beams of his sight are so stedfastly settled." The word "Greyhound" seems to have had no connection with the colour; by some it is thought to have come from the Celtic "Gre"—large or noble. In old illuminations they are always depicted wearing collars, and in the old Welsh laws all greyhounds without their collars lost their privileges. They also were chiefly employed chasing the smaller animals.

(4) Alaunts were another breed. This dog was swift and could hunt by scent alone, and in consequence of their ferocity were used for bears and boars, and were commonly muzzled when not at work. Their best colour was white with black spots about their eyes. Another name was that of "wolf-hound." The Lord Dacre of Fynnys bore on his standard a wolf-dog, or alaunt, argent. In late peerages Lord Dacre's "supporter" is erroneously stated to be a wolf, whereas it was an alaunt or wolf-dog. In the "Royal Wills" (Nicholl) John of Gaunt bequeathed to his "très chere filtz Henry duc de Hertford, Comte de Derby, mon grant lit de drap d'or, le champ piers overez

158

des arbres d'or, et juxte chescun arbre un alaunt blank (a white alaunt dog) liez a mesme l'arbre."

In France, during his imprisonment by the Saracens in Egypt, St. Louis met with a fine breed of dogs said to have come from Tartary. On his release and return to France some of these dogs he brought with him, and they formed the fine breed of hunting dogs that till the Revolution filled the royal kennels (St. Palaye).

As perquisites in medieval hunting, the huntsman had the hide of the animal given him, and the villein who flayed the deer, the head and shoulders. The huntsman often also claimed to take the skin of the fox for his own, and also to claim the skin of an ox in winter for his hounds' leashes, and of a cow in summer for boots. The dogs' reward was called a " quyrrere " (or quarry) because the portion of the prey was eaten on the hide (sur le quir).

The chief music used in hunts was performed on veritable " horns " of slain animals. They were about one foot six inches long and were often elaborately carved. So in the Issue Roll of 10 Ric. II. (1386) : " To the Lord the king in his chamber by the hands of John Bottesham of London, goldsmith, for a knife to be used in the woods and a horn ornamented with gold weighing sixteen ounces less one drachm of gold and made by him for the lord the king for his hunting horn and tassels of green silk for the same."

As the horn of the fourteenth century had only one note, the difference of the blowings was expressed by the duration of that note. The author of " La Chace dou Cerf," written about 1250, mentions " lonc mot," " chasse," " apel," " menée," and " prise." The first explains itself ; chasse appears to have been a number of short notes ; the apel consists of three long moots ; " menée " and " prise " are not explained. Gaston Count de Foix gives some directions for halloing and blowing (huer et corner), but they are brief because he says that the cries differ according to the country in which they are used and according to the beast pursued.

In chasing the wild animals it seemed the usual custom for the knight or his hunter to cry " Soho," thus in the " Book of St. Albans " :

> " All manner of beasts whatsoever chased be
> Have one manner of woord *soho* I tell thee,
> To fulfill or unfill all maner of chase
> The hunter in his mouth that word hase."

There are many entries concerning the keep of hounds by which it appears that the huntsman in the thirteenth and fourteenth centuries kept the hounds and was allowed a halfpenny a day for each dog of all breeds, as in the Wardrobe Account of Edward I. 28, there is a payment of £9 3s. to the king's fox-hunter for the keep of twelve foxhounds at a halfpenny a day each.

In the " Book of Courtesy," written about 1460 to instruct the young pages and varletons in a knight's household, under " De Venatore et suis Carribus," it is said :

> " A ha'penny the hunt takes on the day
> For every hound, the sooth to say

Two cast (handfuls) of bread has the fewterer (keeper)
If two leash greyhounds there are,
To each a bone that is to tell
If I the sooth to you shall spell
Besides his vantage (profit) that may befall
Of skins and other things withal.
That hunters better can tell than I
And therefore I leave it utterly."

We have in " Le Livre de la Chasce," by Gaston Comte de Foix, and in " The Master of Game," written between the years 1406-13 by Edward II., Duke of York, who fell at the battle of Agincourt, 1415, full descriptions of the hounds' kennel. The lodging-room is to be ten fathoms long and five broad, with one door in front and one behind into a green court of the same size, facing the sun. It is to be paved, and to have a fireplace in it and gutters. The bench and room are to be cleaned every day and fresh straw brought in. There is to be a loft over the room to prevent extremes of heat and cold, and a " childe " (young lad) is to live in the lodging-room " to prevent quarrels."

Constantly we find in the old manor-rolls the obligation of the holder to contribute towards the pleasure of the overlord, by lending his hawks or his hounds. Thus William Eugaine holds Pightesley and Laxton under William the Conqueror by the sergeantry of hunting wolves, foxes and other vermin; and in the reign of Henry III. Humphrey de Monte held the Manor of Whitfield by sergeantry of providing a " brache " (hound) for the king whenever he should come to the forest of Whittlebury to hunt hart, hind, buck or doe.

As to the royal falcons, in many places the manors were held " in capite " from the king for preserving them, thus (as only one instance) Philip de Hertrug held certain lands in Hertrug, Co. Beds., which were worth forty shillings a year by the Sergeantry of Mewing and keeping one gos-hawk for the lord the king. (Plac. Cor.)

The servants employed in the chace were generally on foot both in France and England, but the knight rode, and in the greater households, the huntsman. The costume of the servants seem for a very long period to have little changed—not so their master's, which altered with the changing years, but the latter always seems to have worn, whatsoever the colour and fabric, long loose robes, close-fitting caps, probably of cloth, tied under the chin.

It has already been mentioned that nearly the earliest books on the Chace in England are Dame Juliana's " Book of St. Albans " and " The Art of Hunting " by William Twici, Huntsman to King Edward II. There is also for France " Documents relatifs à Jean roi de France." This work is of special interest as it was begun in England when Gace, whose verses are incorporated in it, a priest who was a great falconer, came with King John of France and his fourth son Philip into England after the battle of Poitiers. This work was commenced by the order of King John at Hereford in order that his son might be taught the rules of the chace in 1359. When the Chaplain returned to France it was finished at Paris somewhere about the year 1373. But even earlier than the " Book of St. Albans " in the English

BISHOP WYVIL AND HIS CHAMPION.

From Coulton's Mediæval Garner.

DAYS OF CHIVALRY

tongue is the book referred to in the preceding pages " The Master of Game," written between years 1406-13 by Edward, Duke of York. Another little French work quoted above is " Le Livre de la Chasce " par Gaston III., Comte de Foix, a rare and interesting little book.

A graphic description of a medieval fox-hunt is given in the ancient poem *circa* 1360, " Sir Gawayne and the Green Knight." It has been paraphrased and translated by Kenneth Hare. Two verses describing the end of the hunt are given.

" Nimbly adown to earth doth that lord light,
And caught and overhead bore high his prey,
Thither the nearer huntsmen speed aright
To mark the brave hounds all aloud that bay,
Faint the recheat is sounded far away
Till gathered is that company all whole
Whose loud hallooing closes up the day
While all that ever bore bugle blows his dole
So merry do they raise the Mass for Reynard's soul.

They stroke their gallant hounds and fee them well,
Then turn back home tearing off Reynard's coat,
The purple twilight gathers in the dell,
Their mighty horns they blow with lusty throat
Full stoutly, so they come by ditch and moat
And find a great fire on the floor agood,
And Gawayne and that company of note—
His blue robes trail to ground right as they should
Brave is his furred surcoat and noble hangs his hood."

The fox, the deer, the boar and the wolf were the chief animals of the larger breed hunted by the knights in England.

The fox is with us still, the red deer still left for a time, in diminished numbers, on Exmoor; but the wild boar and wolf are now extinct, the former once abounded in Britain. Traces have been found of its survival in Chartley Park, Staffordshire, in an entry of 1683. This is in an account extant of the then steward of the manor.

The boar is one of the four heraldic beasts of venery, and the well-known badge of Richard III.

As to the wolf, these were numerous in Saxon England. So much so that a patriotic Saxon built a retreat for travellers pursued by them, at Flixton, near Filey, and this probably was one of many set up against their attacks on the unfortunate wayfarer. In Henry III.'s reign grants of lands were made on the obligation attached of destroying wolves on them. In Edward II.'s reign the Peak in Derbyshire is particularly mentioned as infested with them, and so it was down till the reign of Henry VII. (1485-1509) when wolves seem to have become very rare, if not extinct, in England. In the wild hills and glens of the neighbouring kingdom of Scotland, they existed much longer, and it is said that the last wolf was killed here by Sir Evan Cameron of Lochiel in 1680.

In France, the land pre-eminently of Chivalry and its kindred sport—the chace—all these beasts were even more numerous than in Britain, and in Brittany still at night is often heard the weird cry of the wolf. Some such dog employed there for the chace of the wolf was no doubt that in the following quintrain, the earliest notice in the Middle Ages of a dog's name—at the time of the Norman Conquest.

> " William de Conigby
> Came out of Brittany,
> With his wife Tiffany,
> And his maide Maufas,
> And his dogge Hardigras."
> —Prof. ad John de Fordun, Scots Chronicon.

The terms used in " Venerie " were extremely quaint, so, too, was the ceremonial which took place in a well officered chace. To take one instance—to " brittle " or " break " the deer (in French " faire la curée ") meant, in plain terms, to flay and disembowel the stag, a matter on which much precision was required, and the rules of which were ascribed to the celebrated Sir Tristram of Lyonesse. It was an indispensable requisite for the young noble squire to acquire these terms of venerie. Nor did his concern with venison end here; he placed it on the table, he waited during the banquet, and carved it on one of the ponderous trenchers of the period. Much grace and delicacy were supposed to be displayed on these occasions. In one Romance we read of the high birth and breeding of the young squire being ascertained by his scrupulously declining to use a napkin to wash his hands before he began to carve the venison, and contented himself with waving them in the air till they dried of themselves. All the various parts of a stag had its appropriate names couched in the strange jargon of the chace. And if it was so with the stag, so too with the wild boar, and other animals hunted by the knights, each had peculiar and individual terms given them.

For example, it has been mentioned cutting up the deer was called " breaking," but carving a joint of venison at dinner was called " breking," so in Wynkyn de Worde's " Booke of Servinge," " Breke that dere, imbrace that mallard."

A hart was, when skinned, said to be " flean," a hare " cased," a boar " stripped," a buck " skinned," a fox " cased," an otter " cased." Different terms were used to " dislodge " an animal. It was to " unharbour " a hart, to " start " a hare, to " rear " a boar, to " raise " a wolf, to " rouse " a buck, to " find " a fox, to " bay " a marten, to " dig " a badger, to " bolt " a coney (rabbit).

After a hunt if the king were present—if the quarry had been the wild boar—at dinner its tusks were, with its head, presented to him with much joy on his part, " avec grand plaisir." The hunters in his presence recited the chief events of the day, particularly anything marvellous, " qui appretent a rire au Roy," omitting anything in their tale which was not laughable or joyous—hence came the proverb :

> " De chiens, d'oiseaux, d'armes, d'amour
> Pour une joie cent doulours."

The pursuit of the boar was esteemed by the knights the noblest in the chace; minute directions in the old books on " Venerie " are devoted to the subject. We are told a boar should be attacked on horseback, preferably to on foot—that the spear should be long, broad, and sharp; that attacking him is a greater feat than attacking an armed man, " est plus redoutable qui celle d'un homme armé mais la victoire en est aussi bien glorieuse," and what joy, an old writer says, to sup afterwards off him and to hand round the delicious morsels. Then the hunt should be at moonlight, so as to give the dogs opportunity to find him, and these dogs should also be chosen young and strong to seize him by the throat, " colleter avec lui." As to the wolf, a pit or trap in the woods well baited with pieces of meat should be prepared and thorny branches put up to prevent his exit. Then when sighted he should be driven into this trap with loud cries and beating of sticks, for the wolf separated from the pack is always a cowardly beast.

CHAPTER XII

A KNIGHT'S MENIE

As the age of Chivalry progressed, not only in manners but in the way of living, greater refinement crept in. Those wind-entered, grey castles which have been described in the earlier part of this book became better adorned, their chambers with greater comforts, and the "menie" or household they sheltered not, as earlier, a mere throng of rough and mailed men, but servants under the knights, squires, each apportioned to their domestic duties.

Froissart has given us a very striking account of the mode of house-keeping in the family of Gaston, Count of Foix, a prince whose court was considered not only of a noble but of a knightly pre-eminence. Froissart lived in his house about twelve weeks, much recommended to Gaston on account of having brought with him a book containing all the songs, ballads, and virilays which Wencelaus of Bohemia, the gentle Duke of Brabant, had made and the historian himself had compiled or transcribed.

"Every night after supper," says Froissart, "I read therein to him, and while I read there was none durst speak anything to interrupt me, so much did the Count delight in listening." He then follows with some account of the arrangement of this knight's household, which we render in less obsolete English.

"This Earl Gascon of Foix with whom I was at that time, was then fifty-nine years of age, and I declare I have in my time seen many knights, kings, princes and others but I never saw anyone like him in person, not of so fair a form, nor so well made. His countenance sanguine, fair, and smiling, his eyes grey and amorous whenever he chose to cast them; in every way he was so perfect he could not be praised too much. He loved that which ought to be loved, he hated that which ought to be hated. He was a very wise knight, also of high enterprise and of right good counsel. He never had a bad person about him. He said many orisons every day, a nocturn of the Psalter, and matins of Our Lady, and of the Holy Ghost and of the Cross, and a dirge every day. He gave five florins, in small coins every day to the poor about his gate for the love of God. He was generous and courteous in his gifts. . . . He loved hounds above all animals for winter and summer he loved the chace. . . . Every month he took account what he spent. He changed in rotation (to escape fraud) those who received his monies every two months. He had certain coffers in his own chamber out of which

164

ofttimes he would himself take money to give to lords, knights, and others who came to him, for he would have none depart giftless. . . .

"At midnight when he came out of his chamber into the hall to supper, he had ever borne before him twelve torches burning, carried by twelve young pages or squires standing before his table all supper time; they gave a great light, and the hall was ever full of knights and squires, and many other tables set for those who wished to sup. But none were allowed to address him at his own table unless he was called upon to do so. His meat was a little wild fowl composed of the wings and legs only, and during each day he ate and drank sparsely.

"He had great pleasure in musical instruments, on which he himself was a performer, and that right well. So he had songs sung before him, and other musical things as he sat at table . . . none rejoiced more in brave deeds of arms than he did, so there was seen in his hall and courtyard knights and squires of prowess going up and down and conversing in arms and love passages."

The household of a knight was, as before observed, called his "menie," later his "family." This latter did not consist solely, as in modern sense, of his wife and children or relations, but of his whole household of servants and retainers. A great part of the duties which are not relegated to the lower orders of domestics were then performed by pages, damoiselles, and young squires of gentle and often noble degree. Such considered it in the Middle Ages no disgrace to do many services in a brave knight's "menie" which their posterity to-day would utterly refuse to do. One of the most curious and illustrative books dealing with such duties is that edited by the late Dr. Furnivall, entitled "Divers Treatises Touching the Manners and Meals of Englishmen of Former Days." One of these treatises, "The Book of Courtesy," well illustrates this subject. We must suppose from numerous hints and descriptions that an elaborate system of manners and customs prevailed long before they were codified in any treatise such as this. Thus for instance the Bayeux Tapestry of the eleventh century shows a feast, with a page or server kneeling, his napkin round his neck, long before the author of "The Book of Courtesy" prescribing such, wrote and lived (*circa* 1460.)

Dr. Furnivall quotes an old pamphlet summing up the ancient point of view of such a knight and his young squire. "Amongst what sort of people should then a serving-man be sought for? Even a duke's son preferred page to the prince, the earl's son attendant upon the duke, the knight's second son the earl's servant, the esquire's son to wear the knight's livery and the gentleman's son the esquire's serving-man. Yes, I know at this day gentlemen, younger brothers, that wear their elder brothers' blue coat and badge, attending him with reverent regard and dutiful obedience, as if he were their prince or sovereign. The one holding the plough, the other whipping the cart horse, labouring as honest men in their vocation." Indeed under the system of entail and devolution of feudal estates, this was, in time of peace, the only possible livelihood for a gentleman's younger son. Few of knights' sons ever went into the Church, or had any aptitude to study law. Debarred from trade he could only at his family's bidding offer his services to some good knight or lord who by his estate kept up a large household.

In the household of Lord Percy there were nine young " henchmen," noble lads who served him as cupbearers and in various menial offices, in his household. In this same lord's menie, his second son was carver, his third son sewer. Therefore in this " Book of Courtesy " from which extracts are made, the admonitions are to these gentle-born lads who were filling in a knight's house, many of these offices.

De Officiariis in Curiis Dominorum.

" Now of officers speak will we
Of court, and also of their duty (mestiers)
Four men there be that yards shall bear;
Porter, marshal, steward, usher,
The porter shall have the longest wand,
The marshal a shorter shall have in hand."

Per quantum Tempus Armigeri habebunt Liberatam et ignis ardebit in aula?

(For how long shall Squires have Liveries and Fire burn in hall?)

" So long squires liveries shall have
Of groom of hall, or else his knave
But fire shall burn in hall at meat
Until ' Cena Domini ' (Maundy Thursday) men have eat.
There brought shall be a holly keen
That set shall be in arbour green
And that shall be till All-Hallows Day
And oft be shifted as you I say,
In hall marshal all men shall set
After their degree, without let."

De Pincernario, Panetario et Cocis sibi Servientibus.

(Of the Butler, Pantler and Cooks as servants to him.)

" The butler, pantler, and cooks also
To him are servants without mo (more)
Therefore on his yard score shall he
All messes in hall that served shall be
Command to set both bread and ale
To all men that served be in hall,
To gentlemen with heated drink
Else fails the service, as I think.
Each mess at sixpence booked shall be
At the counting-house with other meiny," etc.

De Officio Pincernarii.

" Butler shall set for each mess
A pot, a loaf, without distress (without being compelled)
Butler, pantler, fellows are aye," etc.

DAYS OF CHIVALRY

De Hostiario et suis Servientibus.
(Of the Usher and his servants.)

" Speak I will a little while
Of usher of chamber without guile,
There is a gentle man, yeomen-usher also,
Two grooms at the least, a page thereto."

De Officio Garcionum.
(Of the groom's office.)

" ' Grooms ' (these evidently from other sources were young squires)
Shall make litter and stuff pallets out
Nine foot in length without doubt,
Seven foot certainly shall it be broad
Well watered and bound together, craftily trod
With wisps drank out at feet and side,
Well twisted and turned again, that tide
Unsunken in hollows shall it be made
Both outer and inner so God me glad.
And hooks and loops on bands shall follow.
The valance on a rod shall hang with state
Since curtains drawn within full straight,
That reach even to the ground about.

.   .   .   .   .   .

The counterpane he lays on the bed's feet
Cushions on the side shall meet,
Carpets of Spain on the floor beside
That spread should be for pomp and pride.
Three perchers (big candles) of wax then shall he get
Above the chimney that be set,
In socket each one from other shall be.

The usher (squire) always shall sit at door
At meat, and shall walk on the floor—
To see that all be served aright."

In another little treatise " The Book of Nature," we read what
the young squire of the bed-chamber should also do.   " When he
(the knight) has supped and goes to his chamber, spread forth your
foot-sheet, take off his gown, and lay it up in such place as ye best
know.   Put a mantle on his back to keep his body from cold, set him
on the foot-sheet, pull off his shoes, socks and hosen and throw these
last over your shoulder.   Comb his hair, but first kneel down and put
his kerchief and nightcap around and over in seemly fashion."
(There is no mention here of a dress for the night.   It was the custom
for rich and poor to lie naked in bed.)   " Have the bed, head-sheet
and pillow ready and when he is in bed draw the curtains round
about it and see that there is enough night-light to last the night."
Then follows this amusing direction.   " Drive out the dog and the
cat, giving them a clout; take no leave of your lord, but bow low to
him and retire."

Of course one of the most useful servants in a knightly household was the squire of the stables. So " The Book of Courtesy " goes on and says :

De Avenerio.

" The avener shall provender wisely ordain
All the lord's horses to maintain,
They shall have two cast of hay
A peck of provender in a day.
Every horse shall have so much
At rack and manger that stands with staff
(*i.e.*, a bar before the hayrack).
There is a master of horses—a squire,
Under him avener and farrier,
These yeomen old saddles shall have
That shall be last for knight and knave.
For each horse a farrier shall shoe
A ha'penny a day he takes him to,
Under the grooms and pages many a one
That be at wages every one
Soom at twopence a day,
And soom at three-farthings I you say."

There was much ceremony always at the chief meal in knightly times. The tables were, it is true, only trestles, but very minute directions are given both in this little work quoted above and others for laying and removing the table-cloth.

" At either end he casts a cope (covering)
Laid down on board, the ends turned up
That he assays kneeling on knee.

.   .   .   .   .   .

The announcing squire or else a knight
The towel down takes by full good right."

Again :

" The towel two knights together shall bear
Before the lord's sleeves that be so dear "—

(this is for washing the hands)

" The over basin they hold
While the carver pours water into the nether."

The squire of the table is to have a napkin.

" Small towel upon his neck shall be seen
To cleanse his knives that be so keen."

Then our ancestors ever remembered the poor.

" The almoner by this hath said Grace,
And the alms-dish hath set in place
Therein the carver a loaf shall set
To serve God first without let;

.   .   .   .   .   .

168

DAYS OF CHIVALRY

The almoner a rod shall have in hand
An office for alms I understand,
All the broken meat he keeps I wot
To deal to poor men at the gate,
And drink that is left served in hall
Of rich and poor, both great and small."

The hall was lighted by torches, or candles; the squire who dealt
out and looked after the candles therefore held an important post.
These were made of the poorer sort of tallow, but the rich had them
made of wax, " of wax thereto if ye take tent."

" In hall at supper shall candles burn
Of Paris, therein that all men ken
Each mess a candle from All-Hallows Day.
To Candlemas, as I you say
Of candles delivery squires shall have
So long if it is that man will crave.
Of bread and ale also the butler
Shall make delivery throughout the year
To squires, and also wine to knight
Or else he doth not his office right.
Here endeth the third speech,
Of all our sins Christ be our leech
And bring us to his dwelling-place !
' Amen,' say ye, for his great grace,
   Amen, par charité.''

The chief article on the knight's table was the silver ship which
formed the salt-cellar, for as no salt was used in cooking till a late
period in the Middle Ages, it was needful to be added at the table.
This cellar was called " the Nef." It constituted the gradation of
rank, for the host, his relatives and guests sat above it, his ordinary
" menie " below it.

There were no forks and no instruments for helping from the
dishes. Each person had a knife and spoon which he licked or wiped
upon his bread before using them in the common dish.

The bowl of water which preceded and followed became a
necessity. In some rich households in addition to the chief meal
there was one called a " Void." It consisted in wines and spices and
dried fruits; these latter were many of them brought by Crusaders
to this country. Thus plums from Syria, damsons from Damascus.
Jellies and gingerbread and pickles are mentioned in the letter book
of Edward II. Bread and butter dates from the reign of Edward IV.,
before which dripping was always used.

Chemists in those days dealt in sweetmeats, and spices, and
strange to say, the brewers were always women. About as late as
1470 peers were allowed five dishes at a meal, besides their pottage,
gentlemen three, meaner persons two. The meat was always under-
done, over-cooked meat was thought to provoke the tempers of those
who ate it.

Bread was of many kinds. " Simnel " or " manchet " was the

finest; " wassel " was the best common quality; " cocket " the inferior; " muslin " was made of barley, wheat and oats mixed.

Christmas bread was made of fine flour, eggs and milk. There was also " spice-bread," still found in the north of England. Griddle-cakes were then peculiar to Wales.

Macaroons are as old as Chaucer.

Ale was brewed with hops. Fried beans were greatly used in Lent. Cucumber and melons were extensively eaten during these ages, and lemon juice (after the lemon had been introduced from the south of Europe) was largely used with fish and meat, as acids were very popular with our forefathers.

Another peculiarity in these knightly times as regards food was that not only by the chairs they sat on, the dishes they were served in, was rank marked, but the way the meat was apportioned. A whole animal, whether fish, flesh or fowl, was only for a lord or knight of high degree. When the master of the house and his guests were commoners, everything down to a lark must be " hewed on gobbets," namely, cut into small pieces.

Far on in the Middle Ages, the trenchers on which meat was placed consisted of wholemeal bread, four days old; later these were made of wood, and then of pewter.

Often, for our ancestors loved the open air, their meals were taken out of doors.

A poet later than Chaucer thus describes such a scene of festivity.

> " A hundred knights, truly told
> Shall play with bowls in alleys cold,
> Your disease to drive away;
> To see the fishes in pools play
> To a drawbridge then shall ye
> Th' one half of stones, th' other of tree;
> A barge shall meet you full right
> With twenty-four oars full bright,
> The fresh water to row up and down
> Forty torches burning bright
> At your bridges to bring you light."

So again on a return from a chevaulchie, or a journey, the knight shall find :

> " When you come home your ' menie ' among
> Ye shall have revel, dance and song;
> Little children, great and small
> Shall sing as does the nightingale,
> Then shall ye go to your ' evensong '
> With tenors and trebles among,
> Three score of copes of damask bright
> Full of pearls they shall be pight,
> Your censors shall be of gold
> Indent with azure many a fold.
> Your quire nor organ song shall want
> With contre-note and descant,
> The other half with organs playing
> With young children full fain singing."

DAYS OF CHIVALRY

Referring again to the bedrooms of knightly degree. The bed which we have seen the young squire of the chamber was carefully to prepare, was invariably of the form called a " tester-bed." Its only exception, the pallet-bed the squire slept in, either at the foot of his master's bed or across the doorway outside as a protection. The hangings often were of velvet, silk or worsted. " A green velvet bed embroidered in gold of Cyprus with the arms of England and Hainault was provided for Queen Philippa's churching in 1335." Another of " embroidered baldekyn " with the same arms with three curtains of red sendal (a kind of silk) and ten carpets of red tapestry were described as the property of John, late Duke of Exeter in 1401 (Patent Roll 2, Hen. IV.). Two silk beds with a furred covering of minever were granted in 1400 to the king's sister Elizabeth, widow of the Earl of Exeter. The sheets of the richer knights and their ladies were made of the cloth of Champagne, Flanders, or Rennes, namely, linen or of stamyn, that is linsey-woolsey. For the higher classes they were also set with jewels, principally jacinths which were supposed to have the power of sending persons to sleep. The blankets themselves were of woollen or fustian, the latter most prized. The bedstead itself, which was a mere box without bottom or lid, was filled with straw, and on this the mattress and bed were laid.

Titled persons slept on the bed uppermost, commoners on the mattress; as to the crowd beneath them, a sack filled with chaff upon the floor was thought good enough for such. Despite the meanness of the straw that these box-bedsteads contained, the quilts covering them were generally works of art, frequently of velvet and silk, and embroidered with great care and beauty.

Important items in every bedroom were the " standard " and coffer; two chests large and small. The former held the articles in every day use, the latter contained such things as were too valuable to be trusted out of the owner's sight. The cost of a " standard " in 1388 was thirty shillings, the coffer, more ornamented, cost fifty shillings. Around the walls were hangings called " arras " from the great manufactory at that town. As these hangings projected from the wall, " behind the arras " was the convenient station for eaves-droppers !

The older medieval term for these hangings was " hall." John of Gaunt orders his " hall " of the same pattern to be taken to Rothwell with the blue and white bed (Register II., fol. 46). A black bed and " hall " was sent from Westminster to Bruseyard Priory for the funeral of Elizabeth, Duchess of Clarence, in 1364. The Black Prince gave to Canterbury Cathedral, by will, his " hall " of plumes of ostrich, and of red and black tapestry bordered with swans' and ladies' heads for the purpose of celebrating her anniversary every year (Register of Cant. Cathed. MS. 68).

Washing was performed by the help of articles brought for the occasion and never left in the bed-chamber. Princes and nobles washed in silver basins, the lower classes in wooden tubs. These latter, too, were utilized, as we have noted before, when the ritual bath was given to the neophyte for knighthood. Such too, were used when the knight returned from a battle or tournament and casting off his armour, took his bath, often as we have seen, bathed in it by some industrious maiden. We find in the " Testamenta

171

Vetusta," I., 67, Earl Humphrey of Hereford bequeathed " a silver basin in which we are accustomed to wash our heads," by which term no doubt he meant his face—washing the head being then not practised.

In the Lays and Romances we find many references to the young knights bathing in the rivers and streams when they halted. It seems therefore that the medieval knight was far cleaner than a later generation when in Louis XIV.'s court, the ladies and the aristocratic fops of the period never washed but greased their faces.

That the knight of these times despised the unwashed is borne out in the " Lay of Garin le Lorrain," the typical war poem of the period, where the serf Rigaud is contrasted with his master " his hair bristling, and his face as black as coal. He went for six months without bathing; none but rain water ever touched his face."

The windows of these castles and manors, originally simple open slips—hence it is said the narrow apertures in the earliest Norman churches—were after a time fitted with wooden shutters, and afterwards of skin; yet the use of glass is earlier than many suppose. It is true we read of the glass being taken out of the Earl of Northumberland's windows when he left home and carefully laid by till his return, but in 1252 we find Henry III. commanding the manufacture of " white glass " for the great hall of Northampton Castle; and glass windows in the chamber of his queen in Nottingham Castle, and early drinking cups of glass were in existence but great rarities.

It would be deficient in this sketch of the household of a medieval knight's " menie " and appointments if there was left out any reference to the ecclesiastical.

When Mass was said every day and attended by the knight as regularly as pursuing during the day the chace, or the tourney or the tournament while at home, chapels and oratories were found in each of his dwellings and the domestic chaplain one of his " menie." In royal houses and those of great nobles this private establishment was not unfrequently collegiate with a dean, canons, clerks, and singing men and boys. The royal chapel at Windsor is perhaps the only remaining example. But small chapels and ecclesiastically designed buildings may be found in nearly every old castle and manor-house which still exists, e.g., the chapel of Colchester Castle of the twelfth century; of Ormsbro' Castle of the late twelfth century; that of Igtham Moat in Kent and that of Haddon Hall.

In a wealthy knight's house, beside the general chapel, there was often a small oratory for the use of himself and his wife, in later times called " a closet." These chapels were thoroughly furnished with vessels, books, vestments, according to the means of the owner. From the Household Book of the then Earl of Northumberland we gather that his chapel had three altars and that he and his lady had besides an oratory in which were other altars. Every morning throughout the land the bell sounded for Mass, and evening for Vespers. The priest who served these chapels, was, in his spare times, usually employed, more or less, in secular duties; some engaged in their employer's service, some, if unattached, in those of lords and on royal missions, for as they were the most learned in that age, and most skilled in the diplomacy then known, their services were much sought. So Piers Ploughman says:

" Somme serven the kyng, and his silver tellen
In cheker and in chauncelrie, chalengen his dettes
Of wardes and wardemotes, weyves and theyres
And some serven as servants, lordes and ladies
And in stede of stywardes, sitten and demen."

These chapels and ecclesiastical establishments in the more wealthy knights' and lords' houses were the scene of many offerings at the time of the great Church festivals. Miracle plays took place in them and all who joined in them had their rewards. Here is appended the offerings made on such occasion by the Earl and Countess of Northumberland who, though living far on in the Middle Ages, no doubt, in what they did, merely followed the custom of their predecessors.

A table of what the Earl and Lady were accustomed to offer at Mass on all holy days " if he keep chappell," of offering and annual lights paid for at the Holy Blood of Hailes (in Gloucestershire) Our Lady of Walsingham, St. Margaret in Lincolnshire, Our Lady in the Whitefriars, Doncaster, of my lord's foundation.

(1) Presents at Xmas to Barne, Bishop of Beverley and York, when he comes, as he is accustomed to come, yearly.
(2) Rewards to the children of his chapell when they do sing the response called Exaudivi at the mattyntime for and in vespers upon All Hallows Day. Six shillings and eightpence.
(3) On St. Nicholas Eve six shillings and eightpence.
(4) To those of his lordship's chapell if they do play the Play of the Nativitie upon Xmas Day in the mornynge in my lord's chapell before his lordship, twenty shillings.
(5) For singing Gloria in Excelsis at the mattyns time upon Xmas Day in the morning.
(6) To the Abbot of Misrule on Xmas.
(7) To the Yeoman or Groom of the vestry for bringing him the hallowed taper on Candlemas Day.
(8) To his lordship's chaplain and other servants that play the Play before his lordship on Shrof tewsday at night, twenty shillings.
(9) That play the Play of Resurrection upon Easter Day in the morning in my lorde's Chapell before his lordship.
(10) To the yeoman or groom of the vestry on All Hallows Day syngynge for all Crystynne soles the saide nyhte to it be past mydnyght, three shillings and fourpence."

This gives a good idea of the extensive use churches and private chapels were utilized for in plays of a religious character on the great festivals of the year.

If it seem a wonder that every knight's castle or manor contained a chapel or at least an oratory, let it be remembered how essentially Chivalry in its later development had been fostered by the Church,

A KNIGHT'S LIFE IN

and on what a high ideal had been set the virtues pertaining to Chivalry. Very different to the Protestant or Catholic knight of to-day were the religious practices of those times. The former possibly once a week in the habit of frequenting a church, the latter attending, if at home, a weekly Mass and Vespers. But it was real need to the rough knight of those days that he should do differently. The Code of Chivalry as the " Order of Chivalry " laid down " le parjure, l'orgueil, l'impureté ou l'incontinence, la paresse, l'avarice, la colère, la goumandise, l'ivrognerie doivent être en horreur au Chevalier," and he was bidden to cultivate " la noblesse, de courage à foi, espérance, charité, justice, force, attrempance, loyaulte ; " to foreswear the first, to pursue the latter, needed strong religious convictions and help.

The knights, too, never forgot their brothers-in-arms who had passed away, hence the many Masses for them said and the Chantries founded by them for those departed. Indeed the number of Chantry priests became a scandal, so many to avoid parochial or harder work sought these posts, while the village churches were often left very badly off for ministers.

As to the food that maintained a wealthy knight's house, the " menie " or household was self-supporting and independent of external help to a degree which is difficult to conceive in days of easy supplies and rapid communication. A castle or large manor-house had its own corn lands and pasture, its stacks of corn and hay-granaries and storehouses of all kinds. The owner had mills, cattle byres, slaughter and salting houses ; if the cloth which the household wore was not woven at home, at least the sheep were shorn there and the wool went to be sold or exchanged for cloth at the nearest staple town.

Whatever was not of home manufacture was conveyed from the wood, the quarry, or the town, by pack-horses and barges, or bought from itinerant chapmen at the fairs held periodically through the land.

In these castles and manors, too, great stores, particularly if the owners were rich, of gold and silver plate, jewels and furs and precious raiment were found.

At a time when intercourse with foreign countries was difficult, much capital remained in this country. Sir John Arundel, who was drowned in 1380, lost not only his life, but all his apparel to his body, " fifty-two suits of gold."

The Black Prince left an immense treasure of gold and silver, plate and jewels, besides rich beds and furniture, cloth of arras embroidered with " mermyns de mer," swans, eagles and griffins ; " grand trésor, draps, chevalx, argent et or " (from Will of the Black Prince) and medieval wills even of less princely knights, of which a large number are extant, resemble, in their degree, that of the Prince.

The word " livery " constantly appears in these household expenses. " Livery " (liberatura) properly means " allowance." It did not necessary mean " uniform " but " deliveries," *i.e.*, of rations, or as in case of the squire's fire we have cited from " The Book of Courtesy," fuel for their rooms. However, it did also carry with it the modern idea of " cloth," generally the mark of the owner's colour or arms, and in a knight's " menie " a certain amount of this was served out annually to each member of it. At the festival of Christmas rich and varied robes were particularly given to certain favoured servants. To take an instance from royalty. Edward III. in 1363 had served out at Christmas to six ladies and nine knights, " nine cloths, 10½ ells of long coloured cloth, one cloth, 4 ells rayed cloth, 36 furs, 5 mantles, 6 cloaks, 29 minever hoods, four furs of Calabria, 500 ermines, 4 furs, 8 hoods of white budge, as well as 5 ' cloc,' " a doubtful word which may denote clogs, articles dating from the days of the Saxons, when they were known as " wife's shoes." Nearly the earliest entry found in the " Rolls " on the subject of male costume is an order of King John to provide for his (natural) son Geoffrey, six hoods and tunicles and a cape of russet furred with lamb-skin, two robes of russet with a lambskin cloak, thirty yards of woollen cloth, also hose and two pair of boots. The word " russet," like scarlet, seems to have been used to denote a material as well as a colour. As to " liveries " in the accepted sense of to-day—*i.e.*, peculiar clothing. The baron or knight could not reign as king in his castle but he could make his castle as strong and as splendid as he chose; he could not demand the military service of his vassals for his private war, but he could, if he chose to pay for it, support a vast household of men armed and " liveried " as servants, a retinue of pomp and splendour, but ready, beneath their mail and liveries for any opportunity of disturbance. (Stubbs' Court Hist. III. 469.)

Reference has before been made to the love of gardens and pleasances by the knights and their ladies. When the plain grim feudal keep, as years rolled on, and the returning Crusader had learnt a greater skill in architecture from mixing with more polished nations, was surrounded by other buildings and the simple cobble yard expanded to gardens with the outer walls of the whole castellated buildings —this love of plants and flowers grew apace. As before has been mentioned many new plants were brought from the East by the Crusaders, and the knowledge of medicinal herbs increased by inter-course with the Moors of Spain and the Saracens in the East. In the " Roman de Rose," we have a very good description given of such flowers, fruits and herbs—and the latter, if of healing properties, were assiduously cultivated to ease the wounds of the countless forays, tourneys and wars that these warlike possessors were liable to.

A MEDIEVAL GARDEN. (Thirteenth Century).

Bright green and lush
Around these sparkling streams did push
The sweetest grass. There might one lie
Beside one's love, luxuriously—
As thought 'twere bed of down. The earth
Made pregnant by the streams, gave birth
To thymy herbage and gay flowers,
And when drear winter frowns and lowers
In spots less genial, ever here
Things bud and burgeon through the year.
The violet, sweet of scent and hue,
The periwinkle's star of blue,
The golden kingcups burnished bright
Mingled with pink-rimmed daisies white,
And varied flowers, blue, gold and red,
The alleys, lawns and groves o'erspread,

175

A KNIGHT'S LIFE

Among them grew
Pomegranates filled with seeds and thick
Of skin, most wholesome for the sick;
Strange nut trees, which in season bore
Rich fragrant nutmegs, good for store
And nowise cursed with nauseous taste,
But savouring well.   Near by were placed
Almonds and gillyflower cloves,
Brought hither from hot Ind's far groves,
Dates, figs and liquorice which deals
Contentment, while misease it heals,
And wholesome aniseed's sweet spice,
And much prized grains of paradise,
Nor must rare cinnamon be forgot,
Nor zedoary, which I wot
At the end of great repasts men eat.
In this garden rare
Grew many a tree familiar
As cherry, pear, and knotted quince,
'Neath which a tender tooth will wince,
Brown medlars, plums both black and white,
Apples and chestnuts, peaches bright;
Sorb-apples, barberries, fruit of lote
And many more of lesser note.

CHAPTER XIII

KNIGHTS-BANNERETS

HITHERTO the knights in peace time have been treated of, it is necessary to examine their status in time of war. After all their real avocation was such, tournaments, tourneys were mere intervals in the sterner discipline of camp and field.

Distinctive marks in war have, from the earliest history that has come down to us, been used by men engaged in such, and in the battles of the Middle Ages when contending knights were enveloped in mail and their faces covered by laced helmets, these armorial cognizances, pennons and banners, were not simply used as adornments but necessities. The age of Chivalry in its flower was therefore the age of Banners. Even in naval engagements such were used. The vessels in the Middle Ages, as in ancient times, had frequently gold-coloured and purple sails. The sails of seigniorial ships were generally brilliantly emblazoned with the coats of arms of the seignior; even the merchant vessels and fishing boats had the image of a saint or patron figure of the Virgin, a famous legend or sacramental word, intended to exorcise the Evil Spirits who played no inconsiderable part in the superstitions of the toilers of the deep, painted on them.

Among the most celebrated flags of the French Navy were the " baucents," a name that recalls the " Bauséant," the banner of the Templars. These made of red taffeta and sometimes " sprinkled with gold " were only employed in the most merciless war in hand, for as a document of 1292 says, " They signified certain death and mortal strife to all sailors everywhere." Even as early as the irruptions of the Normans on the coasts of Western Europe, banners were used by them. The poet, Benoit de Sainte-More, tells us that it was in this fashion, covered with seven hundred banners of different colours that Rollo brought his fleet back up the Seine to Meulan. If this was so on the sea, it was even more so on the land. If we could have looked down on a knightly army on march, one would have had to confess with the sun shining on its banners, so numerous, so varied and so rich, that war appeared robbed of half its ruth, and that even, when the mêlée took place between opposing ranks of knights, it seemed, owing to their many banners, not a scene of death, but a flower garden of beauty.

But not every knight was entitled to a banner, though all were entitled to pennons. At first those who were qualified to display a banner were great feudal ones, who could muster so many men to that banner. Afterwards they seem to have fallen into the second rank of the nobility, between barons and knights-bachelors, and were drawn from the ranks of the latter. So a knight-bachelor whose services and

M

landed possessions entitled him to this promotion would apply formally to the commander in the field for the status of banneret. If granted, the heralds cut publicly the tails from his knightly pennon and so squared it into a banner, or the commander himself as a special honour might do this. Thus it happened to the celebrated English knight Chandos. Though he had done valiantly at Poitiers, and in 1365 was the hero and counsellor of the Count de Montfort in his war with the Count of Blois, he had all this time been only a knight-bachelor. Even his seneschalship of Aquitaine had not seemed to justify him claiming to display his banner. But before the battle of Navaret in Spain, whither he had accompanied his lord the Black Prince, he took the title of knight-banneret. He advanced, in front of the armies drawn up opposite to each other for battle, with his banner unfolded in his hand. He presented it to the Prince, saying, " Sir, behold here is my banner. I require you to display it abroad, and give me leave this to-day to raise it, for, Sir, I thank God and you, I possess land and heritage sufficient to maintain it withal."

The Prince and King Peter took the banner between their hands which was blazoned " argent a pile gules," and after cutting off the end, to make it square, they spread it abroad ; and the Prince delivered it to Chandos, saying, " Sir John, behold your banner, and God send you joy, honour and strength to preserve it." Chandos bowed and after thanking the Prince he went back to his own company and said, " Sir knights, behold my banner and yours, keep it as your own." (Froissart.)

But the distinction between a knight-banneret and the knight-bachelor was merely in military rank and precedence, and the former may be considered an institution more of policy than of Chivalry. The knight-bachelor displayed, or was entitled to display, a pennon or forked ensign, the banneret, as in the case of Chandos, had a flag square on all sides, which was the proper emblem of the baron. Du Tillet reports that the Count de Laval challenged Sir Raoul de Coueguen's right to raise a square banner, being only a banneret and not a baron, and adds that he was generally ridiculed for this presumption and called the knight with the square ensign. This circumstance shows that the distinction of a banneret's and baron's banner was not absolutely settled, and in all descriptions, the banneret's banner is described as " square."

The earliest contemporary mention of bannerets in France, a learned writer (Daniel) says, is in the reign of Philip Augustus, and the English writer Selden says in England in the reign of Edward I. But in neither case is reference made to them to suggest that the dignity was then new or even uncommon. Sir Alan Plokenet, Sir Ralph and Sir Philip Daubeny are entered as bannerets on the Roll of Carmarthen Castle in 1280, and the Roll of Caerlaverock (of which more presently) contains the names and arms of eighty-five bannerets who accompanied Edward I. in his expedition to Scotland in the year 1300.

If the question is asked, why bannerets about the times quoted above, appeared so frequently and possibly for the first time (at least under that name), the answer briefly seems to be, they were created possessing the lands to keep the dignity up and the proven bravery in many a hard fought battle when as simple knights-bachelors they had fought and won, to bring order into the shifting components of which a feudal army consisted.

When under the previous iron discipline of the feudal system a kingdom's men and knights had been summoned by the ban and arrière ban to the overlord's assistance, no such knights-bannerets were required, but when that feudal system had become weakened and declining everywhere, by the creation of knights unfettered by its sterner obligations, a means was required to call these free-lances together under a well-known and trusty banner.

To the owner of such banner was entrusted the gathering together under it, not only the men on his own lands, but to induce by hopes of gain and even payments all those brave and unattached knights-errant to serve beneath him, while he, in turn, served his overlord. The times these knights-bannerets appeared were changed times (and hence their need) to those when the overlord's crier said, " Obey my summons or I will burn you " (arrivez ou je vous brulerai). When the ban was published and at the second summons the trumpet rang out in the cross roads, in the streets, and in country places calling the men to arms and to fail to answer the call of the ban was to commit a crime of the first magnitude.

New measures, inspired by new times and the crumbling away of feudality were requisite to get together a medieval army, and these measures were greatly submitted to these newly-created knights-bannerets.

A banneret was expected to bring into the field at least thirty men-at-arms, that is, knights or squires mounted, and in complete order, at his own expense. Each man-at-arms, besides his attendants on foot, ought to have a mounted crossbowman and a horseman armed with a bow and an axe. Therefore the number of horsemen alone who assembled under a banner was at least three hundred, and including followers on foot might amount to a thousand men. The banneret might indeed if he had remained a simple knight have arrayed the same force under a pennon, but his accepting a banner bound him to bring out that number at least.

So strict was this obligation on bannerets that we find in the reign of Charles VII. of France, his nobles making a remonstrance to him that their estates were so much wasted by the long wars with England that they could no longer support the number of men attached to the dignity of banneret, and from that time, as far as France is concerned, these great companies of men-at-arms which had hitherto been led by knights-bannerets became a discarded custom, and if an ordinary knight, by his prowess and skill, was at hand, he led the companies himself. But while the custom lasted it had an excellent effect.

From the constant wars, particularly those of the Hundred Years, the knights-bachelors, landless and impoverished, had often been tempted to lawless courses. The frequent prohibitions of tournaments, by both the Church and the more peaceful sovereigns, had had also its necessary effect in impoverishing these knights of the free lance to whom tournaments afforded one principal means of subsistence.

> " Joust and tourney were forbid,
> All his means of living gone."
> —French Fabliaux.

The licence and vices imported by those too, who had returned from the Crusades, and who had been, from long years of warfare, completely weaned from any peaceful avocations; the poverty also to which noble families, particularly the younger sons, had been reduced by these fatal expeditions, all made a mass of disintegrated " swords," wandering about without leaders, or, if they had leaders, little better than themselves. The class therefore, of able, wise and valiant men such as the bannerets to enlist these free-lances, was of immense value. Their institution at this unsettled period, when old feudal chains were broken and the sterner discipline of a past age decayed, was not only a necessity but a blessing to the overlord and the sovereign.

Oliver Marche, also Froissart, give various examples of the manner of acquiring a banner.

(1) Entre en bannière—that is to say, the first occasion a knight-bachelor entered into the status of a banneret.

(2) Lever bannière—that is when a knight acquired a fief which carried with it a right of banner.

(3) Porter bannière—to march with it to war.

(4) Relever bannière—to succeed by inheritance to a property of extinct bannerets.

(5) Développer bannière—that was to be made (as Chandos was) by a prince or general (on the field of battle) because the banner, previously rolled up, the prince or general displayed for the petitioning knight.

The lands which carried with them the right of levying men and enlisting them to a knight's service in war and so giving him the power to demand a banner were described as " terres a bannière," where on the castle or knight's dwelling the banner flew from one of the turrets.

The small banners which knights carried in war-time and the little " banderolles " which they held in their hands in entering the lists of a tournament, with those with which they made the sign of the Cross before commencing the joustings and also those other tiny flags they often carried on their helmets, afford the origin of those little weather-cocks made in form of a flag so often to have been seen on their dwellings. Immediately a knight acquired such a dwelling, up went his banner fluttering from a lofty staff (arborée le lein le plus eminent). In an enterprise which Saintré undertook with his companions, they bore, we are told in his History, two such little banners on their helmets, between which shone a diamond which was destined for the victor-knight's prize. We also find from the same source when a passage of arms had been proclaimed between Gravelines and Calais that " le Dimanche premier jour du mois et ouverture du pas arrive le dit Seigneur de Bouguincan le matin après le Messe et très-belle compaigne qui fist sur le haut pignon (gable-end) de à une bordure d'argent et crois angleterre ! Saint George ! "

The Church also gave the right of banners to those of her knightly servants who led the men of her various wide-spreading lands and abbeys for defence or war. Such a banner was usually kept in the church and on its return at head of the ecclesiastical retainers, was received with great ceremony by the chiefs of the community.

In the Cathedral of Chartres there is a representation in one of the windows of the knight who was about to lead the Church's men to battle receiving the banner and belt at the hands of the presiding prelate. The knight is clothed in blue, with a cap of scarlet. Many towns also had their banners for the use of those who of knightly rank they had nominated as their leaders and defenders in war. In Italy such a knight entrusted with a city's banner was called " Gonfalioner."

Ménestrier in his " Histoire de l'ancienne Chevalerie " says a chàplet of pearls or a garland of flowers or a twisted wreath of colours wound in, or a little cap (of maintenance?) were worn by bannerets at festal feasts and in the presence of the sovereign or prince, or a cap made of flowers just as the former wore their crowns. Froissart recounts how Edward of England gave the brave French knight (banneret) such a chaplet of pearls, saying, " Monseigneur Eustace, je vous donne ce chapelet pour le mieux combattant de la journée de ceux de dedans et de dehors et vous prie que vous le portiez cette année pour l'amour de moy." St. Palaye says, " other honours were also offered to whet the ambition of the knights-bannerets; they could aspire to the degree of Count, Baron, Marquis, or Duke, and their titles of such, secured to them and their wives, and a fixed rank, whereby recognition was given immediately upon the magnitude and importance of the service they had rendered to the State. A great portion of the decorations they received were originally worn at ceremonies and displayed on their helmets or their dress. Even the dwellings of such bannerets, considered at that time as temples of honour, had to have the proper signs and emblems shown on them of the knight's high rank. The crenellations and towers which served for the defence of the castles also were such outward marks of nobility and has been remarked above, such had the privilege of ornamenting the rooftrees of their houses with weather-cocks."

The banner therefore of knights-bannerets was not merely a decoration but an emblem of authority and order. To these privileged knights was also allowed " crier les enseignes " (Favyn " Theatre d'honneur," p. 24). In other words to use a personal battle-cry—the cri de guerre or cri d'armes. Sometimes it was embroidered on their banner, as the Templars had their battle-cry, " Ha Beauseant," " Montjoye St. Denys " the Kings of France, " St. George for England," " St. George for Guienne," " Montjoye " for Anjou, and " Montjoye au blanc épervier " for the princes of France, so it was the privilege of bannerets to have their own " Cri de guerre." It was a useful privilege, for in the scattered formations of a Middle-Age battle when all about the field companies of men were engaged and scattered, the cry of their own banneret recalled them to his main body when necessary, and these knightly banners provoked an emulation also between the possessors to carry them farthest into the enemy's ranks.

> " ' Charge, Chester, charge,
> On, Stanley, on,'
> Were the last words of Marmion."

The best and most interesting account of an army whose constituent parts were headed by bannerets, with a description of their banners, is found in the "Roll of Caerlaverock," presumed to have been composed by a monk living at that time. In this medieval array are to be found eighty-five knights-bannerets, besides a great number of knights-bachelors, some the younger sons of the lords who marched in it, some gathered together as free-lances by the bannerets to serve the king in his march to Scotland. Subjoined is the first part of the Roll, in Norman-French with its English translation.

LE SIEGE DE KARLAVEROCK

El millime tresenteisime an de
Grace, au jour de seint John
Tint a Carduel Edward grant courte
E comanda q'a terme court
Tout si homme se appareillassent
Ensemble oveoc li alassent
Sur les Escos ses enemis.
Dedems le jour que leur fu mis
Fu preste tout le ost bame
E li bons Roys o sa maisine
Tantost se vint vers les Escos
Non pas en cotes et surcos
Mais sur les gra's chevaus de pris
Por ceo q'il ne feussent surpris,
Arme bien et seurement.
La ont meinte riche garnement
Brode sur cendeaus et samis;
Meint beau penon et lance mis
Meint banière desploie.
E loing estoit la noise oie
Des henissemens des chevaus;
Par tote estoient mouns e vauls
Pleins de sommers e de charroi
Oue la vitaile et la couroi
De tentes et de pavillons.
E li jours estoit beaus e longs.
Se erroient petites journées,
En quatre eschieles ordinées;
Les queles vous deviserai,
Que nulle n'en trespasserai.
Ains vous dirray de compaignons
Toutes les armies et les noms
Des banières nomement,
Si vous volies oier coment.

Henri, le bon Conte de Nichole,
De prowesse enbrasse e acole
E en son coer le a souveraine,
Menans le eschiele primeraine,
Banière ot de un cendall saffrin,
O un lion rampant porprin.

DAYS OF CHIVALRY

Oue li Robert le fitz wautier,
Qe bien siet de armes le mestier
Si en fesoit kanques il devoit,
En la jaune banier avoit
Fesse entre deus chevrons vermaus.

E Guillemes li Mareschaus,
Dont en Irelande ot la baillie,
La bende de or engreillie
Portoit en la rouge banière.

Hue Bardoulf de Grant manière
Riches homs preus e courtois
En azure quint fuelles trois
Portoit de fin or esmère.

Un grant seigneur, mout honore,
Puis je bein nom'er le cinkime,
Phillipe le seigneur de kime,
Qui portoit rouge, ove un cheveron
De or croiselle tout environ,

Henry de Grai vi je là
Ki ben e noblement ala
Ovec son bon seigneur, le Conte.
Banière avoit e par droit conte
De VI pieces la vous mesur
Barre de argent e de azur.

Robert de Monthaut i estoit
Ki mout haute entente i mettoit
De faire a haute honeur ateinte.
Banière avoit en azure teinte
Oue un lyon rampant d'argent.

E compaignes a cele gent
Thomas de Multon se fu
Ke avoit banière e escu
De argent ove treis bars de goules.

Ces armes ne furent pas soules,
De siente en la parellement
Car telles ou resemblement
John de Longaster entre meins;
Mes ke en lieu de une barre meins
Quarter rouge e jaune luppart.

E de celle mesme part
Fu Guillemis li Vavasours,
Ki darmes nest muet ne sours.
Banière avoit bien conoissable
De or fin oue la daunce de sable.

183

Johan de Odelston ensement
Ki bien e adessement
Ua darmes toutes les saisons.
Au Counte estoit si est raisons
Ke nomes soit entre sa gent,
Rouge portoit frette d'argent.

Le bon Robert le fitz Rogier
Ui je sa banière a rengier
Les cele au Counte en cele alée.
De or et de rouge esquartelée
Ove une bende taient en noier.

A Johan son filz et son heir,
Ki de Clavering a surnom,
N'estoit diverse de rien non,
Fors de un labell vert seulement.

Se estoient du retenement
Au bon Conte et au bien ame
Tint cil ke ci vous ai nome.
Ses companis fu li Conestables
Joefnes homes riches e metables
Ki Quens estoit de Herefort.
Banière ot de Inde cendal fort
O une blanche bende lée
De deus costices entre alée
De or fin, dont au dehors assis
Ot in rampant lyonceaux sis.
Nicholas de Segrave o li
Ke nature avoit embeli
De corps et enrichi de cuer.
Vaillant père ot ki getta puer
Les garbes et le lyon prist;
A ses enfauns ensi aprist
Les coragous a resembler
E o les nobles assembler.
Cils ot la banière son père
Au label rouge por son frère
Johan ke li ainsnez estoit
E ki entere la portoit.
Li pères ot de la moillier
Cink filz estoient chevalier
Prue et hardi et defensable.
O un lyon de argent en sable
Rampant et de or fin coronne
Fu la banière del ainsne
Ke li Quens Mareschaus avoit
Mis et service kil devoit
Por ce ke kil ne i pooit venir.
Il ne me puet pas souvenir
Ke baneret i fuissent plus
Mes si le voir vous en conclus

DAYS OF CHIVALRY

Bon bachelers i ot bien cent,
Dont nuls en ostell ne destent
Nulle foiz tant ke il aient touz
Cherchies les passages doutouz
O ens chevauchent chescun jour.
Li mareschal li herbergour
Ki livrent places a logier
A ceus ke doivent herbergier
Par tant ai dit de avant garde
Ki sont dedeinz et ki la garde.

Johans li bons Quenas de Warene
De lautre eschele avoit la rene
A justicier et gouvorner,
Com cil ki bien scavoit mener
Gen seignourie et honnourée.
De or et de azur eschequrée
Fu sa banière noblement.

Il ot en son assemblement
Henri de Perci, son nevou,
De ki sembloit ke eust fait vou
De aler les escos de rampant.
Jaune o un bleu lyon rampant
Fu sa banière bien vuable.
Robert le Fitz Payne sievable;
Ot sa banière flanc a flanc
Rouge a passans lyons de blanc
Trois de un baston bleu surgettez.

Gautiers de Monci ajoustez
Estoit en cele compaignie
Car tuit furent de une maisnie.
Cils ot banière eschequerée
De blanc et rouge coulurée.

Le Valence Aymars li vaillans
Belle banière i fu baillans
De argent et de azure burelée,
O la bordure poralée
Tout entour de rouge merolos.

Un vaillant hom e de grant los
O lui Nichole de Karru
Dont meinre foiz orent paru
Li fait en couvert et en lande
Sur la felloune gent d'irlande.
Banière ot jaune bien passable
O trois passans lyons de sable.
Rogier de la Ware ovec ens,
Ung chivaller sage et preus,
Ky les armes et vermeillectes
O blanc lyon et croiselectes.

De Warwik le Count Guy
Coment ken ma rime de Guy
Ne avoit voisin de lui mellour
Banière ot de rouge coulour
O fesse de or et croissilie.

Jaune o crois noir engreelie
La portoit Johans de Mooun.

Cele de Tateshale a oun
Por sa valour o eus tirée
De or de rouge eschequerée
Au chief de ermine outrement.

Rauf le filz Guilleme autrement
Ke cil de Valence portoit
Car en lieu de merles métoit
Trois chapeaus de roses vermeilles
Ke bien séoient a merveilles.

Guillemes de Ros assemblans
I fu rouge a trois bouz blans.

E la banière Hue Poinz
Estoit barre de viii poinz
De or et de goules ovelment.

Johans de Beauchamp proprement
Portoit le banière de vair
Au douz tens et au sovest aier.

Prestes a lascier les ventailles
Ensi se aroutent les babailles.
Dont ia de deus oi aves
E de la tierce oier deues.

Edward Sires de Irois
De Escoce et de Engleterre rois
Princes Gualois Duc de Acquitaine
La tierce eschile un poi lointame,
Conduit et guye arreement
Si bel c si serrement
Ke nuls de autre ne se i depart.
En sa banière trois luparte
De or fin estoient mis en rouge
Courant felloun fier et harouge;
Par tel signifiance mis
Ke aussi est vers ses ennemis
Li vois fiers felouns et hastans
Car sa morsure nest tastans
Nuls ki nen soit envenimez
Non porquant tot est ralumez

DAYS OF CHIVALRY

De donce debonairete
Quant il requerent se amiste
Et a sa pais veullent venir.
Tel prince doit bien avenir
De grans gens estre cheveraigne.

Soun nevou Johan de Britaigne
Pur ce ke plus de lui est près
Doy je plus tost noumer après
Si le avoit il bien deseroi
Com cil ki son oncle ot servi
Puis se enfance peniblement
Et de guerpi outrement
Son père et son autre lignage
Por demourer de son maisnage
Kant li Rois ot besoigne de gens.
Et il ke estoit beaus et gens
Banière avoit cointe et parée
De or et de azur eschequerée,
Au rouge ourle o jaunes lupars
Dermine estoit la quarte pars.

Johan de Bar iloec estoit
Ken la banière Inde pourtoit
Deus bars de or et fu croissillie
O la rouge ourle engreeillie.

Guillemes de Grant son palée
De argent et de asur surealée
De bende rouge o trois eigleaus
Portoit de or fin bien fais e beaus.

Bien doi mettre en mon serventois
Ke Elys de Aubigni li courtois
Banière ot rouge ou entaillie
Ot fesse blanche engreellie.

Mais Eurmenions de la Brecte
La banière eut toute rougecte.
Après eus ci truis en mon conte
Hue de Ver le filz au Conte
De Oxenford et frère son hoir.
O le ourle endente de noir
Avoit banière e long et lée
De or et de rouge esquartelée
De bon cendal none pas de toyle
Se ot devant un blanche estoile.

Johan de Rivers le appareil
Ot mascle de or et de vermeil;
E par tant compare le a oun
Au bon Morice de Crooun.

A KNIGHT'S LIFE IN

Robert le Seigneur de Cliffort
A ki raisons donne confort
De ses enemis encombrer
Toutes les fois ke remembrer.
Li puet de son noble lignage
Escoce pregn a testmoignage.

Translation

In the year of grace one thousand three hundred, on the day of St. John, Edward held a great court at Carlisle, and commanded that in a short time all his men should prepare to go with him against his enemies, the Scots.

On the appointed day all the host was ready and the good king with his household then set forward against the Scots, not in coats and surcoats but on powerful and costly chargers; and, that they might not be taken by surprise, well and securely armed.

There were many rich caparisons embroidered on silks and satins; many a beautiful pennon fixed to a lance; and many a banner displayed.

And afar off was the noise heard of the neighing of horses; mountains and valleys were everywhere covered with sumpter horses and wagons with provisions and sacks of tents and pavilions.

And the days were long and fine. They proceeded by easy journeys, arranged in four squadrons; the which I will so describe to you, that not one shall be passed over. But first I will tell you of the names and arms of the companions, especially of the banners, if you will listen now.

Henry, the good Earl of Lincoln, burning with valour and which is the chief feeling of his heart, leading the first squadron, had a banner of yellow silk, with a purple lion rampant.

With him Robert FitzWalter, who well knew the use of arms and so used them when required. In a yellow banner he had a fess between two red chevrons.

And William le Marshall, who when in Ireland had the chief command. He bore a gold bend engrailed in a red banner.

Hugh Bardolf, a man of great appearance, rich, valiant, and courteous. He bore azure, three cinquefoils of pure gold.

A great lord, much honoured may I well name the fifth, Philip the Lord of Kyme, who bore red, with a chevron of gold surrounded by crosslets.

I saw Henry de Grey there, who well and nobly attended with his good Lord, the Earl. He had a banner and reckoned rightly you would find it barry of six pieces of silver and blue.

Robert de Montalt was there, who highly endeavoured to accomplish high honour. He had a banner of a blue colour, with a lion rampant of silver.

In company with these was Thomas de Multon, who had a banner and shield of silver with three red bars.

These arms were not single, for such, or much resembling them, were in the hands of John de Lancaster; but who, in the place of a bar less, bore a red quarter with a yellow leopard.

DAYS OF CHIVALRY

And of this same division was William le Vavasour, who in arms is neither deaf nor dumb. He had a very distinguishable banner of fine gold with a sable dauncet.

Also John de Huddleston, who at all times appears well and promptly in arms. He was with the Count, which makes it appear proper that he should be named among his followers. He bore gules fretty of silver.

I saw the good Robert FitzRogers' banner ranged with that of the Earl in the march. It was quarterly of gold and red with a black bend.

That of John, his son and heir, who has the surname of Clavering, was not at all different, excepting only a green label.

All those whom I have named to you were of the retinue of the good and well-beloved Earl. His companion was the Constable who was the Earl of Hereford, a rich and elegant young man. He had a banner of deep blue silk with a white band between two cotises of fine gold, on the outside of which he had six lioncels rampant.

With him was Nicholas de Segrave, whom Nature had adorned in body and enriched in heart. He had a valiant father, who wholly abandoned the sheaves, and assumed the lion; and who taught his children to imitate the brave, and associate with the nobles. Nicholas used his father's banner with a red label. By his brother John, who was the eldest, it was borne entire. The father had, by his wife, five sons, who were valiant, bold and courageous knights.

The banner of the eldest, whom the Earl Marshall had sent to execute his duties because he could not come, was sable with a silver lion rampant, crowned with fine gold. I cannot recollect what the other bannerets were there, but you shall see in the conclusion that he had a hundred good bachelors there, not one of whom would go into lodgings or tent until they had examined all the suspected passes, in which they rode every day.

The Marshall, the harbinger, assigned lodgings to those who were entitled to them. Thus far I have spoken of those who are in and form the van-guard.

John, the good Earl of Warwick, held the reins to regulate and govern the second squadron, as he who well knew how to lead noble and honourable men. His banner was handsomely chequered with gold and azure.

He had in his company Henri de Percy, his nephew, who seemed to have made a vow to humble the Scots. His banner was very conspicious, a blue lion rampant on yellow.

Robert de Fitzpayne followed them; he had his red banner, side by side, with three white lions passant, surcharged with a blue baton.

Add to these Walter de Money, who was in this company because they were all of one household. He had his banner chequered of silver and red.

The valiant Aymer de Valance bore a beautiful banner there of silver and azure stuff, surrounded by a border of red martlets.

With him Nicholas de Carew, a valiant man of great fame, which had often been displayed both in cover and on the plains against the rebellious people of Ireland.

He had a handsome yellow banner with three lions passant, sable.

189

With them was Roger de la Ware, a wise and valiant knight, whose arms were red with a white lion and crosslets.

Guy, Earl of Warwick, who of all that are mentioned in my rhyme had not a better neighbour than himself, bore a red banner with a fess of gold and crusilly.

John de Mohun bore there, yellow, with a black cross engrailed.

Tateshal, for valour which he had displayed with them, has one of gold and red chequered, with a chief ermine.

Ralph de Fitzwilliam bore differently from him of Valence, for instead of martlets he had three chaplets of red roses which became him marvellously.

That which William de Ros displayed there was red with three white bougets.

And the banner of Hugh Pointz was barry of eight pieces of gold and red.

John de Beauchamp bore handsomely, in a graceful manner and with inspiring ardour a banner vair.

The ventailles were soon lowered and the battalion proceeded on their march. Of two of them you have already been told, and of the third you shall hear.

Edward, King of England and Scotland, Lord of Ireland, Prince of Wales, and Duke of Aquitaine, conducted the third squadron at a little distance, and brought up the rear so closely and ably that none of the others were left behind.

In his banner were three leopards, courant of fine gold, set on red, fierce, haughty and cruel; thus placed to signify that, like them the King is dreadful, fierce and proud to his enemies, for his bite is slight to none who inflame his anger; not but his kindness is soon rekindled towards such as seek his friendship or submit to his power. Such a Prince was well suited to be the chieftain of noble personages.

I must next mention his nephew, John of Brittany, because he is nearest to him, and the preference he has well deserved, having assiduously served his uncle from his infancy, and left his father and other relations to dwell in his household when the King has occasion for his followers.

He was handsome and amiable and had a beautiful ornamented banner, chequered gold and azure, with a red border and yellow leopards, and a quarter of ermine.

John de Bar was likewise there, who in a blue banner, crosselly, bore two barbels of gold, with a red border engrailed.

William de Grandison bore paly silver and azure surcharged with a red bend, and thereon three beautiful eaglets of fine gold.

Well ought I to state in my Lay, that the courteous Elias de Aubigney had a red banner, on which appeared a white fess engrailled.

But Eurmenions de la Brette had a banner entirely red.

After them I find in my account Hugh de Vere, son of the Earl of Oxford, and brother to his heir. He had a long and narrow banner not of silk but of good cloth, and quartered gold and red, with a black indented border, and in the upper part a white star.

John de Rivers had his caparisons mascally of gold and vermilion; and they were therefore similar to those of the good Maurice de Croun.

DAYS OF CHIVALRY

Robert, the Lord of Clifford, to whom reason gives consolation, who always remembers to overcome his enemies. He may call Scotland to bear witness of his noble lineage, that originated well and nobly. . . .

The Roll from which the above is quoted contains, as has been said, the names of eighty-five knights-bannerets—in some cases the sons of such are mentioned, who were knights free from feudal obligations, but serving under their fathers' and king's banners. It is interesting as showing how fully developed heraldry had become, and how fully the knights understood the influence of banners inspiring the rank and file of their followers, on march, and in field.

It would, however, be a wrong conception, though it is a very widespread idea, that the most formidable aspect of medieval war was a charge of knights with vizor down and lance in rest; and that these gallant Chevaliers only pranced their horses round and round the outer margin of a medieval castle, or if they did dismount and try to take a fortress by assault, would rage in vain, having only their sword or axe to rely on, against its thick walls and barred portcullis, or, as in the description of a knightly army such as that which the Roll of Caerlaverock portrays, none but knights in mail composed it. The impression, as a thoughtful writer puts it, is no doubt due to the fact that many people read romances, ancient and modern, which concern themselves with the personal adventures of their heroes, but have not read medieval history, which tells—even more than enough—of battles and sieges. The knight was not always in the pomp and pageantry of Chivalry, nor, in the war and sieges he undertook, was he alone the fighting force in the array, nor were swords the only weapons used to bring a people and a beleaguered town into his power. Banners, as we have seen, marked the companies of different leaders—the glittering lances of the knights glanced in the sun in its rising and setting, but fitter instruments than the graceful lance, and weightier weapons than the swift sword were used in reducing walled towns and opposing forces in the field, and a vast number of men-at-arms and rank and file served with the young knights under a banneret's command.

Knights themselves, even the bravest in the lists and the actual battle-field, were supposed to know something of the works necessary to raise against a besieged city, and though we find in the old chronicles very little information about the medieval drill or tactics, it is very possible that there was more of both than is commonly supposed. It is certain that a knight-banneret whose duty it was to command bodies of troops would invent the elements of tactics enough to enable him to combine them in a general plan of battle with his brother-bannerets and to take advantage of the different turns of the fight. It is true that the armies of medieval England and France consisted chiefly of levies of men under the ban or the arriere-ban, who were not marked out for professional soldiers, and the knights as their leaders were chiefly chosen by the extent of their territorial possessions and not by their military excellence; but the men were not unaccustomed to their weapons, and the knights who commanded them, from their earliest youth as pages and afterwards squires in warlike households, were made efficient in everything that befitted a youth admitted to Chivalry. Until the invention of gunpowder, or rather till that of artillery, the whole art of fortification (Prosper Mérimée) consisted in following more or less exactly the traditions handed down by the Romans. The stronghold of the Middle Ages had precisely the same characteristics as the ancient " castellum." The methods of attack against which the engineers had to guard were the assault by escalade, either by surprise or by force of numbers, and the breach caused either by sapping, mining or by the battering-rams of the besiegers. The first work of besiegers was to destroy the outworks of a besieged place, such as the posterns, the barbicans, the barriers, etc. As most of these outworks were built of wood, attempts were generally made to cut them to pieces with hatchets, or to set fire on them with arrows to which were fastened pieces of burning tow steeped in sulphur or some other incendiary composition. If the main body of the place was not so strongly fortified as to render a successful assault by force impossible, it was usual to attempt an escalade. With this end in view the moat generally strewn with calthrops (fine pointed iron pieces) was filled up with fascines on which ladders were reared against the ramparts, and while archers on the brink of the ditch, protected by mantlets, stuck in the ground, drove away any of the defenders who attempted to show themselves above the parapets or loopholes.

If the besiegers thought the town would hold out long, a blockade was the sole remaining means of reduction, though this was a difficult thing to carry on with forces only bound to serve for so many days. It therefore became necessary for the besieger to protect his approaches by wooden, earthen, or even stone works, constructed under cover of the night, and solid and lofty enough to enable his archers to aim right on to the battlements of the besieged place. Wooden towers several stories high were also frequently resorted to, put together piece by piece at the edge of the moat or constructed out of bow-shot and subsequently rolled on wheels to the foot of the walls. At the Siege of Toulouse in 1218, a machine of this kind is said to have been built by Simon de Montfort capable of holding, according to the " Lay of the Albigeois," five hundred men.

Besides these means there still remained sapping and mining. Miners under protection of a body of archers were despatched with pickaxes into the moat. A sloping roof covered with mantlets protected them from the missiles of the besieged. When the mine had reached the walls these were propped up with pieces of timber, and the earth was dug away until they rested on these artificial supports. Combustible materials were then heaped round the wooden props and set on fire and the walls crumbled down, admitting the assailants.

The battering-ram was also advantageously used, a long heavy beam suspended in the centre from a kind of massive trestle. The end which battered the wall was either covered with an iron head, or pointed with brass. Huge catapults were often used which projected great stones from a long distance upon a besieged wall. They were sometimes employed to throw into a stronghold dead bodies of horses and dogs, fire balls and cases of inflammable matter, and were greatly used to shatter the roofs of buildings inside the walls and any wooden shed constructed on the walls.

In the open field at close grip with the enemy, the knight was used with the greatest advantage, and when Chivalry was at its height, the

NURSES AND SUCKLINGS.

From a MS. of about 1300
From Coulton's Mediæval Garner.

common soldier who fought on foot was scarcely valued or considered; it remained for the battles of Crécy and Poitiers to show how invaluable were his services, and on both occasions the English long-bow won the day.

Archers, however, particularly in England from the time of the Norman Conquest, had assumed an importance in all armies under the English banners. The success of the Normans at Hastings was greatly due to the skill and superiority of their archers. The latter are shown on the Bayeux Tapestry, both in hauberks and without, and one is seen on horseback. The bow then seems to be of the simplest construction and the arrow not the cloth-yard shaft of a later age. It became a custom from a very early date for the archer to bear a stake sharpened at both ends, which the front rank drove firmly into the ground with the second and uppermost point sloping from them, while the rear ranks filled up the intermediate spaces with theirs. When protected thus, in front and on both flanks, it was found that the archers of England could defy the charge of the heaviest cavalry, and the prowess of these archers made them renowned throughout Europe.

At the Siege of Messina by Cœur de Lion we are told by the Chronicler, Richard of Devizes, that the Sicilians were obliged to leave their walls unmanned, " because no one could look abroad but he would have an arrow in his eye before he could shut it," while Richard himself did not disdain the use of the bow but used it personally with deadly effect when besieging Nottingham Castle defended by the adherents of his brother John. During the Norman period the infantry as a rule were armed with the bow, though other weapons were placed on the same plane. But when the long-bow proper came into use and the arbalest was invented, the deadly effect of the arrow and the quarrel began to be fully recognized and accepted. The bow which before had been valued chiefly in sieges and defence of mountain passes and strongholds became considered as of exceptional efficacy in the open field. We find in various Statutes of Arms that a number of the military tenants were ordered to be provided with the long-bow and arrows. The Statute of Westminster, for instance, especially mentions the bow. Indeed the practice of archery by the commonalty of England was protected by a long series of legislation. As early as Henry I. we find an enactment—which indicates that such accidents happened then as in these days of rifle shooting—that if any one practising with arrows or darts should by accident slay another, it was not to be punished as a crime. In 1363 Statutes were passed calling on the people to leave their popular amusements of ball and quoits and casting the stone, and the like, on their festivals and Sundays, and to practise archery instead. " Servants and labourers shall have bows and arrows and use the same the Sundays and holidays and leave all playing at tennis, or football and other games called quoits, dice, casting the stone, kailes and other such inopportune games." A later Statute says that the dearness of bows had driven the people to leave shooting, and it therefore regulates the price of bows. Yew trees were ordered to be grown in the churchyards to provide material for such. Every merchant importing merchandise from abroad where bow-staves were exported was bound to send four bow-staves for every ton of merchandise into the kingdom. As to the arrows an immense number were manufactured, the vast flocks of geese in medieval England, and swans, providing the quills.   Each archer commonly carried " under his belt " two dozen arrows.

The equipment of the archer began to be considerably augmented; towards the end of the thirteenth century he who before had merely been defended by his " chapelle-de-fer " was frequently defended by a hauberk and the conical helmet.   A variety of the bowmen proper were the arbalestiers.   The arbalest or cross-bow was a very early weapon and to have been chiefly—at first—used for sport.   It was not till the close of the twelfth century that it was recognized as a military weapon and found illustrated as such in manuscripts. Condemned by Pope Innocent II. in 1139, it was used, as we have before mentioned, by Richard I. in his Crusade.   His body-guard was formed partly of arbalastiers.   In the copious records left by Matthew Paris, the cross-bowman is constantly mentioned.   His particular post was in the forepart of the battle and upon the wings where the heavy quarrels discharged from his weapon were supposed to check the advance of the enemies' knights, and in the thirteenth century scarcely a battle is recounted where the arbalastier is not credited with performing most conspicuous service.   In the battle near Damietta in 1237 a hundred Templars and three hundred cross-bowmen are said to have fallen.   In the contest with Louis IX., Henry III. of England had seven hundred cross-bowmen in his force, while the French had a vastly greater number.

In the time of King John the pay for a cross-bowman on foot was threepence a day, while if mounted he was paid sevenpence halfpenny or fifteen-pence, according as to whether he possessed one or two horses.

The supersession of the cross-bow in England by the long bow was due to natural causes.   It was found that as the long-bow underwent improvements it out-classed the cross-bow in more ways than one.   A powerful and skilful bowman could discharge half a dozen or more arrows during the time the arbalestier was winding up his cross-bow for a second shot.   Also the distance covered by the arrow and its penetrative power was found greater than that of the quarrel.   In consequence of the rapidity of the English archers they invariably beat down the attack of the continental cross-bowmen, where their use was retained much longer than in this country.   The great and growing use that archers in the English battles were found, prepared the way for infantry gradually to oust the mailed knight on horseback in a fight; an instance of this is found at Crécy.

Edward III. was a bad strategist but a good tactician.   He ought not to have been found at Crécy on the 28th August, 1346; but being there, he did the best that could be done.   More than half his army were archers.   He dismounted his men-at-arms and posted his archers as advancing wings on each side of both " battles " of infantry. " From the day of Crécy," writes Green, " feudalism tottered slowly but surely to its grave. . . . The churl had struck the noble." Yet as has been well remarked, it is interesting to note how little Froissart knew of this.   To him, as to the princes and the lords and to Francis I. a hundred and fifty years later, Chivalry and its emblazoned banners were more than the art of war and they failed to realize that the destinies of war were passing, and in some cases had passed already, from the knight in armour to the brave archer and pike-man.

This rapid growth of archers in a feudal army is seen in the battles of the Wars of the Roses which were chiefly fought by dismounted men-at-arms and innumerable archers, some of whom were raised by parliamentary vote, some hired, some mustered as those in the wars of Edward I. against Scotland, as retainers of the great lords and knights mentioned in that Roll of Caerlaverock that we have quoted above, till " villanous salpetre " at last put an end to the superiority of the knightly mêlée and with it the superiority of the " gentle " class. It is not certain when or how the long-bow became the English weapon. The Saxons at Hastings, as well as the Normans, used the short horseman's bow and drew the arrow to the breast and not the ear; this is well displayed in the Bayeux Tapestry. The long-bow is not mentioned in the Assize of Arms in 1181, and there is little account of English archery till the wars of Edward I. in Wales and Scotland.

The Crusaders if they used a bow, chiefly—though against the Papal injunction—used the cross-bow, this because it was smaller so more handy on horseback than the six-foot long-bow. It was Edward I. then " the flower of knighthood, in his home wars who, using and perceiving the great use of the long-bow, in reality, by his adoption of it, introduced the gradual substitution for the good knight's sword and destrier and mêlée, the long-bow and the archer."

The men-at-arms at this period were also important factors in a feudal army. They were part of a knight-banneret's troop or company. They were usually armed with a steel chapelle-de-fer (a steel cap with often a point in front, lined with padding). This covered a chain-mail coif which was part of a continuous hauberk, and the arms and hands were covered with mail of a similar description. Bands of leather round the neck afforded the protection of a gorget, they were affixed to a hauberk composed of leather scales of large size and leaf-like shape showing the mid-rib, while a belt round the waist and pendant leaves on the skirt completed a most effective bodily defence. The legs were enclosed in soft leather chausses protected by metal studs upon which was a cross-gartering of leather thongs. Their usual weapon was the axe.

The rank and file of a knightly army were armed with, and carried with them, for the assaulting of both the enemy and hostile towns, many strangely named weapons. Eustache Deschamps ennumerates such in one of his ballads animadverting on those who manufacture arms—

" De males dagues de Bourdeaulz,
   Et d'espées de Clermont,
   De dondaines, et de cousteaulz
   D'acier, qui à Milan se font
   De haiche à martel qui confont,
   De croquepois, de fer de lance,
   D'archegaie qu'om gette et lance,
   De faussars, espaphus, guisarmes,
   Puist il avoir plaine sa pance,
   Qui me requérra de faire armes.

De canons, de pierres et carreaulz
D'espingales, du feu second,
D'engins, de truye, des mereaulx,
Qu'ilz departent quant ilz s'en vont,
D'art perilleux qui fiert parfont,
Et qui soudainement s'avance,
Puist estre mis jusqu'à oultrance,
Et toujours soit en plours et larmes,
En douleur, en désespérance,
Qui me requérra de faire armes.

Des maces de Damas, de fliaux
Des piques que les Flamens ont,
De haucepiez qui sont ysneaulx
De plommées qui corps deffont
De broches, d'espiez, telz qu'ils sont,
De faulz trenchans sans espérance
De guérir, sont mort ou en trance
Cilz ou tu qu'ilz soies qui t'armes;
Perdre puist honeur et vaillance,
Qui me requérra de faire armes."

(Of evil daggers of Bordeaux
And of Clermont swords,
Of stone-throwers, and of knives
Of steel, which are made at Milan,
Of the hammer-axe which confounds one,
Of crooks and of iron lances,
Of javelins that are cast and thrown,
Of guichards, two-handled swords and guisarmes;
May he have his belly full
Who calls on me to take up arms.

As for cannon, stones and quarrels
Arbalests on wheels, Greek fire,
May they depart whither they are going,
With such perilous skill whoso strikes hard
And whoso suddenly rushes on
May (he) be shown no mercy,
And (let him) always be in grief and tears,
In sorrow and in despair
Who calls on me to take up arms.

By Damascus maces (military) flails
Pikes such as the Flemings use,
Cross-bows which are swift,
Holy water sprinklers that disfigure the body,
Scythes which slice one beyond hope
Of cure, let him die and swoon away
Him and thee, whosoever thou art who dost arm thyself
Lost be (thy) honour and valiancy
Who calls on me to take up arms.)

Several of these weapons were later than the period the book covers, but such are given to show how from weapons less " scientific," if the word may be used, they sprung. Others of them are of very ancient date.

(1) The cannon here spoken of was of the most primitive character, the difficulty which attended its use, and the danger incurred by those who discharged them, caused the old arms to be long preferred to the new ones. The balls they discharged were stone ones.

The first written evidence relating to the existence of cannon is in the Ordinances of Florence in the year 1326 wherein authority is given to the Priors Gonfalionieri to appoint persons to superintend the manufacture of cannon and iron balls for the defence of the camp in the Republic. Barbour, the Scottish poet, quotes an authority for use of cannon by Edward III. in his Scottish campaign in 1327, but the authority is doubtful and the date of the first appearance of cannon in the field is still debated. Some say they were used at Crécy in the year 1346. Certainly in 1382 the men of Ghent carried guns into the field against the Brugeois, and at the combat of Pont-de-Comines in the same year we read " bombardes portatives " were used.

(2) The " dondaines " were something similar, and were used for throwing stones, or arrows, especially for throwing heavy weights a short distance (see Rigaud, Vol. VII., p. 24).

(3) The " hammer-axes " had a sharp edge one side, and a hammer the other.

(4) The " croquepois " were sticks armed with an iron hook.

(5) The " guisarmes " were weapons shaped like scythes. This was a weapon dating from the bronze age and used as late as the seventeenth century.

The " guisarme " usually terminated in a strong sharp point, the two sides were both sharpened to a razor-like edge and various hooks and spikes added.

(6) The " fauchard " resembles a scythe in particular, and was a species of guisarme. So deadly and so ghastly were the wounds inflicted by this weapon that an agitation for its abolition rose in the Middle Ages. (Ashdown, " British and Foreign Arms and Armour," p. 320).

(7) " Espaphus " espadon, was a two-handed sword.

(8) " Carreaulx " were " quarrels," that is great arrows or " bolts " usually discharged from a machine with the extremity armed with a piece of weighted lead; quarrels and bolts were used by the arbalestiers or cross-bowmen.

(9) " Truyes " were " sows "—a machine dating from Roman times, used for throwing stones, also affording shelter when approaching a walled town, and it could also be used as a battering-ram. Such a machine seems to have been used by the ancient Assyrians.

(10) " Espringales," machines like arbalests mounted on wheels, being huge steel bows which threw javelins, spears and darts, and sometimes were adapted to throw stones, two or more, at a single discharge. These latter were vertical springs of steel which were pulled back by ropes and pulleys and when released would throw one missile from a sling at the extremity and another from a cup fixed to the steel. (Ashdown, p. 247).

(11) " Fuseaulx," a kind of stick shaped like a spindle but very long and used for defensive purposes (Godefroi). It seems to have had no connection with fire or even rockets.

(12) " Plommèes " were great balls of lead or iron attached to the end of an iron chain : they were known popularly as " Holy Water Sprinklers."

(13) The military " flail " is allied to the weapon called " The Morning Star," a mace with a spiked head. It consisted of a shaft to which was affixed a staple having a chain depending, and to the end of which a ball of iron, usually covered with spikes, was attached.

Many of these weapons were carried by the rank and file of a feudal army from the earliest times, some were adaptations of more primitive models, while two or three had their origin as far as can be traced by specimens found, to the middle of the fourteenth century. Certainly, without the modern cannon and gunnery, the medieval soldier was not wanting in arms, and so unlike the knight, his leader and overlord, armed only with lance, sword and axe, sometimes with the " misericorde " to despatch his fallen foe, he was provided with arms for every emergency on the field of battle or in a siege.

CHAPTER XIV

PILGRIMAGE AND CRUSADES

PROBABLY the Crusades would have taken place, or, at least would have been attempted, had the order of knighthood never been existant, nor had military saintship become a fashion; but they never would have taken place, if, long before their era, and coeval with them, pilgrimages had not been practised.

This chapter, though it necessarily deals with knighthood in reference to the Crusades, cannot on such an immense subject, devote much space to them, but it may be of use to dwell a little on pilgrimages, which called the remarkable movement known as Crusades into being and activity.

The cause of the first of these Crusades was to free the Holy Places for the use and safety of Christian Pilgrims. That land, hallowed by the presence of the Divine Founder of Christianity, had very early been the object of pilgrimage. Narratives of such have come down to us— one of a Christian of Bordeaux as early as A.D. 333, that of St. Paula, and her daughter about A.D. 386, given by St. Jerome, that of Bishop Arculf A.D. 700, of Willebad A.D. 725, of Saewulf A.D. 1102, of Sigurd the Crusader in 1107.

In our own country even as early as Saxon times, their kings made treaties to secure the safe-conduct of their subjects through foreign lands. There was, in the latter part of this Saxon period, a great rage for foreign pilgrimages. Thousands of persons were continually going and coming between England and the principal shrines of Europe, especially the threshold of the Apostles at Rome. They were the subject of a letter from Charlemagne to King Offa, "concerning the strangers, who for the love of God and the salvation of their souls, wish to repair to the thresholds of the Blessed Apostles, let them travel in peace without any trouble." Again, in the year A.D. 1031 King Canute made a pilgrimage to Rome, and met the Emperor Conrad, and other princes, from whom he obtained for all his subjects, whether merchants or pilgrims, exemptions from the usual tolls exacted on the journey to Rome. To the shrine of St. James at Compostella numbers of English pilgrims annually went. At the marriage of Edward I. in 1234 to Leonora, sister of Alonzo of Castille, a protection for English pilgrims was stipulated, but they came in such numbers as to alarm the French. In the fifteenth century Rymer mentions nine hundred and sixteen licences to make the pilgrimage to Santiago granted in 1428, and two thousand four hundred licences in 1434.

Before any man went on pilgrimage, he first went to his church and received the Church's blessing on his pious enterprise. At the

199

opening of the service he lies prostrate before the altar while the priest and choir sing over him certain appropriate Psalms, *viz.*, xxxv., l. and xc. Then some versicles and three collects for his safety. Then he rises, and then follows the benediction of his script and staff, and the priest sprinkles the script with holy water and places it on the neck of the pilgrim, saying, " In the Name of —— take this script, the habit of your pilgrimage, that corrected and saved you may be worthy to reach the thresholds of the saints to which you desire to go, and, your journey done may return to us in safety." Then the priest delivers the staff, saying, " Take this staff, the support of your journey and of the labour of your pilgrimage, that you may be able to conquer all the bands of your enemy, and to come safely to the threshold of the saints to which you desire to go, and your journey obediently performed return to us with joy." If any one of the pilgrims present is going to Jerusalem, he is to bring a habit signed with the Cross and the priest blesses it, " We pray that Thou wilt vouchsafe to bless this Cross, that the banner of the Cross, whose figure is here signed upon him, may be to Thy servant an invincible strength against the evil temptation of the old enemy, a defence by the way, a protection in Thy house, and may be to us everywhere a guard." Then he sprinkles the habit with holy water and gives it to the pilgrim, saying " Take this habit signed with the Cross of the Lord our Saviour, that by it you may come safely to His sepulchre, who with the Father," etc. Then follows Mass ; and after Mass, certain prayers over the pilgrims, prostrate at the altar ; then " let them communicate, and so depart in the name of the Lord."

There was a certain costume appropriate to the pilgrim. It consisted of a robe, a hat, a staff and script. Du Cange calls the robe " selaxina." It is said to have been always of wool and sometimes of a shaggy stuff. It seems intended to have represented the robe of John the Baptist of camels' hair, and was grey in colour. The pilgrim, whether knight or peasant, who was sent on pilgrimage as a penance seems usually to have been ordered to do so bare-foot. They also often made a vow not to cut their hair or beard until the pilgrimage had been accomplished. But the special insignia of a pilgrim was the staff and script. The staff was usually a long one, some five or six feet long, with a knob at the top and another about a foot lower down, with a hook on it to attach a water-bottle or small bundle. The script was a small bag slung at the side by a cord over the shoulder and contained the pilgrim's food and a few necessaries. Sometimes this script was ornamented. Thus on the grave-stone of a knight at Haltwhistle " a garb," or wheatsheaf (one of the " charges " on his shield) is represented upon his script. But besides the ordinary insignia of pilgrimage, every pilgrimage had its special signs, which the pilgrim on his return wore conspicuously upon his hat or script, or hung round his neck. It followed therefore that the pilgrim who had made a long pilgrimage, paying his devotions at every shrine on his way, might come back as thickly decorated with signs, as a modern soldier who has been through several stirring campaigns.

The pilgrim to the Holy Land even before the Crusades had this distinction above all others—that he wore a special sign from the very hour that he took the vow upon him to make that most honourable pilgrimage.

This sign was a cross made of two strips of coloured cloth sewn on the shoulder of his robe. The English wore the Cross of white, the French of red, the Flemish of green. Some, in their enthusiasm, had the Cross cut into their flesh. In the Romance of " St. Isumbras " we read :

> " With a sharpe knyfe he share
> A Cross upon his shoulder bare."

Others had it branded on them with a hot iron; one pilgrim in the " Miracles of St. Thomas " of Abbot Benedict, gives the reason—that though his clothes should be torn away, no one should be able to tear the Cross from his breast. At the end of the Church's " Office of Pilgrims " a rubrick is, however, placed, that this burning the Cross in the flesh is forbidden by the Canon law on pain of the greater excommunication. This prohibition shows that at one time it was not an uncommon practice. When the pilgrim reached the Holy Land and had visited the usual round of the Holy Places, he became entitled to wear the palm in token of an accomplishment of that pilgrimage, and so was derived the name of " palmer."

Those who had taken any of the greater pilgrimages would probably be regarded ever after their return with respect by their friends and acquaintances, and the agnomen " Palmer " or " Pilgrim " would naturally be added to their Christian name—as William the Palmer, John the Pilgrim—and this doubtless is the origin of the present-day common surnames. The tokens of pilgrimage sometimes even accompanied a man to his grave and were sculptured on his monument. Shells (of the Compostella Pilgrimage) have not unfrequently been found in stone coffins, which, as sacred things, and having a certain virtue, were strewed over the dead man as he was carried upon his bier and afterwards placed in his grave. For example, when the grave of Bishop Mayhew, who died as late as 1516, in Hereford Cathedral was opened some years ago, there was found lying by his side a common, rough hazel wand between four and five feet long and about as thick as a man's finger, and with it a mussel and a few oyster shells. The tomb of Abbot Cheltenham at Tewkesbury has the spandrils ornamented with shields charged with scallop shells, and the pilgrim staff and script are sculptured on the bosses of the groining of the canopy over the tomb. There is a grave-stone, before mentioned, at Haltwhistle, Northumberland, on which is the usual device of a cross sculptured in relief, and on one side of the shaft of the Cross are laid a sword and a shield, charged with the arms of Blenkinsop—a fess between three garbs—probably indicating the dead man was a knight; on the other side of the shaft of the Cross are laid a Palmer's staff and a script bearing also garbs, indicating that the knight had been a pilgrim.

In the church of Ashby-de-la-Zouch there is a recumbent figure of a man in pilgrim's weeds. A hat with scallop-shells lies under his head, his script tasselled and charged with scallop-shells, his staff laid diagonally across the body. The costly style of the monument, the lion at his feet, and above all a collar of SS. round his neck, prove that the knight commemorated was a person of distinction and a pilgrim. In Henry VII.'s Chapel, Westminster, the figure of a pilgrim is frequently introduced in the sculpture of the side chapels, and on the reredos, in allusion, no doubt, to the pilgrims who figure in the legendary history of St. Edward the Confessor. There are scattered also about the country many curious symbols on medieval grave-stones which seem intended for pilgrim staves; yet if every knight and person of lower degree who had made a pilgrimage had had its badges carved upon their tombs we should surely have found many others thus decorated, but indeed we have the graves of knights who were known to have accomplished the great pilgrimage to Jerusalem, who have no such insignia upon their tombs.

A narrative of the pilgrimage made by a distinguished knight, Robert, Duke of Normandy, the father of William the Conqueror, will serve to illustrate the manners and sentiments even the nobles had in entering on a pilgrimage.

When the Norman duke resolved in expiation of his sins to visit the Holy Land as a pilgrim he settled the affairs of the duchy and took his son William, whom he designated as his successor, to Paris, and made him do homage to the king, Henry I. of France. He then set out for the East attended by a large train of knights and others, going barefoot like any simple pilgrim, clad in the pilgrim habit, wearing his script and staff. On coming to any town, he made his train go in first; he followed by himself, meekly enduring the scoffs and insults of the rabble. In a town near Besancon, when the pilgrims were going out of the gates, a brutal porter gave the duke a blow on the back with a stick. His attendants would have punished the offence with death, but the duke said, " Nay, for a pilgrim must suffer for the love of God," adding that he valued more the blow that had been given him, than the best city he possessed. In this manner he passed through Burgundy, Provence and Lombardy. At Rome, as was the custom, he received a cross from the Pope. He then proceeded to Constantinople, where his piety and his liberality won him the favour of all ranks of the people. He refused the presents offered him by the Emperor, and insisted on paying for everything he received. To overcome his delicacy, the Emperor gave orders that no one should sell wood to the pilgrims, but Robert directed his attendants to purchase nuts and dress their food with shells and thus eluded the Emperor's generosity.

Falling sick on his journey through Asia Minor he had himself borne in a litter by the Saracens, and when a Norman pilgrim whom he met asked if he had any message to send home, he said, " Tell my people that thou hast met me with devils carrying me to Paradise." He gave some money to the pilgrim, who went on his way laughing at the reply of his duke. At the gate of the Holy City the duke found a number of poor pilgrims, who could not obtain admittance for want of the requisite money to pay the toll exacted from such. Robert paid a byzant for each and they preceded his entrance into the town. Even the Moslems admired his piety, and the Emir of the city caused all money to be returned to him. The duke instantly divided it among the poor and his followers, and gave rich presents to the Moslems.

Alas, death overtook this worthy knight and pilgrim on his return, at Nicæa, in Bithynia. The relics he collected were brought to Normandy and deposited in the monastery of Cerisy, which he had founded.

Robert of Normandy was only one out of hundreds of knights, who, before the Crusades, made pilgrimage. Houses for the accommodation of such persons, erected either by the piety of princes or private persons, were soon to be seen in every great town; on the banks of streams over which no bridge led, were raised inns in which the weary wayfarers found refreshment and repose. Itineraries were drawn up which directed the steps of the pious from the most remote west to the banks of the Jordan, and amidst the ravages of war the pilgrim's habit was a protection.

Another most remarkable of pilgrimages undertaken as penances by a knight and a nobleman was that of Fulk le Noir, Count of Anjou. This man who had resigned himself to the violent passions which, not uncommonly in that age, produced the most terrible catastrophes, was accused of having, among other deeds of blood, murdered his wife. The public abhorrence, the torment of his conscience, which, in men of his character, is generally of the same strength as their passions, and the fearful visions which his terrified imagination conjured up, conspired to render his existence a torment.

No longer able to endure the agony of his remorse and see himself surrounded with luxury, he bade adieu to his estates, and assuming the habit of a pilgrim, set out for the Holy Land. The storms of the sea reminded him that he was still an object of Divine anger, and crushed under the harrowing sense of his iniquity, when he arrived in Jerusalem, he suffered not himself to indulge in the calm exercises of devotion, but with a cord round his neck, and scourged by his attendants, rushed through the streets, exclaiming, " Lord, have pity on a faithless and perjured Christian, on a sinner wandered far from his own country."

It was not without some degree of art this unfortunate pilgrim obtained permission of the Saracens to worship at the Holy Sepulchre; but when he did, his tears and lamentations were expressive of the most violent remorse; and the chroniclers of his life have not failed to add a miracle to that which may be regarded as the natural effect of his grief. So acceptable was his repentance, they write, that the stone of the Sepulchre, which was hard and solid, became as he kissed it, as soft and flexible as wax warmed at the fire.

But this was the least part of the prodigy—" for the Count bit into it, and carried away a great piece in his mouth, without the Infidels knowing anything of it; and he henceforth visited all the other Holy Places at his ease."

Having satisfied his conscience by the completion of his pilgrimage, the Count performed certain acts of charity to the poor Christians at Jerusalem, and then returned to Europe.

Soon after his return he built a church, in imitation of that of the Holy Sepulchre, and led a very devout life; but his conscience still harassed him with the sense of guilt, and he determined upon performing a second pilgrimage, which he did with the same fervent attention to devotion and charity as on the former occasion.

But on his return, he was enabled to add tenfold to the merit of the expedition, by aiding the Pope in a dangerous difficulty with which he was assailed. For this he received as a reward a plenary absolution, and he reached his estates loaded with relics and papal benedictions.

Still, however, he felt a weight upon his heart, which his pious pilgrimages and all his devout acts had not succeeded in removing. He was therefore impelled to make a third pilgrimage to the Holy

Land. To his own earnest prayers for pardon were added those of his followers, and he once more returned to Europe, hoping that he might now enjoy his home with a peaceful conscience, but before he reached it, he was seized with a fatal malady at Metz, where a tomb was raised to his memory.

That contrition for sins—a desire of expiation for such—entered into many of these knightly pilgrims' hearts, one cannot doubt, but like all earthly good things, gain was soon added, particularly in the monks and lower classes who went on pilgrimage. Relics brought from the Holy Land were held, of course, more in repute than any others. The demand was so great and the supply was so constant, that it is no breach of charity to suppose that the clergy of the Holy City scrupled not to palm counterfeits on many of their Western brethren. The wealthy pilgrim, by purchasing relics and bestowing them on his return on some abbey or church, obtained the prayers of the Brotherhood for himself and family, as a benefactor. The poor pilgrim by laying out a portion of the money given to him in charity, in a little venture of relics, was sure to obtain a large return for his capital by selling them to the founders of some new church or convent. Relics also came to be esteemed as personal safeguards, the smaller sort in little boxes hung round the neck or in the clothing. It is no wonder, the demand so great, they became a regular article of commerce and no longer the pilgrim bent on expiating his sins, but the pilgrim with trader instincts visited the Holy Land and brought back to the West cargoes of these holy relics.

As the seaports of France and Italy carried on an extensive commerce with Egypt and Syria for spices, silks and precious stones, their shipping offered an easy mode of conveyance to the Holy Land and thus accelerated the desire for pilgrimage. Women were often among such, and many persons who preferred a life of rambling to honest industry (hence our word " saunter " from " a la sante terre ") assumed, as time went on, the pilgrim's dress, and went from shrine to shrine, living on the charity of the devout.

Jerusalem was one of the earliest conquests of the Moslems, but the tolerance of successive Khalifs had long thrown no impediment in the way of the Christian pilgrim. The celebrated Haroun-al-Raschid had even presented, in friendship, the keep of the Holy City to Charlemagne. Even when Jerusalem fell into the hands of the Fatimite Khalifs, they were too worldly-wise to stop the hundreds of Western pilgrims who brought money to their coffers, and profit to their citizens. But when the wild hordes from Central Asia penetrated into Syria under Malek Shah these civilities of the Infidels—the Christians in Palestine no longer enjoyed. The barbarous Turks would rush with loud cries and yells into the churches when the pilgrims were at their devotions, jump upon the altars, and throw the sacred vessels about, break the marble pillars and images. They exacted with far more severity than the former Saracens, tolls at the gates of the Holy City, consequently thousands of the poorer pilgrims lay without the walls unable to obtain entrance. It was in consequence of these miseries of the pilgrims that Peter, a native of Amiens in Picardy, known through all Christendom as " The Hermit," preached the First Crusade.

This Crusade, as were the later ones, was in fact a pilgrimage, the only difference in it was that the knights and their followers no longer assumed the peaceable garb of the older pilgrim, but the hauberk, lance and shield of the warrior. And to such, the appeal of Peter had a wonderful charm. Those mimic battles which so long each knight had enjoyed in tourney and tournament, with no object to gain but his lady's approval, and his valour's display, were now transferred to the Holy Land, where the prize held out by the Church was his soul's salvation. And even there his lady's gaze might be displayed in the mêlée of many a hard fought battle. Those martial feats which had so long in his native land been a simple amusement, were now lifted up and dignified and given the holiest of objects for their attainment in the eyes and heart of the knight of the Middle Ages—the rescue of the Holy Place and Holy City where his suzeraine, his lord, had once lived and died.

That they held this view is obvious; they went armed with the same arms to the Holy Land as they did when entering a tournament à l'outrance. On board of the French or Venetian galleys that conveyed them, they slung their shields along the sides of each, emblazoned with their family bearings. In these galleys their destriers, barded and chamfroned, were conveyed as if to one of those picturesque encounters —a tourney.

The banners and pennons on their lances braved the sea and its storms as often as on a wild day at home they had braved the same and waved the same as over some crowded lists at a " pas d'armes." As they embarked on board they shouted out the same war cries they had often done on land before their prince, and if the Crusades represented the tourneys, only shifted to the Holy Land, so, as has been observed, they were the representation and outcome of the many pilgrimages.

As before taking such, the pilgrim had to confess his sins, be present at Mass, be absolved and receive the blessing of Mother Church, so each knight—if an earnest Crusader—ere he set out, did the same. As weariness, hunger, thirst before he reached the Holy Land and City, the pilgrim realized might be his lot, so did the knight when he had sewn on his shoulder the Cross, and leaving, as the pure and simple pilgrim of old, his lands, his houses, and his kindred, took in lieu of a pilgrim's staff, his sword, and instead of a pilgrim's script his shield, and set out on that mighty pilgrimage—a Crusade.

It is unlikely that the knights even realized—so much ignorance prevailed of geography and even of the quality and bravery of the foes they had met—the dangers in all their extent which awaited them; certainly the hordes of the camp-followers, women and lesser soldiery, failed to do so, and yet, taking only to the end of the third Crusade, not less than half a million of warriors, the flower of knighthood, from Germany, France and Britain, it has been computed had perished, and if we take into consideration the small scarcity of population then, in these countries, compared with the present time, it is possible perhaps to realize how much of manhood and chivalry these three Crusades destroyed and ate up.

At the time of the advent of the First Crusade, pilgrimages, to free the Holy Places, were deemed essential to a soul's well-being, for the end of the world was daily expected, and the destruction of all social life. Portents were of daily occurrence. Men's minds dreading the unseen, seized on natural appearances and converted them into Divine intimations. Stars were seen to fall from heaven, thick as hail; northern lights of unusual brilliancy flashed along the sky, and comets displayed their flaming trains. Children were born with double limbs and capable of speech. Shepherds as they watched their flocks by night beheld a great city in the air. A priest as he walked with two companions in a wood saw a huge sword carried along by the wind; and another priest was, in bright daylight, the spectator of a combat in the sky between two horsemen, one of whom smote the other with a great cross, and thus became the victor. All these circumstances or rather portents urged the population to appease heaven by the well-known remedy of a pilgrimage. And to make that pilgrimage successful, the Holy Land must be freed and held by the Christians.

In this atmosphere then of misfortune the Crusade was proclaimed, and fright—the most characteristic trait of the Middle Ages—waited to be appeased. Supernatural forces, superstition under a thousand forms is always at the bottom of individual intelligence and is the common mark of all men. The knight impregnated with the supernatural, haunted by childish fancies, and by visions seen by weakened and fasting anchorites, was convinced that everything was an omen. To him natural scourges were the dread visitation of God on the saints; he must submit, or seek to advert them by long pilgrimages to the Holy Places. All the superstitious practices of antiquity were transmitted to the feudal ages. Vainly did the Church combat many of these survivals of paganism. Superstition stronger than religion, moulded the idea of Christianity to its own use. Even monks who wrote history shared in the belief of their contemporaries.

The Prior of Vigeois in Limousin asserts that one could foresee the ills with which his land was afflicted, for the wolves in the forest of Pompadour howled steadily throughout the day of the Feast of Saint Austoiclinian. In the midst of his wars the Count of Toulouse refused to execute a convention because he had seen a bird, a crow which the peasants call Saint Martin's bird, flying on his left. Later in the century a noble, Roger of Comminges, was going to do homage to his overlord. As the ceremony was about to begin the latter sneezed. Immediately Roger refused to do homage, because the Count had sneezed but once, so everything that day would turn out badly.

Divination of the future by lot, also a legacy of antiquity, was in common use.

A book—the Evangel, the Psalter—was opened and the first lines read as a presage.

Those who went to war or on a pilgrimage did not fail to consult the lots on the outcome of the enterprise. Simon de Montfort, before taking the Cross, had opened a Psalter and sought to obtain a presentiment of his destiny.

The Church did not forbid the practice, she used it herself. On many an occasion when a chapter confronted the question of instituting a bishop or a canon, the Evangels were consulted, and from the verse found by chance a prognostication of the future of the recipient was made.

Later, when Innocent III. was urged to disinherit the Count of Toulouse in favour of Simon de Montfort ("Chansons de la Croisade des Albigeois") he demanded a moment's delay. "Barons," said he,

" take notice, if you please, that I consult." He opened a book, and perceiving from the lot that the destiny of the Count of Toulouse was not evil, attempted to save him.

No less did terrestrial marvels strike the imagination of the brave but in some ways childish knights.

In France, at Rozoy-en-Brie, at the instant of the sacrifice of the Mass, the wine appeared changed into blood, the bread to flesh. In a Church of Limousin several crosses appeared on the altar-cloth. In a Church of Tarn the blood circulated in a statue of the Virgin. At Chateauroux, a brigand (temp. Henry II. of England) who was throwing dice before a church door, in a fit of rage hurled a stone at a statue of the Virgin and Child. The arm of the latter broke off, and a great deal of blood flowed from the wound. This arm King John got into his possession, and kept as a precious relic.

In this human society, excited by daily sufferings and terrors, living in the midst of hallucinations and visions—the preaching of the First Crusade came as a mighty wind blowing away all these mists of fancy and superstition, and gave to the faith of knight and peasant a tangible object for his piety—to free the Holy Land from the Infidel. Even children caught a glimpse of that divine object. A young boy, Stephen—a shepherd near Vendome—had a vision in which God in the form of a poor pilgrim asked him for a piece of bread and gave him a letter charging him to go and re-conquer the Holy Land and deliver the Holy Sepulchre. A little later, when he was driving his sheep home, he saw them kneel before him and beg for mercy. Then it was indeed a divine mission he felt he had received. He travelled over the land uttering the cry of the Crusade, " Lord, God, arouse Christianity! Lord God, give us the true Cross!" and he is said to have worked miracles everywhere, and the Chronicle of Rouen tells us he had join him, as a leader of the Crusade, over thirty thousand other children.

There was also another factor in the knight's life which urged their attempt. Despite their tourneys, their love songs and their gallantry, born from the times they lived in, an undercurrent of sadness and the insufficiency of this world seems to have permeated their hearts. Even in their martial games, the mixture of pain and evil in this life the young knight is reminded of

> " Qui bien et mal ne peut souffoir,
> A grant honneur ne peut venir."
> —Petit Jean de Saintre.

So again Eustache Deschamps:

> " Las! que j'ay veu de tribulacion
> De tempests, et de mortalites
> De haines, de peuples mocion
> De grans orgueils et de grans vanitez
> De traisons et de crudelitez."

Two earlier writers than the author above echo the same view of life. Wace in the " Roman de Rou " writes:

" Tout rien se torne en declin
Tot chiet, tot muert, tot vait en fin
Hom muert, fer use, fust porrist
Tur font, mur chiet, rose flaistrit
Cheval tresbuche, drap viesist,
Tot ouvre fet od mainz perost.''

(All things hasten to decay, all fall, all perish, all things come
to an end. Man dieth, iron consumeth, wood decayeth. Towers
crumble. Strong walls fall down. The rose withereth away. The
war-horse waxeth feeble. Gay trappings grow old. All the works of
man's hands perish.)

So too, Walter der Vogelweide :

" Hie vor do was din welt so schône
Nu ist worden also höne.''

(The world was once so beautiful,
And now so desolate and dull.)

These feelings of the transitory character of human life, of its
miseries, its failures, its evils was the great mainspring that sent the
knights, and hundreds of a lower rank, on pilgrimages to the Holy
Places. When the human heart is sad within it turns naturally to
some object which holds out a remedy, and the more difficult it is to
reach that object, the greater value its supposed consolations are when
attained. Even if it was owing to the knight's battles, his feuds, his
wasting, when on a line of march, the fields of his foe—he realized
the misery—he felt it was abnormal and sad.

" Temps de doleur et de temptacion
Ages de plour, d'envie et de tournient;
Temps de langour et de dampnacion,
Ages meneur près du definement,
Temps plains d'orreur, qui tout fait faussement
Ages menteur plain d'orgueil et d'envie.''

The swiftness of youth's passing was brought to the medieval
mind more than to our own no doubt by the constant pestilences that
raged over Europe—the constant feuds and wars, and the want of
skill possessed by the medical faculty in arresting the ravages of
disease. All these things were in the knights' as well as in their poets'
minds.

" Adieu, printemps; adieu, jeune saison
Que tous deduiz sont deuz à creature
Adieu, Amours; adieu, noble maison,
Pleine jadis de flours et de verdure.
Adieu, esté, autompne qui pou dure,
Yvers me vient, c'est-a-dire vieillesce;
Pour a tristes, te dy adieu, jeunesce.''

DAYS OF CHIVALRY

This ever-present reality of the next world, despite many failings and many lapses from virtue, permeated all ranks of life in the days of Chivalry. Despite their often boisterous living and feastings, their carousals and tourneys, it formed in the knightly character a strange substratum of melancholy; this also influenced even the framers of their songs and their poets. Eustache Deschamps of these latter, though full of the joy of living, constantly relapses into the nearness of the next world and the inevitable passage to it by death.

> " Que tu mourras; tes prédécesseurs voy
> Qui sont tuit mort ou en paix ou en guerre;
> Ayme donc Dieu, sers, obeïs et croy.
> De tel seigneur fait bon l'amour acquerre.
> Car leurs règnes perdent pas cas soudain
> Roy terrien l'un fait a l'autre effroy
> Et par pechié n'ont rien d'uy à demain," etc.

When therefore a Crusade was preached it held out hopes, in its accomplishment, of fulfilling and quelling many of these aspirations and longings in the medieval pilgrim heart—no less in the martial one of the knight.

Is it a wonder that on every side, from castle and town, from village and from palace, the news of it seemed the voice of God, offering a panacea to the troubles and miseries of the age? It became a wonder that any should refuse its summons. " I hold no man a true knight," a poet of the time says, " who refuses to go willingly, with his whole heart and with all the means in his power to the assistance of God who so greatly needs it."

It is impossible to analyse from the few data left us, the spirit in which this vast congregation of warriors entered on the Crusade. According to religious writers of the age, it was one of peace, according to the practice they pursued, one of extermination of the Infidels. The object they had in view was certainly in a sense a peaceful one—to give peace and freedom to the Christians then in the Holy Land, or who should hereafter come there as pilgrims, but the means to effect this was by the sword. Ruthless and unsparing as that sword was when used by those early knights fighting against their Christian foes, more ruthless and more cruel when against the Infidel. No such opinion was held then by each stalwart knight as in latter days—that the unbeliever if true to the light given him could be saved; he was looked upon as unclean and his right to exterminate such as the very enemy of God. The Indulgence published to the faithful at the Council of Clermont contained these words: " Let every one who has zeal for the glory of God unite with us. Let us help our brethren; let us break their bonds. Let us cast off their yoke. Cancel, by a work so agreeable to God, the robberies, the fires, the homicides which exclude from the kingdom of God." Is it a wonder that the spirit which animated each knight that took the Cross was one of hatred against the foe he was about to engage in—even if the reason of it was to produce peace—peace in the Holy Land for the Christian?

To torture prisoners, to slay women and children wholesale, to starve and torture prisoners of war—if such were unbelievers—was held by the Christian knight as lawful as to slay them in the open field.

Quarter was neither asked nor given; cruelty became a duty, and it was a rare instance of clemency when some of the most marketable of the defenders of Jerusalem were preserved alive and sold as slaves. In the time of Godefroi de Bouillon pity was unknown for the Infidel. The practice of such warfare is seen in the capture of Antioch and Jerusalem recorded by clerical chroniclers with their full approbation. Robert FitzGerald, near Antioch, brought back into camp a hundred heads of Turks; three hundred heads were sent down from Antioch to the ports, " a very welcome sight." Saracens' noses and ears were spitted on a lance as a trophy. A boat's load of Greek noses and thumbs were sent to Byzantium as a menace. At Ascalon thirty prisoners marched before Godfrey's procession, each bearing on a spear the head of a slain Saracen. Richard I. carried the same horrible trophies at his saddle-bow. Bohemund killed and roasted some prisoners as a jest, to make the enemy believe the Christians were cannibals.

Some of the Christians (it is stated in their own chronicles) ate the flesh of Turks " making war upon God's enemies both with teeth and hands." (See " The Gesta of Richard Cœur de Lion.") Later, at the capture of Acre the whole garrison being held hostage, for the restitution of the relic of the True Cross by Richard, and it not being forthcoming, he slew all his captives to the number, it is said, of five thousand. The bodies of the victims were ripped up to find bezants and precious stones " annum et argentum multum invenerunt in visceribus eorum."

In such a spirit of fierce enthusiastic warfare the knights who went on the First Crusade carried it to a successful termination. Noble and religious a knight as Godfrey de Bouillon felt the same towards the Infidels. When Raymond of Toulouse saved the lives of his prisoners and Tancred promised to do the same, these were cut down the next day and no protest from Godfrey was ever heard. The chroniclers tell the same story and exalt the praises of Godfrey " nullus et sis vitæ est reservatus. Nec ætati nec sexui nec nobilitati ned cuivis, conditoni miserebantur Christani—neque feminis neque parvulis pepercerunt." Yet this was the man whose servants could find no fault with him except that he would stay too long in church after Mass so that their dinner got cold, and was too fond of reading good books. He was " moult preudhomme et moult aymant Dieu et gens d'église." This was he who refused to wear the crown of gold where his Master had worn the crown of thorns, " il ne volt estre corosné roy de Jerusalem, porce Jésus Christ fils de Dieu porta corosne d'espines le jour de sa passion." It could only be to a mind so good, so noble there was the strong conviction that to kill and maltreat the unbeliever even down to his children was a gallant and pious work for a Christian knight to perform.

Something of this conviction was no doubt bred in such from the feudal doctrines then in vogue. A liege-man was bound to look on the enemies of his lord as his own; the Holy Land was God's, therefore as his liege-man, the knight was bound to look on his enemies in it, as his own. The very titles he often addressed that God with—as has been remarked in an earlier part of this work—were those of a knight addressing his feudal lord; therefore the measures he took to exterminate his Siezweaine's foes were the same as he would have adopted in those intermecine battles constantly waged in Western Europe between lord with lord.

This ruthless policy was even adopted when Jerusalem was taken. Those same knights who on first catching sight of the Holy City threw themselves upon the rocky ground adoring their Lord and Redeemer, Raymond d'Agiler relates, slaughtered so vast a number of unbelievers in the Mosque of Omar when they entered the city, that the reins of their horses were bathed in blood. Strange as it may seem that these knights who could turn a love song and had sworn to defend the widow and the fatherless! Yet not strange if we remember the view held at that time that every Infidel was the direct servant of the Evil One, and sworn foe of God, that therefore every one of such killed, fulfilled the knight's oath on entering Chivalry to beat down the evil and upraise the good wherever he might be. That milder ways to unbelievers should be practised was a doctrine unknown to the Crusader, or even to those bishops who in martial accoutrements took part in their battles, and blest them on the battle-field.

It was only later, in the long story of the Crusades, that the Christian knighthood became tinged with forbearance and Chivalry toward his Moslem foes, and then it arose not from the teaching of the clergy but from the refining example of the Saracens themselves. If the mixture of worldly motives was greater in those later times, there was less violence and more respect of the enemy. If the last Crusades are ennobled by the example of Saint Louis, one of the most pleasing traits in them are these proofs of less violence and less cruelty to the foe. As has been well said, " Godfrey and his companions are Homeric heroes, Louis IX. and his knights are medieval gentlemen."

As Gibbon says there is both cause and effect in this. The development of Chivalry softened manners, and every refinement of manners, effected by external causes, helped to develop Chivalry. The ideals of Chivalry were heightened during the two centuries of the Crusades, and so an ideal knight of the thirteenth century was more complex and refined than his brother of the eleventh century. He was not more devout, more chaste, more courageous or more honourable; but he added a grace to these virtues and had a higher and more conscious aim.

This then was one among others of the benefits the crusading knight brought back—if he returned to his native land—a greater courtesy and less cruelty in waging war. Free intercourse with his more polished foes, often as in Spain, caused the Christian and Moslem knights to meet in martial games. All this softened his rough northern manners, and taught him that even war might be carried on with forbearance, and that even an unbeliever had some virtues.

Another point the English certainly learnt from the Crusades, and that from their Moslem adversaries, was the greater use of bowmen. Medieval warfare in the West had organized itself as cavalry, heavy-armed, on great horses unwieldy except to charge. They learnt from the nimble Saracen the value of archers and light movements in the field. The English learnt well this lesson and so became proficient in the value of the archer. So little had the bow been used that in the Second Council of the Lateran in 1139 the use of arrows and cross-bows against Christians was forbidden under anathema, and Muratori proves that the prohibition was intended to hold equally whether the war was just or unjust. Until that time the French certainly had only used the lance and sword. When they returned from the Crusades they brought back the use of the arrow and the javelin. In our own country this Lateran decree was obeyed by Stephen and Henry II., but it was disregarded by Richard I., seeing the great use the enemy found it, in the many battles he had with them in the East, and his death by an arrow was deemed by Monkish chroniclers, in consequence, a divine judgment on his disobedience to the Church.

As far as the religious influence of the Crusade it tended to break up the individual character of the devout and group them together. It was the same influence which had in secular matters begun to bind men together in co-operations and associations for trade, and which had, in fact, created a public feeling, and in religion was stripping individuals of their individual sanctity and dividing it piecemeal among many. That ardent and aroused spirit of a world disturbed by fear of its speedy dissolution, by signs, by omens, by great plagues and sicknesses, was in full force and required an outlet. So the impetuous burst of devoutness with which the Crusade commenced blended together a thousand currents of religious feeling and rolled onward a mighty stream, destroying the old landmarks of private and even national feeling, and broke in twain more completely than anything else the chains of feudalism and the isolation of the ecclesiastic in his own national surroundings.

The effect of the Crusades was complete revolution in the manners and customs of the Western nations—the suppression of servitude, the founding of free towns, the alienation and the division of the feudal lands and development of the communal system were the immediate consequences of the tremendous emigration of men who went forth to fight and die in Holy Land. The nobles ceased to wage their perpetual private quarrels, knighthood became emancipated from feudal chains and assumed a regular and solemn character, ordeals by arms decreased, religious orders multiplied and charitable institutions, first formed for the pilgrims and crusaders, were established on every side.

Men's minds became more enlightened and their manners softened by becoming more cosmopolitan, with a wider knowledge of other lands and people than their own. A new literature sprung forth all at once from the imagination of troubadours, minstrels, and minnesingers, and the art of war, besides mighty strides in commerce and navigation, made various strides in the direction of progress.

Partly by contact with the Byzantines, partly by conflict with the Mahommedan, the Franks learned new methods too of building and of attacking fortifications. The concentric castle with its rings of walls began to displace the old keep and bailey with a single wall. The common use of armorial bearing and the practice of the tournament may possibly be Oriental in their origin, but the latter has its affinities with the Jerid and the former, though of prehistoric origin, may have received a new impulse from the East.

Always a large part too French, the Crusades on the whole contributed to exalt the prestige of France until at the end of the thirteenth century it stood the most considerable power in Europe, and those connections are still to be traced to-day.

The Crusades also were the means of providing for younger sons of the feudal nobility, and as such they resulted in a number of colonies such as the kingdom of Jerusalem, the kingdom of Cyprus, and the Latin Empire of Constantinople.

Perhaps in closing this brief review of the knight on Pilgrimage and Crusade, no nobler one could be brought before the reader than St. Louis IX. of France.

He was a knight " sans peur et sans reproche," who wore all through his life as " a perfect and very gentle knight " the white flower of a saintly life. In comparison with him Godfrey and Tancred seem uncultured.

Twice he took the Cross, and twice left a mother, a wife, and people who idolized him. Unlike even the noblest of the earliest Crusaders, he neither required to carve out, nor gained in the Holy Land, a kingdom or a princely appanage ; he left, on the contrary, a rich and prosperous one to take the pilgrim's script and the Crusader's Cross. His friend and chronicler, the Sire de Joinville, who lived in the closest familiarity with his master, sums up his character in these words : " Never did layman of our times live so devoutly during the whole of his days. . . . If God died on the Cross so did he ; for he wore the cross when he was at Tunis."

His personal habits were simple yet not austere. He " ate contentedly of what his cooks sent up to him, never asking for any particular dish, and drank his wine mixed with water. Never wore embroidered coats of arms nor rich furs but justified those who did, saying that a gentleman should dress according to his rank, so that neither the old should say ' too much,' nor the young ' too little.' "

His religion was as simple as his life. " My chapel," he said, " is my arsenal against all the assaults (traverses) of the world." When the Greek fire came flying through the air " like a dragon " he stretched his hands towards the Crucifix and said, " Faire Sire God preserve my people." He would not speak to a Saracen lord who spoke French and brought him presents, on learning that he was a renegade, nor when Octai Faress-ed-din, chief of the Mamelukes, begged him to confer knighthood upon him as Richard had done for Saladin's nephew, unless he promised to be a Christian.

The day before he died he was heard murmuring, " Nous irons à Jerusalem," and the next day, having lost the power of speech for some hours, he said, " Lord, I will enter into Thy house and adore Thee in Thy Holy Tabernacle." These were his last words.

Yet pious and holy as this royal knight was, he was no idle dreamer or recluse. For courage and feats of arms Louis IX. would have been worthy to be a brother-in-arms of Richard himself. At Damietta as soon as he heard that the Oriflamme of St. Denys had been borne ashore, he leapt into the water up to his armpits in full armour, and when he got to land and saw the Infidel foe " he clapped his lance under his arm, threw his shield in front of him, and would have rushed upon them had the older knights around not constrained him. His appearance in battle is thus described by Joinville. " Never have I seen so fine a knight (si bel homme d'armes), he towered above all his people, out-topping them by the shoulders, a gilded helmet on his head and a German sword in his hands. It was said we should have been lost that day had not the king been with us, for six Turks seized the king's horse by the bridle and were leading him away prisoner; but he delivered himself from them single-handed, by the mighty sword-strokes he dealt them.''

Yet his was a heart full of piety, yet the heart of a soldier—for those he loved. When De Ronnay after the battle of Mansourah kissed his gauntleted hand and told him his dear brother, the Count of Artois, had been slain, he said '' that God should be praised for the good gifts he gave,'' though as he said it big tears fell from his eyes.

Verily he seems to have been most fitted of man to have recovered the relic of his Master's Crown of Thorns, he who so often in life had cast aside his crown of the Golden Fleur-de-lys in exchange for the thorny crown of the pilgrim and crusader. In him we see Chivalry in its highest and most noble aspect, and the Crusading knight without blemish or stain. It is no wonder that after him all other knights seem on a lesser plane and we feel inclined to call him '' the last of the knights.''

At all events, his life shows us—if it had only been permitted to have its full influence and way—what a noble influence Chivalry could exert in raising man to almost a divine height.

When all is said, the Crusades remain a wonderful and perpetually astonishing act in the great drama of human life. They touched the summits of daring and devotion, if they also sank into the deep abysm of shame—whatever of self-interest may have lurked in them, either worldly motives of procuring salvation for a little price or worldly motives of achieving riches and acquiring lands—yet it would be treason to the majority of man's incessant struggles towards an ideal good, if one were to deny that in and through the Crusades men strove for righteousness' sake to extend the kingdom of God on earth. Therefore the tears and blood that were shed were not unavailing; the heroism and chivalry were not wasted. Humanity is the richer for the memory of those millions of men who followed the Cross in the true and certain hope of an eternal reward.

These ages were not '' dark ages '' when Christianity could gather itself together in a common cause and carry the banner of Faith to the Sepulchre of the Redeemer; nor can we but give thanks for their memory, for Jerusalem is in the hearts still of every one baptized with the Cross.

It is a noble and elevating thought that after this long lapse of ages the brave soldiers from this little Isle of Britain have again rescued the Holy City from the Turk and freed the Christians from their domination, and at last fulfilled the desire of our Angevin yet English kings—that Jerusalem should be delivered.

As a modern writer has remarked, it is easy to say that the Crusading knight was ever allured by an '' ignis fatuus '' that led him, the visionary, to a land of chimeras and that had no relation to the love of God and man or to the misery of the world, and to humble Christian goodness; that it was founded on pride—and at best but a soldier's virtue—a virtue of paradox. At any rate such a knight aimed higher than the common scope of the world. His pride was pride in his order, not in his own deeds; he did not worship himself or his theories, but was a humble son of the old Faith; if it did not make his life as pure as the sentiment which he acknowledged, it was better than the gross licence out of which it sprang and against which it protested, and if after years of battle oversea, the Holy Land remained with the Infidel—yet if the Crusading knight had attained naught else, he set up before the men of his own days and for future generations a pattern of chivalrous self-sacrifice and self-abnegation which the world is the better for.

If we examine the failure of the Crusades and the relinquishment of that Chivalrous Quest, it must be found :

(1) In the gradual extinction of the spirit that animated the Chivalry of the Middle Ages. Its very fervour burnt out its strength, and as the years advanced its flame grew less and at last vanished altogether.

(2) The trading spirit of the great republics of Venice and Genoa and Pisa, which, accompanying the last Crusader, did so for their mercantile betterment, infused into the Christian character of a Crusade the baser metal of trade and self-interest.

(3) The error of not introducing, when the Christian kingdom of Jerusalem was first organized, the Salic law; not having it, heiresses inherited and carried their rights to husbands who, like the Lusignana, feebly protected the assailed kingdom, or else carried it into families who merely held the empty title without unsheathing the sword of Godfrey and Baldwin against the Moslem.

(4) The distance of Palestine from the " base," *i.e.*, the Western nations of Europe who in England, France and Germany formed the recruiting ground of the Crusades, the facility therefore the enemy around the small Christian principalities and the kingdom of Jerusalem possessed in levying and throwing their forces into the cities of Palestine.

So Jerusalem became desolate ; after years of travail, after immense expenditure of life and treasure, after countless tears and prayers, of thousands of knightly oaths and deeds it became possible in the decadent ages of Chivalry for a knight no longer to say, " If I forget thee, O Jerusalem, let my right hand forget its cunning," and hushed in the dust of ages were the once ringing words of Jacques de Vitoy, Bishop of Ptolemais in the thirteenth century : " Jerusalem is the city of cities, the saint of saints, the queen of nations and the princess of provinces. She is situated in the centre of the world, in the middle of the earth, so that all men may turn their steps to her ; she is the patrimony of the patriarchs, the muse of the prophets, the mistress of the apostles, the cradle of our salvation, the home of our Lord and the mother of the faith."

CHAPTER XV

FROM the earliest times of Chivalry knights were wont to enter into a union of companions-in-arms, than which nothing was considered more sacred. These companions were united for weal and woe, and no crime was accounted more infamous than to desert or betray such brothers-at-arms. They had the same friends and the same foes; and as it was the genius of Chivalry to carry every virtuous and noble sentiment to the most fantastic extremity, the most extravagant proofs of fidelity to this engagement were often exacted or bestowed. The beautiful romance of Amis and Amiloun, in which a knight slays his own child to make a salve with its blood to cure the leprosy of his brother-in-arms, turns entirely on this extravagant pitch of sentiment. To this fraternity only two persons could, with propriety, bind themselves. (This league of service may possibly have been the incentive to found those great Military Orders of Fraternity which, embracing a vast number of knights, sworn to obedience and mutual aid, became, during the time of the Crusades, so remarkable; for in nothing did Chivalry show itself more worthy of admiration than in its religious aspect in these famed Orders.) It abandoned on the one hand the renown of the soldier, and on the other the repose of the cloister, and it exposed its votary to the hardships of both by devoting him in turn to the perils of the battle-field and to the labours attendant upon the succouring of the distressed. Other knights courted adventure for the sake of their honour and the lady of their love; these incurred it in order to help the unfortunate and to assist the poor. The Grand Master of the Knights' Hospitallers was proud of the title of " Guardian of the ' Redeemer's Poor ' "; he, of the Order of St. Lazarus, was of necessity a leper, while the knight-companions termed the poor " our masters."

The earliest of these religious and military confraternities was that called " Of the Holy Sepulchre." Several legends cluster round the origin of its formation. One, that St. James the Less, in the year A.D. 60-61 founded it; another, that Constantine the Great and St. Helena; another that Charlemagne, when he regained from the Caliph Haroun al-Raschid the protectorate of the Holy Land. The legend of its foundation by St. James is preserved in the office of the Canonesses of the Order, " de jour de May, la feste de S. Jaques Apostre, frère de Nostre Seigneur, Premier Exeque de Hierusalem et Institeur de l'order du S. Sepulchre de Nostre Seigneur en Jerusalem." Historically the origin of the Order, as in the case with many other great things, rose from a small beginning. When, after the visit of

St. Helena to the Holy Sepulchre, a magnificent church was erected over it, whereupon guards were then needed and a confraternity arose (see Foucher de Chartres, *Historia Hierolymita*). In a document of the ninth century is found mention of this confraternity, when it mentions as Custodian of the Holy Cross, a Treasurer of the Holy Resurrection and a body of officers for different services about the Holy Sepulchre. Jerusalem was taken by assault by the Crusaders in 1099 and Godefroy de Bouillon on the 25th July, the same year, instituted Canons of the Holy Sepulchre to the number of twenty. This was the first establishment of the Order. Their habit was to be white with a sash of purple, and it was enacted that the Order was to take precedence of all other religions in the Holy Land. The Cross patriarchal in red to be placed on their habit and above their hearts.

The Order of the Holy Sepulchre is the most ancient Order of Chivalry, and may be said to be the root from which all the other great Military Orders sprang. To exhibit its pre-eminence in foundation is here appended the various dates of origin of it and other Orders of Chivalry resting on a religious basis in Palestine.

1099. Order of the Holy Sepulchre.
1112. Order of St. Lazarus.
1113. Order of St. John Hospitaller.
1118. Order of the Temple.
1180. Order of Our Ladye of Montjoie.
1190. Order of Teutonic Knights.
1194. Order of the Sword (Lusignan-Cyprus).
1195. Order of St. Catherine of Mount Sinai.

The Canons of the Orders had many privileges and lands and manors and farms granted them in the Holy Land. They had a right of a fishing vessel all the year round on the Sea of Tiberias; freedom of entry to the harbour of Tripoli; a fourth of the town of Joppa; many churches as rich as the one at Tripoli, St. George on the mountains; the fine monastery of the Holy Sepulchre at St. John d'Acre.

To turn to the more military side of this Order. Immediately after the foundation of the Canons of the Holy Sepulchre by Godefroy in 1099, a great number of Crusaders, knights of the Western nations, came spontaneously and placed themselves under the rule of the Prior of the Sepulchre, making to him their vow of obedience and consecrating their lives to the defence of the Tomb of the Lord, and so became knights henceforth of the Sepulchre: kneeling before him he accepted their vows and embracing each, said to each "Proficiat." That the Order fulfilled their promises is apparent. At the battle of Ascalon the Holy Cross was carried by the vice-patriarch Arnould de Rohes and the Sacred Lance by Raymond d'Acquilhes. At the battle of Iberlin in 1123, three prelates followed by many knights of the Order marched in front of the Army, displaying three Relics as a banner. In 1291 the Head of the Order, the Patriarch Nicholas de Hanaper, was grievously wounded after the battle of Ascalon in rescuing the wounded and fugitive Christians. The Crusaders greatly favoured this earliest and most ancient of the religious Military Orders. Robert, Duke of Normandy, after the battle of Ascalon gave them a banner of green studded with gold roundels captured from the Fatima caliph. Gerhard d'Avesne made them an offering of his armour. Sigurd, King of Norway, loaded them with rich gifts. Baldwin II., King of Jerusalem, wished to die in their habit. Alfonso, "The Battler," bequeathed to them part of his kingdom. In the twelfth century this Order had priories in France, Spain, Rousillon, Savoy, Sicily, Cyprus, England, Germany, Hungary, Sweden, Rome, and Constantinople. Their chief priories were at St. Jean d'Acre, St. Luc at Perouse, and Miechow in Poland.

The knights, after the Holy Land was subdued by the Infidel, passed to Europe, where from century to century they have existed up to the present time, becoming like those of the Garter, the Golden Fleece, the Seraphim and others, ordinary Orders of Chivalry under certain very indulgent rules.

An old Saxon saying comes down to us of these various creations of knighthood times : " There are four sorts of knights. Those of the Holy Sepulchre who are most worthy. Those of Mt. St. Catherine and of the Cloudy Star who are most dear. Those of the Bridge of the Tiber at the time of the Emperor's Coronation who are best. Those created on the Field of Battle who are most valiant." The fifth class whom the king chooses is " a carpet knight." The far most numerous creations of this Order were, however, by the princes and lords on themselves and on their followers standing on the Holy Sepulchre at a time of pilgrimage and there bestowing it. This Holy Place has before been mentioned in the chapter dealing with places where knighthood was conferred, and now the English Earl of Essex (Sir John Bourchier), who made the pilgrimage (temp. Henry VII.), a knight of the Order of the Holy Sepulchre, made on the Sacred Tomb several of his followers knights. William Way, Fellow of Eton College, the celebrated medieval English traveller, mentions in his " Itinerary " fourteen knights of the Order created, when he was at Jerusalem, at the Sepulchre.

The banner these knights of the Sepulchre fought under was not a distinctive one of their own, but the royal banner of the Christian kingdom of Jerusalem, which, according to an ancient authority, was white semé of drops (taches) gules, no doubt signifying the Holy Blood. According to Count Pasini Guassorie, the English knights often wore instead of a red, a green Cross of Jerusalem on their vesture. He writes : " Le père Bonami nous donne le portrait d'un Chevalier du Sant Sepulchre en Angleterre, avec le croix patriarcle verte, treflée sur la poitrine. Quant à la croix rouge ou verte, c'était bien la croix Ancienne du Sant Sepulchre." The same writer informs us that this Order was established in England since the year 1189. But this of course refers to the date of the founding of the several priories they had in England. The Book of the Ancient Statutes of the Order mentions the foundation and dress in these words : " Erepta e manibus infidelium sancta civitas a Gottofredo Bullionio tunc pü nonnulli religiosum ordinem militarem S. Sepulchre instituerunt Equites illius militiæ pallium album insuta desuper cruce vel potius guinque crucibus rubris hac figura " (here is the Cross of Jerusalem drawn). " Instituto adigebant ad custodiendum sepulchrum dominum excipere . . . Præterea tenebantur centum armatos equites in aula regis Jerusalem alere ail ipsi ministrandum tum in pace tum in bello."

This latter paragraph gives us a romantic touch of the mailed and ready knights of the Order waiting day and night, in war and peace—ready at a moment's notice to issue forth and do battle for the Holy Sepulchre that they guarded.

The privileges of knights of the Sepulchre were several. They had by Papal Bull conceded to them : (1) Precedence of all the other Orders with the exception of the later Order of the Golden Fleece. (2) They were empowered to legitimize bastards. (3) To change a name given in Baptism. (4) To pardon—if they met such—prisoners on the way to death. (5) To create notaries. (6) To participate in the goods of the Church.

The Canonesses of the Order of the Holy Sepulchre still exist, for this Order, like that of St. John of Jerusalem, had such. In England their house is at New Hall, County Essex.

Another of the great Orders was that of the Knights of St. John or Hospitallers founded a little later than that of the Holy Sepulchre. It arose not as the latter from an ecclesiastical foundation of priests or canons appointed to preserve one of the Holy Places (the Sepulchre) but from the founding of a hospital, which some merchants of Amalfi had obtained permission from the Caliph of Egypt to build and dedicate to St. John, in which were received and sheltered the poor pilgrims who visited the Holy Land. Pierre Gérard, a native of the Island of Martiques, in Provence, proposed, some time after its formation, to the lay brothers who managed it, to renounce the world, to don a regular dress and to form an uncloistered monastic order, under the name of Hospitallers. Pope Pascal II. appointed Gérard as director and granted the Hospitallers many privileges.

This was the origin of the Military Order of St. John, which was to become famous through all Christendom by their chastity and their valour. Imposed on them was the triple vow of Chastity, Poverty, and Obedience, besides the duty of hospitality and the exercise of arms in order that they might defend the kingdom of Jerusalem against all attacks. It was on the death of Gérard, the first Master of the Order, that the military features of it rapidly extended. Raymond Depuy, it was said, " gave back to the brethren the arms they had quitted," for the greater number of them were knights who had retired from the world into religion.

Their combination of devotion, good works, and military prowess was a happy one—it was a new thing in the world, and had good results. In the thirteenth century it reckoned fifteen hundred knights, of whom no member could call anything his own, " not even his own will." They were, in the early ages of its birth, enjoined to be content with bread and water. They were to wear the plainest clothing ; they were to be the servants of the poor and (as their Statutes said) : " It does not become us as servants to be richer than our lords." Their arms were never to wage wars carried on between Christian princes, only against the Infidels.

This restriction kept the Military Orders distinct from the feudal levies or hired companions of the secular princes, and was of immense service in keeping them intact and the most valiant and useful in the Crusades of all the military employed ; and it is worthy of remark that though the knights of St. John were recruited from the proudest houses in Europe, in an age when Chivalry was no bar to incontinence, they do not appear to have sinned grievously, either by pride or luxury, but kept their vows. Though they were bound to poverty and possessed nineteen thousand manors, they were not accused of avarice; in this decay of monastic virtue and the decadence of Chivalry before a world which professed but did not practice it, they seem to have preserved much of the purity of their original institution. Perhaps it arose from the singular vitality this Order possessed over the other Military Orders. Driven out of Palestine, in time, with the others, they carved out a new line of warfare against the Infidel. Retiring to Rhodes and then to Malta, debarred from meeting their old adversaries on holy ground, they met them on the sea, and their galleys and war vessels carrying their dreaded banner swept the waters of the great inland sea for centuries on behalf of the Cross.

The Order was first introduced into England in the reign of Henry I. at Clerkenwell, which continued its principal house, but they also had dependent houses called " Commanderies " on many of their English estates, to the number of fifty-three. These houses of the military knights in England were only cells, erected on their estates, in order to cultivate them for their support, and to form " depots " for their recruits, where they might be trained, not in learning like the Benedictines, or agriculture like the Cistercians, or preaching like the Dominicans, but in piety and military exercises. The Superior of the Order in England sat in Parliament, and was accounted the premier lay baron. The monument of the last English Prior, Sir Thomas Tresham, in his robes as Prior of the Order, still remains in Rushton Church, Northamptonshire.

Vying for a lengthened period with the Hospitallers, and founded but twenty years after their establishment, were the Templars. Hugues de Payens and Geoffrey de Saint-Aldémar having crossed the sea with nine other nobles, all of French birth, obtained from the Patriarch Guarimond and from Baldwin II., King of Jerusalem, permission to form an association, the objects of which were to protect pilgrims and defend the Temple walls, hence they derived their name of Templars. In the first nine years of their existence (1118-'27) they admitted no strangers to their ranks. At the Council of Troyes in 1228 Hugues de Payens accompanied by five of his companions, when they obtained confirmation of their Order and a special Code of Rules drawn up for it under the guidance of St. Bernard were agreeable and thus they were bound to go to Mass three times a week, and to communicate thrice a year; they wore a white robe emblazoned with a red cross. Their original rules were of great austerity. They prescribed perpetual exile, and war for the Holy Places to the death. They were to accept every combat, however outnumbered they might be, to ask no quarter, and to give no ransom. No enemy was so dreaded by the Infidel as these picked troops. Their banner, " Beauséant," half black, half white, was in the forepart of every battle, and on many a well-fought field their chant went up, " Non nobis, Domine, non nobis, sed nomini tuo da gloriam."

The rule allowed three horses and a servant to each knight. Married knights were admitted, but there were, unlike the Hospitallers, no Sisters of this Order. The Order was introduced into England in the reign of King Stephen. At first its chief house, " The Temple," was on the south side of Holborn, afterwards it was removed to

Fleet Street; the round church still remains there. All the Templars' houses were called " Temples," as all the Carthusians were called " Chartereux " (corrupted into " Charterhouse "). This Order had only five other houses in England which were called " Preceptories," and were dependent on the Temple in London.

The resources of the Templars increased in a very short space in a remarkable manner by donations and legacies that some historians declare that the revenue of the Order amounted to four and a half millions sterling, and that they possessed enormous lands in nearly every European country, one item being nine thousand houses. In their keeping was much wealth deposited. In their quarters in London were deposited most of the treasures of the English crown, while Philip Augustus on the eve of his departure for the Holy Land entrusted them with the care of his jewels and archives.

In the field they were magnificent soldiers. The defence of Gaza, the battle of Tiberias, the capture of Damietta, and the Egyptian Crusade, all bear witness of this.

But success in war and wealth undermined their character. The Order at last became so demoralized by luxury and idleness that it forgot the aim for which it was founded, disdained to obey its rules, and gave itself up to the love of gain and pleasure. This was especially the case when driven out of the Holy Land. They took refuge in France and other countries; unlike their brethren of the Hospital idleness brought many attendant evils, and while the knights of St. John were fighting the Infidel on the sea, they remained in luxury at home. Even before leaving the Holy Land their conduct was not without reproach. They signed a treaty of alliance with the " Old Man of the Mountains," the leader of the sect of the Assassins, the most implacable enemy of the Cross; they allowed him on condition of paying them tribute to fortify himself in Lebanon. They made war against the Prince of Antioch and the King of Cyprus and ravaged Thrace and Greece where the Christian nobles had founded states; they took Athens by storm, and massacred its duke—Robert de Brienne.

All this made them unpopular and open to blame, and even as early as 1273 Pope Gregory, on account of their lax belief and morals, had thought of fusing them in the Order of the Hospitallers. It remained, however, for Philip le Bel in the following century to take active measures for their suppression. Space will not allow to go into the long and tedious infamy and trials the Order was subject to, suffice it to say in France a great many of the knights, after examination often under torture, were burnt at the stake, including the Grand Master, while in other countries where their Preceptories were found, they were suppressed.

Evidence produced from torture is always very valueless; certain of those accused under it confessed to the charges of immorality, secret rites and heretical opinions brought against them, but the greater part absolutely denied them. Philip, the King of France, pursued his object in view—the papal suppression of the whole Order—with remarkable audacity and firmness.

Most historians attribute his attitude from his desire to obtain the immense possessions and lands the Order held in the kingdom of France. That that may have had somewhat to do with his ardour may be true, but from the fact that the other great Military Order, that of the Hospitallers who held equally broad lands and wealth, was left untouched and unassailed, and when the Templars were finally suppressed he permitted a great portion of such to be taken over and incorporated by the Knights of St. John, certainly seems good evidence that his measures were directed not solely by self-aggrandisement, but on some well-founded grounds that the Templars in many cases had fallen into culpable and deplorable excesses and faults.

The principal distinction originally between the Templars and Hospitallers had been, that the Templars added to their monastic and military vows no obligations to tend the sick and relieve the poor; their sole occupation as " poor soldiers of Jesus Christ " had been to make war with the Infidel; this occupation ceasing on the Holy Land becoming lost to the Christians, the necessary strictness of their rules became relaxed, and unlike the Hospitallers who on their expulsion turned their warfare to the sea, debarred from the land—sloth, luxury and excesses crept into their ranks. St. Bernard's praises, when first they were constituted, " they neither sit idle nor wander about for their pleasure, they earn their bread by mending their arms and clothes; no insolent words or immoderate laughter are heard among them; they abhor chess (scaccos) and dice, they neither hunt nor hawk; they detest actors, sorcerers, jongleurs, licentious songs and gay spectacles as vanities, falsehoods and follies; they cut their hair short, never adorn, seldom wash themselves; they pride themselves on neglected hair, soiled with dust, and burnt by the sun and hauberk," could, in these latter days, before their fall, no longer be applied to them, and that the charges brought against them were only founded on the avarice of a king, or the weakness of a pope (Clements V.) seem incredible. On the other hand, many of their members, possibly the greater part, were possessed of a better spirit and way of living, for in the British Isles, Spain, Portugal and Germany their knights were either wholly acquitted or little was proved against them.

Their fall met with little condemnation, however, in any of the kingdoms they had houses. The nobles were jealous of their past credit in war and hated them for their arrogant talk as if they had been, and were, the only Christian soldiers; the lower classes listened as they ever do to slanders and believed them to be the servants of the devil and corrupters of society; the popular estimate of them in this country may be illustrated by the grant of Edward II. soon after the suppression of the Order, of a certificate to an English knight that he was no Templar. The knight had made a vow to let his beard grow and feared as they always had been bearded, he might be taken for a Templar and so mishandled (Cornish).

This writer states, " It was believed after the suppression of the Order, on each anniversary of it, the heads of seven of the martyred Templars rose from their graves; a phantom clothed in the red cross mantle came into the churchyard and cried thrice, ' Who shall now defend the Holy Temple ? Who shall free the Sepulchre of the Lord ? ' and the seven heads made answer, ' None, the Temple is destroyed.' "

It was at the Council of Vienne, 1312, Clement V. dissolved the Order. In Spain and Portugal their property was applied to the defence of the Christians against the Moors and Saracens, but the greater portion (as has before been mentioned) of their possessions, particularly those held in France, were transferred to the keeping of the Hospitallers. The serious abuses and crimes which had caused the suppression of the Order had fortunately not vitiated the whole of its members. Most of them when set at liberty, preserving their former rank, enrolled themselves in the Order of St. John. So Albert de Blacas, Prior of Aix, for instance, obtained the commandership of Saint Maurice, as Prior of the Hospitallers, and Frederick, Grand Prior of Lower Germany, retained the title in the Order of St. John of Jerusalem.

Reverting to the more fortunate state of this great rival Order of the Templars, that of St. John Hospitaller. Instead of falling into decay when their swords were no longer employed in Palestine, they commanded the trade of the Levant, and as trade included privateering, they became as bold in their aggressions upon the Infidel fleets as the Infidels themselves. Their seven red galleys were at any time a match for twenty Turkish ships, and holding, as they did in their position at Malta, the middle strait of the sea, they could close the door between the Eastern and Western rovers.

And if in later times a proof of their ancient martial spirit was as fresh as ever, even though it long had been shown on sea and not on land, the glorious defence of Malta in 1565 when the whole power of Islam, consisting of thirty thousand men on board one hundred and eighty vessels, was directed against their island fortress and defeated, proved to a wondering and exulting Christendom that out of six hundred knights who survived, hardly one was free of wounds, and of thirty thousand Infidel invaders, no more than five thousand left the island.

That these three chief Military Orders employed in the Crusades did much in stiffening the cosmopolitan ranks of those who from different Western lands composed the Crusading armies, none can deny.

Prevented from—like many of the secular lords and knights—elevating themselves, by their prowess and swords, to Eastern principalities and seigneuries, their whole object was the defence of the Holy Land and death to the Infidel. Many young knights-errant, who had before found no nobler objects for their Chivalry than the lists of a tournament or the petty warfare of neighbouring barons found, in these warlike Orders, a fitter object for those swords and martial aspirations, and those who enlisted in them best fulfilled the injunctions of Pope Urban, who, at the First Crusade, cried out, " Warriors! ye who hear me, ye who search without ceasing for some vain pretext for war, rejoice now, for here is a legitimate cause for war. The moment is come in which to prove if you are animated with a true courage; the moment is come in which to expiate so many violences committed in the bosom of peace—so many victories disfigured by injustice. . . . Ye are no longer to take vengeance for the injuries done against men, but for those committed against God. Ye are no longer to be employed in the attack of a city or castle, but in the conquest of sacred places. If you fall you will have the glory of dying on the same spot as Jesus Christ, and God will not forget that he saw you in his holy warfare. Let no base affections, let no profane sentiments repress your zeal. Soldiers of the living God! hear no sound but the lamentations of Zion; burst asunder all human ties and remember what the

Lord has said, ' He who loveth father or mother more than me, is not worthy of me; whosoever shall forsake his house or his father, or his mother, or his wife or children or heritage, for my name's sake, shall be rewarded a hundredfold and shall possess eternal life.' " (Speech of Urban at the Council of Clermont.)

On the other hand, if these religious Military Orders possessed advantages in the Crusading war that those not within them lacked, they perhaps promoted more than the rest of the Crusaders the spirit of intolerance to any other foes than those marked with the Cross. The obvious danger of teaching a military body to consider themselves as missionaries of religion and bound to spread its doctrines is that they realize no better way to do so than by their swords and lances. The end is held to justify the means and the slaughter of thousands of ignorant Infidels is regarded as an indifferent or as a meritorious action. The wars of Charlemagne in Saxony, the massacre of the Albigenses in Provence, the long continued wars in Palestine, all serve to illustrate the danger from the doctrine which inculcated religion, not as a check upon the horrors and crimes of war, but as itself its most proper and legitimate cause. Yet even in an age that held this doctrine to perfection, some gleams of a higher duty than that of the sword seem to have obtained. The very fact that the Hospitallers did not share the ultimate fate of the Templars arose not from their swords being less employed in slaughtering the Infidel, but from those hospitals tended and founded by them throughout Palestine and Western Europe, and from their employment of Sisters or Canonesses, affiliated to their warlike Order, who tempered by their womanly influence, their impetuous Chivalry.

Briefly here may be mentioned another Military Order, which not of the pristine fame as the two others—the Templars and Hospitallers —nor the object of their Crusade in the Holy Land, yet carried the Cross among unbelievers and gradually subdued them beneath its teaching.

The Order of Teutonic Knights found in 1128 at Jerusalem by the German Crusaders obeyed the rule of St. Augustin. They were subject to special statutes, somewhat similar to the two preceding Orders. Their first Grand Master, Henri Walpot, established his residence at St. Jean d'Acre. They wore a white mantle with a rather broad black cross, picked out with silver, on their left sleeve. To gain admittance to the Order it was necessary for a candidate to be over fifteen years of age and to be of a strong, robust build, in order to resist the fatigues of war. The knights were bound by a vow of Chastity and to avoid all intercourse with women. They were not allowed to give their own mothers a kiss when they saluted them. They possessed no private property; they always left their cell doors open so that every one might see what they were doing. Their arms were free from gold and silver ornaments, and for a long while they spent their lives in great humility. The most celebrated Grand Master, Hermann de Salza, received in 1210 from Pope Honorius III. and the Emperor Frederick II., whom he had reconciled, large possessions and high honours.

These knights conquered Prussia, Slavonica and Courland and became masters of the whole territory between the Vistula and the Wiemen. As with the Templars so with the Teutonic Knights, success, wealth and unlimited power brought with them the seeds of decay. After the disastrous battle of Goumbald in 1410, the immense lands up to then they owned, gradually were lost to them. Their discipline grew lax, their swords when they should have been drawn, still sheathed; the ancient reason of their existence, the defeat of the pagans and introduction of the Christian religion among them, by the latter's conversion and subjugation, long since uncalled for. The last Grand Master, Albert of Brandenburg, bound by the Order's oaths of the triple vow of Poverty, Chastity, and Obedience, and to free Prussia from being a fief, as it was of the Church, turned Lutheran, and divided the possessions of the Order with his uncle, the aged Sigismund, King of Poland, who for these considerations conferred on him the title of Duke of Prussia. This was the origin of the royal family of Prussia. After this easy acquisition of title and territory the Order of the Teutonic Knights became extinct.

The knights of these Military Orders often assumed on their family coat-armour, the crosses of their respective Orders, sometimes this cross was quartered with his own, sometimes impaled with it. It may be for this reason that compared with other charges on their, and their descendants', shields, the cross appears much less frequently as their private cognizance, as from the fact it was already borne by them as knights of a cross-bearing Order. Independently of bearing the Cross of the Military Orders on their shields, quartered or impaled with their own, other knights added to or changed their paternal coats with crosses or scollop shells or other emblems, denoting they had been Crusaders. Thus the Count of Vela of the Royal House of Aragon making the Crusade, added to his arms on a border azure eight crosses of the Kingdom of Jerusalem (Argote de Molina L. 1. c. 100).

In the reign of Baldwin II. of Jerusalem, the son of the King of Denmark landed at Jaffa and with his followers relieved the Christians there. He then bore the arms of his father, gules three Danish axes, or, but our English family of Berkeleys, who are descended from him, changed this coat for gules, a chevron ermine between ten crosses pattee in memory of this achievement of their ancestor.

The taking of Jerusalem gave rise to the arms of the Duchy of Lorraine. Before the conquest the duke bore a hart, gules, afterwards three alerions upon a bend. This was occasioned by his shooting three of these birds from off the tower of Jerusalem.

Some families changed their old coats for new ones on engaging in the Crusades. The family of Villiers before that bore sable three cinque foils argent. Sir Nicholas Villiers attended Edward I. to the Holy Land and thereupon changed the above for five escallop shells on a Cross of St. George, to show he had made the military pilgrimage.

One of the family of the FitzGeralds having been to the Holy Land, caused his family to change their old bearings for a saltiere argent, on a field gules, between twelve crosslets or.

Some old writers assign the origin of fusils (a charge in heraldry) being borne to the Crusades, and that they were originally given for this reason—at the meeting held at Vezelai, by Louis, King of France, his Queen was determined to attend her husband to the Holy Land notwithstanding the fate of a princess of Austria who had done so and been taken prisoner. Many ladies of her court were induced to follow her example. Mezeria declares they mounted on horseback like

Amazons, and formed a squadron which went under the name of Queen Eleanor's Guard. They sent spindles and distaffs (the French of which is " fuse ") to all the young men of their acquaintance and neighbourhood who had not taken the Cross, which had such effect on them, that in very shame they joined the Crusade. If at this date of time these things seem trivial let it be remembered such was not the view of those in crusading times. They saw symbols and sacraments everywhere, combined with the habit of looking for authority and regulations in everything, where every detail had an inward meaning and was prescribed by authority. As a sacrament might fail in effect if all its details were not performed, so an act of homage, an oath or transfer of a fief might be rendered invalid by some omission of detail; in the same way the changing of the bearings of a knight's shield or his banner had a significance and carried a weight with it, we in these latter times when all that is mystical or symbolic has given way to the commonplace and the literal, cannot understand. Why one religious Military Order should bear an eight-pointed cross when charging the foe, and another the Cross of Jerusalem, and another a plain Latin Cross, seems to us nowadays a childish piece of display— not so at the time they were invented and borne, they each carried a spiritual and real significance to the bearers. Thus an instance, the cross on the mantle given at her installation to a Canoness of the Order of the Hospitallers, it was no mere ornament in the Middle Ages but a symbol that spoke as did the conferrer of it, " C'est le signe de la vraye Croix, on lui commande de le porter continnellement sur les habits, pendant sa vie. Cette croix blanche signifie que toutes nos œuvres doivent être pures, nettes et blanches. Ces huits pointes signifient les huit Beautitudes qui nous sont promises, si nous pourtons ce signe au cœur avec ardeur et ferveur, a cet effet la vous mettons sur le côté gauche, afin que l'ayez toujours sur votre cœur et avec icelui vous devez ensevelir," and so on with the rest of their habit.

Other Orders of great fame were those of Calatrava (1158), Santiago (1175) and Alcantara (1212) in Spain, but as their members were not formed to take part in the Crusades in the Holy Land for the recovery of Jerusalem, a detailed account of them is omitted here. Briefly, the history of all is the same; great prowess in war so long as the Crusades in Palestine and Spain lasted; wealth, dignity, pride of birth, ending in mere heraldry and counting of quarterings. They served their time one by one and sank into the ornaments of a court, preserving to the last something of their ancient military credit, but in other respects sinking into decrepitude and furnishing a provision for the younger sons of noble families. The Knights of Malta alone remained worthy of their ancient glory and their cross and name, and, though now a pseudo order or " langue " in this country, they have in a convulsed and war-stricken Europe carried on their old traditions of nursing the sick and befriending the desolate.

One of the benefits arising from the foundation of these religious Military Orders was the freeing of knights from the bonds of feudalism.

To distinguished soldiers of the Cross the honours and benefits of knighthood could hardly be refused on the ground they did not possess a fief, of which indeed perhaps as heirs to such they had denuded themselves in order to their equipment for the Holy War; and thus the conception of knighthood as of something distinct from feudalism both as a social condition and a personal dignity arose and deeply gained ground. It was then that the analogy was first detected between the Order of Priesthood and the Order of Knighthood and that an actual union of monasticism and chivalry was effected by the religious Orders of the Sepulchre, the Hospitallers, and the Templars. The foundation therefore of these Orders further created that free knighthood which was one of the most glorious forms of Chivalry in its zenith and which the writer of this book has endeavoured to bring before the reader.

These religious Military Orders also showed to the feudal lords that a free knighthood not dependent on fief could fight as well, if not better, than themselves.

By their bravery they took precedence of other knights, and inspired not only a love of glory but a religious zeal which enabled them to maintain that lead in many a hard fought field in Palestine. Then so on the advantage of discipline grounded upon the very foundation of their rule and supported by conscience.

Feudal armies were gathered before and up to this time by chance. They dispersed as irregularly; they were led by lords whose claim up to then to command them came from the number of knights' fees that they owned, all jealous of each other and ready to quarrel for precedence like, as a writer on the subject has pointed out, the Highlanders in the '45 even in the presence of the enemy. The Hospitallers and Templars, though composed of noble youths from many a distant country and possessing no fiefs grouping them together and conferring free knighthood upon them, showed to the world that freedom under discipline was better than servitude under discipline and that religious fervour gave a keener edge to a knight's sword than a love of earthly gain or a fair one's bright smiles.

Another effect of these Military Orders semi-monastic were to link closer still to religion even the secular knights. As has been said the rites on the conference of knighthood more and more followed those in the conference of priestly Orders. It is from the time therefore, of the Crusades we can best trace their growth and the recognition of the dignity of knighthood and its semi-sacred character as a state of life apart from the ordinary one outside Chivalry.

CHAPTER XVI

TROUBADOUR-KNIGHTS

FROM the earliest times song and war, and song and love, have gone through the ages hand in hand. After the fierce fight and the bloody encounter, by the log fire of the north, to the sun-stricken plains of the south, music, whether on the rude harp of the wandering gleeman or minstrel down to the more polished rebeck of the Moor, or the viol of Provence, have beguiled the soldier.

In these earlier days the musicians were a class apart, and generally of the lower orders, it remained for the aged Chivalry to exalt this profession and create knights who, though they could wield well the sword, were adepts in music and song—such a knight's most popular name was that of Troubadour, or in northern France, " trouvere."

These troubadour-knights moved in a very different social sphere from the musicians of to-day, and indeed from all minstrels and musicians before or since.

Different from the latter, they never pursued their calling for hire. Not only did they participate in no way in money given to music, but they constantly employed servants of their own to assist at the apt rendering of their compositions. To these servants of the troubadours, called gleemen or jongleurs, the same disparagement of class attached as does to the professional musician of modern times, and in considering the knights as troubadours or proficients in song and music it is essential to bear in mind the difference between them and the jongleurs. It was very rare indeed for a jongleur to advance to be the troubadour, and although from exceptional abilities a few were enabled to do so, the exceptions are extremely rare. The expenses attaching to the troubadour's life alone would be sufficient to deter most men from trying to mount up to this higher social scale. As knights, the troubadours were nearly all of them nobly born, and educated far better than their brother-knights. They were expected to entertain lavishly wherever they might be, far more so than the usual lord or seigneur. They were expected to give numerous fêtes and invent for them new amusements, to serve as examples how these festivals should be rightly carried out. Among the nobility of his district the troubadour was looked on as the arbiter of fashion and refinement. This often led him into disastrous pecuniary difficulties, and the castles and lands he had inherited from his ancestors were obliged to be parted with to meet his debts. Bernardus Silvester, a medieval writer, tells us " that such a man intent only on such a life, soon weds a wife called ' poverty,' whose child born to her inherits the name of ' derision.' "

A KNIGHT'S LIFE

The usual expedient in such predicaments (for fortunately the impoverished troubadour possessed a knightly sword) was to go overseas to Palestine as a Crusader. In some few cases the troubadour from his poverty sunk into the rank and pay of a jongleur. In the Chronicles it is stated that a certain troubadour could not maintain himself and thus became a jongleur. " Pierols no se poc mantener per cavallier e vene joglars," so too, the Seigneur de Marveis and several more " E'l senher de Marveis si'l fes cavallier . . . no poc mantener cavalaria, si se fes joglar."

The popular opinion has so mixed up the idea of troubadours and jongleurs (Saxon gleemen) that it is necessary to emphasize again that they were perfectly distinct classes.

The troubadour was expected to have passed through all degrees of knighthood and attained the position of Chevalier, and so entirely was this understood to be the case that often the terms " troubadour " and " chevalier " were treated as identical. " No se poc mantener per cavallier, e vene joglars." Among their numbers could be reckoned counts and dukes and princes, e.g., Henry the son of Henry II. of England, and the celebrated Richard I. and Alfonso, King of Aragon. All these, from being troubadours, were considered on a footing of social equality and fraternized freely together with the others. Besides his faculty in musical composition the leading and characteristic feature in a troubadour's life was that he was expected " to go through the world " (allar par le mon). Another phrase likewise applied to this necessary custom was " to go from court to court " (allar par les cortz). (Every lord's castle was called in its social aspect a " court.") The troubadour, therefore, if he was to be entitled to the name, as soon as spring sounded, had to make his visits and journeys of music and of song throughout the land.

These travels of the troubadour-knights were most conspicuous (as the home of romance) in Southern France. Here indeed a charming picture of medieval society was presented (because in touch with Moorish refinement and learning) spread through Languedoc and Provence. The table was often laid before the door of the castle for all comers. Amidst a society gay, sceptical and licentious, the troubadour-knight was the arbiter of taste, the oracle of the populace, the idol of women. The mistress here of the wandering bard was always the wife of a noble and not unfrequently a princess of high lineage. To her was addressed his passionate homage, often in strains whose expressions are too passionate for translation. The life of the fair one addressed was passed in an intoxicating atmosphere of music, flattery and amorous intrigue. His power over society was not less important than that exercised formerly by the clergy. The adulation he lavished in song upon the object of his affections, represented in it the personification of every physical grace and every mental accomplishment, could not fail to fire the romantic imagination of the ladye in whose veins coursed the hot blood of the South, and whose vanity caused her to recognize in his extravagant flattery and devotion the highest tribute to her charms.

Around the troubadour in the knightly circles of Arles or Carcassonne was grouped a mirthful and appreciative audience—ladies in brocade and jewels, knights in burnished armour, or emblazoned surcoats, pages in silk and gold. In that animated assemblage the

restraints of rank, never rendered irksome by the exactions of ceremonials, were for the moment entirely suspended. Inspired by such
surroundings the troubadour-knight arose and began the recital of one
of his amorous Lays. Young, slender and handsome, his physical
appearance alone might well elicit female admiration. His long dark
locks fell in ringlets on his shoulders. A gold chain of knighthood
hung about his neck. His fingers—seldom employed by the sword but
by the lute—glittered with gems. From his belt an enamelled poinard
was suspended. His picturesque doublet of silk, his cloak of velvet,
his tight hose, set off to advantage the graces of his person. All eyes
were turned upon him, for he was above the jongleurs and their master
in every music they knew—and the Lays he sang frequently his own
composition. These he chanted to tunes, we should now consider
ecclesiastical pæans, but beneath his touch on the viol or harp,
they were now ardent, now pathetic, now caustic and now humorous,
and his audience swayed by conflicting emotions, broke forth into tears
or laughter. His ambiguous expressions, his licentious images, were
received with the greatest manifestations of approval by them, and at
its end the knight or his ladye gave him sometimes a gold chain,
sometimes a rich furred cloak, sometimes a richly caparisoned
palfrey. As a sort of chorus to his higher accomplishment, the
jongleur often joined in. The latter, generally, was a retainer of the
knightly troubadour and occupied a position analogous to that of
esquire and knight. Sometimes he accompanied the poet upon the
harp or guitar, sometimes he recounted the legends, the martial
exploits, and the popular romances so popular in the Middle Ages.
His rank was ordinarily far beneath that of his companion, yet it was
not unusual for the two professions, at this time (we say " at this
time," for later the jongleurs descended in the scale of rank and ended
in being mere mountebanks), to be combined, and there are instances
when their positions were reversed through the vicisssitudes of fortune,
as has been before mentioned.

The extraordinary privileges enjoyed by these wandering troubadours and jongleurs were by no means entirely owing to the amusement their talents afforded in many a dull and lonely castle or fortified
town.

Their compositions were the sole medium by which public opinion
could be aroused and the abuse of powers or excesses of depravity
restrained. They may be said to have taken the place of the modern
press. The satires they dwelt in on the clergy, the lord, and the
people themselves, by the vehicle of their songs in a fortnight, became
familiar to a hundred communities. These songs evinced no admiration of the beauties of nature, the stanzas in them often isolated and
without continuity, and though a common similarity of type and ideas
pervaded them all, they were everywhere received with avidity. And
yet in delicacy of sentiment, in vigour of expression, these compositions are not excelled by the lyrics of any nation.

This poetry of theirs was not only an art, but life. It had substance as well as form, and, besides the idea of literature, it embodied
the idea of love.

Substance as well as form had a widespread influence, indeed the
two could not be separated. England was but slightly affected and
Scandinavia not at all, but the rest of Europe received a general

indoctrination, and the sentiments of love and ideas of Chivalric love became part of modern life.

If we blame the degeneration of medieval love, Chivalry itself is largely responsible both by ignoring to a great extent the marriage tie, and by substituting for it an essentially unnatural relation between men and women. By way of compensating for the sordid and feudal marriages which were contracted for the preservation of the few and its military obligations, Chivalry stepped in, and encouraged a connection between knight and lady into which love and love alone entered. In it the lady's mission was to incite her lover to noble deeds, the lover's to strive, to the uttermost, to win her praise; and while glorying, at a distance that nothing could bridge over, in the perfections of his lady, his greatest reward was the joy of service and of wooing. That such an ideal could last long, few were the cases, from the infirmity of human nature, where it did not derogate into a lower plane; and what might in its conception have been pure, as time went on, became the reverse.

According to Fauvel the ceremonial that took place on a lady's definitely accepting a knight for love was modelled on that of a vassal pledging himself to his lord : the lover kneeling down before his lady, and with clasped hands vowed fidelity to her. She then lifted him up and gave him a ring and kissed him in token that she " retained " him, as it was called. Such a union was so solemn a matter as to be often blessed by a priest, or dissolved by him. If we remember that the greater part of these ladies were wives, makes the affair more curious, particularly when often the husband was perfectly aware of the loving liason, while he himself did elsewhere the same. There are, however, cases where the husband was not so accommodating, but when such was known great was the outcry from his brother-knights and their ladies. A case in point is the celebrated one in troubadour-story, of the knight Guillem de Caberstaing, of the County of Roussillon. " He was," the old Chronicles say, " right goodly to look on, renowned in arms and Chivalry and knightly service, and in his country there dwelt a lady—my Lady Soremonda by name—wife of Sir Raymond of Castel-Roussillon, a knight of high descent, puissant and proud and cruel and base and hard of heart. Now Guillem of Caberstaing greatly loved the lady and made his songs of her, and the lady, who was young and fair and gay and noble, bore him greater love than to any soul on earth. And the thing was told to Sir Raymond of Castel-Roussillon and he, as one jealous and full of wrath, made inquiry into it, and when he knew it was true, set watch upon his wife. And it fell upon a day that Sir Raymond of Castel-Roussillon found Sir Guillem of Caberstaing hawking without great company, and he slew him and caused his heart to be taken from out his body and his head to be cut off. Then he caused both head and heart to be brought to his dwelling, and the heart caused to be roasted and seasoned with pepper and to be set before his wife to eat it. And when the lady had eaten of it, Raymond of Castel-Roussillon said to her, ' Know you of what you have eaten ? ' and she said, ' I know not, save that the taste is good and savoury.' Then he said to her that what she had eaten of was in very truth the heart of Sir Guillem of Caberstaing, and caused the head to be brought before her, that she might the more readily believe it. And when the lady had seen and heard this, she straightway fell into a swoon, and when she was recovered of it, she spake and said, ' Of a truth, my lord, such good meat have you given me that never more will I eat of any other.' Then he, hearing this, ran upon her with his sword and would have struck at her head, but the lady ran to a balcony and cast herself down, and so died. And the news spread through Catalonia and Roussillon how that Sir Guillem of Caberstaing and the lady were thus foully done to death, and how that Sir Raymond of Castel-Roussillon had set before the lady the heart of Sir Guillem. Then there arose sore weeping and lamentation in all the counties round about, and the outcry that was made of it came to the ears of the King of Aragon (Alfonso II.) who was liege lord of Sir Raymond de Roussillon and of Sir Guillem de Caberstaing. And the king came to Perpignau in Roussillon and commanded that Sir Raymond be brought before him. And when he came, he caused him to be bound, and took from him all his castles and had them razed to the ground; and took from him likewise all that he had, and cast him into prison, and he caused Guillem de Caberstaing and the lady to be taken and brought into.Perpignau, and, to be laid together in a tomb before the church door; and he bade men inscribe upon their tomb the manner of their death, and likewise he bade all the knights and ladies throughout all the County of Roussillon to come thither each year and hold solemn festival to their memories. And Sir Raymond died miserably in the prison of the King of Aragon.''

The importance of this story lies in the fact that seemingly not the cruelty of the Count was so much considered as his breaking the rule of complaisance towards his Countess and her lover. It was transgressing the code of Love held as binding at the time in Chivalrous circles. With his rude behaviour he broke in on

" Those sweet reveries, that love doth ofttimes gives,"

(Li doutz consire, qem don amors soven.)

as the unfortunate lover had sung.

A much more charming story, showing this romantic love, untinged with anything of a gross character, is that of the troubadour, Jaufie Rudel of Blaia (1140). " He was a right noble knight, and it chanced that though he had not seen her, he loved the Princess of Tripoli (one of the small Christian states set up by the Crusaders) for her great excellence and virtue, whereof the pilgrims who came to Antioch spread abroad the report, and he made her fair songs with fair melodies, and with short verses, till he longed so greatly to see her that he took the Cross and embarked upon the sea to gain sight of her, and lo! in the ship there fell upon him such great sickness that they who were with him weened he was dead therein. Nathless they brought him with them as one dead to a hostelry in Tripoli, and the thing was made known to the Princess, so she came to his bedside and took him into her arms. Then he knew that it was she, and sight and speech returned to him, and he gave praise and thanks to God who had preserved his life until his seeing her. And so he died in the arms of the Princess, and she gave him honourable burial in the Temple-house of Tripoli, and on that self-same day she gave herself to God and became a nun, for love of him and for grief at his death. And so here are some of his verses :

DAYS OF CHIVALRY

" When May-days come, full tunefully
The birds do carol from afar,
Yet when I needs from thee must be
Where dwelleth my sweet love afar,
As drear to me as winter's snow,
Are songs of fairest flowers that blow,
So sad the heart within my breast.

No happiness I love to see
Fail I to win that love afar,
I know of none so fair as she,
Her worth above all worth doth stand
And captive in the Paynim's land
I'd gladly dwell at her behest."

The fact of Rudel loving a lady he had never seen is no unusual incident in the pages of knightly lives. It was a deed applauded by the Code of Chivalry; it gave to love a test nothing else could of self-abnegation and sincerity, it put a bar between love and its false sister carnal desire. So in the Chronicles it is frequently stated how these troubadours and these knights-errant of song devoted themselves to the service of a never-seen mistress, nor was it an unusual incident in the tourneys and jousts of the French and English, the " favours " of a lady were carried into the mêlée by a knight who had only heard of her perfections by rumour or some wandering traveller's report.

Sometimes after serving his lady to the best of his ability in song and joust, she threw her lover over. This was an action always reprimanded by the Courts of Love.

" Arnaut of Mavoil ' loved,' " the old Chronicles assert, " the wife of the Viscount of Beziers named Tallifer. Now Arnaut was of goodly face and form and sang right well, and could read romances, and the Countess greatly honoured and advanced him, and he loving her full well sang her praises in his songs . . . and the Countess shunned not his love but harkened to his prayers and favourably received them, and she furnished him with goodly apparel and other gear and spake him fair and favoured him at her court, and he dwelt there esteemed and honoured of men. Nathless she bore him such goodwill that King Alfonso, who also was her lover, came to know of it and became grievously vexed and jealous, so that he accused her of too great love for Arnaut, and so much did he say and cause to be said of her that she sent Arnaut from her. So Arnaut departed and got him to his trusty friend Guillem of Montpellier, where in tears and sadness he made the song which says :

" Molt eran dous miei cossir."

(How sweet to me was e'en my sorrow.)

Before he left her and as was usual with the troubadours before her court, he sang :

" Ah ! sweetest lady, might it chance
Whate're the hour or circumstance
That, once in life thy faithful slave
That rapture know, he long does crave—
233

Of clasping thee within his arms
And gazeing on thy peerless charms,
Kissing thine eyes, thy red lips sweet
That mine in one long kiss should meet."

This strange romantic love did not, however, satisfy some of these troubadours by expression in words, it tempted them to show it in strange deeds. Pierre Vidal was one of these, an extraordinary mixture of sense and folly, yet one of the most distinguished of the Provençal poets. Brave, restless, impressionable, boastful, with a background of wisdom and penetration, he had all the qualities commonly attributed to the Celtic race, together with others peculiarly his own. His canzones are simple and graceful and devoid of the metaphysical subtleties and hard rhymes that were the snare of the style.

"Now he fell to loving Loba of Penautier (' Loba ' means she-wolf). Now Loba was of Carcassonne and Pierre Vidal made himself to be called ' Lop ' (wolf) for love of her, bearing a wolf in his coat of arms. And in the mountains of Carbaret he made men hunt him forsooth with dogs, and with mastiffs and with greyhounds, even as men hunt a wolf. And he donned the skin of a wolf to make the shepherds and dogs believe him one.

"Then the shepherds with their dogs hunted him, and so evilly dealt with him, that he was brought as one dead to the dwelling of the she-wolf of Penautier. And when she saw that it was even Pierre Vidal, she made right merry over his folly, and laughed greatly and also her husband, and she welcomed him joyfully, and her husband bade his servants take him and lay him in a privy chamber, and give him gentle usage, and bade a leech be sent for, and had him tended till he was healed of his wounds."

That Pierre needed no trumpeter this verse shows:

" Of Chivalry and Love I am the flower,
Bravest among the brave—in lady's bower
Is none more courteous and more debonair,
Nor in the battle-field of greater power,
So that my enemies in terror cower
At thought of me, nor to confront me dare."

Sometimes the patience of the lover was worn out by the cold-hearted responses and vanity which thrust upon him perilous enterprises.

" At the court of one of the German Emperors, while some of the court were looking into a den where two lions were confined, one of the ladies purposely let her glove fall within the palisade which enclosed the animals and commanded her lover as a true knight and minnesinger to fetch it out to her. He did not hesitate to obey, jumped over the enclosure, threw his mantle towards the animals as they sprang at him, snatched up the glove, and regained the outside of the cage. And when in safety, he proclaimed aloud that what he had done was for the sake of his own honour and not for that of the fair lady who could, from her vanity, sport with a lover's devotion,

and with applause of all that were present, renounced her love for
ever."

This, however, was an uncommon circumstance. In general, the
lady was supposed to have her lover's character as much at heart as
her own, and to mean by pushing him upon enterprises of hazard, only
to give him an opportunity of meriting her good graces, which she could
not, with honour, confer upon one undistinguished by deeds of
Chivalry.

We are left greatly to our own conjectures on the appearance
and manners of these haughty beauties, who were wooed with sword
and lance, and by the sweet songs of their troubadour-knights, whose
favours were bought at the expense of such dear and desperate perils
often, and who were worshipped in the most extravagant way in deed
and word.

The character of the ladies of the age of Chivalry was probably
determined by that of the men to whom it sometimes approached.

Most of these ladies were educated to understand the treatment
of wounds, not only of the heart but of the sword. They sometimes
trespassed on the province of their lovers and actually took up arms.
The Countess de Montfort in Bretagne is celebrated by Froissart for
the gallantry with which she defended her castle when besieged by
the English. In a far-off land Black Agnes of Dunbar held out the
castle of that name against the Chivalry of Edward III. She
appeared on the battlements with a white handkerchief in her hands
and wiped the walls in derision where they had been struck by stones
from the English arbalests. When Montague, Earl of Salisbury,
brought up to the walls a military engine, like the Roman " testudo "
called " a sow," she exclaimed in rhyme :

> " Beware, Montagou,
> For farrow shall thy sow."

A huge rock discharged from the battlements dashed the sow to
pieces, and the English soldiers who escaped from its ruins were called
by the Countess in derision, " Montague's pigs."

Yet despite these many who in fearlessness among the medieval
women, took even up arms and met the horrors of a beleaguered town
and even the arduous pilgrimages to the Holy Land of the Crusading
armies, to cause these sweet songs of the troubadours there must have
been gentler and more lovable characters among the ladies of this
period. Such figures as Godiva, Griselda, Beatrice, Laura, la reine
Berthe, Una, could not have been conceived without the ideals of these
songs and romances, being found in actual life ; under these ideals
grew up in fact St. Elizabeth of Hungary, Blanche and Eleanour of
Castile and Philippa of Hainault among many others—even their
appearances if hard and rough as the ancient Frankish women described
by Tacitus, could not have evoked these sweet sirventes of the troubadours unless the greater part of the fair ones they saw had not sweet
and gentle faces and demeanour ; such as the Northern poet, Jehan de
Meung, of the Roman de la Rose describes :

> " As the moon makes candles of the stars, her noon
> Paled all her fellows, as the dew
> Her flesh was tender ; and ne'er new
> And blushing bride more simple seemed ;

> Where'er her skin peeped forth it gleamed
> As white as fleur-de-lys; her brow
> Was clear as virgin snow.
> The while her form was tall and slight.
> No need had she her face to dight—
> With paint or other vain disguise,
> As women somewhiles use; despise
> And scorn might she such false allure
> In nature's decking bright and pure.
> So plenteous grew her golden hair
> That near her heels it reached I swear."

So again :

> " Of skin so delicate and pure and white
> As hawthorn bloom, or June-tide rose,
> Her long locks blond."

As to her dress, the same poet says :

> " In her gentle hand
> She grasped a mirror, and a grand
> Quaint carven comb her tresses held,
> She had tired her in
> A costly coat of cloth of Ghent,
> On which much labour had been spent
> In broidering, while her sleeves around
> With silken cords were laced and bound,
> And when that she her raiment fair
> Had donned and tired her golden hair
> The day for her was done."

Again :

> " The purple broidered with great store
> Of orfreys, rich with golden ore,
> With forms of mighty men it shone
> Renowned in ages past and gone—
> Great dukes and kings and such as be
> Writ large in ancient history;
> The golden band around her neck
> Did many an orlèd shield bedeck
> Silver, on ruddy gold, ennealed—
> Illumined each bright quartered shield.
> Then o'er her robe and round each hem
> Shone many a lustrous priceless gem."

" In all this mass of romantic literature a rule of life is inculcated or assumed " (Cornish). Courage, devotion to love are its virtues; cruelty, false honour, licentiousness are the corresponding vices. One notable fact, written in scathing lines on the monks and clergy, is that religion is absent. There are religious poems, it is true, and the knights and ladies perform their religious duties, but a religion of the heart formed no part of the life of these knights and ladies. " They are as pagan as if Christianity did not exist " (Cornish). Perhaps it could not be well otherwise, for though knighthood was a sacrament and its vows consecrated by religion, its chief amusement—the tournament— was not sanctioned by the Church, and the worship of women according to the rules of troubadour Chivalry stood in contradiction to all those principles of purity which the Church never fails to impress upon her children. " Chivalry," as the writer above quoted well puts it, " for all its high ideals, was, in practice, an affair of the world." These Southern poets preached the doctrine of Free Love, which under their pleasant tuition became the governing principle of their knights and ladies and treated it as a rule of virtue, not as an indulgence of human frailty.

It was to establish and regulate all this free Philosophy of Love, those curious courts, or Parliaments of Love, were set up and became the vogue. The countries were divided into a number of duchies and counties, the rulers of which were practically independent, though some acknowledged the overlordship of the French, some of our Angevin kings. Each of these princes and lords had his own court at which he welcomed as many troubadours who liked to visit him, and this especially in Provence and Languedoc. It was therefore an easy matter for a prince to allow in his midst these parliaments devoted to the claims of Love.

The foundress of these Courts may rightly be considered a princess closely linked with England—Eleanor of Guienne. In her was found the brave heart of a man, and yet the romantic spirit of a woman. Even before her marriage with our Angevin king, Henry II., she had gone to the Crusades along with her husband, Louis VII. of France. Attired in a surcoat, hauberk and helmet, and gathering a troop of ladies around her silken banner, she rode off to the Holy War. Arrived in Palestine, she diversified the fatigues of war by romantic episodes of love with the Saracen warriors and particularly with a youthful emir in the service of Sultan Noureddin (Suger, in Duchesne). It is little wonder a granddaughter of the great troubadour, William IX., Count of Poitou and Duke of Aquitaine, Eleanor, inherited these chivalrous tastes. An ever open asylum for those unfortunate in love and fortunate in war was her court when still Duchess of Normandy before her second husband, Henry II., had succeeded to the English throne. Nor a wonder that she attracted to herself a special troubadour-knight, Bernard de Ventadour, to sing her charms and his love. In a beautiful sirvente Bernard has celebrated Eleanor's departure for her new kingdom. He declares that " though absent from his beloved lady, her image will always be engraved on his heart." He speaks further of the nightingale which wakes him in the morning by chanting of his love, and thus recalls to him the lovely Eleanor. The sweet thought of her is far sweeter than the pleasures of sleep, and he lies awake in the morning hours dreaming of her alone (Le Parnesse Occitanien). So beloved was she by her grandfather William IX. that for her he abdicated his immense dominions and Eleanor became the heiress of Gascony, Guienne, Poitou, Seuritonge and Toulouse. These domains unite nearly the whole of Southern France and therefore the home of song and of the troubadours. Rightly therefore must be attributed to her, not only from her tastes but the influence she possessed as heiress over this country of love and song, the initiative in setting up the Courts of Love.

As has been said these Courts were set up to bring into order those excesses of the romantic love then prevalent. To regulate the conduct of ladies whose harshness and severity brought their knights—as we see it did in the case of Pierre Vidal—into danger and absurdity; to again legislate on all questions of the affections, to arrange disputes between lovers, to pass sentence on any lover who was in the wrong, and generally to establish a system of jurisprudence which might arise between lovers themselves and so render unnecessary any appeal to the Courts, except as a last resource.

Of these Courts the most celebrated were those of Queen Eleanor of England, of the Ladies of Gascony, of the Viscountess of Narbonne, of the Countess of Champagne and of the Countess of Flanders. There were also several Courts in Provence, those of Pierrefeu, Signe, Romanin and Avignon being the most celebrated.

The lists of the Courts of Romanin, Avignon and elsewhere disclose the fact that nearly all the ladies who acted as judges were married women. Rowbotham, in his valuable work on the troubadours, says he can discover in the Court of the Ladies of Romanin the name of only one unmarried lady, Jugonne de Sabran, daughter of the Comte de Forcalquier, and in the Court of the Ladies of Pierrefeu perhaps one lady who might be a spinster. (" Jusserande de Claustral Nostredamus," p. 27.)

The general rule was that all the ladies should be married or widows, and also of the higher nobility. In the Court of Pierrefeu we find the majority were wives of seigneurs. While a countess, a viscountess and a daughter of a count are found in the ranks of the jurors.

A large number of ladies assembled to constitute a court. Of the Countess of Champagne's Court it is said, by the chief chronicler of these Courts (André, " Livre de l'Art d'aimer ") " Quam plurimarum dominarum consitio." On one special occasion we find sixty ladies were assembled. " She summoned sixty ladies," says André, " as jury and assessors and then passed sentence." The complete assent of all the ladies present was necessary for a verdict. So again he writes in relation to the verdict of the Court of Gascony, " de totius curiœ assensu."

Before giving some instances of trials, it may be well to state " The Laws of Love," on which their verdicts were based.

(1) Marriage cannot be pleaded as an excuse for refusing love.

(2) A person who cannot keep a secret can never be a lover.

(3) No one can really love two people at the same time.

(4) Love never stands still; it always increases—or diminishes.

(5) Favours which are yielded unwillingly are tasteless.

(6) A person of the male sex cannot be considered a lover until he has passed out of boyhood.

(7) If one of two lovers die, love must be foresworn for two years by the survivor.

(8) No one, when once a lover, can be deprived of his title without a very good reason indeed.

(9) No one can love, unless the soft persuasion of love itself compel him.

(10) Love is always an exile where avarice holds his dwelling.

(11) It is not becoming to love those ladies who only come with a view to marriage.

(12) A true lover never desires the favours of anyone but his own lady-love, out of real affection.

(13) A love that has once been rendered common and commonplace never, as a rule, endures very long.

(14) Too easy possession renders love contemptible. But possession which is attended with difficulties makes love valuable and of great price.

(15) Every lover is accustomed to grow pale at the sight of his lady-love.

(16) At the sudden and unexpected prospect of his lady-love, the heart of the true lover invariably beats.

(17) A new love affair banishes the old one completely.

(18) It is only worth and excellence that make a man worthy to be loved by a lady.

(19) If love once begins to diminish, it quickly fades away as a rule and rarely recovers itself.

(20) A real lover is always the prey of anxiety and malaise.

(21) The affection of love invariably increases under the influence of jealousy.

(22) When two of the lovers begin to entertain suspicion of the other, the jealousy and the love increase at once.

(23) A person who is the prey of love eats little and sleeps little.

(24) Every action of a lover terminates with the thought of the loved one.

(25) A true lover thinks there is no happiness except in pleasing his beloved.

(26) Love can deny nothing to love.

(27) A lover never can be surfeited with the consolations which his beloved may offer him.

(28) A moderate presumption is sufficient to justify one lover in entertaining grave suspicions of the other.

(29) Too great prodigality of favours is not advisable, for a lover who is wearied with a superabundance of pleasure is generally, as a rule, disinclined to love.

(30) A true lover is enthralled with the perpetual image of his lady-love, which never at any moment departs from his mind.

(31) Nothing prevents one lady being loved by two knights, or one knight by two ladies. (André, " Livre de l'Art d'aimer," Vol. 103.)

In their earlier inception plainly enough, as Rowbotham in his work on the troubadours says : " The original audiences of these sorts of love-disputes would be the lords and ladies of the castle in which these troubadour-knights exhibited their musical and poetic powers." In the punctilious etiquette, however, of the age which delighted to give nicest form to everything—these matters being debated with profound seriousness—the chance and ordinary audience of a feudal castle was not considered formal enough to give the necessary prestige to these contentions. In this way these Courts of Love gradually grew up. (Soderhelm's " Anmerkungen um Martial d'Auvergne.")

Again, the form these Courts were conducted in—of alternating disputings between defender and prosecutor—were undoubtedly founded on the manner of conducting their " tensions " by the troubadours. These tensions were contentions between two troubadours, a habitual and favourite form of art among the minstrels of Arabic Spain and all the Semitic nations. So in Hebrew minstrelsy the singing of their Psalms, divided by a colon at each verse, was a mode used by two singers of question or answer. This carried over from the East by the Moors to Spain, where the Provençal knights derived their inspirations from, extremely resembled the questions and answers on love demanded in its Parliaments. This way of opposing themselves alternately in their tensions is well described by two troubadours present at the bridal of Prince Robert of Sicily. The first says :

> " Quant je suis à court et à feste
> Car je sai des chansons de geste."

The other replies :

> " Je suis juglère de vièle
> Je sai de muse et de soestèle (cystole)
> Et de harpe et de chifonie," etc.

The other replies :

> " Je sai contes, je sai fableaux
> Je sai conter beaux ditz nouveaux.
> .   .   .
> De Charlemagne et de Roulant
> Et d'Olivier le combatant," etc.

The other replies :

> " Je sai porter consels d'amors
> Et faire chapelez (couronner) de flors
> Et cainture de druerie (galanterie)
> Et beau parler de cortoisie
> A ceus qui d'amors sont espris."

Here, as in the Parliament of Love, one pleader defends himself against the other.

A few lines may be given here, before illustrating the procedures of the Courts of Love, as to whom the compiler of them, André the chaplain, served. Frederic Diez, a German author, says he was such to Eleanor of Aquitaine, others give Robert de Dreux as his employer, son of Louis le Gros, or Robert, Count of Artois, son of Louis VIII. Meray, in his work on the times of the troubadours thinks his patron was Robert de Dreux and says, " La reine Eleonore d'Aquitaine était sa belle sœur et Marie de Champagne fille du Louis VII. et femme du Comte Henri Ier de Champagne fait surtout époque dans cette affaire, c'était la grande inspiratrice d'André qui cite à presque toutes ces pages." This supposition of Meray's seems the most likely as Marie, Countess of Champagne, holding herself one of the chief Courts of

Love, would naturally get a good scribe such as one of the clergy, who, in that age were nearly the only ones competent to take down the causes brought before her Court and draw up its procedure.

From his " Livre de l'art d'Armour " will now be given a few examples of Trials in these Parliaments of Love.

" On the 29th of April, 1174, the following case was brought before the Court, presided over by the Countess of Champagne : ' Can real love exist between married people ? ' The question was debated in the usual style, and at the conclusion of the proceedings the Countess of Champagne pronounced judgment as follows : ' We declare and affirm agreeably to the general opinion of those present that love cannot exercise its powers on married people. The following reason is proof of the fact : Lovers grant everything mutually and gratuitously, without being constrained by any motive of necessity. Married people, on the contrary, are compelled as a duty to submit to one another's wishes, and not to refuse anything to one another. For this reason it is evident that love cannot exercise its power on married people. Let this decision, which we have arrived at with great deliberation, and after taking counsel of a large number of ladies, be held henceforth as a confirmed and irrefragable truth.' "

" The following was tried before the Court of Love presided over by Queen Eleanor of England : ' A lover to whom the lady-love had accorded the last favours in her power, requested from her the permission to bestow his homage on another mistress. She granted his request, and very soon he ceased to feel the tranports of affection for his first and former lady. After a month, however, he returned to his old love and declared he never besought any indulgences or desired any favours of affection from the new mistress whom he had so obsequiously courted, and that his sole idea had been to put to this proof the constancy of his best beloved and first loved friend. She, however, on his coming to her with this tale, deprived him of her love, declaring that he had rendered himself unworthy of it by the mere act of soliciting and accepting permission to leave her.'

" The question was much debated. It was a difficult one to answer. At length the Queen gave sentence : ' Such is the Nature of Love ! Very frequently lovers pretend that they desire the affection of someone to whom they are not really attached simply in order to assure themselves of the fidelity and constancy of their beloved.'

" ' It is an offence against all the laws of love and rights of lovers to refuse, on such a pretext, any tenderness or favour, to the lover who desires it again, unless that lover can clearly be convicted of having broken faith, or proved disloyal to his duties.' " (André, fol. 92.)

" Another judgment of Queen Eleanor was on the following ' cause célébre.' A lover entreated a lady for her love, but was never able to overcome her reluctance to grant it to him. In order to win her over to his wishes he sent a number of presents which the lady accepted with much grace and delight. Nevertheless, she did not diminish her severity to the sender, and persistently refused, after receiving all his presents, to display any kindness to him, or grant him the slightest favour. He accordingly brought the matter before the Court of Love, and pleaded that he had been deceived by false hopes with which the lady had inspired him by accepting his presents.

" Queen Eleanor gave judgment as follows : ' A lady who is determined to be inflexible must either refuse to receive any gifts which are sent, or she must make compensation for them, or she must be content to be classed as a courtesan.' " (André.)

" Before the Court of Ermengarde, Viscountess of Narbonne, the following case was tried : ' Can the greater affection, the more lively attachment subsist between lovers or between married people ? ' The Viscountess pronounced the verdict of the Court as follows : ' The attachment of lovers are sentiments both in form of nature and of morality completely different. There can therefore be no just comparison between objects which have not the slightest resemblance or relation one to another.' "

" Another case brought before her Court was this. A lady who was attached to a knight by a recognized union of love, married. ' Has she a right to reject her former lover and to refuse him the favours which he was accustomed to receive ? '

" This important question was carefully weighed by the Viscountess and her ladies, and the following judgment was pronounced : ' The addition of the marriage tie by no means annihilated the former love affair, unless the lady decides to say farewell to love for ever, and to love no one in future.' " (André, fol. 94.)

" Here is another case. A lady had imposed on her lover the condition of never praising her in public, no matter what might be said to her detriment. The knight performed his promise well until one day, finding himself in a company of others, who, with one consent began to speak ill of his lady-love, he could contain himself no longer, and burst out into a passionate defence of her, declaring if need be he would defend her honour à l'outrance.

" The Countess of Champagne, on the question being brought before her, gave judgment : ' The lady has been too severe in her commands. The condition, to begin with, was illegal ; for it is not right nor possible to reproach a lover who yields to the necessity of rebutting calumnies and slanders hurled against his lady.' " (André, fol. 91.)

" The Countess of Champagne decided also the following : ' A knight loved a lady, and not having much opportunity of speaking to her, arranged that by means of his steward they should communicate with each other. By this means they contrived to conceal their love in perfect secrecy. The steward, however, forgetting his duty to his master, pleaded his own suit with the lady, and so well that she gave him her complete affection.'

" Filled with indignation at their conduct the knight denounced their love-intrigue to the Countess of Champagne, who having convoked her Court of sixty ladies, pronounced the following judgment : ' Let the crafty knave who has found a mate worthy of him enjoy his stolen pleasures, since the lady has not had sufficient shame and modesty to keep her from such a crime. But we decree that both of them be in future excluded from the love of everybody ; that the lady never be invited to an assembly of ladies, nor the man admitted to an assembly of knightly men since he has broken the laws of honour and she has violated all the precepts of womanly modesty in stooping to the love of one so low.' " (André, fol. 96.)

" A decision, unanimous and for perpetuity, was pronounced by the Court of Ladies of Gascony which held jurisdiction in the English dominions. The cause was this : ' A knight divulged the secrets of his most private moments with his lady-love, and was brought before the Court by the unanimous voice of all lovers of the district, who demanded his exemplary punishment for fear that the example might become contagious.'

" Judgment was given as follows : ' The criminal to be deprived in future of every hope of love. He is to be disowned in every assemblage of the knights and their ladies, and if any lady has the audacity to violate this edict she is to be denied the friendship of every honourable woman.' " (André, fol. 97.)

" Another instance brought before a Court of Love was this : ' A knight-troubadour had loved a lady from her earliest childhood. In those days he had been passionately fond of her, and when she grew up to girlhood he had felt emboldened to declare his love. She promised to grant him the privilege of kissing her whenever he came to see her. But when she became a woman, and he was anxious to take regular advantage of this permission, she refused to grant him the favour, declaring that when she made the promise she was too young to understand the consequences.'

" The Court pronounced judgment in favour of the appellant, the knight, and therefore that he should have the kiss, only on condition that he immediately restored it."

" A far less serious case than those cited above was that of a lover who sued a lady in one of the Courts of Love for pricking him with a pin while she was kissing him. The lady defendant pleaded first, that the kiss was forced from her; secondly, that the pricking was done by accident. But all her artfulness was of no avail. The Court called in a leech and demanded he should inspect the wound if it existed; on his evidence that it did, the Court condemned the lady to kiss the place, when required, until it had healed." (Browne, " Chaucer's England," p. 162.)

It will be seen by the above cases brought before these Parliaments or Courts of Love what the theory of love, as understood by the knight-troubadours and their lady-loves, consisted in. It rested on the fact that the lover was to show his devotion and to convince the lady of his choice of its sincerity by means of a course of behaviour reproachless as far as love was concerned, but often branching out into extravagances and affectations. Again, to endeavour to check these latter phases, these Courts which founded their decisions on the Code given above, endeavoured by their decisions, to do. It would be well in criticizing such, to listen to one of the best modern writers on the subject : " That we must beware not to confound the spirit of the age we live in with that far-off and distant time, when punctilious etiquette was the very essence of all behaviour, and when romantic extravagances were as common in life then as they are rare at present, and that there is nothing so contrary to reason or to true historical sympathy as to pass an adverse judgment on the actors in a drama because the dresses and the scenery are different from those to which we ourselves are accustomed." (Rowbotham, " Troubadours.")

It is necessary, to realize this spirit animating many of men and women who lived in this atmosphere of love, to give them their due. As in all things well conceived, evil creeps in, so it is hardly worth saying this conception of platonic love was in many cases ruined and tainted by lower and regrettable incidents, but that many of those fair ladies and troubadour-knights did receive and did keep the original ideal unspotted by carnal intercourse, many histories of the troubadours evince. For instance, the touching and romantic history that has been briefly tendered above on the troubadour, Jaufre Rudel of Blaia (1140) cannot be read without recognizing his was a devotion to a woman he had never seen of a spiritual and pure kind.

In Swinburne's verses on it:

> " There lived a singer in France of old
> By the tideless, dolorous, midland sea;
> In a land of sand, and ruin, and gold
> There shone one woman and none but she;
> And finding life for her love's sake fail
> Being fain to see her, he hasted, set sail,
> Touched land, and saw her as life grew cold
> And praised God, seeing; and so died he.
> Died, praising God for His gift and grace;
> For she bowed down to him, weeping and said—
> ' Live,' and her tears were shed on his face
> Or ever the life in his face was shed;
> The sharp tears fell through her hair and stung
> Once, and her close lips touched him, and clung
> Once, and grew one with his lips a space
> And so drew back, and the man was dead.
>
> Oh, brother, the gods were good to you,
> Sleep, and be glad while the world endures,
> Be well content as the years wear through,
> Give thanks for life, O brother, and death,
> For the sweet last sound of her feet, her breath,
> For gifts she gave you gracious and fair,
> Tears and kisses—that lady of yours."

In the same way this refined and pure attachment of two lovers existed between Raymond the troubadour-knight, called Viscount of Saint Antonin and his Ladye. " Now the love they bare one another," the Chronicler says, " was out of measure great; and it chanced upon a time that the Viscount had made ready his harness, and there was a great combat, wherein he was wounded to the death, so that his enemies said he was dead. And the tidings of his death reached his lady— she was the wife of the Lord of Pena of Albigeois, a castle mighty and strong—and she, for the great grief she had of it, straightway entered into the Order of the Heretics (Albigensians). And God so willed that the Viscount recovered of his wound, and no man would tell him that she had entered therein. And when he was whole he gat him into Saint Antonin, and it was told him how the lady had become a nun for the sorrow she had on hearing of his death. And at this he left off all gladness and merriment and joy, and was given over to tears and lamentation and woe." (Farnelle, " Lives of the Troubadours," p. 286.)

So, too, of a son of song—a jongleur, Guillem de la Tor—" He took a wife, full fair and young, the which fled away and left him. And he bear her greater goodwill than to all the world besides. And it came to pass that she died, whereat he made such great dole that he became mad, and weened that she feigned her dead to rid herself of him. Wherefore for ten days and ten nights he left her lying on her tomb. And each evening he went to her tomb and uplifted her, and looking upon her face, kissing and embracing her, and praying her to speak to him and tell him whether she were alive or dead." (*Ibid.*)

Another such Galahad among the troubadour-knights was Pons of Caponoil (1180). " He was a noble baron of Puy St. Marie, who made songs and violed full well. And he was valiant in battle and courteous and chivalrous, and of great statue and comeliness. And he loved my Lady Azalais, wife of my Lord Ozil of Mercuer. Much did he love and praise her, and many a fair song did he make of her, and loved none other while she lived, and when she was dead he took the Cross and passed over to Holy Land, and there he died." (Mahn's " Die Biographieen der Troubadours.")

Here is another example seemingly of a perfectly pure love. Under the title of " Chatelain de Couci," a troubadour-knight of the name de Couci, in a sirvente in that collection thus addresses his beloved mistress before parting with her, probably for one of the later Crusades :

> " Je m'en voiz, dame, à Dieu le creator
> Commant vo cors, en quel lieu que je soie.
> Ne sai se ja verroiz maiz mon retor ;
> Aventure est que jamaiz vos revoie.
> Mon cuer avez en la vostre manoie ;
> Faire en povez del tot vostre talent,
> Ma douce dame, à Jhesu vos conmant !
> Je n'en puis maiz
> Certes se je vos laiz."

No one, unless giving the composer the worst of characters, can believe—as he commends his beloved lady to the care of God and His Divine Son—even though she was wife to another, but that his love was simply romantic and harmless. To give his words in the modern French : " Je m'en vais, dame ; à Dieu le createur je commande votre personne, en quelque lieu que je sois ; je ne sais si vous verrez mon retour, il est douteux que je vous revoie jamais. Mon cœur demeure en votre garde, vous pouvez en faire tout ce qu'il vous plaira. Ma douce dame à Jesus je vous recommande. Ce n'est pas ma faute, certes, si je vous délaisse." De Couci, this troubadour-knight, lived about the end of the twelfth century.

These examples certainly demonstrate that the strange romantic love cultivated in song and romance, whose ethics were laid down so carefully by the Parliaments of Love, were held by many in the manner they were originally planned for—a romantic but innocent attachment.

The Middle Ages were also ages of " symbolism par excellence." The Church herself which entered into all the social life of that time cultivated symbols which the ignorance of succeeding ages often interpreted into facts. Then many of the symbols that age gave to virtues of her saints—as the lion placed by some beatified person's statue, symbolizing his fortitude in life; the eagle by another for his heavenly soul gazing on eternity; the stag lying at another's feet, symbolizing his fleetness in evangelization—became the basis afterwards in the future for the legends of how one saint tamed a lion, the other had as companion an eagle. Here facts a later age demanded and so interpreted the symbols of the past into such.

Again, take the symbol of St. Christopher, which originally represented the spiritual redemption by Christianity of some strong man passing through the waters of baptism, bearing on his shoulders henceforth the yoke of Christ; this was turned into the literal fact of a ferryman bearing a child over his river.

Such saints as St. Malo, Corbinian, Humbert of Marolles, having the figure of a bear or wolf assigned to them as typifying they had overcome the powers of evil (which these animals in the Middle Ages were symbols of) became facts, as, for instance, that St. Corbinian made a bear his beast of burden.

The stag was a symbol and, as such, found in the catacombs of the early Church—to symbolize the words, " As the hart desireth the water-springs, so my heart desireth Thee, O God," and as such assigned to the Saints Hubert, Julien, Eustache and others for their unworldly lives and love of the Cross, these aspirations became turned into facts—that between the antlers of a stag they saw a crucifix. In a word, in this age of the troubadours and trouveres what had been used as innocent symbols before of spiritual things, became gross facts, and were so believed.

In the same way many of these harmless things, such as a lady giving a ring to her lover, and a kiss on accepting him as such, or bestowing her favours on his lance and helm, were innocent symbols of an innocent and romantic attachment which a later and grosser age, having divested itself of symbolism, looked on as facts of immorality. On no other ground but that most of these lovers, both knights and ladies, considered their love perfectly innocent—that is, unless they were self-deluded hypocrites of the worst description— could they so constantly in their sirventes and romances call for the aid of God and the Virgin to further them in their amorous passages.

To take one instance, the troubadour-knight, Arnaut de Marvoil, ends one of his sirventes to his love :

> " I'll pray no more—God yield thee grace,
> And never turn from thee His face,
> So please thee, give me health to know,
> Since love for thee has laid me low,
> May Love who conquers everything
> Eke thee a captive to me bring—Lady ! "

So again he sings :

"That day and night to God on high
I pray to win thee or to die
If God thy love to me do give."

This was addressed to the wife of the Viscount of Beziers and she, we are told, " shunned not his love, but hearkened to his prayer." It is obvious, unless both this knight and lady looked on their attachment in a symbolical and platonic way, that calling on God to bless it, they must have been conscious offenders of all their religion taught them.

Perhaps one of the greatest examples of how a later age interpreted early symbolism into fact of the grossest kind (and though it has nothing to do with the ethics of this romantic love fostered by the troubadours, yet shows how a symbol may be wrested into a fact) is that in the indictment of the Templars. The offence they were charged with which raised the greatest indignation and was least capable of disproof was that in their reception into the Order they spat on the Crucifix and trampled on the sign of our salvation. Nothing can be plainer than that this—at the first formation of the Order—had been a symbol which in the course of years had lost its significance and interpreted into a hideous fact. It was at first introduced into their ritual as an emblem of Peter's denial and of worldly disbelief to be exchanged, when once they were clothed with the Crusader's mantle, for unflinching after-service and undoubting faith—a passage from death into life ; this had been retained long after its symbolism had been forgotten, and nothing is so striking as the confession of some of the younger knights, of the reluctance, the shame, and the trembling with which, at the order of their superior, they had gone through this repulsive ceremony. In a word, in that later age a fact was without warranty born of a symbol. (Wright's " Eighteen Christian Centuries," 1863.)

It has been before mentioned how the growing tendency of the cult of the Blessed Virgin raised the position of women in the feudal ages, but in doing so a great familiarity arose with subjects that in the past had been treated with the greatest reverence. This, by the legends prevalent of the Virgin's interposition in purely secular matters, tended to break down the wall subsisting between supernatural and natural love, and is probably one reason why the knights and ladies of the days of the troubadours had no hesitation in asking God and the Virgin's help in their amours. We have in past pages given an instance how the Virgin is supposed to have taken a knight's place in a tournament. We will give here two other instances how she is said to have entered into a love affair. The first is the story " du Varlet qui mist son anel au doict de l'ymage." A young varlet on his way to a contest came to a Church where he found an image of the Virgin. He had on his finger a ring recently given him by his sweetheart and the idea came to him, in order to save it being lost while he was contesting in the coming games, to place it on one of the buttresses of the Church. However, the image of Our Ladye was both new and beautiful, and his heart beating with love, he was the more moved by it, and instead of placing the ring on the buttress, he placed it on the finger of the Image. Then something happened. The marble bent and the fingers closed on the ring so firmly that

" Nul home ne l'en pooit retraire
S'il ne voulait l'anel deffere."

Astonished and delighted he consulted his friends who advised
him to pay his vows to Mary, but though he did so, he did not forget
his former vows to his sweetheart and was married to her, and retired
with her on his wedding night. The Virgin thereupon glided into the
nuptial chamber between these two who were about to embrace each
other. Without speaking a word, Mary showed him the ring he had
placed on her finger, reproaching him for his disloyalty to her. For
a moment the youth, ashamed, repented, but human love was too
strong and he again turned to his earthly bride. Thereupon a second
time the Virgin came displaying such anger that the young husband
finally abandoned his young wife and took the habit of a hermit.

" Du lit saut sus, plus n'y demeure
Si l'inspira la douce dame
Qu'onc n'eveilla hom ne fame
Ains s'en fouy en hermitage
Et prist habit de moniage."
(Meray, " La vie au temps des Trouveres.")

The second story is more scandalous but bears out the contention
that the excessive cult of the Virgin at this time induced the trouveres
and troubadours by bringing her as a helper and intervener into
doubtful human love, to inspire the knights and ladies who listened
to their Lays and stories to appeal to celestial power to help them on
in their amours, and that without feeling they were the least
irreverent.

Jehan de Conde relates, " de l'abbesse que ses nonains
accusèrent "—how this young abbess, after giving way to loving
advances from a youth employed about the abbey, fell into sin; and
after a time expected a child to be born to her. The nuns saw her
condition at last and hastened to tell their bishop the scandal. He
instantly began to set out on his journey to their abbey. But as it
happened the Virgin was not unmindful of all that had happened to
her erring daughter, and the night before the bishop arrived, the
child was born while she slept, and the Virgin with the aid of an
angel conveyed the infant away secretly to a hermit, who brought the
foundling up, nourishing it on goat's milk. When the bishop did
arrive, he found no sign in the young abbess of her late illness, and
nothing was left to him but to hector her nuns with bringing a false
charge against their superior. (Meray, p. 302.)

So far did this abasement of the Virgin to human affairs at this
period prevail, that certain of the contemporaries of the trouvere,
Gautrer de Coigni, did not hesitate to add to the Litanies addressed
to her, " Queen of the Fairies, pray for us " (Meray, p. 302).
Indeed at this period the queen of saints and the saints themselves
were inextricably mixed up with all those half supernatural beings—
faunes, elves, and demons—and as the latter were supposed to enter
into the family life of the knights and their ladies, into their
pleasures and their sicknesses, warding off sometimes the one and
bringing another, so the Virgin and her Son, in the amours of the

time, were supposed to enter into them and to hear the prayers addressed to them by these loving hearts, often shielding them by semi-divine interposition from the penalties attached to human frailty.

At all events, regrettable as it seems, it shows among the frailties current at this period, a firm belief in the supernatural and a trust that the Creator ruled all the affairs of human life—a belief and a trust greatly wanting in the present age.

With all these amorous Lays of the troubadours and trouveres before us, it is a strange fact that in a great many of them a contrary spirit seems often to display itself alien to any sort of love. It is as if these Lays had, as a French writer observes, a " double inspiration," a contradiction, a two-fold struggle. On the one part is that idolatry of love which had become a very principle in Chivalry, on the other that older and lower estimation of the female sex which altered the tone of the lay entirely. In a word, there is a conflict to be observed of these two views of considering the fair sex, in many of these chansons of the knight-troubadours and more northern trouveres. One of the most remarkable cases of this is to be found in the Lay or Romance of " Amadas and Idoine." The maker of it paints his heroine as loyal and beautiful, then a little further on he describes the sex to which she belongs as

> " Volages sunt et poi estaules
> Et sans mesure enfin canjaules.
> Fols est qui en nule se fie
> Encontre raison et droiture
> C'est de femme droit nature
> D'ouvre toujours—
> Por ce si est de femme fine
> Bonne, loial, enterine,
> Une des mervelles du mont."

(They are flighty and little constant and in a word, without measure changeable. . . . It is the true nature of a woman to be always swaying between reason and right. Therefore to find a woman faithful, good, loyal, and trustworthy is one of the wonders of the world.)

This disparagement of women is found most generally in the trouveres of the North, as if the ancient way of treating women as inferiors could not always be suppressed, even by these singers who had received their inspiration from the Crusaders and troubadour-knights of Provence. It was not so long ago that Matilda of Flanders had been dragged by the hair of her head by the Conqueror when she refused to marry a bastard. Nor was the age over when the Queen of Troubadours, Eleanor of Guienne, was long shut up in durance by her passionate and despicable husband, Henry II. Even in Spain, the brutal treatment of the Cid's daughters by the Infantes of Carrion, whether historical or not, point to the same fact that till the troubadour-knights' influence spread from Provence over the adjacent lands their ideal of the sanctity and high place of woman in the world was greatly needed.

The life we have just attempted to describe speaks of a singular ease and freedom of social intercourse, and exhibits in a peculiar manner the softening and refining influence of poetry and song on what hitherto had been the rough character of ancient Chivalry. But it would be a mistake to think that the troubadours' influence was always directed to love and never to the more manly business of war, or that their songs, though often composed in the service of love, were not also composed for the sword and for the battle. We have drawn a picture of the youthful troubadour-knight singing after a banquet, or in the open garden of some castle, in his rich dress of peace, but his ordinary costume was far more manly when travelling from one of these scenes of peaceful song to another in his wanderings. If he was a troubadour, he never forgot he was also a knight. Strange as it may seem, yet the military relations of these musical errants were always kept up in knightly armour, down to the latest time we hear of them. It was as if they prided themselves as much on their martial prowess and capabilities as they did on their music. At any rate, although their errand to every castle was a peaceful one and lutes—when they arrived there—and not swords, were the weapons they handled, they invariably rode from castle to castle in full armour; mounted on a war-horse and with lance in bucket at their horse's side, ready to be placed in rest should occasion arise. Even when going to an amorous rendezvous it was usual to don full armour (see the Preface to the " Romance of Hughes Capet," p. 65. Paris, 1864).

Some people might argue that this peregrination in full armour was entirely intended for purposes of safety, but if such had been the case how was it that the jongleurs who always formed a peaceful company behind their lord—the troubadour—possessed no weapons of defence? The conclusion seems to be that the troubadours as knights-errant were compelled by the laws of Chivalry to wear knightly armour as well as from their individual choice to show the world that though they choose to be singers and composers of love songs, they no less were like the lords and knights they amused—of the high and sacred order of Chivalry.

On those visits they made to a castle where special festivities took place, a tourney or tournament would certainly be one of the chief attractions, and in these contentions of gallantry the troubadours were as eager as any other of their brother-knights to prove to the eyes of the spectators that they were able to do battle for their lady with their sword as well as with their lute. Arrayed therefore in full armour, the same knight who the evening before had discoursed to a crowd of admiring ladies and knights on his lute of Love, and Love's obligations, next day's dawn saw mounted on his war-horse in full armour and with lance in hand ready to support his challenge that his lady was, of all, most perfect.

However, a difference when a troubadour-knight tilted, from the tilts and tourneys of other knights, was this—that the jongleurs were always stationed in some conspicuous place outside the barriers of the lists, who when their master started in the onset, set up a chorus of instruments and voices, singing and playing war music of his composition, to cheer him on to the charge, and to excite the attention of all the spectators round the lists to the warrior who was no less expert with his sword than with his songs (Justinus Lippiensis). These songs continued during the tourney and the jongleurs in order to make the music peal above the noise of the stamping steeds and crash of the contending weapons, often performed the accompaniment to the words on horns and bells, and even stranger instruments which they had learnt when they followed their master to the Holy Land.

If the troubadour fell in one of these encounters it was the jongleurs' duty to carry his dead body from the lists after the mêlée was over.

Many of these knights of song did not confine their prowess alone to the lists of a tournament but like their brother-knights crossed the seas to join in the bloody battles of the Crusades. If—as he always is considered to be—Richard Cœur de Lion was a troubadour, then he must be reckoned the greatest of these crusading knights of song. The Count of Poitiers who is the earliest troubadour mentioned, and at the age of fifteen one of the most powerful princes of his time, in 1101 headed a large army on Crusade to the Holy Land. Pierre Vidal, another troubadour-knight, accompanied Richard Cœur de Lion on his Crusade. Pons Capaduoil in 1180 went also on Crusade, so did Raebaut of Vagueiras in 1180 and Gaucelin Faidit in 1190, besides a great many others. These knights of song were accompanied on their warlike pilgrimage by their ever faithful servants, the jongleurs, who enlivened many of the Crusaders' camps in Palestine by their music. Nor did the troubadours confine their talents exclusively to the service of love—martial in spirit—frequently taking the Cross themselves—many of their songs and romances were written and sung to inspire others to take that Cross. One of the earliest was that composed by the before-mentioned Count of Poitiers, entitled, " A Crusading Song." It is to sorrow over the necessity, as a Crusader, of leaving his fair dominions and his son behind.

Subjoined is a chanson or song for the Crusade which in an historical point of view is of great interest as it is the first of the many composed for and evoked by the Crusades. The author is unknown, though it is found included in the rhymed Chronicle of the Dukes of Normandy by the Trouvere Benoit.

It was seemingly composed about the year 1145-1147 when King Louis le Jeune took the Cross. The translation can hardly be called a translation into English like the literal ones given in this work of Eustache Deschamps, and gives only the general sense of the composition in order to show the reader somewhat of the fire—which is lost in a strict translation—with which the troubadour-knight would sing his verses.

> " Parti de mal e à bien aturne
> Voil ma chancun a la gent faire oïr
> K'a sun besuing nus ad Deus apelé ;
> Si ne li deit nul prosdome faillir.
> Kar en la cruz deignat pur nus múrir
> Mult li doit bien estre gueredoné
> Kar par sa mort sumes tuz rachaté.
>
> Cunte ne duc ne li roi coruné
> Ne se poent de la mort destolir,
> Kar quant il unt grant trésor amassé
> Plus lur covient à grant dolur guerpir.
> Mielz lur venist en bon vis departir ;

A KNIGHT'S LIFE IN

Kar quant il sunt en la terre buté,
Ne lur valt puis, ne chastel ne cité.

Allas ! chetif, tant nus sumes pené
Pur les deliz de nos cors acumplir.
Ki mult sunt tost failli et trespassé,
Kar adès voi le plus joesne envieslir.
Pur ço fet bon paraïs deservir,
Kar là sunt tuit li gueredon dublé ;
Mult en fait mal estre desherité.

Mult ad le quoer de bien enluminé
Ki la cruiz prent pur aler Deu servir.
K'al jugement ki tant iert reduté,
U Deus vendrat les bons des mals partir,
Dunt tut le mund trembler e fremir
Mult iert huni ke i serat rebuté ;
Ki ne verad Deu en sa maesté.

Si m'ait Deus ! trop avons demuré
D'aler à Deu pur sa terre seisir,
Dunt li Turc l'unt eissieslié et geté
Pur nos pechiez ke trop devons haïr,
Là doit chascun aveir tut sun desir
Kur ki pur lui serad la richeté
Pur voir aurad paraïs conquesté.

Mult iert celui en cest siècle honuré
Ki Deus dorat ke il puisse revenir ;
Ki bien aurad en sun pais amé
Par tut l'en deit menbrer et suvenir.
E Deus me doinst de la meillur joir
Que jo la truisse en vie e en santé
Quant Deus aurad sun afaire achevé ?

Qu'il otroit à sa merci venir
Mes bons seigneurs, qu jo ai tant amé
K'a bien petit n'en oi Deu oblié."

(Take the good and cast the evil
Listen people to my song,
For 'tis God for whom I'm speaking
Ye the valiant and the strong.
Take the Cross, the Cross He died on,
O repay Him as ye may
For by dying He's redeemed us,
Can we give Him less to-day ?

Counts and princes they may spoil us
But their spoiling stays at death,
What the treasures of their hoarding
When they give their final breath ?

DAYS OF CHIVALRY

Better far to up and rally
In the good cause I proclaim,
Where at death are earthly honours?
Lost for ever, lost in shame.

Cowards! spending time and labour
For your bodies, for a wage,
All shall pass and all shall wither
Soon the youth shall turn to age.
But the guerdons of true virtue
O they live for ever more,
O the bitterness of losing
Of their everlasting store.

He to whom the light is given
He will up for Holy Land
At the day of Judgment scathless
When the good from evil stand.
When the world shall mighty tremble
O that soul shall fearless be,
Quailing, never such before Him
Coming in His Majesty!

Help me, God, in this my pleading!
Tardy have we been to free
That Thy Cross and that Thy country
Where the Infidels mock Thee.
'Tis our sins that have delayed us
Let us cast them and be free,
Leaving everything behind us
Finding Paradise with Thee.

Such an one will all men honour,
If returning God decrees,
Sweet in absence is his country,
Sweeter if once home he sees.
Living still his lovely ladye
As he left her hardly won,
O he'll joust for her sweet favour
Now his task for God is done.

L'envoy

O my good knights may God keep ye
Whom I've loved so ever more,
That in loving ye I've almost
Oft forgot my God of yore!)

If it is asked, did these troubadours compose the songs they sung, the romances they chanted, the crusading chants or songs they delivered? Though certain of the written romances must be placed to the pen of some monkish writer, who in a lonely retreat thus beguiled his time, yet these were exceptions and the Chronicle of Bertrand

Guesclin distinctly attributes the most renowned Romances, or Chansons, to the composition of the trouveres or troubadours by whom they were sung. After enumerating those of Arthur, Lancelot, Godfrey de Bouillon, Richard and other champions he sums up his account of them as being the heroes " de quoi cils minestriers font les nobles romans." Indeed the slightest acquaintance with Romances of the metrical class shows us that they were composed for the express purpose of being chanted or recited by the authors to some simple tune or cadence for the amusement of a large audience. It is true these knightly minstrels did not compose all the Romances of an historical type, but many did, and to them we must attribute various ones that dealt especially with the heroes they held up as patterns of Chivalry before their knightly audiences.

As time went on these same champions who had first caught the natural ear were still retained in order to secure attention, and backed up by the same assertions of authenticity and affected references to real history. France and England, and also Germany, came at length to adopt a cycle of heroes peculiarly associated with their own land— those of France and England from their close relationship under our Angevin kings had such constantly extant in each. Thus from England—or rather Wales—came the Arthurian cycle of romantic Lays; from France, the Carlovingian of Roland and Charles the Great; from Germany the Nibelung which has supplied the groundwork of so many Teutonic romances. A common ground, however, for all these were those Romances or Lays which dealt with the Crusades and among both the knights of Provence, the knights of France and England, appealed most to their warlike hearts—these were chiefly:

1. The Lay or Romance of the Knight of the Swan.
2. Of the Infancy of Godfrey de Bouillon.
3. Of the Cowards (chétifs).
4. Of the Siege of Antioch.
5. Of the taking of Jerusalem.
6. Of the death of Godfrey.
7. Of Baldwin.
8. Of the bastard of Bouillon.

That of the Siege of Antioch is the oldest and most remarkable, probably composed by the trouvere, Richard of Picardy, who went himself on the first Crusade.

The influence of the Crusades, in a word, exercised at the time a great influence among the trouveres of the north of France, and the troubadours of the south, forming the subject of these songs, and aspirations, for the ears and hearts of their warlike audiences. That these high tales in which the virtues of generosity, bravery, devotion to his mistress and zeal for the Catholic religion, carried to the greatest height of romantic perfection in the character of the hero, united with the scenes passing round them, exercised a salutary effect on the chivalrous hearers, none can doubt.

The verse most frequently employed by these knightly composers was the " sirventes "—a term which is thought to come from the word " servir," and means that the poem was made by one who served. These troubadours also employed the " ballada "—which was a song with a long refrain.

Most interesting of all perhaps was the " tenson," which was a lyrical dialogue between two persons who discussed in it some rule of amorous casuisty, or on a metaphysical or satirical subject. The troubadours composed their songs in the ecclesiastical scales or modes which were the lineal musical descendants of the Greek system of music. Nor did they write the music of their songs for one musician alone. If they deigned to sing such themselves they altered it for one voice, but, in general, they committed the performance of their songs to a company of their faithful companions—the jongleurs. In such a song the jongleur with the best voice sang the " aria " alone, and the remainder, standing by, accompanied their comrade's voice by the music of their instruments. Sometimes the troubadour-knight took the part of both author, instrumentalist and singer himself, when his usual instrument was the guitar or lute. Sometimes, though more rarely, he ordered his jongleurs to accompany him or one of them alone to accompany him who was possessed of a good voice. Such was the general way of musical performance in vogue among these knights of song. Though the music of the troubadours was of a highly culti-vated and elaborate form of art in comparison with the general music of that day, it was always kept subordinate to the poetry. No trouba-dour, as Rowbotham in his work well says, worth the name would ever have studied—as is so much the modern fashion—to exalt and elaborate his music at the expense of the poetry. If he had done so, he would have ceased to be a troubadour and would have been reckoned a mere jongleur or maker of tunes. Reciting romances, weaving in song sirventes or tensons the troubadour-knight not only kindled but kept to its height all those chivalrous feelings the knightly hearer possessed. All those extravagant ideals which really existed in the society of the Middle Ages, became, in turn, the glass by which the youth of the age dressed themselves; while the spirit of Chivalry and Romance thus gradually threw light upon and enhanced each other.

The Lays of the troubadours—themselves knights and frequently of high and noble lineage—exhibit a true picture of the manners which existed in the age they lived in, and are an invaluable mine of informa-tion for the latter-day historian. Many of the incidents—such as wild beasts, strange flowers and vegetation, savage men, imported into their Lays—show an extensive knowledge far beyond the usual monks' chronicles. They demonstrate the wide wanderings of these knights of song through little known regions, and the facility that art gave them to gather material besides their own knowledge from the homeward-bound pilgrim or brother-knights, far travelled. With the true artist's eye to seize on the most salient points of such travellers' stories, they incorporated them into their Lays, while many of them on their return from fighting in the Crusades brought back valuable itineraries for future wayfarers. If the young knight-errant with his lonely squire was the means of creating a brotherhood among the lands he visited in his adventurous quests, far more was the educated and refined trouba-dour, who, from castle to castle, from land to land, took his way, his welcome, his song and lute, his defence, his knightly sword and hauberk, and if this varied knowledge the returning Crusading trouba-dour brought back, it seems highly likely that the first idea of constitut-ing the Courts of Love, described in this chapter, he also brought back from the East, and we have already seen that the " tenson " form of question and answer was derived from Eastern lands and was adopted in these courts. A curious account of one of the assemblies held by the Moslems in the reign of the celebrated Haroun al-Raschid exists where, not philosophical or theological subjects were discussed, but Love—Yahya ibn Khaled who presided said, " You have inquired if the dignity of the Imam be of divine appointment, you have probed to the bottom of all metaphysical questions. Occupy yourselves then to-day with a description of, and on, the subject of Love." (Masoudi, Vol. VI., p. 368.)

Here, but discussed by men (women, of course, being secluded in the East) the same subject that the Courts of Love afterwards occupied themselves with, is found the matter for a wise assembly's investigation.

As to the quality of the Lays and Romances which were composed by the trouveres and troubadours, as compared with the " moralities," farces and jesting compositions of the fifteenth and sixteenth centuries —in taste, in delicacy of form and in " finesse "—they are far superior. There is hardly anything in these songs of theirs, tinged as they are with medieval thought and art, which does not contain some pleasing and gracious description, or some bright and living thought of true poetry which we seek for in vain in those of succeeding centuries. In an age which was full of robbery under arms and confusion, the small poems of these troubadour-knights exhibit models of honourable dealing, and in the midst of a corrupt and half-barbarous age, examples of pure love and where a delicacy of feeling, even shrouds the most amorous of sentiments. Again in such we find instructions of moderation and tolerance at the very time that force was paramount in the world, and when defenceless women and children could only claim their rights by the point of their champions' lances or swords. It was during this age of song that the pathetic story of Griselda, which Boccaccio after incorporated and popularized, had birth, from either a nameless troubadour or else possibly from the trouveresse, Barbe de Verrue. Then, too, the graceful and charming Lay of Aucassin and Nicolette had its origin from the facile and graceful improvization of an unknown trouvere or troubadour. In their Tableaux in which they often described semi-fabulous beasts and semi-fabulous humans there is in those formed for recitation, in some castle or hall, a sober beauty of form and a very high standard of invention. The idiom they are composed in is always true and clear, and expresses under such, clear forms, constant and original thoughts, which gives their poetry an unusual charm. As the French writer Meray (" La Vie au temps des Trouveres ") well says, " La vers généralement riche de rime y est souvent ciselé comme l'or des chasses, rehaussé de vives couleurs comme les images des psautiers et les vitraux des verrières gottigues," or like the emeralds, their bright thoughts—such as ladies carry on their girdles and chatelaines. If too, as often many of their Lays are quoted which only deal with the love and one unacquainted with their literature should conclude this was the sole subject they dwelt on, anyone who has read their delicate chansons on Nature, her changes in the varying seasons, her flowers and birds, fountains and skies, would soon be disabused. Here is one beginning,

DAYS OF CHIVALRY

" Quant veirent la sayson que l'herbe reverdore
Que de fleons clérets la terre aime s'ondoie
Qu' esjoissent oysels de lors gracieuxl Chantez
Li bois et le prée et li chamez."

So of other subjects—their strange and great knowledge of Nature mixed with fable—the trait of the age, in dealing with the unknown in Nature was exemplified in many of their Lays. The learned trouvere, Richard de Fournival (temps. Philip Augustus) composed a " Bestiare d'amour." After describing the animals then known, he fantastically applies their different virtues to his lady. So, too, another Guilhelm Osmond in 1220 composed his " Volucrairy," a wonderful collection of marvellous fantasies in reference to birds, also a Lapidary describing the mystic value of precious stones. These few examples show how varied and diverse was the knowledge not only in the intricacies of love, but in the outside world of the troubadours, trouveres and jongleurs at a time when the age itself was, as compared with modern times, in its infancy.

As there was a difference of rank between the jongleurs and the troubadours, the former generally the servants of the latter—the former of low degree, the latter of knightly—so the decadence of both was different. The jongleurs were extinguished by slow decay, the troubadours by sudden catastrophe. That catastrophe happened in Provence and, by their cruel extermination there, paved the way to the rapid extinction of their class. During the period they flourished four hundred of them (not, of course, reckoning those of a third or fourth rate rank in song and music) flourished from Guilhem de Poitiers down to Guerant Riquier (1236-1294). At the courts of Alfonso X. of Castille and of James I. of Aragon in the middle of the thirteenth century, and even at the court of Frederic of Sicily at the end of that century, and at Venice and Genoa at the beginning of the fourteenth, troubadour-knights might still be found, but they were the scattered and inconsiderable residue of that great company which had well-nigh been extinguished, when the catastrophe referred to ruined them in Provence.

Strange as it seems, this extinction of their order arose on the ground of religion. Who, seeing them in the halcyon days when from castle to castle, from court to court, among light hearts the lightest, making love while the sun shone and where ladies were kind and love was their life-breath and their glory, could have foretold that not for love in their hearts, but for heresy lurking there, they would be among the slain or fugitives. That these swords of theirs which so often had warred for the recovery of the Holy Land should be shattered in their hands for disobedience to the Church that had given them the Cross and blest those shining blades. Yet so it was. A sect of heretics known by the name of Albigenses from the place where they first appeared arose and formulated their doctrines rapidly owing to the secrecy and expertness of their propaganda and spread over the lovely land of Provence, mixing infidel opinions of Eastern mysticism with the old revived heresy of Manichæism and the duality of the principles of Good and Evil. By the peasants not alone, but by the idle pleasure-loving upper classes and by their beloved troubadours, a strange credence was given to this sect.

To the troubadours and their lady friends much in these strange doctrines appealed. If Evil, as these new teachers taught, was everlasting, what need of virtue and of self-restraint since to practise them was to oppose the principles of Eternal Nature. These principles were caught up and repeated in those gay and happy assemblies as very consonant to their feelings. The long sympathy of Provence to the art and music of the Moors prepared the way for a welcome when this offshoot of Eastern religious thought made its appearance among them. Religious contentions on all sides arose between the orthodox and unorthodox. The musical knights seem to have flung themselves into the breach with the same gallantry and recklessness of consequences as they manifested in the tilt-yard or in the Crusades.

Most curious, as Rowbotham informs us in his work on these troubadours, was the musical war they carried on at this juncture. They used to send their trusty jongleurs into the market-places on market-days and at fair times to sing odes and pasquinades dealing with the main points of the Christian and Albigensian religions and lampooning most severely their adversaries. The jongleurs despatched on their strange errand acquitted themselves but too well, and striking their lutes or touching up their violins they soon attracted a crowd of listeners. Their usual method was that called a " tenson " or contention. The same writer gives an instance, " If the Holy Ghost who took the form of man," sang one troubadour, appealing to the great deity of the Albigenses, " listens in aught to my prayers, I will stop thy mouth. O Rome, in whom all the perfidy of the Greeks is revived," thus maintained in song William de Figueira. On the other side a troubadour of the opposite party (Germonda) cried, " Rome, thy laws ought to be strictly adhered to for ever. Cursed are these heretics who dread no vice and believe in mystery."

It was estimated by the contemporary Chroniclers that all the principal troubadours except two, Isarn and Fulke, the troubadour bishop of Marseilles, were on the side of the heretics. It is little wonder the Faithful were horrified at the rapid spread among the cultivated and uncultivated classes in Provence of this heresy. A crusade, as all know, was proclaimed, and after many battles, many sieges and inhuman reprisals, this fertile province was left a desolation, its vineyards trampled down, its gardens and fields a waste, town and cities a heap of stones; its gay and educated massacred, and not least, for those who love song and music, its troubadour-knights every one slain, or left wanderers on the field of Europe. All the stimulus to poetry and song was taken away by the slaughter of this bright and glittering society which had been the minstrel's chief inspirer and genial patron. The gay reign of Love and the troubadours was over for ever.

The leaders of the troubadours assembled to meet this religious Crusade, which had been called into existence by Innocent III., were the Counts of Toulouse and Foix, the Counts of Bearn and of Comminges, the Vicomte de Beziers, Guy de Cavallore, Guillaume de Montagnogent, Arnold de Comminges, Raymond de Miravals, Guillaume Rairiole d'Apt, Bertrand de Marseilles and other troubadour-knights of lesser fame. The town of Beziers belonging to the Vicomte of that name was early marked out by the enemy for destruction, who surrounded the walls by their military engines all surmounted by huge crosses. At a short distance off stood the orthodox clergy singing psalms. The town meanwhile kept up its reputation for being the centre of song, for inside it, the jongleurs paraded the streets singing, on viols and guitars, to the desperate people, their masters' songs. The town was taken by storm, and soon after Carcassonne shared the same fate.

One powerful prince alone came to the assistance of the troubadours, Pedro, the king of Aragon, himself a troubadour. Having defeated the Moors at Navas de Tolosa he hastened to his brother-knights' assistance. Accordingly he first sent a sirvente or war-song to the camp of the enemy, entrusting its delivery to one of his jongleurs, who was bidden to sing it to the assembled crusaders as the message of the king. The jongleur, we are told, proceeded to the performance of his task and was happy in his song till he came to this phrase in his lord's composition, " For the love of my lady I am coming to drive ye out, barbarians, from that beautiful land that ye have ravaged and destroyed." Hereupon one of the crusaders called out, " So help me, God! I do not fear a king who comes against God's cause for the sake of a harlot." This brought the jongleur's song to an untimely end.

The assistance King Pedro brought was of short duration. He was defeated and slain himself at the battle of Muret.

Though no one but must confess this subjugation of Provence stayed a pestilent heresy from spreading over Western Europe, few can contemplate without regret the ruthlessness it was performed in, at least those who have a regard for literature and refinement. The country subdued was where the beautiful language " Oc " was spoken. That country, singularly favoured by nature, was, in the twelfth century, the most flourishing and civilized portion of Western Europe. It was in nowise a part of France. It had a distinct political existence, a distinct national character, distinct usages, and a distinct speech. The soil was fruitful and well cultivated, and amidst the corn-fields and vineyards rose many rich cities, each of which was a little republic, and many stately castles, each of which contained a miniature of an imperial court. It was there that Chivalry first laid aside its ruggedness, first took a graceful and tender form, first appeared as the inseparable associate of art and literature, of courtesy and love. The other vernacular dialects which since the fifth century had sprung up in the ancient provinces of the Roman empire, were still rude and imperfect. The sweet-toned Italian, the rich and energetic English were abandoned to artisans and shepherds. No clerk had ever condescended to use such barbarous jargon for the teaching of science, for the recording of great events, or for the painting of life and manners.

But the language of Provence was already the language of the learned and polite, and was employed by numerous writers, studious of all the arts of composition and versification. A literature rich in ballads and war-songs, in satire, and above all in the amatory poetry, which has been described in former pages, animated the whole world of cultivated minds beside the banks of the Rhone and Garonne. All this was trampled under foot when the overthrow took place of those fair regions for heresy. Even now that literature, though little studied, unconsciously is a factor in our present busy lives, for from the far East and certainly from the far West and Provence, through the medium of Chivalry as proclaimed by her troubadour-knights long dead, the Christian world became aware that woman was worthy to be accounted noble and respected, and that life without love was a barren wilderness. Knightly gallantry, as we have seen in the foregoing pages, had thought proper to elevate the feminine ideal and clothe with virtues the heroines of many fictitious romances of the knight-troubadours. It made woman the aim and arbiter of all achievements. The principal seat in hall and festival was reserved for the softer sex, which hitherto had been considered scarcely worthy of reverence or companionship. Perhaps this courtesy to women on the part of the knights and nobles returned from the Crusades began in opposition to the wife-secluding habits of the Infidels against whom they fought, as at an earlier date, the maintenance of images by the Western Church had been for a protest against the unadorned worship of the Moslems. Perhaps it arose from the gradual expansion of wealth and the security of life and property which left time and opportunity for the cultivation of the female character. Women were early constituted too, chief of societies of nuns, and were there obeyed with implicit submission. Large communities of maidens were presided over by widows still in the bloom of youth, and so holy and pure were these Sisterhoods considered, that Brotherhoods and monks (as the Gilbertines in England) were only separated from each other, even at night, by an aged Abbot sleeping on the floor between them. The greater Cult of the Blessed Virgin, as has frequently been noticed in these pages, also gave a greater dignity to what had been called the inferior sex. But another thing conspired to still further enhance women's position—the death of whole families in the Crusades had left daughters heiresses of immense possessions. In every country but France (and that probably was not anciently the case) the Crown itself was open to female succession and henceforth it became impossible to affect a superiority over a person merely because she was corporally weak and beautiful, who was lady of strong castles and could summon a thousand retainers beneath the banner of her House.

For this alone then, if for no other gifts and graces, the traces of which we can still find in our higher civilization of to-day, was it worth while that those far-off ages submitted to the discipline of Chivalry, and for her troubadour-knights to have so sung as to have raised for ever more in Western nations, the status of the weaker sex.

From the opposition to Simon de Montfort in his crusade against Toulouse, and the attachment the troubadours had for its unfortunate House, with so many, as we have seen, infected by the Albigensian heresy, the greater part of them perished, but it would be false to assert all did so. Those who escaped chiefly made their way to Catalonia and Aragon, where they planted deeply the literature of Provence, which served not only as a model for the poetry, but the literature of the Aragonese. The time of their advent was peculiarly favourable, for peace was then reigning in Aragon, maintained by a line of wise and liberal-minded princes. James the Conqueror himself composed the memoirs of his illustrious reign—Ramon Muntanes—a dramatic recital of the chief events of the thirteenth century, particularly the struggles between Peter of Aragon and Charles of Anjou. King James himself composed several poetical pieces after the fashion of Provence—an allegorical chanson composed by Peter of Aragon, young brother of Alfonso III. was recited, in the style of Provence, at the king's coronation by the jongleur, Romaret.

But the Aragonese princes did more than afford an asylum to the deposed troubadours and jongleurs of Provence. In the reign of King Martin (the last of the line of Barcelona) in 1400 an embassy was despatched to Charles VI. of France praying him to despatch from the consistory of Toulouse (which apparently still kept alive to some extent the ancient Troubadour tradition) certain skilled men who might establish at Barcelona a school of the gay science (gai savoir) conformable to the ancient rules of such.

The foundation of the University of Toulouse had been imposed by St. Louis on Raymond, second Count of that territory, by the Peace of 1229.

The King of France assented to Martin's request and four learned professors in the art of love and song were sent, and founded at Barcelona a duly constituted court. A full account of the opening ceremony was given by Henri de Villena writing to the Marquis of Santillane. Henri was himself of the Royal House and was appointed president of the Court about to be formed. The four envoys from Toulouse and the troubadour-knights then in Aragon assembled at the Palace. A procession was formed, preceded by mace-bearers carrying the books that contained the rules and procedure of love and song. On a raised seat Henri sat with the four envoys on either side. On a raised table like an altar were placed, covered with a cloth of gold, the books (los libros del arte e la joya). On the right hand of the Court was a place prepared for the king. In the semi-circle of the hall sat the troubadours. From another account we gather who the judges were. One a knight, another (strange admission!) a master in theology, another a doctor of law, and the last a well-known burgess. The opening speech was made by the master in theology, who made his subject the " gay science." After this the competing troubadours were bidden to bring forward their several compositions on the subjects which before had been laid down for the contest. Two sessions were held—one in camera, when everyone was sworn to give an impartial judgment on the several compositions, one in public when the successful troubadour recited it in open court. The victor was acclaimed and crowned, and with music and cheers taken in procession to the king's palace, where he was regaled on wine and spices.

This account ends up with this curious and aristocratic remark, which certainly would not suit the temperament of our own age. " E monstravase aquel avantage que Dios e natura ficieron entre los claros ingenios e los obscuros." This (i.e., this ceremony) holds up to glory the distance that God and nature have placed between men of education and the vulgar throng and ends up : " E no se atrevian los ediotas," so ignorance learns to give due respect (to the merit of the educated).

If we analyse this Provençal growth transplanted into Aragon, it is in a great measure more picturesque than so many of the old sirventes of Provence and Languedoc. It is frequently in the form of the " ballada," and by its simplicity and graphic touches akin to our own minstrelsy of the Border.

Though the jongleurs penetrated into Aragon, even their songs holding up to ridicule Chivalry and the Church, had to be moderated in their new-found asylum. Chivalry was still a power in the Peninsula with the Moors still holding many places under their rule, and the Church though having more liberty from the Roman autocracy than any other Christian kingdom, was piously defended and guarded by the kings of Aragon and Castille.

To show the readers somewhat their style one or two are subjoined.

" Si n'eran tres doncelletas—assentades en un banc
Totas tres s'enrahonaban—els llurs galants quant vindran
En respon la mes grandeta—' El meu ne trigara un any.'
En respon la mixaneta :—' El meu no trigara tant ''
La petita ix en finestra—ya'n veu veni el seu galant
En duya la sella verda—y dos criats al devant.
Las primeras parauletas—' marit que trigaban tant ? '
Las segonas parauletas—' Quinas joyas em portan ? '
—Las joyas que yo t'en porto—no se si t'agradaran
No son sabatas ni mixtas—ni chapins valencians
No son fetas d'argenters—ni tampoc de cristians
Son fetas de rey de Moros—que son d'or y diamants
La soguilla que te'n porto—n'es de perlas y brillants
L'ha feta reina de Moros—que hi ha treballat set anys.
M'han dit que no la portessis—sino tres vegadas l'any
La una per cinquagesina—y l'altre per St. Joan
L'altre per Pascua florida—quant els roser floriran.''

(There were three young girls living in their manor who together communed, and asked themselves, " When will our betrothed return ? " " I have waited for mine for a year," said the eldest. " Not so long have I waited," said the younger one. But the youngest went to the window. She saw her betrothed come. He rode on a saddle all gold and two pages preceded him. " Friend," she cried, " why have you tarried so long ? " These were her first sweet words. " What gift have you brought me ? " These were her second. " The presents I have brought you," quoth he, " I do not know, my fair one, if they will please you, they are not stockings nor shoes, nor a mantilla of Valentia, nor beautiful coverings for the hand, of silver or ' chretien.' It is a bandeau I bring you, embroidered with diamonds and pearls. It is the work of the Queen of the Moors, she worked at it for seven long years. You must only wear it three times a year—at the Quinquagesima, at the Feast of St. John and on Palm Sunday, when the roses are in flower.")

Another is still more like the questions and answers in our own Border Ballads—an excerpt is given from it.

" A la bora de la mar—n'hi ha una doncella
Que broda d'un mocador—la flor mes bella
Quant ne fou a mita brodat—li faita seda
Veu veni un berganti y diu—' Oh de la vela ! '
' Mariner, bon mariner—qu'en portau seda ? '
—' De quin color la voleu—blanca o vermella ? '
' Vermelletta la vuy yo—qu'es mea fineta

DAYS OF CHIVALRY

Vermelleta la vuy yo—qu'es per la reyna '
' Entra dintre de la nau—triareu d'ella
Quant fou dintre de la nau—la nau feu vela.'
Marine's posa a cantar—canso novella;
Ab lo cant del mariner—s'ha adormideta.
Ab lo soroll de la mar—ella's desperta
Quant se desperta's troba—Uuny de sa terra
· Mariner, bon mariner—portaume en terra
Qu'els ayres de la mar—me dona pena.'
' Aixo si que no ho fare—qu'heu de ser meba.' "

(On the shore of the sea there was a young girl who was embroidering a handkerchief with scattered flowers. When she came to a certain piece of the embroidery, she wanted some more (embroidery) silk. Thereupon a brigantine hove in sight and she cried out to the ship, " Sailor, good sailor, do you bring silk ? " " What colour want you, wilt thou have white or rose ? " " Rose, I wish," (quoth she) " it is so beautiful, rose I wish, it is for the queen." " Enter," he replied, " lovely one, my ship, and come and take thy silk."

When the lovely one had entered it, the ship immediately sailed. The sailor began to sing, he sung a new song—and while he sang his song, the lovely one fell asleep. When she awaked from the tossing of the waves she was a long way from land. (So she cried) " Sailor, good sailor, put me on shore, I suffer from the wind and sea." (But he answered) " I will not put you on shore for you now belong to me.")

The above is a literal translation of this ancient Catalan poem; below we give, in order to show the reader how nearly it approaches our own old ballads, a free rendering of it as it was probably sung by the later troubadours and jongleurs who had migrated into Aragon.

" Good sailor, good sailor,
 Have you silks to sell,
I prithee, kind sailor,
 Of your kindness tell ? "
" Oh, I have silks
 From lands far away,
What colour, fair maiden,
 Do you want, I pray ? "

" Good sailor, good sailor,
 'Tis of rose I need
To weave a fine robe
 For the queen indeed."
" Oh, roses I have,
 Dear maid, never fear,
They're like the lips
 Of my ladye dear."

" Good sailor, kind sailor,
 O show them me."
" Step on my ship,
 My store you shall see,

Spices and silks
   You shall have them there,
And if you don't pay me
   Should a sailor care? "

   .   .   .   .

She stept on board,
   And she saw each ware,
For the spreading sail
   She had not a care,
For the anchor up,
   Or the land away;
O woe is me
   For the maid that day!

The sailor he sings
   O rich and rare
His voice rings out
   To that Ladye fair,
The sun is hot
   And the music sweet,
And soon in sleep
   She lies at his feet.

" O sailor man, good sailor man,"
   She cries when her drowsy eyes awake,
" The ship is tossing and the wild winds blow
   And the planks and the masts they all shake and quake,
O put me on shore, good sailor, pray,
Shorewards, good sailor, up and away."

But the sailor he laughed,
   " You're mine, my dear,
You're home is gone
   But with me what fear?
We'll sail away
   You shall be my love,
To isles far away,
   With the stars above."

Such naïve and simple ballads were very different to the complicated sirventes the original troubadours sung in their native Provence; the ballad style so adopted by the Moors, who were still the near neighbours of the Aragonese and Castillians soon modified the artificialities of the original troubadours, and as we soon find those who had escaped into the haven of Aragon dying out, these ballad forms of song were so suited to less educated capabilities that they were adopted readily by the jongleurs who roamed over both Aragon and Castille. As for the school of the " gai science " set up by King Martin at Barcelona, if the " gai science " was taught there it was of a pedantic kind and became very shortly after its institution more of a literary society of poets and scholars—who studied the provincial literature and versification, less as vehicles of love and adventure than as interesting relics of the past.

DAYS OF CHIVALRY

At all events, though several of the Aragonese princes were composers of Chansons and were of knightly degree, we can find no trace of themselves or any knight of song, wandering from castle to castle, court to court, as those knights of Provence had done, and though the jongleur or minstrel still did so, the noble and highborn knight-troubadour, despite the cultivation of his literature and the imitations of his songs, became as extinct in the Peninsula as he had become in Languedoc and Provence.

In this book dealing with knighthood, the composers therefore of the songs of Spain cease to be of interest. This only may be said: the " Ballada " introduced by the advent of the troubadour, afterwards allied with those of the still extant Moors of Granada, formed in time a literature of Ballad Poetry which in its dramatic force and yet in its vigorous simplicity, can better than any other country of Europe vie with that store of Ballads of our own Borderland and of Scotland.

CHAPTER XVII

KNIGHTS' DEATHS AND OBSEQUIES

THE particulars concerning the deaths and funeral obsequies of the ordinary knight are found few and far between in the Chronicles of the Middle Ages, simply because their deaths were nothing extraordinary nor the debt they paid to nature other than all mankind. Again greatly different to the men of the present day the thought of death was ever present with them. The tumultuous days they lived in, the constant feuds, the inefficacy of medical science, even the many mortuary masses they attended for their departed brother-knights, made death a very familiar thing to them. As has been before mentioned they very frequently welcomed it as bringing them that gift the age they lived in could not give—Rest.

For this reason the few instances given here of deathbeds are those of highly-placed knights and of royal birth, but these instances are so far useful as they show us what no doubt was the usual trend of mind in the presence of death, of their brother-knights of a lower rank, for " death," as it has been well said, " makes all men equal." One feature in all these instances is common to them—that whatever errors they had committed in their past, at the prospect of death they became sincerely penitent. Nor is this to be wondered at, for unlike many of the present age, they thoroughly believed in another life beyond the grave and a Judge who would then take account for all their earthly life. The age which was accountable for the " Dies Iræ " did not let even the most worldly forget its dread teaching.

A happy issue to death was often expected by a knight on account of having taken the Cross to the Holy Land. In the Lay or Romance of the " Two Crusaders," who try to persuade on their return, two stay-at-home knights to go likewise crusading, it is the thought of performing a deed to solace their latter end that chiefly moves them. The Crusader says to the non-Crusader :

> " Tu ne redoutes pas la mort,
> Si seiz que morir te convient,
> Et tu diz que la mers t'amort ;
> Si faite folie dont vient ?
> La mauvistiez qu'en toi s'amort
> Te tient a l'osteil, se devient
> Que feras se la mort te mort
> Que ne ceiz que li tenz devient ? "

266

A KNIGHT'S LIFE

(You do not fear death, you know that you must one day die, and you say that you fear the sea. Whence comes this folly? The cowardice that has taken root in you holds you here, that is the truth. What will you do if death seizes you, you who do not reckon how time (swiftly) passes.)

The lagging knight at thought of death portrayed by the Crusader, determines to also take the Cross. He says:

" Biaux sire chiez, que que dit aie
Vos m'aveiz vaincu et matei
A vos m'acort, a vos m'apaie
Que vos ne m'aviez pas flatei
La croix preing sans nule delaie."

(Good, then Lord all that I have
Said (against taking the Cross)
You have conquered and rebutted
I agree with you, with you I will make peace
Just because you have not flattered me
I will take the Cross without delay.)

And then the converted knight says his future expectation:

" En non don haut roi glorieux
Qui de sa fille fist sa meire
Qui par son sang très precieux
Nous osta de la mort ameire
Sui de moi croizier curieux
Por venir à la joie cleire;
Car qui a s'ame est oubleux
Bien est raisons qu'il le compeire."

(In the name of the high (and) glorious king
Who of his daughter made his mother,
Who by his most precious blood
Has delivered us from the bitterness of death,
I am wishful to take the Cross
And so at length to attain to the joy celestial,
Because it is only just that he who neglects his soul
Should bear the punishment of it (hereafter).)

Many a knight to save his soul gave up much he loved to take the Cross—it was not only William of Poitou who said:

" J'abandonne donc joie et plaisirs
Le vais, le gris et le sembelin
Adieu brillants turnois, adieu grandeur et magnificence."

If a knight had been unable in life to perform his vow and gain absolution of his sins by pilgrimage or by taking the Cross, often on his deathbed he commissioned one of his friends or household to perform this obligation after his death for him—thus young King Henry, son of Henry II. dying, " gave to William Marshal, one of his household, his cross to bear to Jerusalem." (Hoveden, Vol. II.)

Others thought their deathbeds could be eased if they had not been able to go to the Holy Land, by paying for a grave in the holy earth of the Campo Santo at Pisa, from whence the Pisans made a good profit. A very frequent custom to obtain the pardons granted to members of religious orders was in extremis to assume and die in the habit of a pilgrim or a monk. So Raymond of Toulouse (1221) took the habit of the knights of St. John in *articulo mortis*.

That these " post-obit " pilgrimages for the good of the testator's soul and to ease his conscience in death by hoping to participate in the fruit of them, are not uncommon, the wills of the twelfth to the sixteenth century prove. In the earlier instances they were mostly directed to Rome or Jerusalem, but in later times, like other pilgrimages, they were more commonly made to domestic shrines; even knights' ladies provided for such. One such is given in an old History of Norfolk, who provided for a pilgrim to visit after her death no fewer than eight different shrines in that county. In the will of Lady Cecily Gerbridge, dated 1418, ten marks are bequeathed for a pilgrim, on her behalf, to visit Rome, and Bishop Gardiner of Norwich left twenty marks for a like purpose. In some cases the executors of a will were directed to give certain sums of money to all pilgrims who were willing to undertake an assigned pilgrimage for the deceased.

A few instances of such are here given from the " York Wills."

In 1400 Roger de Wanderforde of Tereswell, in the county of Nottingham, left money to support a pilgrim " to visit the glorious Confessors there resting," to whom he made a solemn vow when he was tossed about in the greatly troubled sea between Hibernia and Norway, and nearly drowned.

In 1404 William Boston of Newark, chaplain, left 26s. VIIId. for a priest to make a pilgrimage for him to Bridlington, Walsingham, Canterbury and Hales.

In 1472 William Ecop, Rector of the Parish Church of Heslerton in the East Riding, ordered a pilgrim in his will to visit the shrine of St. John of Bridlington and seventeen other holy places named, and the pilgrim to pay four-pence at each holy place visited for the good of the testator's soul.

In these Middle Ages, the performance of religious duties and penances by proxy was no doubt largely resorted to by many who, cut off by death, had not themselves been able to perform their vows and religious obligations. It would be interesting to know whether the monks, to whom so many gifts and alms by the dying, both in money and real estate were made, accepted them without disturbing themselves about their source, without inquiring to what extent the donor had rightfully or wrongfully acquired the gifts he made or sent by his executors.

The truth is, this scruple did not worry the monks very much for the very simple reason that, at bottom, the great mass of the faithful were convinced that giving to a saint or to God was a pious deed which in itself justified everything. It mattered little whether the source of the gift was pure or impure; from the moment that the Church was enriched even with possessions wrongfully acquired, the sin was expiated and the wrong repaired. A letter which a certain Simon of Namur addressed to Henry, Bishop of Villiers, in the first years of the thirteenth century on that delicate subject, was answered after many reservations, that if the donor's possessions be of a mixed nature (mixta bona) that part of it was gained honestly, part dishonestly, in such a case the monks may always accept, as they can go on the hypothesis the thing, money or lands, was honestly acquired, it being impossible for them to show to the contrary.

As it was the monks who performed usually the service of interment for the dead, and the knight always, if he could, desired to be bestowed in an abbey, and was happy—as has been noted—if he could before death assume the monastic habit, it was always well for the dying knight to stand well with them. Garin, in the chanson de geste of his name, said to the Abbot of Saint Vincent of Læon, " Let the bodies of my good friends, who have just been killed, be collected, enshrouded and buried. I shall raise funds so that God may show them mercy." Likewise Hervis of Metz sent for the Abbot of Saint Seurin, " Seignior Abbot," said Hervis, " I have sent for you to bury two varlets (young esquires) before the high-altar of Saint Seurin." " If you wish," answered the abbot. Immediately bathing the corpses he took them to the monastery of Saint Seurin to the place the duke had named.

But not only did the religious houses receive from the knights and landed proprietors gifts of money from the dying, or " post mortem " benefactions by their wills and at the hands of those they had therein designated, but they received all kinds of properties— lands, woods, meadows, vineyards, wheat, barley, oats, flocks, even iron and coal, also rights to pasture, to mills and judicial rights. From 1164 to 1201 the Abbey of Clairveaux alone received nine hundred and sixty-four donations. At Vauluissant, one of the ancient abbeys of the order of Citeaux founded in 1127, in the cartularies between 1180-1213 there are sixty which mention such gifts to the monks.

And the motives nearly always the same. Here a woman enriched Vauluissant " for the salvation of her soul, for that of her husband, her children and of her ancestors." Some made donations " for the expiation of their sins," others because they were leaving for the Crusade. In 1216 a noble knight " on the point of setting out against the Albigenses made his will and the priest made him give the abbey six pieces of land." A point is that a great many of these donations—as those left in wills—were only to come into operation when the knight who was the testator, died. They were only valid " post mortem."

As the vows, unfulfilled in lifetime, to go on a pilgrimage or to take the Cross were afterwards performed by deputy, the efficacy to the soul passed away, and was supposed to be benefited and freed.

But the knights and their ladies did not leave money alone; those who wished that their souls should not suffer too long in the other world left endowments for distribution of food. They instituted what were called " pasts " or " stations "—this is, distributions of bread, of wine, and of meat to the canons and clerics of a collegiate or cathedral church. In the " Cartulaire de Notre Dame de Paris " there is a rule of 1230, only seven years after the death of Philip Augustus, which exhibits the arrangements made by the canons of this Church in matters of this kind. At Easter and at Christmas the clerics of the Choir received one hundred half-pints of wine and one hundred large loaves; at Pentecost the " stations " of pork consisted of one hundred and thirty-seven portions of meat, or " frustra," which the canons and clerics divided, the highest in dignity, as always, receiving a double portion. On the feast days of SS. Gervais and Protais nine rams were distributed; each ram was cut into fifteen pieces which the clerics assisting at the office, carried home. It is hard nowadays to associate religious services with the distribution of food and money; to harmonize the uninterrupted sound of chanting with the clinking of money; to conceive of Chapters which seemed like counting houses and restaurants, where the canon need only appear and sing a mass for the departed benefactor to be well paid and well fed, but the Middle Ages and its Church, though their outward pomp was great and enclustered with romantic legendary lore, was also eminently practical and gave nothing for nothing.

Strange to us as it seems, some of these knightly benefactors, though knowing all the directions they left would only come into operation when they had departed this life, gave minute directions. Thus in 1177 a Count of Champagne founded, in view of his speedy death, a memorial service for himself in the collegiate Church of Notre Dame of Oulchy. He directed it should consist of two dinners which should follow his funeral service. At the first dinner all the clergy who should present themselves should be served and the menu was fixed by the donor; the first course a dish of cold pork; the second course, a dish of goose; third course, chicken fricassee, " garnished," says the deed of foundation, " with good sauce thickened with the yellow of eggs." The second dinner resembled the first, except that beef was served in place of the cold pork. Each guest had the right to half a pint of wine and the quality the donor directed was to be " good and drinkable, between the most delicate and the cheapest." In 1203 Blanche, Countess of Champagne, much to the displeasure and sadness of these well-fed clergy, commuted these meals into a money distribution. If it is realized all these strange banquets arose from a knight's or count's desire to obtain at his death an easy entrance into the invisible world, the gravity of death, side by side with the festivities of those he had benefited, seem strangely out of place. (See " Social France " by Achille Luchaire.)

It was a strange age of contrasts—this age of Chivalry—it is therefore no wonder that when one of its upholders—a good knight— was dying, these incongruities often occurred. To the actors they did not seem strange—they were every day usual incidents—it is only time and a different age that makes the reader amazed at reading of them. To us a clergy wearing, as the canons of their cathedrals did, red or green clothes, slippers and short flowing cloaks, and if on horseback using golden bits and spurs, having hawks in their houses and carrying out of doors falcons on their wrists, would be abhorrent, to the knight of those days there was no such feeling. The Council of Paris in 1212 and that of Monpellier, it is true, in 1214 aimed several rules against these luxuries in the clergy, but seemingly without avail, and the very prohibition of these councils shows how much they were indulged in. Yet to the medieval knight as long as the clergy could say a Mass for his soul and sing a dirge at his funeral, their moral behaviour was very little taken notice of; that was chiefly left to the songs and pasquinades of the jongleurs and gleemen.

Having either at the time of death, or long before, by will, directed that his vows unaccomplished in life were to be performed by his friends or dependents—having also given lesser or greater benefactions, in money, lands or movables to some church or monastery —the dying knight frequently directed his body should be clothed in some monastic habit, and laid on a bed of ashes, to show the humility with which he wished to appear before his Maker. Thus in the death scene of Prince Henry, crowned king in his father's lifetime, son of Henry II., he realizing his death imminent, summoned the bishops and religious men who were there, into his presence, having first secretly, and then before all, made confession of his sins, and gave to William Marshal, one of his household, his Cross to bear to Jerusalem (in his stead). After this, laying aside his fine garments, he placed upon him hair-cloth and fastening a cord around his neck, said to the bishops and other religious men who stood around him, " By this cord do I declare myself an unworthy, culpable and guilty sinner, unto you, the ministers of God, beseeching that our Lord Jesus Christ, who remitted his sins to the thief when confessing on the Cross, will through your prayers and His ineffable mercy have compassion upon my most wretched soul." To which all made answer, " Amen." He then said to them, " Drag me out of this bed by this cord and place me on that bed strewed with ashes," which he had caused to be prepared for himself, on which they did as he commanded them, and placed under his head and feet two large square stones ; and all things being thus duly performed he commanded his body to be taken to Rouen in Normandy and there buried. After saying this and being fortified with the viaticum of the Holy Body and Blood of our Lord, in the fear of the Lord, he breathed forth his spirit. (Hoveden's Annals, Vol. II., p. 27.)

Another deathbed scene, showing how a previously proud and cruel heart, death softens, is that afforded by the last hours of Richard, Cœur de Lion—shot in the arm fatally, by an archer, at Chalons, called Gurdon.

" All his jewels he devised to his nephew Otho, the King of Germany, and the fourth part of his treasure he ordered to be distributed among his servants and the poor.

He then ordered Bertram de Gurdon, who had wounded him, to come into his presence, and said to him, " What harm have I done you that you have killed me ? " On which he made answer, " You slew my father and my two brothers with your own hand and you had intended now to kill me, therefore take any revenge on me that you may think fit, for I will readily endure the greatest torments you can devise so long as you have met your end, after having inflicted evils so many and so great upon the world." On this the king ordered him to be released and said, " I forgive you my death," but the youth stood before the feet of the king, and with scowling features and undaunted neck, did his courage demand the sword. The king was aware that punishment was wished for, and that pardon was dreaded. " Live on," said he, " although thou art unwilling, and by my bounty behold the light of day. To the conquered faction now let there be bright hopes and the example of myself." And then after being released from his chains, he was allowed to depart and the king ordered one hundred shillings of English money to be given him. Marchadés, however, the king not knowing of it, seized him, and after the king's death, first flaying him alive, had him hanged.

The king then gave orders that his brains, his blood and his entrails should be buried at Chalons, his heart at Rouen, and his body at Fontevraud, at the feet of his father. (Hoveden: Annals, Vol. II.)

The Chronicle of Winchester gives a different version of Gurdon's death. It says that this ruffianly Routier Marchadés gave him over to Joanna, the king's sister, and that she tore out his eyes and killed him by cruel tortures. If this be true, it shows how cruel was the age, and how great forbearance and forgiveness the dying Richard had displayed in setting him free.

The death of another—King Louis-le-Gros—was very edifying. He distributed all his gold and silver, giving even his clothes and the rich hangings of his bed away. He received the last sacraments. He caused some tapestry to be spread on the ground, and ashes, in the form of a cross, to be strewn over it, and upon this bed of penitence he expired in the act of making the sign of the Cross.

In like manner, Henry III. of England, after confessing his sins at first privately, and afterwards in public before all the bishops and monks around, caused himself to be placed on a bed of ashes, on which he expired.

One of the finest examples of a dying knight is of a much later age. To Villars the French Marshal, wounded at the battle of Malplaquet, it was proposed to give him the viaticum privately. " No, no," said he, " since this army has not been able to see Villars die like a hero it shall see him die like a Christian."

Charles V. of France, on the day he was dying, desired to see the relic of the Crown of Thorns (Christine de Pisan) and his own coronation crown. When both were brought before him he placed the Crown of Thorns before him, crying, " O precious crown, diadem of our salvation, how sweet, how precious is the mystery comprised in thee." Then turning to the crown of France, " O crown of France, precious art thou considering the mystery of justice contained in thee, but vile and viler than all things if one regards the labour and anguish, torment of heart and conscience, yea peril to the soul thou bringest those who bear thee."

Ulrich Baier, a knight of the Teutonic order, died in battle in 1281, fighting against the Infidels in Prussia—his wish was that he might die as his Saviour with wounds in hands and feet and side—and so it was, he received from the enemy exactly those wounds. (Dusburg, c. 101.)

It was at the attack of Brescia by Gaston de Foix that he was dangerously wounded, finding himself so, he exclaimed, " Jesus, my God, I am a dead, dead man." He then kissed the Cross of his sword, repeated some prayers aloud, and no priest being present, made his confession to his house-steward; he then caused himself to be laid at the foot of a tree with a stone under his head, with his face towards the enemy, showing, in that last hour of his life, he would not turn his back on them. When the Duke of Bourbon stood weeping over him, he cried, " Weep not for me, I die in the service of my country—you triumph in the ruin of your own and have far more cause to lament your victory, than I my defeat by death."

DAYS OF CHIVALRY

Sometimes before death knights of an order of Chivalry voluntarily degraded themselves of such, so impressed were they with the humility necessary to approach the next world. Thus the Emperor Charles V. renounced, before retiring into the convent of St. Just, his membership of the Golden Fleece. He gave it to his son and successor with the words, " Reçevez, mon cher fils, ce collier de la Toison d'or, que Philippe Duc de Bourgogne, surnommé le Bon, notre ayeul voulut être un monument éternal de sa foi et de sa vénération pour l'Église Romaine."

So again, Philip, Count de Joiqui, in his old age and preparatory to death, retired from the world, and renounced his knighthood of the " Saint Esprit." (Sainte Marie, " Chivalry Ancient and Modern.")

Sometimes knights on the other hand, voluntarily, in preparation for death, entered an order whose statutes were formed for this object, e.g., the Order of the Star (l'ordre de l'Étoile) founded in 1352 by John, King of France. Among other regulations they were to abstain from all wine, all game, all sweet dishes, and lead a life of abstinence, though living in the world, " pour la glorie de Dieu, et le bien de leur âme." (Sainte Marie, p. 200.)

Sometimes those unjustly condemned to death were apt to cite their judge or judges to appear at a given date before the Eternal Judge. Several instances of this occur in the Middle Ages. Thus in 1312, Ferdinand, King of Spain, was summoned by two brothers, Peter and John, of the knightly order of Caravalla, who were by him unjustly condemned to death, to appear in thirty days before the Eternal Judge—upon the thirtieth day the king was found dead in his bed.

Walter, Bishop of Poitiers, thus summoned Pope Clement V., who had unjustly deposed him.

Philip, King of France, was solemnly cited to appear before the Divine Judgment within a year by the Grand Master of the Templars. He died on the 29th November of the same year.

Francis, Duke of Brittany, cast his young innocent brother into prison on returning from his education in England and afterwards put him to death. The young prince cited his persecutor to appear before the Eternal Judge within the year. Duke Francis died within the same year.

Rudolph of Austria unjustly condemned one of his knights to death, throwing him enclosed in a sack into the river by his castle. The knight, ere expiring, cried out to the duke in a loud voice summoning him before the Judgment Seat of God. The duke laughed at the threat, but before the end of that year died in horrors.

The Emperor Otho, being reproved by his son, the Bishop of Mayence, for his marriage within the forbidden degrees with Adelaide his wife, casting the bishop into prison, was summoned by him to appear along with himself on the same day before the Eternal Tribunal. He was shortly struck with sudden death, and the bishop his son had ceased to live a short time before. (" Tribunal Christi," Bk. II., cap. 3.)

Sometimes, not only as we have seen, did the dying noble and knight make provision for vows unfulfilled in his life, to be fulfilled for him by others after his decease, but he left directions how he should be buried and the anniversaries of his death celebrated. Such a one

s

was Edward the Black Prince—in his will still extant in the register of Archbishop Sudbury at Lambeth, directs : " Et paramont la tombe, soit fait un tablement de latone suzorrez de largesse et longure le meisme la tombe, sur quel nouz volons qu un ymage d'overeigne levez de latoun suzorrez soit mys en memorial de nous, tout armez de fier de guerre de nous armez quartillez et le visage mie, ove notre heaume du leopard mys dessouz la teste del ymage. Et volons qu sur notre tombe en lieu ou len le purra plus clerement lire en veoir soit escript ce qe ensuit en la manere qe sera mielz avis a nos executors—

Tu qe passez ove bouche close, par la ou cest corps repose
Entent ce qe te dirray, sicome te dire la say,
Tiel come tu es, Je au ciel fu, Tu seras tiel come Je su,
De la mort ne pensay je mie, Tant come j'avoy la vie.
En terre avoy grand richesse, dont Je y fys grand noblesse
Terre, mesons, et grand trésor, draps, chivalx, argent et or
Mes ore su je povres et cheitifs, perfond en la terre gys
Ma grand beauté est tout alée. Ma char est tout gastée
Moult est estroite ma meson. En moy na si vérité non,
Et si ore me veissez, Je ne guide pas qe vous deçisez
Qe j'eusse onqes hom esté, si su je ore de tout changée.
Pur Dieu pries au celestien Roy, qe mercy eit de l'arme de moy—
Tout cil qe pur moi peieront, ou a Dieu m'acorderont
Dieu les mette en son parays, ou nul ne poet estre chetifs."

One of the most singular orders connected with burial was the command of Edward I. that at every return of the anniversary his coffin should be opened and his corpse wrapped in a new cerecloth. This precept was obeyed until the deposition of Richard II. in 1399.

Henry VII. agreed with the abbot and convent of Westminster that there should be four tapers burning continually at his tomb—two at the side and two at the ends, each eleven feet long and twelve pounds in weight; thirty tapers, etc., in the hearse, and four torches to be held about it at his weekly obit : and one hundred tapers nine feet long, and twenty-four torches of twice the weight, to be lighted at his anniversary.

The cost of these anniversaries varied greatly. The expenses of four obits are recorded of Blanche, Duchess of Lancaster. In 1371 the amount came to £38 18., in 1374 to £45 4s. 10d., etc. (Register of John of Gaunt, 1 fol. 147.)

Sixty-eight shillings and twopence were expended on the obit of Queen Philippa in 1390 for wax torches to burn on and about the tomb on her anniversary and for white cloth to clothe the poor men holding the torches.

But besides leaving directions for vows to be fulfilled and arms and lights to be placed around their graves and Masses said, in these ages of Chivalry there was hardly a church in the kingdom which had not one or more Chantries founded in it and endowed for the perpetual maintenance of a Chantry priest to say these Masses daily for ever for the soul's health of the founder and his family. The churches of the large and wealthy towns had sometimes ten or twelve such Chantries. All Souls College at Oxford was founded as such for the souls of the knights who fell at Agincourt. These Chantry chapels were sometimes built on to the parish church and opening into it; sometimes it was only a corner of the church screened off. In some cases the Chantry priest had a special house assigned him. Richard III. commenced the foundation of a Chantry in the Cathedral of York of one hundred chaplains, when his death at Bosworth Field interrupted it. Beside these Chantry priests there was a great crowd of priests who gained a livelihood by taking temporary engagements to say Masses for the soul of the testator, for these many priests were required free from parochial duties.

So Chaucer in the Canon Yeoman's tale mentions such a one :

" In London was a priest, an annueller
That therein dwelled hadde many a year."

An " annueller " was one who sang annual or yearly Masses for the dead.

Funerals were often much longer delayed in the Middle Ages than now, especially in the case of the highest knights and nobles.

The Black Prince, who died 8th June, 1376, was not buried till after Michaelmas; and his consort Joan, who died 7th August, 1385, was still unburied on the 7th December following.

One important item at a funeral was the torch-bearers clad in white, paupers to the number of the years of the deceased person. The record that twenty-four torch-bearers held the pall of Blanche, Duchess of Lancaster, sets at rest the otherwise disputed date of her birth. This princess had one of the costliest tombs on record in England, no less than £486 having been paid for it to Henry Yeuley, Mason of London.

For her mother-in-law, Queen Phillipa, " the iron tomb over the grave of the Venerable Father Michael, late Bishop of London, outside the western door of the Cathedral Church of St. Paul " was bought at a cost of £40 and adapted for its new tenant. (Issue Roll 50, Ed. III.)

It is difficult to know the cost of ordinary knights' funerals. We can only judge by halving or quartering the costs of more exalted persons, records of which are left.

Thus for the infant Princess Blanche and the prisoner in England, Count Robert of Artois, in 1343, each cost £85 6s. 11d. That of Queen Anne of Bohemia, 1391, was £14 13s. 1d.; that of Katherine Mortimer, daughter of Owen Glyndeur and her daughters, prisoners of State in 1413, were only 20 shillings.

The paltry sum of £33 6s. 8½d. was paid for the funeral charges and Masses for poor Henry VI., whose memory was further outraged by the presence of two torch-bearers instead of forty-nine, the number of his years. (Issue Roll 2, Ed. IV.)

A catafalque, then termed a hearse, was usually set up in the church where the burial had taken place, and remained sometimes for a lengthened period. The cost of those erected for Henry IV. at Canterbury, where he was interred, and at Westminster was 26 shillings and 8d. each, while that of his son Thomas, Duke of Clarence at Canterbury, was no less than £85. (Issue Roll 9, Henry V.)

Round these catafalques or hearses candles were kept constantly burning. It is probably such—and not her actual grave—that Hoveden refers to in connection with Fair Rosamund; he writes:

" In the same year Hugh, Bishop of Lincoln, while making his visitation of the houses of the religious in his diocese in 1141, came to the Abbey of the Nuns of Godstow which lies between Oxford and Woodstock. On entering the church to pray, he saw a tomb in the middle of the choir, before the altar, covered with clothes of silk, and surrounded with lamps and tapers, on which he asked whose tomb it was, and was told it was the tomb of Rosamond, who had formerly been the mistress of Henry, King of England, son of the Empress Matilda, and that her love of her had shown many favours to that church. The bishop ordered the tomb to be removed outside of the church." (Hoveden's Annals, Vol. II., p. 257.)

In many of these directions, which are cited, can be seen how many lights and candles, and in some cases lamps, were to be used, irrespective of the ritual tapers used at a mortuary Mass.

The custom of lighting candles (and in some cases, lamps, to burn a long while) round a dead body, and watching at its side all night, was originally owing to the belief that a corpse was specially liable to the assaults of demons. The practice of tolling a bell at death must have had a similar origin, for it was a common medieval belief that the sound of a blest bell had a similar efficacy to drive off the demons who, when a man dies, gather near to waylay his fleeting soul.

It was also a belief that demons raised storms and tempests in the material world. St. Thomas Aquinas gives his sanction to this belief:

" Pluvia et venti et quæcunque solo motu locali fiunt, possunt causari a dæmonibus." (Part I., art. 2.)

Blest bells were therefore used to allay tempests. Albert le Grand in his " De Potentia Demonum " says of such bells, " Every time that they sound they chase far away the malignant spirits of temptation, the calamities of storms, and the spirits causing tempests." The office of consecrating bells is still found in the offices of the Catholic Church, and is still used.

The custom of tolling was slightly varied in England and France. In England the consecrated death-bell was tolled after the death, according to the custom of the time of Bede. In France it tolled at the time the soul was departing. It was rung according to the great liturgist Durandus, thrice to denote the absolution which had been given to the penitent for the three modes of sin—by thought, word and deed; while for a clerk it was tolled as many times as denoted the number of his orders.

For a like reason—to keep off Evil Spirits from the dead—the consecrated wafer was often buried with the dead, and St. Basil is said to have specially consecrated a Host to be placed in his coffin.

It was probably also the fear of such demoniacal assaults that inspired, for one reason, the custom of burying the dead under the floors of churches and as near as possible to the altar. Another reason is probable from the usage handed down from the primitive Church of burying their dead in the Catacombs where their place of worship was carved out, with those who had departed lying all round it in their niches. Another reason may have been to protect their graves under the consecrated walls—the graveyards during the time of our Plantagenet kings being, despite the clergy, continually used by the villagers and townspeople for their rustic games, while in it the Lords of the Manor frequently convoked their Courts. At all events this intramural practice has preserved to us many beautiful tombs which otherwise would long have ceased to exist.

Sometimes, particularly in the case of religious of a high rank and in the case of knights, and probably for the same reason that bells were tolled to ward off Evil Spirits, a lamp was lighted and placed burning in a crevice of the tomb itself. Camden relates that at the demolition and suppression of the abbeys in Yorkshire, burning lamps were found in many tombs, the flame of which, it was said, could not be extinguished by wind or water. So Scott describes the grave of Michael Scott at Melrose Abbey:

> " Lo warrior ! how the cross of red
> Points to the grave of the mighty dead,
> Within it burns a wondrous light
> To chase the spirits that love the night."

For the same purpose the knight when dying often held, in his shaking hand, the candle blest at Candlemas, the office for which feast has the words, " That Thou wouldst vouchsafe and bless these candles for the service of men and for the health of their bodies and souls, whether upon the earth or on the waters."

The great Emperor Charles V., Grand Master of the Knights of the Golden Fleece, in his retirement at the convent of St. Juste, when dying, thus, we are told, met death with one of these consecrated tapers in his hand.

Though not dealing with the belief in demoniacal power at the moment of death, another belief in such, to show how much this power was supposed to be exercised during the ages of Chivalry, may be mentioned here. During these ages there prevailed in various parts of Europe a custom generally termed " jus prima noctis " which has been greatly misunderstood and perverted into a proof of a licentious seigniorial privilege, with which in reality it had nothing to do ; the custom far from originating in licence, appears, on the contrary, to have taken its rise in an austere practice of Chastity, which was inculcated by the early Church, as we learn from a decree of the fourth Council of Carthage A.D. 398, which enacted that " when the bridegroom and bride have received the benediction, let them remain that same night in a state of virginity out of reverence for the benediction." This custom of abstention afterwards was prolonged for three nights. This rule St. Louis observed. Several rituals of the fifteenth century, particularly those of Liege, Limoges and Bordeaux enact it. As late as the sixteenth century St. Carlo Borromeo inculcates its observance.

Dispensations were often obtained to avoid it. Such are extant from the Bishops of Amiens. Now when we examine into the origin of this most frequent prohibition of the Church, and her zeal in enforcing it, we find it is to be found in the " Book of Tobit," taught by the Angel who directed Tobit's marriage, in order to frustrate the power of the demon who had been the means of seven previous husbands of his bride dying on their wedding nights. " Thou," said the Angel, " when thou hast received thy wife and hast entered into the chamber, abstain from carnal intercourse with her for three days and give thyself up to nothing but prayer with her." This is the true source of the " jus primæ noctis," a rule the knights, particularly in France, frequently observed and whose origin was, in its inception, based on the malefic power of demons, only frustrated by prayer and chastity on the day of the bridal and following two days.

In this story of Tobias, as related in the Vulgate, the practice of continence it will be observed is enjoined, not primarily as a means of pleasing the Almighty but for the purpose of defeating a jealous devil. The same custom for the same reason—escaping demoniacal influence—obtains in several other lands, thus among the Vedic Indians, the Javanese, the Dyaks, the inhabitants of the Celebes Islands. (See Sir James Frazer's " Folklore in Old Testament," Vol. I.)

Probably owing to the frequency of sudden deaths—caused by the constant feuds and rivalries of adjacent lords and knights—the bodies of those dead in order to show their retainers their deaths were natural ones, were exposed for some time previous to burial. Round these thus exposed, it was the custom, particularly if the dead knight or his family had been benefactors of their house, for the monks of some adjacent abbey to kneel night and day in the chamber of death, and offer prayers for the departed soul. If, owing to the rapid decay of the corpse, it could not be long exposed, waxen effigies were used in its place—the real body itself placed under it in a coffin.

It seems from an instance given by St. Palaye, that sometimes a living person was induced, by payment, to figure on the bed in lieu of the dead knight himself. He quotes Vaissesse in his " History of Languedoc," for such an instance of paying a man to don the defunct knight's armour and lie in state on his bed and so receive the mourners. That in the household accounts of the noble family of Polignac in 1375 is an entry of five sols given to a certain Blaise for counterfeiting at his obsequies Jean, son of the Viscount of that family. It is more than probable that this was a case before referred to, where the dead young knight's death was suspected to have been brought about by unnatural or unfair means, and it was necessary to display the body unscathed to put an end to such rumours and suspicions.

As to the coffins the knights were placed in—they were chiefly of lead, shaped like the mummy cases of ancient Egypt. Iron coffins are extremely rare. In the earliest years of the Middle Ages stone coffins in England were frequently used, but only by the nobility and wealthy. When about to be buried it was customary to place their feet and faces towards the quarter where their future was hoped to be spent. Thus the Indians buried their dead towards the setting sun (the West), on the other hand from the earliest times the Christians placed theirs towards the rising sun (the East) because according to the old tradition that is the attitude of prayer and because at the last trump the holy dead will hurry Eastwards. So in Eusebius (Hist. Eccl. 430, 19) a martyr explains to his pagan judge that the heavenly Jerusalem, the fatherland of the pious, lay exactly in the East—and towards it, all Christians were buried, and waited in rest for the Resurrection summons.

DAYS OF CHIVALRY

Even before death it seems from some passages in the Lays of the period to have been the custom to turn the dying head towards the East (just as the altars are placed Eastwards). Thus in the " Lay of the Death of Tristan " :

> " Si se turne vers Orient
> Pur lui prie pitusement
> ' Amis Tristram quant mort vus vei
> Par raisun vivre puis ne dei ? ' "

(She turned towards the East and piteously prayed for him, " O my friend Tristan, since I see you dead it is not right that I should linger here.")

Previous to burial the entrails and heart were usually removed to the nearest Church, or one where the dead knight knew his gifts in life would purchase the suffrages of the community. These entrails were " en d'épaisse stoffes de paille " (wrapt up in thick swayths of straw) (Gautier). The body was washed in spiced wine and water, a cross placed in the hands or on the breast ; the coffin, as has been noted above, left open till the day of burial, often with an elaborate silken pall, brought back, if the knight had been crusading, by him, for this very purpose, from the Holy Land.

In the room where these last offices were rendered to the dead many tapers were burnt, and incense also. It is difficult, as has before been said, to reckon the number of candles or torches that were burnt for a simple knight, however gallant had been his life ; they amounted probably to about a quarter of those bestowed on a royal person. Four hundred torches of wax, each weighing six pounds, were burnt before the coffin of the Queen of Charles V. of France.

If the knight had fallen on the field of battle, unless his squires brought his body home for burial, many of these elaborate ceremonies were perforce wanting.

A nephew of the Earl of Essex who had fallen in 1391 at the siege of Rouen, his English following, after the town had been taken by their arms, brought back overseas to his native land for interment, but very often where the knight fell he was either buried on the spot or conveyed to the nearest church for that purpose.

From the Lays and Romances it seems a very usual practice when a knight thus fell on the battle-field for his companions, when he succumbed, to make a short prayer over him—thus in the early Chanson de Geste of " La Mort de Roland," the hero finds Turpin, the celebrated archbishop of the Carlovingian Cycle, fallen, and so he cries :

> " E ! gentilz hom, chevaliers de bon aire,
> Hoi te cumant à l'Glorius celeste ;
> Jamais n'iert hum plus volentiers le servet.
> Des les Apostles ne fut *mais* tel prophete
> Pur lei tenir e pur humes atraire.
> Ja la vostre anme nen ait *doelne* suffraite !
> De pareïs li seit la porte uverte."

(Alas, gentle soul! Knight of noble lineage,
I commend you to the glorious Heavenly Father,
Never shall I serve a man with greater willingness,
With the exception of the Apostles no one has been a greater prophet
To maintain the law and to attract men.
May your soul endure no evil or suffering,
May the gate of heaven be opened to you.)

Sometimes the departing spirit of a knight dying on the battle-field itself makes a prayer—as in the same Chanson—Roland thus prays :

> " Veire paterne, ki unkes ne mentis
> Seint Lazarun de mort resurrexis
> E Daniel des lions guaresis
> Guaris de mei l'anme de tuz perilz
> Pur les pecchiez que en ma vie fis."

(Our true Father who never speakst falsely,
Who raised from the dead St. Lazarus,
And protected Daniel among the lions,
Deliver my soul from all perils
That through my sins I have in life contracted.)

And praying thus, he is said to have stretched forth his mailed hand to God, as if calling on his Maker to witness he had fought in his service a good fight, and that never more, the wild horn of Roland, mortal ears would hear at the pass of Ronsevalles.

The good knight buried, the task of describing his obsequies finished, it remains to enter a little into the memorials, either of armour found over his tomb, or the valuables, chiefly brasses, laid over his remains on many a now-forgotten church-wall or aisle, but which, examined by a discerning eye, are most valuable both for family history and for heraldry. The remains in this country of any armour found suspended over a knight's tomb are few and far between ; the best known is that of the Black Prince in Canterbury Cathedral, but one part of armour—the helmet—is found frequently in that position.

As helmets were always a knight's peculiar cognizance, it seemed fitting therefore, over his last long sleep, they were so often suspended. Even while living it became a custom peculiar to this country to use them as a token of hospitality outside the dwellings of the gentle-born, to denote to the wandering brother-knight or his lady therein they would meet with both fraternity and lodging.

The author of the " Roman de Pierceforest " frequently mentions this practice, " estoit une costume en la grant Bretagne . . . tous gentils hommes et nobles dames faisoient mettre au plus hault de leur hostel ung heaulme en signe que tous gentils femmes trespassant les chemins, entrassant hardyamont en leur hostel comme au leur propre."

Though but a small proportion of the vast number of suits, helmets, and weapons that have come down to us can be assigned to definite wearers, most of these owe their origin to this ancient and poetic custom of hanging the arms of knightly persons over their tombs, a custom linked with the still older dedication of arms and armour at the obsequies of the dead, by either placing them in the grave or in the temples of the Gods.

This reality of the connection between the pagan and the Christian customs is apparent by such incidents as that of William of Toulouse early in the thirteenth century, who dedicated his helmet, shield, and sword to St. Julian, hanging them over his shrine; or that of the King of France, who, after the battle of Cassel in 1327, presented his victorious arms to the neighbouring church. Unfortunately the old veneration for the person of the dead, which led to the consecration of the armour and weapons he had actually used, hardly survived the thirteenth century.

Cupidity induced the clergy to claim such as a perquisite of the burial function, as when the Prior of Westminster received £100 as ransom for the horse and trappings of John of Eltham; while the temptation natural to the survivor to retain the finely-tempered weapons and armour, whose quality had been tested in many a hard-fought action, had always to be reckoned with. The reluctance to part with such is beautifully expressed in some of the old ballads, as those on the death of Arthur. Armour was, moreover, specially devised by will to be kept as heirlooms. Thus Thomas Beauchamp, Earl of Warwick (temp. Henry IV.) left his son Richard, by will, the sword and coat of mail said to have belonged to the celebrated Guy, Earl of Warwick, he having received them from his father as an heirloom. Sir Thomas Poynings, in 1369, devised to his heir the helmet and armour which his father devised to him. The custom grew up extensively, of leaving the undertaker to provide property-helmets and arms in place of those the dead knight had himself used, also this is another reason which tended to lessen the interest of even the arms which yet remain with us.

That the helmet of Henry V. was thus provided by the undertaker, is well known, and that he continued to provide arms down to Elizabeth's time is shown by accounts of funerals, such as Lord Grey de Wilton in 1562, when among the items of the undertaker's bill are a " cote of arms," " banner and bannerolles," a " helmet of stele gylt with fyne golde," with a crest gilt and coloured, a " swerde with the hyltes, pomell, chape, buckle and pendant, likewise gylte with a gurdle and sheathe of velvet." (S. Gardner, " Armour in England," p. 8.)

This custom, of substituting spurious insignia at the solemn interment of the knightly dead, was set by the Church who consigned mock croziers and chalices of no intrinsic value to the graves of the most exalted prelates. However, of the true and the spurious armour alike—time, rust, and above all changes of religious sentiment in regard to the Churches—have spared little beside an occasional helmet.

> " These good knights are dust,
>   Their swords are all rust,
>   Their souls are with the Saints, we trust."

Yet neglect and depredations notwithstanding, the preservation of nearly all the English fighting helmets known, from the time of the Black Prince to that of Henry VIII., and many swords of early date, is due to their having been deposited in churches. Knights not only in their lifetime hung their arms up in churches, and at their deaths they were often hung up over their graves, but so much honoured was their order that even their horses, after the death of their masters, participated in their glory. The horses of Ralph, Lord Neville, who died in 1347 and who was buried in Durham Cathedral, were honoured for his sake. The body of the dead knight was conveyed in a carriage drawn by seven horses as far as the churchyard, thence carried on the shoulders of knights into the nave of the cathedral where the Abbot of St. Mary's of York performed the funeral service, at which, as alms, were offered eight of Lord Neville's horses, four for war, attended by four men-at-arms, and four for peace, and at the same time three cloths of gold interwoven with flowers.

So in the history of Bertrand de Guesclin who died in 1380. His body was carried to the grave followed by four princes of the blood, and his horses were presented to the officiating bishop as alms, who thereupon laid his hands upon them and blessed them.

As has above been mentioned, the helmet and sword were frequently displayed over a knightly tomb, but only a knight who died on the battle-field was allowed in the days when Chivalry was at its prime, to have his banner (if a banneret) or pennon (if a simple knight) displayed over his last resting-place.

From early times in the Middle Ages it was a frequent custom to place small hearts in the hands of the knights and ladies commemorated on brasses, just as the Chalice was placed in those of priests, either to indicate that the deceased had been enabled to fulfil some vow, or simply to suggest that the heart was given to God, a new heart desired, or of a complete trust in the Sacred Heart of Jesus.

Thus figured a brass at Buslingthorpe, Lincs. (1290). At Aldborough, Yorks., of William de Aldeburgh in armour (1360). At Broughton, Lincs. (1370), of Sir Henry Redford and his wife; and a great many other instances in different counties in England.

The brasses of the period during the Wars of the Roses have a peculiar interest heraldically, as it became usual for knights and squires to wear tabards-of-arms over their body-armour, even for the ladies to appear in heraldic kirtles and mantles.

The metal used was " latten," not brass at all, but an alloy consisting of about 60 parts copper, 30 zinc and 10 of lead or tin, making a hard metal resisting much rough usage. (Macklin, " The Brasses of England.")

Although knights and squires, on their brasses, almost always wear armour, there are a few instances in which they appear in civil dress. One of the best of these is the brass of Sir Thomas and Lady Brook (1437) at Thorncombe, Devon. Sir Thomas has the usual belted gown, though it is apparently lined and edged with fur and a collar of SS. about the neck. His lady wears kirtle and mantle, horned headdress, and the same collar. A dog lies at the knight's feet, and it is a remarkable fact that its collar is buckled and clasped in exactly the same way, though there are no SS.

These dogs at the feet are occasionally intended to represent actual favourites. Thus at Deerhurst in Gloucestershire (1400), Lady

Cassy has a dog in a collar and bells with its name " Terri " attached;
and there was once a " Jakke " with Sir Bryan de Stapleton at
Ingham, Norfolk, unhappily destroyed in 1800. From a drawing we
find the dog had a sharp nose, a Pomeranian ruff, and a smooth body,
and was evidently a portrait.

A curious custom sometimes obtaining in knightly burials was to
attach to them so-called " Crosses of Absolution "—such in our own
country have been found at Bury St. Edmunds, Chichester and Lewes.
They were not only records of absolution to the dying knight, but
granting an indulgence to the passer-by, who should pray at his tomb.
Such was appended to John, seventh Earl Warren's tomb in Lewes
Priory. It was in verse, and ended with the following couplet:

> " Ki pur sa alme priera
> Trois mil jeurs de pardon avera."

So on the brass of Reynaud Alard, 1354, at Winchelsea:

> " Qe pur salme priera L jours de pardon avera."

It would require a more elaborate description than this chapter
will admit to endeavour to bring before the mind's eye one of these
abbey-churches where the knights loved to be thus buried and their
obsequies performed, one of those abbeys before its spoliation, when
the sculptures were unmutilated and the paintings fresh, and the
windows filled with glorious stained glass, and the choir hung with
hangings, and banners and tapestries waved from the arches of the
triforium, and the altar shone gloriously with jewelled plate, and the
monuments of abbots and nobles were still perfect, and the wax tapers
burned night and day in the hearses, throwing a flickering light on the
solemn effigies below, and glancing upon the tarnished armour and the
dusty banners which hung over the tombs, while the cowled monks sat
in their stalls and prayed. Or when on some high festival the convent
walked round the holy aisles in procession, two and two, clad in rich
copes over their coarse frocks, preceded by cross and banner, with
swinging censers pouring forth clouds of incense, while one of those
angel boys' voices, which we still sometimes hear, chanted the solemn
litany, the pure sweet-ringing voice floating along the vaulted aisles,
until it was lost in the swell of the chorus of the whole procession:
" Ora! Ora! Ora! pro nobis! " The spoliation under Henry VIII.
and afterwards the Cromwellian soldiery, defaced or removed many of
these interesting memorials of the knightly dead in this country, and
in France, a sister home of ancient Chivalry, the insensate fury of the
Revolution destroyed perhaps still more. Witness the wanton
destruction of the Royal tombs at St. Denys, but enough are left for
the thoughtful wayfarer to remind him of those who lived, loved,
fought and died in the far-off days of Chivalry, and before such a one
from whom he is perhaps descended or whose noble life he remembers
to say:

> " A braver soldier never couchéd lance,
> A gentler heart did never sway a court;
> But kings and mightiest potentates must die
> For that's the end of human misery."
> —Henry VI., II., p. 2.

It will be seen from the moment of baptism, when the future knight was brought into a church, these edifices were the scenes of many episodes in his life. Here he was girded as a youthful squire—these dark aisles saw him later watching his armour, before the dawn, ere his knighthood was given. Here before some altar in his adventurous life, he often knelt and made his vows; here after some triumph in the tourney or battle-field, he returned his thanks, and gave his offerings; here when he came to die he was with pomp and honour laid.

It seems well, ere closing this chapter, to say a few words further about these churches themselves. Edifices set aside for worship are still used, and still built, but the knightly edifices of the medieval Church were constructed, not alone for worship, but for instruction, and that instruction conveyed by visible objects. The walls we see to-day grey, and unadorned, in a knight's age and to his eyes being blazoned with Biblical history, were to him a living language—the different parts of the church all spoke to him of the mysteries of his faith. The long succession on, or round, the walls of clustered images, was instruction to such a one, who often could neither read nor write, who only knew how to wield a sword and never a pen. These churches then, to such, were stories in stone. So John Gerson wrote: " Images are made for us for no other reason than to show to simple folk what they are unable to know from Holy Scripture, and yet what they ought to believe." So the second Council of Nicea, " in speaking of the image of our Saviour—we place His figure in our houses, in our churches, in pictures, on certain vestments, in a word, everywhere, so that by continually contemplating such in our minds we may never be forgetful." So, too, Gregory the Great: " What to those reading books of Scripture—so are pictures to the ignorant. By them they see what they ought to follow and read such though ignorant of letters."

The very arrangement of the churches conveyed to the unlearned knight a spiritual lesson: faced towards the East, such recalled the birthplace of his Saviour; generally built on an elevated spot of ground he learned the superiority of Divine things over terrestrial; the porch, the choir, and the sanctuary were emblems to him of the way of penitence, of the Christian life, and of the saintly and heavenly Beyond. Or possibly he had been taught the other mystical interpretation of these portions of his Church: the door, the earth; the nave, the sea; the sanctuary, heaven; the great rose window, the air or ether on which glowed on its rosy surface, the figures of angels and archangels. High above the principal door was the figure of God the Father, over His head the Dove of the Paraclete, while the Christ on his Cross the Father held on his knee; below an innumerable number of saints and angels, the latter often playing on musical instruments. Or perhaps instead of these august figures over the entrance was carved the scene of the Last Judgment, this latter being extremely frequent in the twelfth century, to combat the unbelief of the people who, having expected when the thousand years from the birth of the Redeemer had been accomplished, that the world would come to an end, needed this reminder that the words and prophecy they expected it from, pointed rather to the Last Judgment.

It was perhaps this teaching power of carved stone, painted glass, soaring pillars and wondrous doors, in an age illiterate, made knights and serfs, noble born and base born contribute to rear these magnificent cathedrals and churches in France and England, not alone for the glory of God, but because they found within their mystic walls, and outside their portals, that education alone in spiritual things they could only learn by the eye conveying it to their souls.

CHAPTER XVIII

" Where is the King Don Juan ? Where
Each royal prince and noble heir of Aragon ?
Where are the courtly gallantries ?
Their deeds of love and high emprise,
    In battle done ?

Tourney and joust, that charmed the eye,
And scarf, and gorgeous panoply,
    And nodding plume,
What were they but a pageant scene ?
What but the garlands gay and green
    That deck the tomb ?

Where are the high-born dames and where
Their gay attire, and jewelled hair,
    And odours sweet ?
Where are the gentle knights that came
To kneel and breathe love's ardent flame,
    Low at their feet ?

Where is the song of Troubadour ?
Where are the lute and gay tambour
    They loved of yore ?
Where is the mazy dance of old,
The flowing robes, inwrought with gold,
    The dancers wore ? "

The Spanish poet, Coplas de Manrique, asks these questions anent
the decadence of Chivalry. In this chapter it is necessary to find an
answer for the decay of an institution which so long and so gloriously
held up before the eyes of men a higher standard of life and a great
influence on the then civilization of Europe.

Chivalry began to dawn in the end of the tenth century. It
blazed forth with high vigour during the Crusades, which indeed
may be considered as exploits of national knight-errantry on the
same principles which actuated the conduct of individual knights-
adventurers. But its most brilliant period, though its decline set in
rapidly from that period, was during the wars between France and
England. It was then that the habit of constant and honourable

opposition, unembittered by rancour or personal hatred, gave the fairest opportunity for the exercise of the courtesies required of him whom Chaucer terms " a very perfect knight."

This standard of knightly elegance and courtesy became intensified in proportion as its virile powers decayed. In the same way as the increased civilization and luxury imported into the monastic establishments, though they bestowed a greater pomp and stateliness upon them, gradually paved the way for their final dissolution. Yet at this period few could perceive Chivalry's coming decadence. A Du Guesclin in France, a Walter Manny in England, gloriously upheld its honour; a chivalrous king like Edward III. gave fresh laurels to its past wreaths. Courtrai was fought, and Amadis of Gaul written at this time, and the Black Prince embodied the old courtesies of his order, when he waited, after the battle of Poitiers, upon his captive and overlord, John of France. The outward courtesies of war were more observed, few knights or those of gentle blood were slain deliberately in a battle; more and more such encounters were looked upon as lucrative expeditions where ransoms could fill the pocket of the captor. Defensive armour having been brought to such perfection, this desire could easily be satisfied, for once a horse threw his rider, he lay helpless to rise till assisted to do so by his victor.

That this commercial value of a noble prisoner more and more penetrated the army of opposing knights, Froissart bears witness to, when the phrase constantly is occurring in his pages in describing the after-result of one of these battles " many rich prisoners." It was now the abstemiousness of the ancient knight became also forgotten in the extravagant banquets that followed every tournament and courtly function—the fruits, spices, and dainties brought by his crusading fathers from the East all helped to stimulate gluttony and licence. Gambling with dice and other games of chance, despite the Church's warning, became more and more practised. While, in a word, all Chivalry outwardly looked prosperous, there was a canker at its roots.

The Crusades over, nothing but idle trifling and licentious assignations diversified by the chace or a tournament was left to fill up the want which the Crusades had supplied to the knights. Religion, too, became less and less the pursuit of Chivalry. It was in her churches her sons had received the accolade; it was for her, and the fatherless, and widow, they had sworn to do battle, yet that great religious movement—the Crusades—over, coldness to religion swept over Europe, the very vows in her name the knight now took in this time of Decadence, he either forgot or wilfully neglected. Eustache Deschamps calling to mind the good old days and seeing the evil around him, thus wrote:

" Les Chevaliers du bon temps ancien
  Et leurs enfans aloient à la messe;
  En doubtant Dieu, chascun vivoit du sien.
  L'en congnoissoit leur bien et leur prouesse,
  Et li peuples labouroit en simplesse;
  Chascuns estoit content de son office,
  Religion fut de tous biens l'addresse;
  Mais aujourdui ne voy regner que vice.

Li jeune enfant deviennent rufien
Jouers de dez, gourmans et plains d'yvresse
Hautains de cuer, et ne leur chault en rien
D'onneur, de bien, de nulle gentilesse,
Fors de mentir, d'orgueil et de paresse,
Et que chascun son vouloir acomplisse;
Le temps passé fut vertu et haultesse;
Mais aujourdui ne voy regner que vice.

A ceuls qui font ainsis viennent bien
Temporelment; Chevalerie cesse,
Car les vertus sont de foible merrien,
Le labour fault, religion se blesse,
Et valliance veult estre larronnesse;
Ainsi convient que tout honour périsse;
Lemonde aussi, se Dieu tout ne radresse :
Mais aujourdui me voy regner que vice."

(Knights of the ancient days
And their children went to Mass
In the fear of God, each subsisted on his own (property)
Their worth and prowess they realized;
And the lower classes led the simple life,
Everyone was content with his station in life,
And religion was placed of all things first
But nowadays one sees vice only rule.

The young lad has become a very ruffian,
Players at dice, gluttons, inebriates,
Proud of heart and fired with no spark of honour,
Goodness or gentle breeding,
There is nothing except lying, pride and laziness,
Everyone does as he likes,
The time has gone by for virtue and high-mindedness,
But nowadays one sees only vice rule.

For a brief while these things last. Chivalry ceases
Because its virtues can offer only a frail resistance;
Work fails; religion is wounded; and valiancy
Dissolves itself into robbery, so it comes to pass
All honour perishes; the world also, unless God
Should redress it all. But to-day one sees nothing but vice rule.)

   . Some of this Decadence in Chivalry must be traced to the false conception of Love, which the trouveres of the North, the scholars in song, and the successors of the skill of the Southern troubadours, innoculated the knights of France and England with. For that strange Platonic Love—sung, read, practised by the knights of the South—the trouveres of the North, their successors, failed to understand. Take for instance the following :

    Towards the close of the thirteenth century a Society of Knights and Ladies was established in Languedoc, called the " Confraternity of Penitents of Love." Never in religion was a point carried to such extravagance. Both ladies and knights tried how they might display best their enthusiasm for love. Their object was to prove the excess of their love with an invincible courage which was no less enduring in suffering as to brave the extremes of cold and heat. It followed, therefore, that the knights and squires, the dames and the demoiselles who had the fortitude to assent to these hard rules, accustomed themselves during the heats of summer to wear the warmest and thickest clothing in order to follow out the dictum of the old poets that love could change the nature even of the seasons. Contrary-wise, in winter, they put on the thinnest of garments; on the intensest day of frost it was held to be a crime to wear a fur, or cloak, or mantle. As the flame of Love was sufficient warmth, all fires were banished from their apartments, in lieu of such they dressed them with green boughs. When all around was covered with thick ice, they slept without a single covering over them. At the same time and in bitter weather they wandered from castle to castle as well as many of their imitators, of whom there were a great number, and during these arduous pilgrimages they bewailed the cold, very martyrs to their vows to Love. (Vaissette's " Hist. gen de Languedoc," IV., p. 184.)

Strange as all this may seem, its very extravagance demonstrates the Platonic and harmless form love was held in by the Southern troubadour, but to the Northern trouvere such a conception, or such a Society, would have been impossible, without giving both a licentious colouring and purpose.

In the " Lai d'Ywenec " of the celebrated trouveresse, Marie de France, who is generally supposed to have lived in the middle of the twelfth century and whose Lays were well known and sung in the castles of the North, occurs this incident: A knight, finding in a castle a fair prisoner, and wishing to corrupt her in order to induce her to assent to his criminal wishes, conceives the best way to gain the Ladye's confidence is to receive himself the Blessed Sacrament.

> " Si a le prestre demandé
> Et cil i vint cum plus tost pot;
> Corpus Domini aportot
> Li chevaliers l'a receu,
> Li vins del chalice a beu;
> Li chapeleins s'en est allez,
> Et la vieille a les huis fermez.
> La dame gist lèz son ami
> Unkes si bel cuple ne vi."

> (He has asked for the priest
> And he came as soon as he could;
> The Body of Our Lord he brought,
> The knight has received thereof,
> The wine from the Chalice he has drunken,
> The chaplain has gone thence,
> And the old dame has closed the doors,
> The lady lies down with her lover,
> There never so fair a couple was seen.)

Compare this low conception of morality and religion with the older writers on knighthood, as to what was required of them. Thus in the " Lay of Lancelot du Lac," the virtues of ancient Chivalry are "force, hardiesse, beauté, gentillesse, débonaireté, courtoissie, largesse, et force d'avoir (good means) and d'armis." So, too, another —" Le Jouvencal "—in his list, has, " le sobriété, de la continence et des autres vertus requises au métier des armes." The " Order of Chevalrie " enters into greater details, as we have previously in another part detailed. " Noblesse, de courage a foi, espérance, charité, justice," etc.

Religion, so wanting in Chivalry in its decadence, was in its ancient prime first thought of

> " Chevaliers en ce monde-cy
> Ne peuvent vivre, sans soucy;
> Ils doivent le peuple defendre
> Et leur sang pour la Foi espandre."

> (Knights in their world
> Cannot live without care,
> For the people they must defend,
> And their blood for the Faith expend.)

The nauseous and fatal corruption of a platonic doctrine of Love extolled by the trouveres and jongleurs invaded the sterner Chivalry of the North, rendering their swords but playthings, and their lances but ornaments, and their very tourneys, no longer held for true love, but for her darker sister, licence, had much to do with the decadence of ancient Chivalry, while that ardent Catholic faith, once professed, became weak and inoperative, and was no longer the cause of the knight's strong arm, nor of his resistless charge under her consecrated banners.

The jongleurs (after a time the tawdry successors of the troubadours and trouveres), whose practice it was to roam about the country far and wide, attending fairs, country merry-makings, village bridals, were not insensible to the gradual decadence in morality and religion of the knights, their masters, any more than perceiving the same in the friars and monks, of whose frailities and ignorances they were fully cognizant. With this knowledge of both the orders—the knightly and the monastic—they compiled songs against both and in the vulgar tongue, easily learnt by their audience—the townsfolk and villagers—wherever they went. Gradually, like drops of water wearing out a stone, these jongleurs' foolish little songs wore down any of the ancient respect the people had for the Chivalrous order above them. It is no wonder then one factor of knighthood's gradual decay came in from the ridicule and want of respect it challenged; by its lapses from its old standards of religion and morality. From being looked upon as a body sworn to defend their widows and their orphans, to challenge their oppressors, to beat down the evil in the land, and raise up the good, men found all this wanting in the proud and glittering knight of their day, and began to ask what good such a thing as Chivalry, false to its oaths, could be?

That the jongleurs at the decay of the troubadours attained greater influence and so were enabled to spread their songs ridiculing often knighthood and the Church, is manifest even as far as Aragon, when about twenty years after the dispersal and overthrow of the troubadours in Provence they were constantly seen in that kingdom and Castille. In 1329 Don Alfonso of Aragon was crowned, and jongleurs at the feast appeared, and the king presented to each in turn the surcoat and mantle of cloth of gold, bordered with ermine and embroidered with pearls, which he assumed at intervals throughout the banquet—as many as ten sets of these garments were bestowed upon these jongleurs. It was a custom in vogue then throughout Europe.

> " Robe de vair et erminettes
> De conin et de violettes
> D'escarlate de draps de soie,"

were the customary rewards of that art.

We read in romances of the period of mantles heaped at the feet of these wandering minstrels. A writer of the time of Philip Augustus speaks with undisguised contempt of " princes, who after having spent thirty or forty marks on garments which were veritable works of art, marvellously embroidered with flowers, give them away, a week later, to some jongleurs, those ministers of the devil as soon as they open their mouths." More than seven thousand mantles taken off by the guests were thus bestowed on the jongleurs playing at the marriage of Beatrice d'Este and Galeazzo of Milan. A young gentleman of rank is advised :

> " Comme tu vendras en hautez lieux
> Aux heraux et aux menestreux
> Ou qui vendront ou tu seras
> Dons convenables leurs feras,
> De robes d'or ou de monnaie."

As time went on the gross and coarse sensuality which we have seen grafted upon the romantic professions of an earlier Chivalry became finally so predominant as altogether to discard all marks of true sentimental attachment, and from the time of Catherine de Medici, who trained her maids of honour as courtezans, the manners of the Court of France (England for a time, till the advent of the Stuarts, was spared) seem to have been inferior in decency to those of well-regulated bagnios. The spirit of devotion, which the rules of ancient Chivalry inculcated, was so openly disavowed that the reason assigned for preferring the character of Sir Tristram to that of Sir Lancelot, was because the former is described, in romance, as relying upon his own arm alone, whereas Sir Lancelot, on engaging in a fight, never failed to commend himself to God and the saints, which, in the more modern opinions of the Chevaliers of France, argued a want of confidence in his own strength and valour.

Appeals to arms by two knights falling out, when they took place, were no longer fought in the lists, or in presence of the marshals of the field, but in lonely and sequestered places—inequality of arms was not regarded, however great the superiority of one side might be. " Thou hast both a sword and dagger," said Quelus to Antregust as they were about to fight, " and I have only a sword." " The more thy folly," was the answer, " to leave thy dagger, we came to fight not to adjust weapons." The combat went forward and Quelus was slain.

If these were some of the moral reasons of Chivalry's weakening influence owing to the decadence of that high standard in them attained by the ancient knights, this decay must be attributed also to outside changes then developing.

(1) The first was the rapid change in the constitution of the medieval armies. In dealing in a previous chapter with the armour of the period, we called the reader's attention to the fact that foot soldiers, at that time nearly exclusively archers, were supplanting (with the mounted men-at-arms) the mailed knight. After the battle of Poitiers, where the greater part of the French Chevaliers were slain and routed by the English bowmen—and so, too, by the use of the cross-bowmen at the battle of Bouvines—it began to dawn more and more, and at first much against the aspirations of Chivalry, that charges of cavalry stood little chance against a strong phalanx of foot soldiers. It is true, often the knight, both in a tourney and in a battle, would fight on foot, but his own peculiar place was on horseback making impetuous charges, and these, the now better armed, better trained, and disciplined foot soldiers, began to prove their superiority in the actual battle.

(2) Though the long-bow continued, after proving its usefulness, long to be the favourite weapon, as far as the English armies were concerned, now field pieces gradually, owing to every successive improvement in them, became more perfect and more decisive in the fate of battles. The use of such not alone began to take the place of the impetuous charges of the knights, or their antiquated measures to reduce a walled town, but affected the mail of the knight himself. It was found that however much heavy armour might be efficient against lances, swords and arrows, it afforded little protection against cannon. The armour of the knight was gradually curtailed to a light head-piece, a cuirass, and the usual defences of the men-at-arms. In France the young nobility especially became weary of the unwieldy steel in which their knightly ancestors sheathed themselves, and adopted the light armour of the German Reiters or mercenary cavalry. They also discontinued the use of the lance, and as these light-armed Cavaliers (for much depends on outward show and circumstance) did no longer carry the weapons or practise the exercises of knighthood they laid aside, at the same time, the habits and sentiments peculiar to the old Order of Chivalry.

As early as 1443 we find complaints made at the Court of France to Charles VII. of the discontinuance of tourneys, of the lords and knights becoming like women, that instead of jousting they diced, or followed the chace or danced. " No longer they held tournaments nor feats of arms for fear of wounds (pour paour des lezions), in a word, the Chivalry of France have become as women." (Le Labourer.)

So much had a discontinuance in such taken place in the few years between the reign of Charles VII. and that of Henry II., who had been mortally wounded at a tournament by Montmorency, that when the Queen-Mother was prevailed on to allow the lists to be set up for a tourney it was with difficulty any present knew, or were adept in, the ancient rules for such.

Later still, in 1589, the then Archbishop of Bourges made a speech at the Assembly of the States, pleading as a remedy for the grievances that were affecting the country, for a revival of Chivalry such as it was under Francis I. " and composed of the nobility," " ut equestus ordo per bella civilia intermortuus in aliquam splendorem restitutur equitatus Gallicus, toto orbe olim formidabilis, qui nobilitati constare debet, restituta disciplina instauretur." But the times had passed, and were passing, for the Prelate's impassioned appeal to bear any fruit—the ancient spirit of Chivalry burning so brightly in the Crusades had left only from its very ardour in then lighting up, by its watch-fires, martial Europe—dead and dying embers behind. In England, however, the appearance of knighthood and its bravery lasted longer than in the sister country of France. Its habiliments as time went on became more and more extravagant, and came to a height in the reigns of Henry VIII. and Elizabeth. The knights dressed up in ridiculous disguises and assumed absurd titles. It was mere buffoonery compared with its ancient and stately ceremonies; it became a gorgeous covering to an already dead body. To the unthinking, Chivalry was thus in its perfection at the " Field of the Cloth of Gold " in 1520. Lances broken—banquets were given and heraldry gave its fictitious colouring to the pageant, but it was all to exalt three sovereigns—a bravery of processions, armour and devices —not a contest of ancient Chivalry. There was no seriousness in it all. The knights now only played a fantastic game, though a former of our kings had tried for a while to revive its life. In Henry V., himself truly chivalrous, could have done so, it would have been done, but even his ardent spirit could not reawaken its dying glory. Here and there, on the outskirts of the world—as a modern writer well puts it—the knight could " chevaucher " as of old, but few and far were such. Even the friends of young Harry Hotspur before the battle of Otterburn never gave the counsels their gallant old forefathers would have given—" not to adventure himself abroad in the field against the power of Scotland; it is better to lose one pennon," they said, " than two or three hundred knights and squires." Odds in the good old days were never counted; the greater the danger the greater the glory; it was only a decadent Chivalry that tendered such advice.

(3) Another reason for the decay of knighthood was the custom that crept in, both in France and England, of conferring the accolade on those, often of the burgher or non-knightly families. This grew more and more common as time went on, and by lowering its dignity and status formed one element in its decadence. In its pristine state Chivalry being looked on as a sort of ennoblement, its ranks were seduously kept for the higher classes. In Languedoc it was only per-mitted by special grace of the king for one of the citizen class to be knighted. Those of servile birth could never be made such without express leave of their lords and masters. Even till long after the Middle Ages a king of Hungary could not, without permission of the overlord, confer knighthood on any vassal. When, therefore, these prohibitions of ancient Chivalry were broken through in France and England by the sovereign, in order cheaply to reward the services of a person of the middle or lower classes, admitting him to knighthood, not only did it lower Chivalry but admit persons who by their posi-tion, of trade or profession, were unable to perform its military obligations.

Charondas, a French commentator, writing in 1603, tells us—so low had the order of knighthood become that there were innumerable persons calling themselves knights and their wives arrogating the title of " Madame " who had never been knighted at all, except by themselves. The summoning of knights of the shire to sit with the burgesses in the royal courts held by our Angevin kings also had the same deteriorating influence on Chivalry—by lowering its dignity it gradually lost its influence, and by losing its influence, it fell before other and stronger ones—such as the rise of the communes abroad, the rise of the Commons in England and chartered townsfolk throughout the realm.

Again if we look at the foundation of Chivalry it must be regarded as an institution founded on a condition of perpetual war. One of its death-blows, therefore, was when Louis IX., after a long struggle, forbade private war in all his lands (1257). Philip le Bel renewed the prohibition, and the last enactment was by Charles V. in 1380. In England under our Plantagenet and Angevin kings it had before been summarily proscribed and only tolerated when the royal power was too weak to combat it. The only exception was on the Scottish Border where, for the defence of the realm, the northern barons and knights were allowed to keep a war-like state.

War being the " daily bread " of Chivalry—though for a lengthened period the effect of these enactments did not show themselves—they no less gradually depleted the ranks of knighthood, and the kings, to appease those that existed, created decorative orders such as the Garter, the Saint Esprit, the Golden Fleece, which added no duties to life and no war-making obligations on their members.

In France, perhaps the greatest factor in the decay of Chivalry, however, arose from the institution of bands of gens-d'armes or men-at-arms, constituted expressly as a sort of standing army, to supply the place of bannerets, knights-bachelors and squires, and other militia of early times. It was in the year 1445 that Charles VII. selected from the numerous Chivalry of France fifteen companies of men-at-arms called " Les Compagnies d'ordonnance " which were to remain in perpetual pay and subordinance and to enable the king to dispense with the tumultuary forces of Chivalry, which arriving and departing from the host—after serving forty days often—collecting too their subsistence by ravaging the country and engaging in frequent brawls with each other, rather weakened than aided the cause they were professed to support. Till this time, so ravaging had been the former undisciplined men-at-arms that there was a saying abroad among the people:

> " Si Dieu étoit gendarme
> Il feroit pillard."

The regulated companies, which were substituted for these desultory feudal levies, were of a more permanent and manageable description. Each company contained a hundred men-at-arms and each man-at-arms was to be what was termed a " lance garnie," that is, a mounted spearman with his proper attendants, four archers and a varlet called a " coustillier " from the knife or dagger with which he was armed.

Thus each company consisted of six hundred horse, and the fifteen bands, to fifteen thousand cavalry. The charge of national defence was thus transferred from the Chivalry of France whose bold and desperate valour was sometimes useless by their independent wilfulness and want of unity to these new levies of Charles VII. At first the officers and often the men were of gentle birth, and no doubt some of the knights-bannerets headed them, and the officers were men of the highest rank, while the archers and even the varlets often of honourable birth. But in the reign of Charles IX. we find a further change natural to a new order of things. The king was content to seek as qualifications men whatever their rank, if they were possessed of personal bravery, strength, and adepts in the use of weapons. Monluc informs us in his " Commentaries " that he made his first campaign as an archer in the Marechal de Foix's company, when " it was a situation much esteemed in those days when many nobles served, but at present (when he writes) the rank is greatly depreciated." The old knights and nobles complained that valets and lacqueys were recruited in companies which were put on the same footing as the old men-at-arms, who had been of gentle birth. These complaints joined with the charge against Catherine de Medici that she had, by the creation of twenty-five new members of the Order of Saint Michael, rendered its honours as common as the cockle-shells on the seashore, serve to show how early the rude attempt at establishing a standing army operated to the subversion of all ideas and privileges of Chivalry and how much this movement provided one of the chief elements in the decadence of ancient knighthood in France. Now as that country had always been the nursery (if we may call it so) and pattern for Chivalry to other countries, even though these new measures of her kings did not spread beyond her frontier, they could not help having an effect on ancient ways and thoughts in other knightly lands and that of a most depressing character for Chivalry.

England from her insular position and having no land frontiers to protect, nor Free Companies to ride rough-shod over her green field, was not in the same position as France, and a standing army such as Charles IX. began to form would have been utterly repugnant to the liberty-loving Englishman. Indeed, later in the ages—it was a charge brought against the last reigning Stuart king—he was trying to set up a standing army. Feudality and with it the obligation of knight-service remained, therefore, much longer in this country, but, from a very early period, the independence of the knights over their vassals had been greatly restricted by the royal power.

As early as 1086 William the Conqueror took a step which was a direct violation of feudal principles, and by doing so provided a class of men he and his successors could always, in case of war, summon to his standard. In a great meeting at Salisbury of vassals, whoever they might be, and to whomsoever they might own vassalage, he made them all submit and become " his men " and swear " to be faithful to him against all others."

Thus was provided a direct tie between the crown and all freeholders which no intermediate tie would justify them breaking. Upon this body of men who comprised all males between the ages of fifteen and sixty, and who were legally bound to have by them a helmet and leathern cuirass and spear—long before Charles IX. formed his standing army—the English sovereign had a body of stalwart and soldierly men to rally to his call, and, by these measures even in early times, the power of the knights and overlords in this country was greatly circumscribed when compared to those of France, Germany, and Spain. Their influence was further weakened, and, so their decadence became more marked, by the famous Statute passed in the reign of Edward I. known as " Quia Emptores," prohibiting any vassal from granting any land to be held in fee-simple under himself, and enacting that if he wished to sell he must do so out and out, and so that the purchaser henceforth should hold of the same chief lord as the seller did. Thus the formation of the infinite chain of lord, vassal, and sub-vassal was checked, till in process of time, it came about that nearly all freeholders in England held of the Crown.

This act destroyed the disruptive force of feudalism and with it in a great measure the former powers and privileges of the knights who held their lands in fief. These—the old military tenures— remained even up to the reign of Charles II., though their ancient owners would have hardly known them, so circumscribed were their rights, so obsolete their privileges.

This act of " Quia Emptores " provided therefore another factor in the gradual disappearance of ancient Chivalry in England, and it was helped too, by another circumstance—the internecine Wars of the Roses were waged exclusively by the nobility and those of knightly order; the battles were so hardly contested, so frequent and so sanguinary, and at the close of each so frequent the executions at the hands of the victors, that the whole class for which ancient Chivalry in this country had subsisted—was nearly exterminated. It is true a nobility succeeded, but raised from a class generally who had no long centuries behind them to inspire them by the deeds of their chivalrous ancestors, no scruples founded on traditional education in arms to get rid of. The stern school of feudality had never reared them as its scholars—therefore all the more ready they were to accept new ethics in military matters, new ways of forming a battle, and not to the Church whose influence was weakening in Europe—but to the sovereign—they readily dedicated their swords and their consciences. Rapidly the sacrosanct character of the knights died out and their ancient vows became—except in individual cases—totally forgotten, " to defend the widow and the fatherless and the Holy Faith."

Knighthood's titles, it is true, remained, and remain to the present day—but as decorations carrying with them little of the old knights' characteristic services in arms.

Shall we say then that the Spirit of Chivalry is altogether dead, dead perhaps after the field of Bosworth-fight? Not if looking back through the ages we hear the battle-cry of the Cavaliers at Marston " for God and the King "; not if later we go up to the far north and see many a noble of Scotland laying down his life for a hopeless cause because it was his Prince's; not if we stand proudly to-day and count our noble dead who for duty and their country, giving up all, lie with their deathless honour on the battle-wrecked fields of Flanders.

INDEX

INDEX

INDEX

INDEX